PRIVATE JUSTICE

Books by Terri Blackstock

Cape Refuge (Book 1 in series)
Emerald Windows

Newpointe 911

Private Justice
Shadow of Doubt
Trial by Fire
Word of Honor

Sun Coast Chronicles

Evidence of Mercy
Justifiable Means
Ulterior Motives
Presumption of Guilt

Second Chances

Never Again Good-bye
When Dreams Cross
Blind Trust
Broken Wings

With Beverly LaHaye

Season of Blessing
Seasons Under Heaven
Showers in Season
Times and Seasons

Novellas

Seaside

NEWPOINTE
9 1 1

PRIVATE JUSTICE

TERRI BLACKSTOCK

ZONDERVAN™

GRAND RAPIDS, MICHIGAN 49530

This book is lovingly dedicated to the Nazarene

ZONDERVAN™

Private Justice
Copyright © 1998 by Terri Blackstock

Requests for information should be addressed to:

Zondervan, *Grand Rapids, Michigan 49530*

Library of Congress Cataloging-in-Publication Data

Blackstock, Terri, 1957–
    Private justice / Terri Blackstock.
        p.   cm.
    ISBN: 0-310-21757-1 (soft)
    I. Title.   II. Series: Blackstock, Erri, 1957–   Newpointe 911 ; bk. 1.
PS3552.L34285P75   1998
813'.54—dc21   97-36571

Published in association with the literary agency of Alive Communications, Inc., 7680 Goddard Street, Suite 200, Colorado Springs, CO 80920.

Interior design by Jody DeNeef

Printed in the United States of America

---

02 03 04 05 06 07 /❖ DC/ 26 25 24 23 22

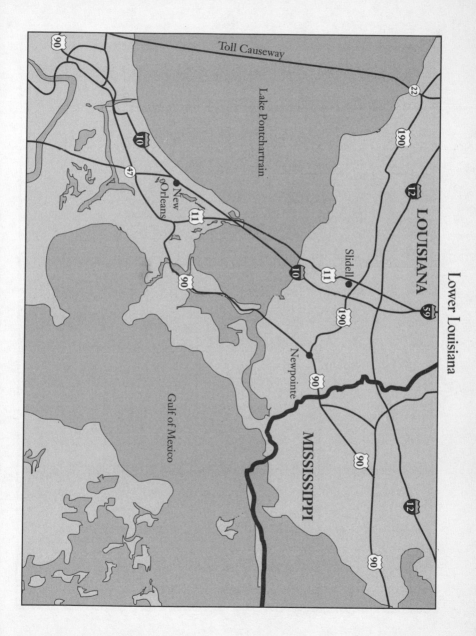

Lower Louisiana

Newpointe, Louisiana

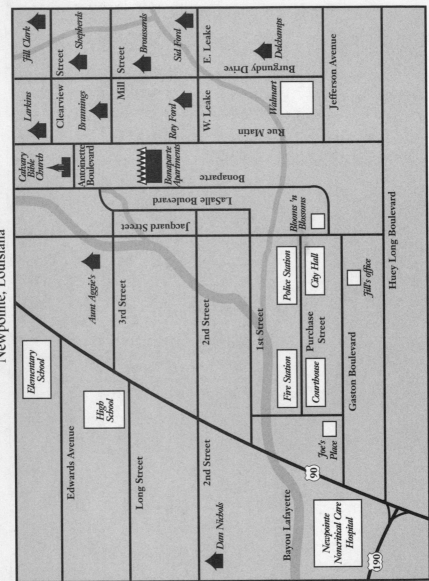

Acknowledgments

• • •

In March of 1996, my neighboring town of Jackson, Mississippi, was shaken to the core when one of our firemen walked into Central Fire Station and killed four district chiefs. He then wounded several other firefighters and a cop in his effort to get away. Shortly thereafter, police discovered that he had also murdered his wife.

The event was a tragic one for our community. A gaping hole was left in the Jackson fire department, and suddenly the town became aware of how important those men and women in our protective services can be.

It gave me the idea for the Newpointe 911 series, in which the close-knit community of firefighters, paramedics, and police officers in my fictitious town of Newpointe struggle together against the dangers that threaten their town. I wanted my readers to have a new appreciation for the individuals who make up these forces—individuals with families and friends and beliefs and values. Individuals who hurt and grieve and bleed like we do, but who must go on, because they've sworn to protect us. This series is a salute to those real individuals who live from emergency to emergency, and often put our lives before their own.

Thanks to my stepfather, Bill Weathersby, retired Jackson firefighter, who fought fires because it was what he loved to do. He gave me answers to many questions—both simple and complicated. I couldn't have written this if he hadn't been just a phone call away.

Also, thanks to Dr. Harry Kraus, who doesn't report me to the FBI when I ask him questions like, "How could I shoot a person in the head without killing him?" Being a novelist himself, he patiently talked me through the scenarios I needed to set my story up. I hope I can someday return the favor.

Thanks to my agent, Greg Johnson, for not putting money above the calling. How wonderful to work with someone who shares my vision.

Thanks to Mike Hoffman, Zondervan webmaster, who gave me a map of cyberspace and opened a whole new world of research for me.

And finally, a huge thanks to the best fiction team in publishing today—Dave Lambert, Lori Walburg, and Sue Brower—for their tireless work to make my books something we can all be proud of. I probably put us all through the wringer on this one!

Chapter One

● ● ●

The competing sounds of brass bands, jazz ensembles, and zydeco musicians gave Newpointe, Louisiana, an irresistibly festive atmosphere, but Mark Branning tried not to feel festive. It was a struggle, since he stood in a clown suit with an orange wig on his head, preparing to make the long walk down the Mardi Gras parade route. Already, Jacquard Street was packed with tourists and townspeople here to chase beads and candy being thrown by drunken heroes. In moments, he and his fellow firefighters, also dressed as clowns, would fall into their sloppy formation on the town's main drag, followed by the fire truck that carried even more painted firemen.

It was what promoters advertised as a "family friendly" parade—unlike the decadent bacchanalian celebrations in New Orleans, only forty minutes away. But Fat Tuesday was still Fat Tuesday, no matter where it was celebrated, and it always got out of hand. It was the time of year when the protective services in Newpointe had to be on the alert. Last year, during the same "family friendly" parade, a man had been stabbed, two women had been raped, and they'd been called to the scene of four drunk-driving accidents. It seemed to get worse every year.

Just days ago, Jim Shoemaker, police chief of the small town, and Craig Barnes, fire chief, had appealed to the mayor that the town was better served if their forces remained on duty on Fat Tuesday. Mayor Patricia Castor insisted that the community needed to see their emergency personnel having fun with everyone else. It fostered trust, she said, and made the men and women who protected the town look more human. At her insistence, and to Shoemaker's and Barnes's dismay, only skeleton crews were to remain on duty, while the rest of the firemen, police officers, and paramedics were to dress like clowns and act like idiots. "It's a religious holiday," she drawled, as if that sealed her decision.

Mark slung the shoulder strap of his bag of beads and candies over his head, and snickered at the idea that they would call Fat Tuesday a religious *anything*. The fact that it preceded Lent—a time for fasting and reflection as Easter approached—seemed to him a lame excuse for drunken revelry.

A police squad car pulled up beside the group of wayward firefighters, and Stan Shepherd, the town's only detective—still unadorned and unpainted—grinned out at him. "Lookin' good, Mark," he said with a chuckle.

"So how'd you get out of this?" Mark asked him, ambling toward the car. "I thought Newpointe's finest were supposed to dress like demonic bikers."

"Makes a lot of sense, doesn't it?" Stan asked with a grin. "Pat Castor wants us to show the town how human and accessible we are, so she makes us wear makeup that could give nightmares to a Marine."

"Hey, what can you say? It's Mardi Gras. You still haven't told me why you're not made up."

"Because I refused," Stan stated flatly. "How's that for a reason?"

Mark leaned on the car door and stared down at his friend. "You mean that's all it took?"

"That's all. Plus I read some statute to her about how it was illegal for someone out of uniform to drive a squad car."

"You're not in uniform, Stan."

"Yes, I am. I'm a plainclothes cop. This is my uniform." Stan looked past Mark to the others milling around, waiting impatiently for their chance to ruin their reputations. "Speaking of nightmares, check out George's costume."

"You talkin' 'bout me?" George Broussard asked, coming toward the car. Mark grinned at the Cajun's gaudy three-colored foil wig and the yellow and purple-polka dot shirt he wore. It was too little for him, and the buttons strained over his protruding gut. His hairy belly peeked out from under the bottom hem of the ill-chosen blouse, and someone had drawn a smiling pair of lips under his navel and crossed eyes above it.

"Yep. The stuff that bad dreams are made of," Mark agreed.

"Yeah, and you got lotsa room to talk," George returned. "Just 'cause you don't got the canvas I got to work with . . ." He patted his bare belly again, and Mark turned away in mock disgust.

Mark was glad he had lost weight since he and Allie had split up. The wives gleefully wielding the face and body paint were particularly cruel to those midlife paunches. His costume did, at least, cover all of his torso without accenting any glaring flaws, though he could have done without the flapper fringe that some sadistic seamstress had applied in rows to the polyester shirt.

"Is Allie gonna be here today?" Stan asked Mark.

Mark glanced at George, wishing Stan hadn't asked that in front of him. He hadn't broadcast the news of his separation from his wife and figured there were still some in town who didn't know about it. That suited him just fine. George, who had only been in Newpointe for the past year, wasn't a close enough friend for Mark to air his dirty laundry with.

As if he sensed Mark's discomfort, George wandered off and blended back into the cluster of clowns.

"How would I know what Allie's gonna do?" Mark asked.

"Don't give me that garbage," Stan said. "You keep closer tabs on your wife now than you did before."

"Estranged wife. I don't know if she'll be here. I doubt it. It's not her thing." He straightened, unwrapped a Jolly Rancher, and popped it into his mouth. "Then again, I did kind of think she might swallow some of her self-righteousness today to come help the wives paint us up. It's a power thing, you know. They love to make us look ridiculous. Allie's devoted her life to it."

"At least you're not bitter."

The barb hit home. "Bitter? Why should I be bitter? Actually, I feel great. I love my new bachelor life. Did I tell you that I picked up some great furniture at Kay Neubig's garage sale? Mid-century relics complete with the original stuffing coming out from the tears in the authentic vinyl. And my apartment has ambiance. The building's foundation is going, so the whole place slants. It's hard to keep gravity from pulling the kitchen cabinets open, and I worry a little when the train that comes by at two A.M. every night makes the building sway and vibrate— but like I said, ambiance. You know how I live for ambiance."

"So you're ticked about the apartment. Do you miss your wife?"

Mark was glad his face was painted so the heat moving to his cheeks wasn't apparent. Stan was a good friend, but he was crossing the line. He decided to change the subject. "Let's just say I'm aware that she's not here. I'm also aware that *your* wife isn't here. Why isn't Celia wielding a paintbrush today with the other cop wives?"

"Because we're boycotting the whole makeup idea. She's here. I'll pick her up when the procession gets up to Bonaparte, and she'll ride the rest of the way with me."

"I thought only uniformed cops could ride in the squad cars."

"She's dressed just like I am—in plainclothes." Stan grinned and winked, then put the car into drive and skirted the band and the motorcycles up ahead.

Mark turned back toward the firemen and saw George dancing to the jazz band. That face painted on his stomach gave him a comical double-decker look that had the women among them doubling over in laughter.

"If Martha could see you now!" one of the wives yelled.

"She will, darlin'," George said. "She's bringin' the baby. They're probably in the crowd as we speak."

"Poor kid," Mark muttered with a grin. "Only six months old, and he has to see a thing like this."

• • •

The noise of the sirens, revving motorcycles, and brass bands playing three streets over almost drowned out the screams of the six-month-old baby in the Broussard house, but Reese Carter, the old man who lived next door, pulled himself up from his little rolling stool in his garden and wondered why the baby's mother hadn't quieted him yet. The parents—George Broussard, a local fireman, and his pretty wife, Martha—were attentive, and he rarely heard the baby crying for more than a few minutes. But this had gone on since the parade had started—probably more than half an hour now.

Not one to intrude where he wasn't invited, he tried to mind his own business and concentrate on the weeds he pulled from his garden. He wished the parade would end, so that he could have peace again. The conflicting sounds of jazz and marching bands, drum corps from the high school, tapes playing on floats, and sirens blaring were making him wish he'd picked today to visit a relative out of town. But most of his people lived here in Louisiana, and he doubted there was a place in the state that was immune to Fat Tuesday.

Despite the parade noise, he could still hear the baby screaming. He pulled his gloves off with a disgusted sigh, trying to decide whether to go inside where he couldn't hear the baby's cries, or check to see if things were all right next door. His first instinct was to go inside, but then he remembered that last Christmas, after his wife died, when he'd expected to spend the day alone mired in self-pity, Martha Broussard had knocked on his door and invited him over to share Christmas dinner. He hadn't wanted to go—hadn't been in a festive mood and didn't want to pretend he was—but she had insisted. So he had gone, and several hours later he realized that the day was mostly over and he hadn't had time to feel sorry for himself.

If something was wrong next door now, he owed it to them to see if there was anything he could do. Maybe the baby was sick, and he could go to the drugstore for some medicine. Or maybe Tommy just had colic and couldn't be comforted, in which case Reese could show Martha some of the tricks that his wife had used on their children and grandchildren.

He dusted off his hands, then rinsed them under the faucet on the side of his house and dried them on his pants. He caught a faint whiff of smoke in the air. Someone must be breaking the city ordinance about burning limbs in their yard. Fat Tuesday seemed to give people license to do whatever they wanted, he thought with disdain as he headed down his driveway, cut across the Broussard yard, and trudged up the porch steps to the door. He rang the bell and waited. No answer.

Now that he was closer, he could hear that the baby wasn't just crying—he was screaming wildly. Reese leaned closer to the door and called, "Martha? Are you there?"

He knocked hard, hurting his arthritic knuckles, then raised his voice. "Martha! It's Reese Carter, next door. Martha, are you there?"

But all he heard in reply was the baby's gasping wails against the background of jazz music three blocks away.

•   •   •

The jazz band in front of Mark and the other firemen changed tunes, and some accordions launched into a zydeco tune. Trying to keep himself and the rest of the firemen in the spirit as they waited for their turn to march out onto the parade route, Mark led some of the others in an absurd chorus-line kick dance that fit perfectly with their attire. As he clowned, he scanned the other firemen and wondered how much beer they—and the rest of the parade participants—had already guzzled in the spirit of the festivities. It was only ten o'clock in the morning, yet trays and trays of drafts in plastic cups had been doled out to those waiting to participate.

Some of the wives still milled among the firemen, finishing up the outlandish makeup jobs. Jamie Larkins, with a cup of beer in one hand and an eyeliner pencil in the other, was swaying to the beat as she painted Marty Bledsoe's face. Susan Ford, a pretty black woman who wouldn't touch alcohol even if she were dying of thirst, finished Slater Finch's bare back—on which she'd drawn Betty Boop eyes and lips and applied a fake nose. She saw Mark horsing around and said, "You better stop that sweating, Mark Branning, you hear me?" The sweet demand cut through the laughing voices as Susan approached him with her makeup tray. "Look at you. Your smile is dripping. Our king of choreography is losing his looks."

"Me? Never," Mark deadpanned. "You may note that I have the least amount of face paint on. They knew not to mess with a good thing."

"Either that, or you already fit the bill without it."

Mark looked wounded. "Susan, you slay me. I believed you when you said I looked like George Clooney."

"Loony, Mark, not Clooney. And I never mentioned a George."

He grinned as she reached up with a tissue and wiped the smear from his mouth. "You're a mean woman, Susan Ford."

"You bet I am. And don't you forget it." Her smile faded as she touched up his face. "By the way, I saw Allie yesterday."

"Speaking of mean women?" he asked.

She wasn't amused. "She looked awful lonesome, Mark."

Again, he was glad that his face paint hid the heat rushing to his cheeks. He didn't know why every conversation these days seemed to lead directly to Allie. If Allie looked "lonesome," it was because she'd chosen to be alone. They'd been separated for over two months now, and although neither of them had made a move to file for divorce, there was no movement being made toward a reconciliation, either.

Susan seemed to realize she'd hit a nerve. Reaching up to press a kiss on his painted cheek, she whispered, "Sorry, honey. Didn't mean to bring you down."

"It's okay. No problem." A bone-thin majorette passed with a tray of beer, and he eyed it this time, wondering if he should drink just one to keep his mood from deflating completely. But Susan was there, as well as others from his church who would pass immediate judgment. He let the tray pass and wished the parade would hurry up and move so he could get the morning over with.

•   •   •

At Midtown Fire Station on Purchase Street, where all of Newpointe's protective services were located side by side, right across from city hall and the courthouse, Nick Foster paced the bunkroom and rehearsed his sermon for his little church's midweek service. It was tough being a bivocational pastor, juggling practical and spiritual duties. Sometimes it was impossible to separate his ministry from his profession. Today was one of those times. Whenever he dared to buck the mayor's authority and refuse to participate in something he believed to be immoral—as he had today—he risked losing his job as a fireman. Without it, he wouldn't make enough to pay his rent. Though Calvary Bible Church had its share of supporters, there weren't many families in the body who had much to give. Newpointe, as a whole, was not a wealthy town. Most of the tithes and offerings went to pay for the building they'd built two years ago, plus the missions projects he'd started. There wasn't much left over for him, which was fine as long as he had firefighting to keep his refrigerator stocked. He lived in a trailer across the street from the church. "The parsonage," his church called it, even though neither he nor the church owned it.

He got stuck on one of the points in his sermon, went back to his notes, made a quick change, then began pacing again. What did you tell a town whose residents had been brought up on voodoo and Mardi Gras? Even though he'd made it a point to preach a series of sermons on idolatry in the weeks preceding Mardi Gras, he was still astounded at the number of his church members who made themselves part of the infrastructure that upheld the holiday. Half of his congregation was in the parade, and the other half was watching.

He stumbled on the words again and sank onto a bunk, feeling more frustrated than usual. Did it really matter if he got the words right, if no one really listened?

Taking off his wire-rimmed glasses, he dropped his head and stared down between his feet for a moment, feeling the burden of all those souls weighing on his heart. Finally, he closed his eyes and began to pray that God would make him more effective, that he'd open their hearts and ears, that they would see things clearly . . .

He heard the door slam shut and looked up to see Dan Nichols, one of the other firefighters holding down the skeleton crew.

The tall blonde man was drenched in sweat and breathing hard, but to Nick's amusement, he went straight to the mirror and checked the receding hairline that seemed such a source of preoccupation to him.

"Has it moved any?" Nick teased.

Dan shot him an annoyed look. He slid the towel off of his neck and began wiping his face. "I wasn't looking at my hair."

Nick forced back his grin. Though he knew that he and Dan were considered two of the most eligible bachelors in town, Dan was by far the first choice of most of the single ladies. He was athletic and physically fit, something no one could say about Nick. And Dan had something else Nick didn't have. Money. Lots of it. He was one of the rare breed of fire-fighters who didn't have to work a second job to make ends meet. Dan had come from a wealthy family, had a geology degree, and could have been anything he wanted. But all he'd wanted was to be a fireman.

"You been out jogging?" Nick asked, a little surprised that he'd risk being away from the station when they were under-staffed.

"I didn't go far," Dan said. "If we'd gotten a call, you would have seen me as soon as you pulled out."

"So is it crazy out there yet?"

"Gettin' loud, I'll say that." He dropped down on the bunk across from Nick, still panting. "You know—" He hesitated, as if carefully weighing his words. "I know it was right for us to take a stand and not participate in Mardi Gras, but part of me feels like a stick-in-the-mud."

"Sure, I know," Nick said. "It's just a parade, right? No big deal, just a day of fun that's no harm to anybody. Don't buy into that lie, Dan."

Dan grinned. "It's just that everybody's there. I'm human. I grew up on Mardi Gras. It feels weird not being part of it."

Nick fought his disappointment. "Tell you the truth, I was surprised you stood with me on this. Why did you?"

Dan patted his shoulder and grinned. "Because you're right. You know you are." He stood up. "I think I'll go take a shower."

The door opened again as Dan headed for the bathroom, and Craig Barnes, the fire chief, shot in.

"Hey, boss," Nick said. "Thought you were at the parade."

"Yeah, I'm going," he said. "I'm hoping to avoid the blasted makeup. You won't see Mayor Castor prancing down the street with floppy shoes and a big nose. No, she gets to ride in a convertible and hang on to her dignity, and she expects me to hoof it with a bunch of drunken firefighters whose goal it is to make this department the laughingstock of the town."

Nick thought of echoing the sentiment, but in this mood, he doubted Craig would appreciate it. The chief wasn't one to pal around with his subordinates. He rarely vented, but when he did, it was usually meant to be a monologue.

"Where's everybody, anyway?" Craig demanded as he went to his locker and pulled out his cap. "Don't tell me you're the only one here."

"Dan's in the shower, and Junior is sweeping out back. You know, Craig, if you didn't show up, it might make a nice statement."

"With all those other bozos falling all over themselves to be in the parade? Some statement. No, I've got to grin and bear it." He slammed the locker and started out. "If anybody calls looking for me, tell 'em I'm on my way."

"Sure thing," Nick said.

As the fire chief headed back out the door, Nick sighed. So much was being made of so little. The mania itself ought to be a wake-up call to those who made themselves a part of the custom.

But all he could do was preach and pray, and hope that someday, they would start listening.

♦   ♦   ♦

The city employees' float, decorated like a pirate's ship, pulled into the street several positions in front of the firemen, cueing them that it was time to get into formation. Laughter erupted from some of the wives milling among the firemen, some already tipsy, others sober yet giddy as they prepared their husbands for the parade.

Lonesome, Mark thought with contempt. He couldn't say why Susan's description had ruined his mood.

He remembered another parade: the July Fourth parade last year, when Allie had been there among them, part of the fire family and the other half of himself. She had dressed like Martha Washington, and he'd been Uncle Sam. It had been a fun day, even in the sweltering heat.

He winced as Jamie Larkins, another fire wife, was swept away on a gale of raucous laughter. Cale, her husband, had been stealing sips from her draft, too, and Mark wondered if the effects would wear off before Cale went on duty tonight. He hoped so. A drunk or hungover firefighter was the last thing they needed on Fat Tuesday.

As the parade began to move, the brass band in front of them kicked into a newer, faster cadence and began dancing their way toward Jacquard Street. The firemen all looked at each other with comical dread before following. Some of them were jollier clowns than others, having been siphoning the beer that had been circulating like water since they'd gotten there that morning. It was the one day each year when the mayor footed the bill for something that wasn't an absolute necessity. Nick Foster, Mark's pastor, had protested the use of funds and asked her to spend it on much-needed bulletproof vests for the cops, a new pumper for the fire department, or updated rescue units for the paramedics. But as usual, she paid no attention.

Mark had considered taking Nick's stand and refusing to be in the parade, but part of him *wanted* to join in the fun, even though he'd voiced his righteous indignation just for the record. Part of him felt like a hypocrite—pretending to be spiritually offended by the parade even though, as everyone knew, he hadn't attended church since he and Allie had separated. It wasn't that he didn't want to—it was just that it was too uncomfortable with his wife there, all tense and cold, and with all of the members who had been his close friends offering advice that he neither needed nor wanted. If Mark had chosen to follow his pastor's lead, he was sure Nick would have used their time alone at the station to lecture him, again, about the mistake he was making in letting his marriage fail—as if that were his choice.

In a whirlwind of noise, the siren on the ladder truck behind them went off, and the motorcycles carrying the cops with faces painted like demonic rock stars roared louder. Another siren farther back, presumably from a rescue unit, moaned at migraine-level volume. Mark tried to shake himself out of the depression threatening to close over him; impulsively, he reached for one of the passing trays. He grabbed a draft and threw it back, then crushed the cup in his hand and dropped it to the ground. It did nothing to improve his mood, but he noticed Susan Ford and her husband, Ray—one of Mark's closest friends and the captain on his shift—watching him with sober, concerned faces. He wished they would both just mind their own business.

As the parade moved, the firemen scuffed onto Jacquard Street in their oversized shoes and undersized ruffled shirts, waving and tossing beads and candy to the cheers and pleas of hyperactive children and intoxicated adults, begging, "Throw me some beads!"

For the sake of goodwill in his community, Mark plastered on a smile and tried to have a good time.

Chapter Two

● ● ●

The baby's vibrato cries grew hoarse, but the level of urgency in his tone seemed to heighten as Reese Carter banged once again on Martha Broussard's door. Should he go around back? Maybe Martha was hanging laundry or working in the yard with one of those carry-around stereos with those despicable headphones that young people seemed to love these days. That wasn't like her, though. Martha wasn't that young, and she wasn't that irresponsible.

The smell of smoke grew stronger, and finally his fear that something was terribly wrong overcame his reluctance. He tested the knob, found it unlocked, and pushed the door open.

Feeling as if he were intruding in a place where he had no right to be, he stepped hesitantly inside. "Martha? Is anyone here?"

The baby's hoarse voice choked out louder and more desperately, so he headed down the hall to the baby's room.

Martha wasn't there. The baby's face was crimson and wet, and his eyes were swollen from the tears. It had been a long time since Reese had picked up a baby, and again he worried that Martha would think he was intruding, but something was obviously wrong. He leaned over the crib and lifted the baby out.

Tommy had been crying too hard to stop, so his pattern changed from screams to hiccup sobs as the old man rocked him. "Martha?" Reese called again.

He carried the baby back down the hall and peered into the living room. There was no sign of her, but a packed diaper bag lay on the floor, some of its contents spilled out. He stepped toward it, peering from the living room into the kitchen. "Martha?"

It was then that he saw the splatters on the blue carpet, the brownish-red spray that was easy to miss at first, then the darker red blotches. He caught his breath.

His heart began to pound painfully against his chest. The baby still cried, and Reese held him tighter as he followed the drops across the carpet and into the kitchen, toward the back door that stood open. His mind raced with possibilities. Maybe she had fallen and hit her head, then gotten up, confused, and wandered outside, where she had passed out in the yard.

He stepped carefully around the blood and pushed open the screen door.

The yard was filling with smoke, and he doubted that it was coming from someone burning tree limbs. He turned back into the kitchen and, with trembling hands, set the baby in the swing and locked the seat belt. As Reese stumbled outside, the baby began to wail again, but he couldn't go back. There was an old storage building at the back of the Broussard yard, and flames were shooting out of the roof.

The door to the structure was partially open, and thick smoke poured out. Coughing, he kicked the door open and tried to see inside. Between the lawn mower and a bicycle, he could barely make out the shape of a woman's legs.

"Martha!" Stomping out the flames over the threshold, he stepped in, reached for her feet, and pulled her out. It wasn't until she was out of the reach of the flames, lying on the grass, that he was able to see her face.

Martha Broussard had a bullet hole through her forehead.

Reese fell back in horror, then turned and ran, tripping on the step as he rushed into the house for the telephone. The baby kept screaming as he grabbed the phone and dialed.

"911, may I help you?"

He tried to speak, but the words choked in his throat. "Uh ... yes ... please, help. Martha ... Martha Broussard ... has been shot ... and there's fire."

Clutching the telephone in his shaking hands, Reese gradually became aware of the raucous strains of "When the Saints Come Marching In" mingling with the screams of the baby whose mother lay dead.

Chapter Three

• • •

Stan Shepherd's wife Celia leaned out the passenger window
of his squad car, tossing "What Would Jesus Do?" bracelets
and gospel tracts to the frolicking onlookers as he drove slowly
along the parade route. It had occurred to Stan that he could
get fired for sharing his faith from a squad car. But he had
decided to allow himself that freedom to make up for having to
be in the parade in the first place. Besides, Celia wouldn't have
taken no for an answer.

The roar and clash of the parade almost drowned out the
radio call from Dispatch, but he heard the name Martha Broussard and just enough more to make his face go pale. He
reached across the front seat for Celia's shoulder and pulled her
back into the car. "Honey, you've got to get out."

"Why?"

"I've got a call. Possible homicide."

Celia got out, closed the door, and trotted alongside, asking
through the open window, "Who was killed?"

He didn't want to alarm her—and besides, he still hadn't
confirmed the identity of the victim—so he didn't answer. "I
don't know how I'll get out of here," he said instead. His siren
and lights were already on for the parade, so there was nothing
he could do to let the crowds know he had a real emergency.

"Stan?" Celia asked again. "Who is it?"

"I don't know yet," he shouted over the noise. "Get back
now. I have to find a way through."

Celia fell back, and he tried to inch his way to the side of the road—but there were people crowding the roadside. Up ahead, one of the motorcycle cops had heard the call and was turning his bike around and ordering people out of the way. He yelled something to the other cops in the parade, who stopped their parade maneuvers and skirted the side of the parade up to where the firemen clowned.

Up ahead, Stan saw the fire truck pull out of the line and make a path through the crowd toward an intersection that wasn't on the parade route. He wondered if anyone who'd heard the call had told George Broussard yet.

He picked up the radio mike and told the dispatcher he was on his way. As he inched his way through the crowd to the next intersection, where he could escape the parade route, he saw George Broussard standing stock-still in the middle of the parade, his face painted in a surreal smile and his belly poking out from under his shirt with a face painted on it. One of the cops straddled his bike next to George, shouting into his ear, breaking the news. George's face went slack as he reached up and pulled off the foil wig he wore, then spotted Stan in the approaching squad car and launched toward him.

The music played on, festive and upbeat, as the distraught fireman reached Stan's squad car and dove into the passenger seat. "My wife!" he cried.

"We're on our way, buddy," Stan said. Finally reaching the intersection, he stomped the accelerator.

● ● ●

At the Midtown Station, Nick Foster, Dan Nichols, and Junior Reynolds pulled the pumper out of its stall and raced to the address the dispatcher had given them. Something about Martha Broussard—had the dispatcher said she'd been shot?

Nick pulled on his oxygen tank and set the mask over his head as the truck approached the Broussard house. As the truck slowed and he leaped off, he prayed that Martha Broussard wasn't this year's first casualty of Fat Tuesday.

Chapter Four

● ● ●

The fire at the Broussard house had been small; the crew on duty had put it out quickly. In no time, the modest home had been converted into a crime scene. Yellow tape cordoned off the yard and the street for a block in either direction, and a handful of cops in clownwear came and went from the front door, most with smeared paint on their faces, since none had taken the time to remove it.

Mark Branning, still dressed in his flapper fringe and baggy ruffled pants, stood back among the firemen awaiting further instructions. None of the usual post-fire policies could be observed, since the blaze was connected with a shooting. The police department was in charge now.

Nick, who'd been one of the first firefighters to reach the scene, had told him that Martha Broussard had been found in the fire with a head wound from a gunshot. Two paramedics were still in the backyard—saving her life, Mark hoped, but as time passed and they didn't rush her out to the ambulance to be helicoptered to the hospital in Slidell, his fears rose that the news wasn't good.

The faces were sober as cops and crime photographers came and went from the house. The air was charged with smoke and apprehension.

"She's dead, don't you think?" Ray Ford asked him in a dull monotone.

Mark shook his head in sympathy. "Poor George. Who could have done this?"

"Could be anybody," Ray said. "We don't really know them that well."

That was true. The Broussards had lived in Newpointe for only a year. George had grown up here, but had lived in Monroe for most of his adult life. They had moved back to be closer to his aging parents. The fire department had accepted George's experience with wide-open arms, making him a shift captain. They had seemed like nice people—kept their yard neat, went to church, minded their own business . . .

But this murder changed everything.

"You don't think they was runnin' from somethin' when they come here, do you?" Ray asked him.

Mark glanced at him, surprised. "I thought Susan and Martha were friends. Wouldn't she know?"

"She thought the world of Martha. Loves that baby. She gon' be sick."

Mark stared back up at the house as Stan came out the front door, got behind the wheel of the car he'd driven in the parade, and radioed something in. The baby's cries grew louder, and Mark looked back at the front door. George stood in the foyer with that stupid clown shirt hanging open, his burly chest and the face on his belly exposed as he stared into space.

Mark wondered if Allie would be frightened when she learned that there was a killer on the loose. He thought of asking Stan if Martha was, indeed, dead, and if they knew who did it. But Stan was busy.

"I still say they was runnin' from somethin'," Ray Ford muttered. "George's got some enemy did this. Maybe a gamblin' debt."

"Does George gamble?"

"I don't know. But it makes sense."

Mark glared at the black man who was one of his closest friends. "Anybody ever tell you you watch too many movies? You don't even know if the man gambles, and you're convinced that his wife was murdered because of a gambling debt. If you leave here and tell *anybody* that, so help me, I'll strangle you."

Ray looked offended. "I ain't no gossip, Mark. I'm just sayin'—it looks a little suspicious."

"Hey—maybe George did it," Mark muttered sarcastically.

Ray's eyebrows shot up. "No! You don't think—"

Mark rolled his eyes. "Stop speculating, Ray. The man's wife was killed. That doesn't make him a gambler *or* a murderer, and it doesn't mean he was in the Witness Protection Program, and it doesn't mean he's an underworld spy. It's Fat Tuesday, and bad things *always* happen on Fat Tuesday. Leave it at that and let the cops do the detective work."

Ray bristled and ambled back to the fire truck.

Chapter Five

● ● ●

Allie Branning put the finishing touches on the last purple Mardi Gras centerpiece she had made for the Krewe of Janus Ball tonight at the Newpointe High School gym. Sweeping her blonde hair behind one ear, she checked her list to see which hospital arrangements she needed to do first. She couldn't make any deliveries until after the parade, because it cut through the center of town, making it impossible to get from her little flower shop, Blooms 'n' Blossoms, to the tiny noncritical care hospital on the other side of town. At least she could take consolation in the fact that the steady stream of customers she'd had yesterday had stopped, if only for the duration of the parade.

The bell attached to the front door clanged as someone came in, and she peered from the back room to the front. It was Jill Clark, her closest friend. "Come on back, Jill," she called. "I've got a ton of things to do. These Mardi Gras parties are killing me."

"Enjoy it and just *make* a killing," Jill said, purloining one of the peppermint sticks that Allie kept in a container beside the cash register. Peeling off the wrapping, she stuck the tip in her mouth and strolled to the back room. The candy gave her a youthful, pixie look that belied the fact that she was the most respected attorney in town. "You know, I think you're the only business in all of Newpointe that's open today," Jill said.

Jill was wearing jeans and tennis shoes rather than the usual dark suit that seemed to be her dress code in the courtroom.

Her short brown hair looked more relaxed and less polished than usual.

"Did you take off today?" Allie asked.

"Well, not really, but when no one made any appointments and court wasn't even in session, I figured I might as well kick back and take it easy. You want to have lunch?"

"Can't," Allie said. "Too many deliveries to make after the parade is over, and no help. I've called every part-timer who's ever worked for me, and they all considered it cruel and unusual punishment to make them work on Fat Tuesday. Last year, I had Mark to help me. But things were different then: Pat Castor didn't force the firemen to observe this oh-so-solemn religious holiday, and we weren't in the middle of a divorce—"

"Divorce?" Jill took the peppermint from her mouth. "Allie, you said that wasn't an option, that you didn't believe in divorce."

"Well, I've been thinking about it, and I've decided that it believes in me," she said, clipping the flower stems with a vengeance in the sinkful of water. "I have biblical grounds."

"What biblical grounds?"

"Adultery."

Jill stepped up to the table where Allie stood and touched her wet hands, stopping her work. Allie met her eyes.

"Allie, I know you. Biblical grounds or not—*adultery* or not—divorce will make your life worse, not better."

Allie held her gaze for several moments. Outside the shop, she heard the upbeat music of the parade passing by, children shouting and revelers laughing. She wondered if Mark was at the beginning of the procession or the end—and if he'd even give her a second thought as he passed the business they had built together.

"What choice do I have?" she asked Jill. "What am I supposed to do? There haven't been any grand gestures or any noble attempts to reconcile."

"From you *or* him," Jill pointed out.

"I'm the one who was wronged."

"You aren't even *sure* about that, Allie."

"Oh, I'm sure, all right. Jill, the ball's in his court, and he's not going to play it."

"Do you really *want* him to play it?"

"I don't know." She smiled sadly. "Maybe I just want to ram him in the head with it."

"He's a stubborn man," Jill conceded. "But I don't really think you want to lose him."

"I have already." Allie picked up a long-stemmed rose and tapped the white petals against her lips. They'd had white roses shaped in a cross as the centerpiece of their wedding, when they'd vowed to love each other until death. The death of what, she wondered now. "Problems can be worked out, but when your husband just stops loving you . . ."

Jill took the rose out of Allie's hand. "See, I don't think he really has stopped loving you. Not entirely. It's a miserable, unhappy man that I see walking around town these days. He covers it with jokes and barbs, and all that Branning sarcasm and charm, but there's a lot of pain in his eyes."

"He's not proud of our failure," Allie said. "Neither am I."

"Then don't fail."

Allie met her friend's steady, pull-no-punches gaze. Jill would never change.

The front door jingled again as someone came in. "Allie, are you here?"

Allie and Jill came out from the back room and saw Celia standing at the door, perspiring as if she had just run two miles, and gasping to catch her breath. Outside, the jazz of the parade mixed with jubilant shouts and motorcycle engines and horns honking. "Celia, what is it?"

"There's been a murder," she said, trying to catch her breath. "They're saying it's Martha Broussard."

Allie's eyes widened. "Really?"

Celia went to the small water tank and filled a paper cup with water. She took a drink, then tried to go on again. "The whole crew left. Cops, firemen, paramedics. The parade was gutted."

Allie looked at Jill, then back at Celia. "Celia, are you sure?"

"No," Celia admitted, "not about who the victim was. But Ray Ford told Susan that the call had been to the Broussard address, and that Martha had a gunshot wound. I'm telling you, it gets worse every year. I just hope Stan can figure out who did it before the creep gets away. All we need is to have a killer loose on the night of Fat Tuesday."

"Poor Martha," Allie whispered. "I can't imagine . . ." She looked at the other two women. "Did either of you know her very well?"

Celia shook her head. "I kept meaning to have them over."

"Yeah, me, too," Allie said. "But with Mark and me separated . . ."

"Maybe it's not too late. I'll hear from Stan as soon as he gets back to the station," Celia said. "Maybe she's still alive. You know how news can get distorted in this town."

A while later, Allie tuned to the Newpointe radio station as she returned from her deliveries. Details about the shooting were sketchy, but the announcer seemed certain that Martha had been murdered, that there were no leads on the killer, and that someone with a gun and a heart to kill was still roaming the streets. Allie drove back from the high school gym by rote, down Second Street, then right on Jacquard to Bonaparte. The parade was over, and broken beer bottles, cigarette butts, plastic cups, and confetti of every shape and color lined the streets. She pulled into the parking lot in front of Blooms 'n' Blossoms, turned off the van's ignition, and sat there for a moment.

She had never been one to enjoy being alone, and this murder wouldn't make things easier. As it was, she had trouble sleeping nights. Every creak in their old house, every whistle of the wind, every car that drove by woke her.

Tonight she'd probably be up all night, listening for killers.

Summoning the numbness that had anesthetized her for the past two months, she got out of the van and hurried in, tied her apron back on, and began to furiously design the last of the arrangements that had been ordered. If she could just keep busy, keep her hands working and her mind racing, keep her schedule full and hours packed, she wouldn't have to let the horror of the news sink in. She would finish the arrangements, make the deliveries, then come back and clean up here. The floor in the front of the shop needed mopping, and it was time to clean the bathroom, even though no one but employees ever used it. And those curtains in the windows were getting dusty. She should wash them tonight, then iron them and hang them back up. There was so much to do that it would be hours before she stopped hurrying and settled into the quiet. After that, maybe she'd be exhausted enough to sleep.

The telephone rang, startling her; she knocked a glass vase off her work table, and it shattered all over the floor. She stood still, staring down at the sharp fragments as if they formed a picture of her life blowing apart.

She made no move to answer the phone. She couldn't talk right now, not about Martha or George, not about murders or marriages, not even about parades or flowers.

Eventually, the phone stopped ringing, but she remained frozen. *I've got to move*, she told herself. *Got to keep busy. No time to think.*

But she *couldn't* move, couldn't organize her thoughts enough to clean up the glass or find another vase or arrange the flowers.

She heard the bell on the front door as someone came in, and she wished she had put the "Closed" sign out and locked the door behind her.

"Allie?"

Mark's voice startled her again, but there was nothing nearby to knock over.

"Allie, are you in back?"

"Here," she said, surprised at how hollow her voice sounded. "I'm here."

He came into the doorway.

"Stop!" she said. "You'll step on the glass. I broke a vase."

He looked down at the pieces all around her feet. She realized it must look odd to him, the way she just stood there, not making any attempt to clean it up, but she still couldn't manage to make herself move. "I . . . have so many deliveries to make. So many arrangements still . . . and now this."

She realized how absurd it sounded, as if in the course of her busy day a broken vase rated higher than a murder.

She made herself look at him, at the redness in his eyes and the remnants of white face paint around the edges of his unshaven face. He was wearing a pair of jeans and a pullover golf shirt. Despite the paint, he looked good—as good as he had when she'd first met him. And he stood silently looking at her, as if he had something to say but couldn't find the words. Looking away from those eyes that seemed to see straight into her, she tried to make a list. Get broom, sweep up glass, finish the arrangement, load the van . . .

As if he sensed her distress, he got the broom and the dustpan and began to sweep up the glass. She stayed where she was, watching him empty the dustpan into the trash, then come back for a second round of sweeping. "There," he said quietly. "No harm done."

She nodded like a robot. "Thank you."

He regarded her carefully. "You heard about Martha Broussard, didn't you?"

She nodded again. "How is George?"

"Not too good. You're not either, are you?"

She felt her face flushing and reached for another vase. "All this business about murder," she said. "It's just shaken me a little."

"I thought you might be afraid." He got the vase and held it under the sink, filled it halfway with water. He set it back down in front of her.

She began to stick the flowers in the vase, with no regard for color or symmetry.

She looked down at her watch, but the time didn't register. "I have to get back to the high school. They're already decorating for the Krewe of Janus Ball. I've taken one load over there already. They're probably waiting."

"I thought you'd decided not to sell to them. Idol worship, you said, since Janus was a mythical god and all."

She might have known that he'd throw her words back in her face. "I had to do it anyway," she said. "I needed the money. It's not easy maintaining two households. You said you were going to boycott Mardi Gras," she told him. "Guess neither of us is too good at following our convictions."

"Or keeping our commitments."

Her eyes whiplashed up to his as she wondered how he dared make a comment like that when *he* was the one who had broken his vows. "Like I was saying," she bit out, "they're waiting for me at the high school."

"The Krewe can wait, Allie. I need to talk to you."

Not today, she thought. *Not now.* The last thing she wanted was to cry in front of him.

He rubbed his face and took a deep breath, but kept his eyes on the floor. "I was wondering something, Allie. I was wondering if you would go to the funeral with me."

She felt transparent and wondered if he saw the million conflicting emotions battling on her face. "Why?" she asked. Though the question seemed confrontational, Allie couldn't help asking it. Did he want her with him for image control—so people who didn't already know about their breakup wouldn't find out now?

He swallowed. "I just thought we could put our differences aside for George's sake. And . . . well, it's not going to be an easy day."

Maybe he needed her, she thought. He was certainly closer to George than she was to Martha. But that idea raised questions.

"Is she going to be there?"

"Who?" he asked in a flat voice, but she didn't doubt for a moment that he knew.

"Isabelle Mattreaux. Oh, that's right. You call her Issie." She said it so bluntly that she surprised even herself. For so long, they had talked *around* the name, as if uttering it would somehow unleash things that were better left contained.

He looked slightly indignant. "Everybody calls her that. And I would imagine she'll be there. The whole town will be there. What difference does it make?"

She tried to think. *Did* it make a difference if she was there? Wouldn't Allie go anyway? Would she rather be *with* Mark or *without* him when she faced her? Would she rather look like the independent, strong woman who'd gone on with her life, or the wife who still hadn't quite let go?

Mark watched the struggle on her face. Finally, he said, "Never mind, Allie. Just forget it. I thought it would be nice if we went together, for George's sake, but never mind." He started for the door.

For a moment she thought of letting him go, but something told her that, if she did, it would become one more thing to add to her list of regrets.

"Mark?"

"What?"

"I'll go with you."

He swung around. "Don't do me any favors, Allie."

"Do you want me to go, or not?"

"Yes! That's why I came here. That, and to see if you were all right. To tell you to lock up carefully, and not answer the door if you don't know who it is."

The tears that had threatened her, that she had managed to hold at bay, pushed into her eyes now. She turned away and closed her eyes, pressing her tear ducts to keep her tears from falling.

He stepped slowly back into the room.

"Do they know who did it?" she asked, not sure if real curiosity triggered the question or if she was merely trying to get the focus off her feelings for Mark. "Do they have any idea?"

"No. There are very few leads." His words were delivered in a soft monotone, all business. "We know that it wasn't a forced entry. Her back door was wide open, and the killer probably just came in through the unlocked screen. He didn't take anything, so robbery isn't the motive, and there was no rape. They took fibers and prints and blood samples, and they're all at the crime lab now."

"So there's somebody out there who could walk in and shoot a woman in the forehead for no good reason."

"Probably somebody who came to town for Mardi Gras. The whole holiday seems to bring out the absolute worst in society. Wouldn't bother me if Newpointe refused to celebrate it."

"We'd be evicted from the state of Louisiana."

He shrugged sarcastically. "A murder here, a rape there—small prices to pay to boost the economy."

She wasn't amused, but she knew he didn't mean for her to be.

"Well, I'll let you know if they find out anything. And we'll make firmer plans when the time for the funeral is set."

She nodded. "Yeah, okay."

He gazed at her a little longer, then finally looked away. "Are you gonna be all right?"

"You know me," she said without much feeling. "I'm always all right."

He started to respond to that, then stopped himself. Finally, he said, "Keep everything locked, okay? Even the shop. I'll lock up on my way out and put out the 'Closed' sign. You have enough to do without any new customers today, anyway."

She nodded agreement. "Are you on duty tonight?"

"Unofficially. It's not my shift, but I'm gonna go in and help out for a while. We're expecting a little more activity tonight."

They held each other's gaze for a moment longer, and finally, Mark headed out of the shop.

As she heard him locking the door, Allie sank down onto her stool and covered her face with her hands.

Chapter Six

• • •

As expected, the 911 lines stayed lit up the evening of Fat Tuesday as brawls broke out in barrooms and drunk drivers rammed trees. Some addict on PCP tried to fly from a two-story building and wound up breaking his back and both legs. A group of pot-smoking teenagers gathered leaves and sticks to start a campfire in the elementary school's playground, only to find that the wind was too strong and caught the school on fire. The firefighters had put out the fire before too much damage was done, while the police dispatched to the scene had arrested the youngsters and the paramedics had treated them for smoke inhalation and a few minor burns. Almost every call required a collaborative effort among the town's emergency teams, and tonight, they were all hopping.

But none of the emergency personnel in Newpointe wanted to answer these emergency calls when there was a killer on the loose. Every one of them wanted to be out searching the town for the man who had killed Martha Broussard.

Since Mark wasn't officially on duty, he left the station just after ten and headed to the bar a couple of blocks away, where many of the cops and firemen hung out after work. It was unusually crowded as the Fat Tuesday-ers crushed in to celebrate. Their cigarette smoke left a haze over the room, and the low roar of voices competed with the jazz band playing in the corner.

There had been a time when Mark had hated this place. But then he and Allie had begun having problems, and he'd dreaded going home. He had started coming here after work with Cale

Larkins, one of the firemen on his shift. He hadn't come to drink—he'd always gotten a soft drink while his buddies indulged in their choice of spirits. Now, looking back, he couldn't remember exactly when he'd made the transition from Sprite to vodka, but it had happened some time after he and Allie split up. Now his visit to Joe's Place was almost a nightly event.

He took a stool at the bar and looked around. Some of the off-duty cops sat at a table, probably talking about the murder. He wondered if they'd learned anything about the killer yet.

Joe Petitjean, the proprietor, pointed to him. "Where y'at, Mark?" It was the typical Cajun greeting, and even non-Cajuns like Mark responded appropriately.

"Awright," Mark said. "Vodka, straight up. Double."

Joe turned back, unfazed, and poured the drink. "Was you at the Broussard's house today when they found her?" he asked, leaning across the counter to be heard when he handed him the drink.

"Yeah," he said.

"Ever'body's talkin'."

"Anybody saying who could have done it?" Mark asked.

"Not yet. No leads, what I hear."

Joe went back to work, and Mark swiveled on his chair and scanned the patrons. He sipped on his vodka, let the liquid burn down his throat, and told himself that soon he wouldn't be thinking about the murder or his marriage, or any more of a million things that could keep him awake nights.

The door opened and cool air spilled inside, providing a little relief from the smoke. He glanced over his shoulder and saw Issie Mattreaux coming in with two girlfriends. She saw him immediately, said something to her friends, and started toward him.

She wasn't in uniform, the way he usually saw her, and in her jeans and sweater she looked almost like a teenager. Her nickname suited her well. No one could ever call her Isabelle with a straight face. Her silky black hair hung straight to her shoulders, and she wore a small barrette on one side to hold it back from her face. But around her eyes were tiny lines, lines that belied her youthful look and gave away the fatigue and worry on her face since the murder. He wondered if Allie would still be threatened if she could see Issie now.

She came up behind him, set a hand on his back, and leaned around him to Joe. "Give me a Diet Coke, Joe," she said.

Mark lifted an eyebrow and looked back at her. "Diet Coke? On Fat Tuesday?"

She knew him well enough to know that his question was sarcastic. "I'm not in the mood to drink," she said, pulling up onto the stool next to him. She nodded at the glass in his hand. "I see you are, though."

He grinned. "Whatever gets you through the night."

She turned so that she was facing him, and asked, "You okay?"

"Sure, why?"

"Well, it was a rough day. Martha and everything ..." Her voice trailed off. "I saw your car at the florist this afternoon. Is Allie all right?"

"I guess." He looked down at the bar and tried to rub a spot off the wood. He knew she wasn't really concerned about Allie's state of mind. More likely, she just wanted to get the scoop on what had happened between them today. But he couldn't blame her—before his separation from Allie, he'd accommodated that curiosity plenty.

"So ... are you two trying to work things out?"

It annoyed him that she would ask such a thing.

"You don't have to answer if I've hit a nerve," she said, starting to get up. "I know it's none of my business."

"No, that's not it," he said. "I mean ... I'd talk about it if I had any answers. I just don't."

He felt her gaze on him, but he didn't dare meet it. He had managed to keep his distance for the past few weeks, even though he saw her frequently at the fire station. But he kept her at arm's length, didn't look her in the eye, and avoided any heartfelt conversations that he'd feel guilty about later.

"Has either of you filed for divorce?"

He shook his head. "I don't believe in divorce."

"Just separation?"

He rubbed his eyes. "No, I don't believe in that, either. But sometimes you don't have a choice."

"Are you still going to counseling?"

He knew he should never have told her about that in the first place, but she had been there when no one else had, and he'd needed to talk. "No. When she threw me out, she refused to go back. Said I wasn't being honest and it was a waste of time." He took a gulp of his drink, then grinned up at her, trying to shift the conversation away from such serious matters. "Speaking of wasting time, can we talk about something else?"

"Honest about what?" she asked, ignoring his question as she sat back down.

He couldn't tell her that it was all about her, but he knew she realized it. That was why she questioned him so hard. She wanted him to state the obvious, so that their relationship—or whatever it was—could move to a higher level.

Either that, or she was just genuinely interested in seeing him reunite with his wife.

Yeah, right.

"You don't really care about this. It's too sad for a stand-up act and too boring for a country song."

"Come on, Mark," she said, leaning toward him. "It's me you're talking to. What did she think you weren't being honest about?"

He turned away from her and scowled, frustrated. He didn't like being put on the spot. "Got me."

She leaned forward on the bar and took a sip of her drink, pondering what he'd said. He glanced up at her, saw her expression. "What?" he asked. "You have something on your mind. What is it?"

She shook her head. "Just something I've wanted to ask, but haven't had the nerve." Their eyes locked. Was this where he was supposed to tell her to go ahead and ask? No, no need. She would find the nerve somewhere.

"Mark, this may come out sounding like a real arrogant question, and if it does, then I'll just have to look like a jerk."

"You should become an ambassador, Issie. You're the queen of diplomacy. All those great lead-ins ... I want to ask, but I don't have the nerve ... this may come out sounding real arrogant, *but* ... I can hardly wait for what all these lead-ins are leading up to."

"It's about Allie," she said, ignoring his sarcasm—which she had said she found charming anyway. "I've run into Allie a few times, and I feel a little bit of a chill from her, and I was wondering ..."

His stomach tightened, and he brought the glass to his lips, seeking the burn it could bring.

"Mark, are you sure your breakup doesn't have anything to do with our friendship?"

"Are you kidding?"

She frowned. "Mark, I'm serious."

He set the glass down hard, and Issie jumped. Mark took a deep breath, trying to calm himself, then looked her in the eye. Lowering his voice so they wouldn't be overheard, he said, "My wife caught me with my arms around you in the bunk room at the fire station. She drew a conclusion—a mistaken one, but it had some pretty serious repercussions."

"But the breakup came weeks later, and you said it had nothing to do with me."

"I lied. I didn't want you to feel bad, when nothing really happened."

"She should have trusted you enough to know that. Even I know you better than that."

He looked into his glass, recalling how Issie had cried on his shoulder about being jilted by her pseudofiancé. He had closed the door so she could cry in private, and they had sat on the bunk while she bared her soul to him. She'd told him he was her best friend, the only one she trusted, and when she'd been overcome with emotion and grief, he had held her to let her cry.

So much for being a nice guy.

Just his luck that Allie had surprised him with a visit to the fire station, that the other guys had innocently directed her to the bunk room, that she had walked in on that little scene. He had tried to explain, but she wasn't interested in explanations. Only in what she thought she had seen.

The fact that Issie seemed so concerned now galled him. She hadn't cared that much at the time.

"I could talk to her," Issie said. "I mean, if it would help."

He almost laughed. "Trust me. Having you call Allie is the fastest way I can think of to get the divorce wheels turning. Allie would turn the wheels, and they'd run right over me."

"Don't worry, Mark. I'd be there to rescue you."

He met her eyes and saw that she meant exactly what he thought she did. Something about that pleased him.

The door opened, and several other off-duty firemen spilled in and made a beeline for him. *Talk about rescue*, he thought. They just might be rescuing him from himself.

Chapter Seven

● ● ●

Jamie Larkins was already nursing a hangover at 10:30, about the time most of the town was getting their second wind. She was also cursing herself for getting ripped so early in the day. She took two Tylenol and tried to sleep. It had occurred to her that she could keep drinking—even that she should, since she planned to give up alcohol for Lent tomorrow and needed to get the partying out of her system—but the murder had doused her plans. Her girlfriends who had planned to go out partying with her tonight after Cale reported to work had all backed out, mostly out of fear because a murderer was on the loose.

She went to her purse and dug out the vial of cocaine, and with a great sigh dropped it into a drawer in the end table next to the couch. She had hoped to talk Cale into sharing it with her tonight, even though he was so paranoid about random drug testing and losing his job. But she knew that he liked a good time as much as she did, and with the right coaxing, he would come around. It didn't matter now, though, since he'd had to work and she felt too lousy right now to waste it.

Unable to sleep, she sat on her bed and turned on the television with the remote control. She combed her fingers through her hair to pull it out of her eyes and flipped channels until she came to channel 4, a New Orleans station doing a live broadcast from Bourbon Street. The reporter seemed to be living it up himself, and in the background drunken, laughing partyers crowded in behind him while music from street musicians kept the mood upbeat.

If Cale hadn't had to work tonight, the two of them would be there now, right in the middle of things as they had been so many times before. Mardi Gras was her favorite time of year, and the Southshore—New Orleans—was her favorite place to celebrate it. That far from home—over forty miles—they needn't worry about his reputation as a public servant. Besides, she knew they wouldn't be doing drug testing for a while yet, since they had just tested Cale's shift last week.

But Cale had wound up working tonight, and her friends had all backed out. She couldn't believe she was sitting at home alone on Fat Tuesday. The phone call they'd shared half an hour ago was no substitute for his being here.

She picked up the phone and dialed the number of the fire station, hoping Cale was available and would have a minute to talk. The phone rang unanswered, and she guessed they were out on a call.

She hung up the phone and leaned back on her pillows, watching longingly as the television cameras zoomed in on Pat O'Brien's, where revelers in bawdy costumes brandished Hurricanes in their trademark glasses. As she watched the cameras pan the French Quarter, she heard a noise in the living room. She sat up, wondering if Cale had sneaked away and come home to check on her, or if he, too, was feeling so hungover that he'd convinced someone from another team to swap shifts.

She cut off the television and listened. "Cale? That you?"

There was no answer, and a chill of apprehension shivered down her back. But then her cat came strolling in and leaped up on her bed. Relieved that the noise hadn't been an intruder, she reached for the cat. She could have sworn she had let him out, but with her hangover and pounding headache, she had probably forgotten letting him back in.

She heard a sound again. Her hand stilled on the cat's back, and she felt its fur rise. "Cale?" she called again. "Cale, this isn't funny."

"No, it's not funny." The voice was not Cale's, and she screamed and grabbed the empty beer bottle on her bed table.

The man was hidden in the shadows of the hallway as the first shot rang out, shattering the bottle in her hands. The second hit her in the chest, knocking her back against the headboard.

Fog closed over her as she struggled to catch a breath. Her last grasp of awareness was the smell of diesel fumes, but she was powerless to move or escape the death that had come to take her before she was ready.

Chapter Eight

● ● ●

The A Shift had just returned to the station from a wreck on Bonaparte, one that hadn't really required their help, when the alarm sounded again. Still dressed in their fire gear, they headed back to the pumper, listening to the dispatcher's orders as they took their places.

"Fire reported at 1302 Clearview Street . . . a neighbor reports that someone may be in the house . . ."

Cale Larkins reacted immediately. "That's *my* house, man!"

Though they would have hurried for any call, the team made a special effort to screech out of the firehouse and fly to the scene.

"Is Jamie at home?" Nick asked, leaning forward in his rear seat as he slipped on the shoulder strap for his oxygen tank.

"I think so," Cale shouted. "She was when I called around ten. What if she's in there? What if she's sleeping?"

"Take it easy," one of the guys yelled over the siren. "She'll probably have the fire out by the time we get there."

● ● ●

Mark and Issie heard the sirens heading past the bar, and instinctively they threw down their tab and hurried out to the parking lot. Mark had a scanner under his dashboard and turned it on to listen as Issie stood at the driver's side door. The dispatcher was still giving orders to the cops on duty. "Clearview Street," Mark said. "I'm going."

"Me, too." She jumped in, and he pulled out of the parking lot and headed in the direction the trucks had gone.

Mark flew, and they caught up to the trucks and pulled up to the curb right behind the pumper. With a shock, Mark realized that it was Cale's house. By then, one side of the house was dancing in flames, and that side of the roof was engulfed. Cale leaped from the pumper before it had stopped completely and bolted inside. Mark slipped on his bunker coat and tank, which lay on the back seat of his car, and followed Cale as the rest of the crew unwound the hose and began dousing the flames.

"Jamie!" Cale shouted as he ran from room to room. "Jamieeee!"

He headed for the bedroom, which was black with smoke and popping with flames, and Mark knew that nothing in that room could have survived.

Cale screamed his wife's name as he bolted into the bedroom, and the anguished wail that followed shook the house even more than the flames. Mark rushed in after him. Cale had found his wife and was rolling her in the bedcovers to smother the flames. When they were out, he lifted her and carried her from the house.

The ambulance was there, as were several squad cars, and Issie ran up the walk with the other two paramedics to take Jamie from his arms. They laid her on a gurney and unrolled the blanket, but her burns were so severe that she was nearly unrecognizable.

"Do something!" Cale screamed. "She's not dead! She can't be dead!"

But Mark could see from Issie's strained face that she was. "Cale . . . I'm sorry. . . ."

"No she's not!" he screamed again. "Do—" He gestured hopelessly. "Something!" He reached for his wife and lifted her up. Her hair was seared and her skin was charred, but as he crushed her against him, Mark saw the blood soaking her back.

"Issie," he said, and she, too, saw the exit wound the bullet had made.

"Oh, no," she whispered.

Chapter Nine

• • •

The house at 1302 Clearview Street was handed off from the fire department to the police department and marked as a homicide scene. Stan Shepherd, the detective who had been the first cop on the scene at the Broussard house earlier that day, stepped through the wet, smoldering rubble of the bedroom, looking for empty shells or lodged bullets, while in the part of the house that hadn't burned, others dusted for prints and vacuumed the carpet for possible hair follicles.

As the only detective on the Newpointe police force, Stan considered this second murder to be a personal failure. If he'd caught the guy who'd killed Martha earlier today, Jamie would still be alive. But Stan had mistakenly assumed that the killing was an isolated event.

He picked up some of the charred wood from the wall and smelled it. The faint scent of diesel confirmed how the fire had started. From the evidence they'd already collected, he knew there was a psychopath out there somewhere with a .38, a can of gasoline, and a deadly intent that could not be predicted. He was glad Celia had gone to stay with her Aunt Aggie tonight. He didn't want either of them to be alone.

He heard Cale wailing in the yard and cursed the fact that a homicide investigation called for such cruelty. He would rather have let the ambulance take Jamie Larkins away, but instead, they had to leave her there, in the front yard where the paramedics had put her, until they'd recorded all of the evidence.

And Stan knew that Cale wouldn't leave—not until the medical examiner came to remove her body from the scene.

"The two women were friends," Jim Shoemaker, the police chief who had just gotten to the scene, said. "This can't be a coincidence."

"No," Stan said. "No coincidence. Can't be."

"Stan?" Officer Anthony Martin called from the living room, which hadn't entirely burned. Though everything had been damaged by smoke and water, most of the living room was still intact.

"Yeah," Stan asked.

"I just found something you might want to see."

Stan stepped through the wet, smoldering rubble, and Jim followed, until they were back on the smoke-stained carpet. Anthony showed them the vial full of white powder still lying in the drawer of an end table.

Stan frowned. Cale liked to drink, but he wasn't a druggie. If he had been, he could never have kept his job at the fire department. They had random drug testing every few weeks. Cale had never had a trace of it in his system.

Jamie, on the other hand, had been through drug rehab a couple of years ago. Apparently, she'd slid back into her old habits.

"Tag it," Jim said. "That just might be the key to what's going on here."

"What?" Stan asked. "You think it was a drug deal gone bad?"

"Might be."

"But what about Martha Broussard? You don't think *she* was buying coke."

"No telling."

"No way," Stan said. He went to church with the Broussards, and there wasn't a doubt in his mind that George and

Martha were both devout believers. "Not Martha. Jim, you knew her."

"Not that well, Stan. There's got to be a connection. Maybe Martha knew something. Maybe she saw something. Maybe Jamie told Martha something she wasn't supposed to, and somebody had to shut them both up."

"A lot of speculation; no real evidence."

"We have to start somewhere."

Stan looked around him as the other cops took pictures and videos and collected what evidence they could find amid the soggy, charred rubble. "I don't know, Jim. But I do know that whoever it is has got to be found, and fast."

"We've already called in every cop in town to set up road-blocks."

"It's Fat Tuesday, man. All we're going to find is a bunch of drunk drivers and dopers, and we'll be backed up until November with paperwork to process."

"Can't help it. We can't let 'em go."

"No, we can't. And maybe we'll find him." He looked through the damaged wall into the front yard. Ray Ford, Mark Branning, Craig Barnes, Dan Nichols, Nick Foster, and the others were clustered around Cale, trying to keep him calm as two cops questioned him.

"Yeah, if he's a tourist, we'll catch him in the roadblocks," Jim said.

"And what if it wasn't a tourist?" Stan asked quietly.

Jim looked up. "No way," he said.

The men locked eyes briefly. If it wasn't a tourist, then the person who had done this was someone from Newpointe, someone they all knew. Unable to deal with that possibility, Stan turned and continued sifting through the rubble.

Chapter Ten

● ● ●

Mark Branning felt as though he hadn't slept in days. The combination of alcohol and murder had seeped the energy right out of him, and if there had been an extra bed at the station, he would have stayed and slept there tonight. But the shift was fully staffed, and it seemed that all of the firemen felt as he did, though many of them had grumbled about the futility of trying to sleep on a night when Newpointe seemed to be at its worst.

At three A.M. he was too tired to stay and help out anymore, but the unease in his soul made him dread going home to his barren, lonely apartment. With finances so tight now that he and Allie were maintaining two separate homes on already meager incomes—and because he'd originally thought it would only be temporary—he'd furnished the apartment with just a twin bed, a forty-year-old couch that someone had been about to throw away, a couple of chairs, and a half-dozen cardboard boxes that served as end tables, cupboards, and ottomans.

The bar usually provided a comfortable transition between the depression following a long shift and his lonely return to the apartment, but in the wee hours of the morning, he wasn't in the mood to return to that smoke-filled room and all the noise and gossip.

The truth was, he longed for his real home, the home he'd shared with Allie. It was a tiny little house, only two bedrooms, one bathroom, a kitchen, and a den, but it had been all they could afford on a fireman's salary and the pittance they got from the florist shop after all the bills were paid. It had been the most desirable place on the planet for him at one time, though, because of Allie's knack for decorating. Flowers and plants bloomed all over the house, casting a pleasant and soothing scent. The furnishings, too, though inexpensive, were inviting and comfortable; they had saved for years to buy them. He supposed that, if their marriage ended in divorce, they would find some way of dividing the spoils, but for now, he'd chosen to leave them in their home. He didn't know why, since the separation had been Allie's idea. He should have taken at least half of what they'd accumulated together. But Allie was more materialistic, and she would probably fight tooth and nail for the things she had coveted for so long. He just wasn't up for that kind of fight.

Still, he missed the house, the things they'd filled it with—and worst of all, he missed his wife. He didn't like that, didn't want to acknowledge it. But having seen George grieving over Martha and Cale mourning over Jamie, he'd felt a sick void in his heart, a smothering despair.

What if he'd answered a call to his own house and found his own wife shot to death and surrounded by flames?

Suddenly he wanted to see her, despite the hour. He wanted to touch her and talk to her, tell her about Jamie, make sure she was all right.

He headed out the back room of the fire station and pushed through the kitchen door on his way to the parking lot—then stopped dead in his tracks. Issie was hunched in a chair in the corner of the kitchen, still wearing blue jeans and that teenager blouse she'd been wearing earlier, but there was blood and soot on it from Jamie's body. She looked tiny sitting there, staring off into space, her skin pale and her eyes vacant.

"Issie?" he asked. "Are you all right?"

She looked up at him and managed to nod. "Yeah. I was just thinking."

"About what?"

"I was thinking . . . what a horrible way to die."

Her eyes were dry, though clearly distraught. He stepped toward her. "Why don't you go home? Get some sleep?"

"I'm a little scared," she whispered.

He could understand that. As soon as the town found out about the second murder, there would probably be a panic among all of the women of Newpointe.

"Look, I'll be glad to follow you home, if you want. Make sure you get into your apartment all right."

"Would you?" she asked, looking hopefully up at him with tear-filled eyes that had a little too much power over him. She reached for his hand.

He knew he should have recoiled and stepped back out of her reach. This was how it had started before—tears, need, a touch . . .

His marriage was ending over it.

But he didn't disengage his hand.

"I mean, I can do it alone," she whispered. "I just . . . this has kind of got me strung out. You know, like there's a murderer lurking in every shadow . . ."

"Come on," he said, pulling her to her feet.

She grabbed her bag, and he walked her out into the night. The stars were brilliant, as was the moon, lending a false sense of security to the night.

"My car's still at Joe's Place," she said. "Will you walk me over?"

He walked her across the street to her car, opened the door for her, and locked it before he closed it. Then he trotted back across the street and got into his own.

His mind raced as he followed her the few blocks to her apartment. He had avoided this in the past, worried that getting this close to her home might be too tempting. Tonight was an exception, though—any of the guys at the station would have wanted to watch out for her. It was a Good Samaritan thing, he told himself. Not a lust thing.

She parked in the parking space in front of her apartment, and Mark got out of his car to walk her up to her door. She locked her car carefully, then looked nervously up at him and headed for her door.

He walked a step or two behind her. Wanting to look at her in the moonlight, he forced himself instead to walk with his hands in his pockets and his head cast down—just a good guy doing his masculine duty to protect the fairer sex. She stopped when she reached the door and unlocked it, then turned back to him. "Mark, come in for a few minutes. We could have a drink and talk . . ."

It seemed so innocent, so tempting. Just a few minutes in a warm apartment, talking with a good friend over a glass of wine that would relax him and help him to sleep later . . .

But something inside him resisted. Until now, he'd denied Allie's accusations of being involved with Issie by insisting that nothing had ever happened between them. And until now it had been true. But if he stepped through that door . . .

"I can't," he said, wishing he could. "I need to go."

She looked up at him, her doleful eyes meeting his, and for a moment, he wished she'd coax him, persuade him, ask him one more time. They were both lonely, and it had been a traumatic day. What could be more natural than two people who'd shared such experiences winding down together and talking things over?

"I'm not going to beg, Mark," she said softly. Silence passed as she waited, and he waited, thinking, weighing, wondering . . . Finally, she sighed, releasing him from the decision. "Thanks for following me home," she said matter-of-factly, breaking the mood.

Deflated by the disappointment that she hadn't tried harder, he said, "Sure. Lock up good, okay?"

She nodded and went in, closing the door between them.

He stood in the darkness for a moment, his heart pounding, wondering what he had let slip through his fingers—then wondering what he had escaped.

Allie. I need to see Allie.

The irrational need drew him back to his car, and the soul-deep fatigue and confusing emotions made him sit and stare out the windshield for a moment. He didn't know what he wanted tonight, didn't know where he belonged.

But as he cranked the car and pulled back out into the street, he drove by rote to his own home, where Allie lived, where things had once seemed so secure and so clear, where he'd known right from wrong and love from hate and security from fear.

He pulled into the driveway, turned off the ignition, and sat still for a moment, wondering what he would say when he woke Allie up and she came to the door. Would he tell her about Jamie? Or could he somehow put that off until morning, and just convince her to let him stay here where he could make sure she was safe, where he could *feel* safe, not from the killer, but from the world that seemed to be tugging at him, tearing him apart?

He didn't know, and didn't wait for answers. He made his way to the side entrance, pulled open the screen door, and rang the bell. He still had the key and knew that he could just go in, but he had to offer her some degree of respect since they were no longer living as man and wife.

He knocked. Knowing she was probably afraid to answer or to even call "Who is it?" he leaned close to the door and said, "Allie, it's me."

She still didn't answer, and he rang again as a sense of sick dread fell over him. Where was she? Had someone gotten her, too? Could she be lying in there, another victim of the psychopath who didn't give his targets a chance?

Trembling, he sorted through his keys, trying to find the right one. He tried to insert it into the dead bolt, but his hand was shaking too badly.

Suddenly, the knob turned and the door opened. Allie stood inside the kitchen, her long white cotton robe pooled around her bare feet. In the dim glow cast from the night-light on the stove, she looked angelic, sweet, innocent in contrast to the ugliness he had seen tonight.

"Mark? What is it?"

He couldn't stop the pounding in his heart, and he stumbled in and closed the door behind him, quickly turning on the light to make sure that she was safe and whole, unharmed.

"Mark, what's going on?" She sniffed—of course, she would smell the smoke from the bar, the alcohol on his breath. Why hadn't he thought of that? She stepped back, putting distance between them. "Mark, have you been drinking?"

"It's not about that, Allie," he said quickly, defensively. He shook his head and tried to find the right words, then gave up and just blurted it out. "There was another murder."

Her face showed no expression. She was bracing herself, marshaling her energy, processing the words. "What do you mean, another murder?"

"Jamie Larkins."

She caught her breath and took another step backward. "Oh, no."

"She was shot, just like Martha, and there was a fire."

"Oh, dear God." The words caught in her throat as she asked, "Who's doing this?"

"They didn't know anything when I left," he said. "But I'm sure everything's being done to find the killer."

She lifted her chin and tried to think it through. "Why Martha and Jamie?"

"They found some cocaine in Cale and Jamie's house. Cale seemed genuinely surprised to see it. I don't think he knew it was there. They're thinking maybe a drug deal went bad, and that Martha might have known something. There's no telling."

"Jamie wouldn't have confided in Martha. They were too different, and Martha was at least fifteen years older than Jamie. It's not like they hung around together."

"I know. It doesn't make sense. But until they find him, I don't think anyone is safe. Allie, I'm not going home tonight. I'm staying right here, with you, just to make sure."

He could see the protest forming on her lips, but just as quickly, it died. She was as frightened as he was, and she didn't want to be alone.

"I'll sleep on the couch," he said.

She stared at him for a long moment, and he felt a dread coming over him, coupled with an urgency that he didn't think she'd understand. Was she going to be so stubborn that she'd send him home?

The telephone rang, startling them both. She reached for it, keeping her eyes on him, and he felt exposed, transparent, as if she could see right through him. Sometimes he thought she really could.

"Hello?" she said tentatively. She kept the phone far enough from her ear that Mark could hear the voice on the other end.

"Allie, honey, this is Susan. You're not gonna believe what just happened! Jamie Larkins—"

"I know," Allie cut in. "I've already heard."

"Allie, this is getting scary, and Ray and I got to thinking about you being there all by yourself with a killer on the loose, and honey, we want you to come stay with us tonight. Ray will come and get you, but you don't need to be by yourself—"

"I'm not alone right now, actually," she said, and her eyes locked with Mark's.

"You're not?"

"No." She swallowed, and Mark took a step toward her. The alcohol on his breath seemed to hit her again, and she looked away. "But I do appreciate the invitation, and if you don't mind, I think I will come over. I don't really want to sleep here alone, and the alternative seems—" Her eyes shot up to Mark's again, and he waited for her to finish her sentence. "Well, there really isn't an alternative."

The remark stung him, as it was meant to, and he took the phone out of her hand. "Susan, this is Mark. I've already told Allie that I would stay here tonight. I don't want her here alone, either, so thanks—"

She grabbed the phone back and twisted away from him. "Susan, I'll come right over. But you don't have to send Ray."

"Honey, I don't want to interfere with you and Mark—"

"No, no," Allie said. "Really, I'd rather stay with you."

Mark was almost too angry to talk. "At least tell her that I'll bring you."

Allie put her hand over the phone. "No, Mark, I'd rather drive myself. You've been drinking."

"Allie, for pete's sake, I had one drink! I didn't even finish it. You're just using that as an excuse—"

"I'll drive myself, I said!"

"Fine, then!" he shouted. "You can drive yourself in my car, but I'm going with you!" He jerked the phone back from her and tried to calm his voice. "Susan, I'll bring her over. She'll be there shortly."

Susan's voice was dripping with apology. "Mark, I'm so sorry if I interfered. I didn't know you were there."

"It's okay, Susan," he said. "She'd rather face murder than have me in the house. I'm glad you called."

He hung up the phone and looked down at her, standing in her white robe tied at the waist, with her bare feet peeking out beneath it. She had no makeup on, and her hair was sleep-mussed, and something about the whole picture made his anger melt. He was still drawn to her, no matter how their ardor seemed to have cooled. But he couldn't act on it, not when her tongue was so sharp with accusations and allegations.

"Go get your stuff," he said quietly. "I'll wait for you."

She started into the bedroom, but he stopped her. "Allie, I did drink tonight, but it was only because it's been a lousy day."

"There've been a lot of lousy days lately, Mark." She looked down at the carpet beneath her feet. "I remember when they were about to build Joe's Place, and you were one of the loudest opponents in the meetings at city hall, protesting the fact that it was being built too close to the church. They made him build it somewhere else. Who would have thought that you'd become a regular patron?"

"That's not what I am, Allie. I just stop in there now and then, when things are really rough."

"Maybe things wouldn't be so rough if you didn't stop in there," she said. Her eyes were direct, clear, penetrating as she nailed him with her next question. "Tell me something, Mark. Was Issie there tonight?"

That anger rose again, and he looked away. "What if she was?"

"That's what I thought."

"I didn't go there with her, Allie. It was Fat Tuesday. Everybody in town was at that bar."

"Not everybody," she said.

"Don't be self-righteous, Allie."

"I'm not, Mark. I'm just stating a fact. Did you take her home?"

He looked away again, indignant. "Actually, we were called away by Jamie's murder," he said, hoping his words had the same sting hers did. "And I'm here, aren't I? Not with her, but here." The fact that he evaded her question only bothered him a little. So he had followed Issie home. It didn't mean a thing. He was still innocent. In fact, he probably deserved a trophy for not succumbing to temptation on a night like tonight. If Allie just weren't so bitterly pious, she'd realize it.

"So why *are* you here?" she asked.

"Because I was worried about you. No underlying motive, Allie, as evil and deceptive as you think I am. I wanted to make sure you were all right."

They stared off for a long moment, and finally, he said, "You'd better hurry. No need to keep the Fords up any longer than we have to."

She nodded quietly and went to pack.

••• • •••

At the Fords' house, Allie climbed out of Mark's car, then waited while he dragged her bag out of the trunk and carried it to the door where the porch light was on. Mark set the bag on the porch. She felt him looking down at her, but she didn't look back. Instead, she focused on a button on his shirt.

"Well . . . thanks for bringing me."

"I didn't bring you," he reminded her. "You brought me."

"Well, anyway. Thanks."

"Don't mention it," he said, and she heard the sarcasm in his voice. They were behaving like strangers. Part of her wanted it that way; the other part despised it.

"Allie . . ."

She looked up at him, finally, but the moment she did, he looked away and seemed to lose his train of thought.

She started to knock, knowing that inside, Susan probably waited for her, not wanting to break the moment between them. Poor Susan, she thought. She had such hope for their reconciliation. More hope than Allie had.

But Mark caught her hand, and she hated the fact that his touch still caused a little electric jolt to shoot through her, as it had when they'd first met. "Allie, don't always think the worst of me. I haven't done anything wrong."

"That's exactly the problem," Allie said.

"What? That I haven't done anything wrong?"

"No, that you won't admit it." She felt her cheeks growing hot, and hoped he couldn't see them reddening in the dim light.

"Allie, I can't admit to something that I haven't done. Do you want me to lie?"

"Why not?" she asked. "You've been doing it for months." The words weren't uttered in anger, but in deep sadness, and she looked away as she said them, hoping he wouldn't see the tears filling her eyes.

He lifted her chin, made her look at him. "Allie, I've never lied to you."

She moved her chin away from his fingertips and took a step backward. "No, Mark, it's yourself you lie to, mostly. That way you can convince yourself that what you tell me is the truth."

He rubbed his stubbled jaw and looked up at the night sky, as if he could find some logic, some rationale there. "I remember when you thought the best of me."

"I remember when you *were* the best."

The implication that he no longer was seemed to pierce him, and the pain on his face brought a pang to her own heart. She didn't enjoy hurting him. But for some time now, their conversations seemed to consist of both of them saying things that hurt.

He turned his back and stood on the edge of the porch, looking out into the night. He smelled of smoke, as he often did, and his big shoulders, normally so strong and capable, looked slumped beneath the weight of all that had occurred that day. For a moment, she thought of touching his back, or reaching up to press a kiss on his stubbled cheek. But she wouldn't allow herself to. Several silent moments passed, and finally he turned and said, "Make sure you aren't alone in the store tomorrow. It's easy to let your guard down in daylight, but don't forget Martha was killed in the morning."

She nodded.

"And if you need me, you know where I'll be."

Their eyes met again, and this time, he leaned over and kissed her cheek. "Good night, Allie."

"Night." She waited for him to leave, then realized he wasn't going to until she was inside. She rapped lightly on the door, and Susan answered it.

"Hey, honey, come on in."

Allie stepped inside as Mark trotted down the porch steps and back out to his car.

Susan closed the door and locked the dead bolt. "Is everything all right?"

Allie shook her head. "No, not really." She pulled in a deep sigh. "I really appreciate your inviting me over."

"Isn't it awful about Jamie? And Martha . . . oh, Allie."

The two women hugged. Ray, who was usually jovial, came into the room looking more solemn than she had ever seen him, and as tired and shocked as Mark.

"Ray, have you heard any more about Jamie's murder? Any leads?"

"No, 'fraid not. I just got off the phone with my brother Sid."

Sid was a lieutenant on the Newpointe police force, and likely to know how the investigation was going.

"He said they're pretty sure the murders have somethin' to do with the drugs they found. They've set up roadblocks and are hopin' to catch the guy leavin' town."

"But that doesn't make sense," Susan cried. "Martha would never have touched cocaine. And she wouldn't have known anything about Jamie taking it, either."

"How is Cale?" Allie asked.

"Stunned," Ray said. "He wasn't even s'pose to work tonight. Swapped with somebody at the last minute. Wonder if anything woulda been different if he'd been home."

"Maybe he would have been killed, too," Allie suggested.

"Maybe."

Susan wiped her eyes, breathed deeply, then released it. "Well, we'd better turn in. Tomorrow's gonna be a long day. I made up Ben's room for you, Allie," she said, referring to her son who was away at Louisiana State. "Just make yourself at home, hear?"

Allie went into Ben's room and dropped her bag on the bed. The room was decorated with posters of sports heroes and pennants of his favorite colleges; a basketball hoop hung on the wall. She caught a glimpse of herself in the mirror as she scanned the room, and quickly turned away. She didn't like seeing herself lately.

The fact that Mark had wanted to protect her confused her. What did it mean? She couldn't believe he still loved her, not after two months of separation, when he'd made so little effort to set things right again. He didn't seem to care how she felt about his "friendship" with Issie—or anything else. Why, now, did he suddenly care?

She went to the window and peered out. His car was gone, and she wondered whether he'd go back to the bar or to his apartment. Would he go to see if Issie was all right, since she, too, lived alone?

The thought sickened her. Trying to shove down the emotions welling up inside her, she sat down in the chair across from the bed. Closing her eyes, she cried out to God.

She prayed for Mark, that he would be safe tonight, and that the thoughts he had of her as he drifted into sleep would not be cold, angry thoughts. She hoped they were tender thoughts, the way they used to be.

Where had they gone wrong?

She asked that question of God, but no answer came. Troubled and confused and frightened and exhausted, she finally fell into a shallow sleep.

Chapter Eleven

● ● ●

Jill Clark was awakened from a sound sleep at four A.M. by a
ringing telephone. Reaching blindly for it, she managed to
bump the touch-me lamp, and the light came on. Squinting
from the sudden, unexpected brightness, she picked up the
phone. "Hello?"

"Jill, you gotta help me."

The man's voice was not familiar, so she sat up in bed, trying to clear her brain. "Who is this?"

"Joe Petitjean," he said.

For a moment she struggled to put a face with the name,
then remembered—he was the owner of Joe's Place, the town's
favorite bar. "What is it, Joe?"

"I need a lawyer. I'm down to the po-lice station, and they
questionin' me 'bout Jamie Larkins's murder. Jill, I don't have
nothin' to do with that, and I did *not* sell her the bag of cocaine
she had in the house."

"Jamie Larkins was murdered?" she asked, sitting straight
up. "Joe, it's Martha Broussard who was killed—not Jamie."

"Both of 'em, Jill. I'm tellin' you, they tryin' to pin somethin' on me, even though they said they just brought me in for
questionin'. And I ain't the only one."

She had her pants on and was reaching for a pullover
sweater. "What do you mean?"

"I mean they got at least twenty others in here. They got
some kind of roadblock set up and they catchin' every pot-
smoking, beer-drinkin' yo that tries to leave this town. You

come down here, you better be ready to stay a while. I ain't the only one gonna need a lawyer."

Jill hung up and hurried to the bathroom. She washed her face and brushed her teeth, then grabbed her shoes and hopped as she put on one at a time on her way out.

It wasn't until she was in the car that the horror of what Joe had told her finally penetrated. Jamie Larkins was dead?

She wondered if Allie knew. Digging her cellular phone from her purse, she punched in Allie's number with her thumb as she drove, hoping Allie would have a few details Jill might need. The phone rang five, six, seven times before Jill pushed "end," terminating the call attempt. Where could Allie be?

She tried to think. She needed some background information before she burst into the police station. Someone at the fire department would know something, she thought, since they were usually dispatched to all of the calls at the same time the police were.

She dialed information, got the number for the Midtown Fire Station, and waited as it rang. The voice that answered was subdued and muffled.

"Hello?"

"This is Jill Clark. Who's speaking, please?"

"This is Dan Nichols, Jill," the voice said, and she had an instant image of the tall blond fireman with bright blue eyes.

"Dan, I'm on my way to the police station, but I needed a little information about Jamie Larkins's murder. Can you tell me anything about it?"

"I can tell you what I know," he said. "I wasn't on duty when they got the call. I just came in an hour ago to take Cale's place. But whoever did it shot her through the chest, then set the house on fire."

Jill's stomach jolted, but she tried to stay calm. "What's this about cocaine?"

"They found it in her house—in the part that didn't burn down. They're thinking that maybe there's a connection."

"Okay, that makes sense," she said, thinking out loud. "So now they're rounding up anyone who saw her today, trying to find witnesses. Dan, do they have any leads at all?"

"I couldn't say, Jill. But for now there is a killer on the loose, and I wouldn't be out there alone if I were you."

She turned onto Purchase Street, where the police station and fire station were located. "Thanks, Dan. But I'm almost there."

"I'll meet you outside and walk you in," he said.

She smiled. "I don't think that's necessary. No one's going to attack me right outside the police station."

"It's four-thirty in the morning, Jill, and we know for sure there's a killer in town. I'll meet you outside," he said.

He hung up. Smiling, she clicked off the phone and dropped it back into her purse. As she pulled up to the front of the police station, she saw him coming out of the open garage of the fire department adjacent to the building. Grabbing her purse and briefcase, she got out.

"I appreciate this, Dan," she said.

"Not a problem."

He walked her up the steps to the police station doors and opened the glass door for her. "If you want me to walk you out when you leave, just holler," he told her. "Unless I'm on a call, it's no problem to pop over here."

She touched his arm in thanks. She had heard that he was arrogant, vain, and self-centered. But to her he just seemed like a nice guy, and she hadn't had much experience with nice guys lately. "Thanks, I will."

He disappeared back into the night.

Jill stepped through the next set of glass doors, surprised at the amount of activity in the usually sleepy station. It looked as if every police officer in Newpointe had been called in to work tonight and half the town had been dragged in for questioning.

She spotted Joe sitting outside one of the interrogation rooms. Before she could reach him, though, someone else called her name.

"Jill, thank goodness. I've been trying to call you."

She stopped as she saw Lisa Manning, Jamie Larkins's best friend. Her eyes were swollen, and she was wiping her nose with a wadded tissue. "Lisa, what are you doing here?"

"They came and got me for questioning," she said. "I already told 'em everything I knew, but they won't let me go home yet. I didn't think to call you until a few minutes ago."

Joe was standing now and waving impatiently across the room at her, but she touched Lisa's shoulder. "What did you tell them, Lisa? What *do* you know?"

"*Nothing*. At least, nothing about the murder. I want the killer caught as much as anybody. All I knew was about the coke. She bought it this morning—or yesterday morning—at the parade. She saw some guy she knew and bought it right there on the spot, in front of God and everybody. I didn't even know what it was until later, I swear."

"Did you know the guy?"

"No, I've never seen him before. He had like a black buzz cut, and this gross tattoo of a spider on his neck. Really gave me the creeps. He was about five eleven, I guess, early twenties. She said she knew him from when she used to party on the Southshore a lot. That's all I can remember, but I told them I'd recognize him if I saw him again. Jill, should I have called you first?"

She glanced toward the interrogation room from which two cops were coming, and she shook her head. "I think you're all right, Lisa. You're a witness, that's all. They're trying to get as many leads as they can so they can catch the guy."

"Do I need a lawyer?"

"If they want to talk to you any more, I'll go in with you," she said. "Just sit tight and wait. I have to go talk to Joe."

Lisa sank back into her seat, among the others who had been brought in. Some were handcuffed and leaning back drunkenly against the wall. Most were out-of-towners; she recognized few of them. They were probably people who lived too far north of New Orleans to make the trip all the way in, so they'd come here to do their partying. Some of the bars in town had advertised special events tonight to draw the crowds. Apparently, it had worked.

She made her way to Joe and saw the fear in his eyes. "They wanted to question me, but I told 'em to wait till you got here."

"All right," she said, sitting down. He did the same. "Joe, they must think you know something or saw something. Had Jamie Larkins been in your bar tonight?"

"Not tonight, but she was in this afternoon, all shook up about the murder. She wound up tyin' one on."

"Did you see her talking to anybody?"

"Couple of her girlfriends. She's a wild one, but I never seen her with any men except Cale."

Jill looked Joe in the eye, carefully trying to phrase her words so she wouldn't set him off. "Joe, I have to ask. Is there any reason for the police to believe that she might have gotten the cocaine from you or someone who works for you?"

"No! You kiddin'? I sell booze, not dope."

"All right." She stood and looked around for the nearest cop. Stan Shepherd was just coming out of the interrogation room. "Stan?" she called.

Stan nodded. "Hey, Jill. I see Joe called you."

"Yeah. You want to question him?"

"Sure do."

"All right, let's get this over with. It's late."

He ushered them both into the interrogation room, called in another cop, and set up a tape player in the middle of the table. Jill coached Joe through Stan's questioning for the next hour.

Chapter Twelve

• • •

Just outside of town, miles of traffic at the junction of Highway 90 and I-59 sat backed up as police checked each car for a man who fit the description Lisa had given them. If they could come up with any reason to legally search a vehicle, they made the driver pull over and checked for drugs and guns—specifically a .38 caliber handgun, which had killed both Martha and Jamie. A dozen cars had been pulled over to the side, and officers were arresting their passengers. Several had been caught with drugs, from marijuana to heroin, though they were all possession cases since the quantities of the drugs were small. One guy had been caught with a handgun that they'd determined was, indeed, registered to him, and three others had been caught with illegal weapons. Several others walked invisible lines, trying and failing to prove that they were not too drunk to drive. Though all eight of Newpointe's squad cars were on the scene, fifteen cops had been called to work the roadblock.

As they filed those arrested into the van that was quickly filling up for the third time, they still had gotten no closer to finding the suspected killer. Drunken revelers stewing in their stalled cars were getting angrier, and some were yelling out the windows at the cops who, undaunted, continued going from one car to the next.

Vern Hargis waved a carload of college-aged girls past, and stopped the next car in line, a gray Plymouth that looked as if it had seen better days; the driver was the only one inside. Vern shone his beam into the car as he stepped close to the window. The man had a buzz cut, just as Lisa Manning had described. But so had a couple dozen other guys who'd come through tonight.

"May I see your drivers' license, please, sir?"

The man pulled out his wallet, slid out his license, and handed it to him. "Rounding up all the drunk drivers?" he asked.

Vern noticed the spider tattoo on his neck. "Please get out of the car," he said. The driver opened the door and stepped out. Vern snapped the cuff on one of his wrists. Before the man could react, he had the other one on, and yelled across the roof of the car, "Captain, I've got something!"

Two cops came running as Vern spread-eagled the suspect against the car and began to frisk him.

"What is this? I'm not *drunk!* Can't you see that I'm as sober as you are?"

"He fits the description!" Vern said. "Check out the tattoo." He reached into the man's pocket and slid out three vials of cocaine. "Look at this!"

The other two cops began to search the car. When they found a backpack in his trunk holding at least twenty grams of cocaine and $4,000 in cash, they knew they had their man.

"You're under arrest, pal," Vern said, jerking him over to his squad car, which was parked in the grass on the side of the highway.

"For *what?*"

"Take your choice. Possession with intent to distribute, or murder one."

"*Murder?* Hey, I didn't kill *anybody!* Is this about that Broussard woman?"

That was as close to a confession as Vern needed. This guy was as guilty as the serpent in Eden. "Radio back to the precinct and tell 'em we've got our man."

Chapter Thirteen

● ● ●

The smell of something cooking in the kitchen woke Allie just as the first light of dawn softened the gray outside. She quickly showered in the hall bathroom, then dressed and headed for the kitchen. Susan was busy stirring something in a mixing bowl as her fifteen-year-old daughter, Vanessa, gathered her books for school. "Mama, please!" Vanessa argued. "What good is it to have your learner's permit if you never get to drive?"

Not wanting to interrupt their discussion, Allie stopped just short of the kitchen doorway.

"Not today," Susan said. "Ride with your car pool."

"But Mama! *I* can drive the car pool! My friends never seen me drive before. I been waitin' my whole life to drive and you won't *ever* let me!"

"You're gon' have to wait one more day."

"If it wasn't for the murders you'd let me."

"Young lady, I said *no!*"

"But Mama, don't let these murders get you all unreasonable and paranoid. Some of us still have a life!"

Thinking she'd waited long enough, Allie reluctantly stepped into the room. "Good morning."

Susan looked up from her mixing bowl. "Hey, girl. I hope Vanessa didn't wake you. If she did, she's sorry, ain't you, Vanessa?"

"She didn't wake me," Allie said before the girl had to answer. "Good morning, Vanessa. I love your hair."

The compliment changed the girl's tone, and she ran her fingers through the long weaves that gave her a movie star look. "Thanks. It took hours. Allie, how old were you when your parents let you drive?"

"Uh . . ."

A horn sounded outside, and Susan grabbed Vanessa's sack lunch and thrust it at her. "Your ride's here. Go."

"Shoot!" Pouting, she took the lunch and rushed out the door without saying good-bye to either of them.

Allie grinned, and Susan chuckled lightly. "She's got a tough life. And to think we were both awake all night worrying about murderers running loose . . ." Her smile faded, and she went back to stirring. Susan's eyes were tired, and Allie wondered if her friend had slept at all last night. From the looks of the casseroles cooling on the stove, she doubted it. But it was Susan who asked, "Did you sleep okay?"

"As much as can be expected," Allie said. She went to one of the dishes and pulled the tin foil back to see what was in it. A broccoli casserole that smelled like heaven. "How long have you been at this?"

"Oh, a couple hours. I couldn't sleep." She kept stirring, harder and longer than Allie thought she needed to. "I thought I'd make myself useful and take some casseroles over to George and Cale, so they wouldn't have to worry about what to eat."

"George is with his parents, isn't he?"

"I'll take it to them," she said. "Heaven knows they'll have enough on their minds without having to think up meals to fix."

Allie gazed at Susan. She was so pretty and petite that Allie had always envied her, and she seemed to have unlimited energy and enough compassion to comfort the whole town. "That's sweet of you, Susan."

"Well, it's the least I can do." She drew in a deep breath and kept stirring. "I just don't know what George is gon' do. With that little baby . . ." Her eyes filled with tears, and she looked up at Allie. "Allie, I just don't understand this. I know God's in control, but George and Martha prayed fifteen years for that baby, and it was to God's glory when Tommy was born. How can Martha's murder be for good? How can it be part of the plan?"

"Maybe it isn't part of God's plan," Allie said weakly as she sank into a chair and stared down at the floor.

"But that would mean that God's *not* in control."

"He's in control," Allie said, thinking it through as she went along, "but he allows some things to happen."

"Why?" Susan's voice cracked with the question. "Why something like this? That's what I don't understand."

Allie's own emotions began to well up in her throat, burning her eyes, and she shook her head and got up. "I don't know, Susan."

Susan abandoned her bowl and came to Allie, and the two women embraced and held each other for several moments.

"Well, I guess that's where faith comes in," Susan said finally, stepping back and wiping her eyes. "We just have to pray that God'll help us understand."

"We may never understand," Allie whispered. "Maybe the best we can hope for is peace about it."

"Peace," Susan said, turning back to the bowl. "That seems so impossible right now, with some maniac on the loose and two friends dead." She pulled out a pan that she had already greased and poured the batter into it.

Ray came to the door of the kitchen, just wakened, though he was fully dressed in khakis and a pullover knit shirt. "I just got off the phone with Sid. He's still at the police station," he said. "He been there all night. Says they caught the perpetrator."

"What?" Allie asked, spinning around. "Really?"

Susan stopped pouring the batter. "Who was it, Ray?"

"Some dope dealer they caught on his way out of town. He's from Bogaloosa. Name's Hank Keyes. Been I.D.'d by one of the witnesses who saw Jamie making the deal with him yesterday."

"And they think he's the one who killed Martha and Jamie?"

"They do."

Allie breathed a huge sigh of relief, and turned to Susan, who was staring at Ray with a poignant look on her face. "Do they know why yet, Ray?"

"He's denyin' everythin'," he said. "They can't get nothin' out of him."

Susan pulled out a chair and wilted down. "I wish I could talk to him."

"What would you tell him, Susan?" Allie asked.

"That he blew a terrible hole into this town yesterday. That he didn't just hurt the husbands and the little baby, but he hurt all of us."

"He wouldn't care," Ray said.

"No, he wouldn't," she said. She drew in a deep breath, got back up, and returned to her cooking. "I'm gonna ask Brother Nick to open up the church today," she said. "We need to pray for that man."

Allie didn't say anything. But she didn't think she could pray for a killer.

Chapter Fourteen

● ● ●

Hank Keyes's apartment in Bogaloosa looked as though it had been ransacked, but it was soon apparent to Stan Shepherd and the other officers with him that Keyes had left it this way. Dishes in the sink in the kitchen had week-old food dried on them, and the half-filled glasses scattered around the room looked like science experiments Stan had done in high school—green fuzz covered the contents and climbed up the sides. The apartment reeked of decay and neglect.

They stepped over dirty laundry and wadded papers on the floor, looking for a place to start the search that might prove definitively that Hank was their man.

Before they'd gotten past the living room, the door opened and a bearded, greasy-looking man came stumbling in wearing a black T-shirt with the sleeves cut off. His eyes were blood-shot, and he smelled of vomit, booze, and body odor. He didn't look surprised to see strangers, only mildly annoyed. "You friends of Hank's?" he asked.

"Police officers," Stan said, flashing his shield. "We're from Newpointe, but Officer Cockrell over there is from the Bogaloosa P.D. We're going to have to ask you to leave. We're in the middle of an investigation, and we can't allow any of the evidence to be disturbed."

"I can't come into my own apartment?" the man bellowed.

"You live here?" Stan asked.

"Yeah, I live here. Who'd you *think* lived here?"

"We were told that Hank Keyes lives here."

"Well, he does. We share it." Aggravated, he rubbed his eyes, as though it would somehow clear his thinking. "Who'd you say you were?"

"Police officers," Stan repeated. He noticed the spider tattoo on the man's neck—just like the one their suspect had. "What's your relationship to Hank Keyes?"

"We're roommates," he said. "You got a warrant? 'Cause if you ain't got a warrant—"

"We've got one, pal." Stan showed him the warrant, and the man wilted.

"*Man!* What'd he *do* to get the cops to swarm this place?"

Stan ignored him. "Do you own any guns of any kind?"

"No. None. Come on, man. Whatever you're lookin' for, we ain't got it."

One of the cops who'd started perusing the closets cleared his throat. Stan turned around and saw the guns sitting on the top shelf. "Want to change your story, pal?"

"Man . . ." The guy shook his head. "I thought you meant unregistered guns. Those guns are registered."

"To who?"

"To me."

The same cop who had found the guns began riffling through some boxes on the floor in the same closet. "Man, that stuff's personal. Don't open that!"

The cop on the floor opened the box and looked up at Stan. "It's personal, all right. His personal stash. There's enough cocaine here for every high school kid in Newpointe High."

"That's Hank's stash, not mine. I didn't even know that was there!"

"Right." Stan snapped his handcuffs on the man, and hoped he didn't have to be the one to take him back. He'd never get the smell out of his car. "You weren't by any chance in Newpointe with your buddy last night, were you?"

"No, man. I been in New Orleans all night. Why? Wha'd he do?"

"He killed two women."

"*Hank?* No, man. He couldn't have. I had nothin' to do with that, man. I have witnesses who saw me in the Quarter. A girl I was with can tell you. Her name was Wanda something. I was with her all night."

Stan gave a dry laugh as he led the man to the door. "Hey, Cockrell. Look up Wanda Something in New Orleans. That ought to clear things up."

Chapter Fifteen

● ● ●

Before he headed back to Newpointe, Stan Shepherd stopped in at the only tattoo parlor in Bogaloosa, where he surmised that Hank and his roommate may have gotten their tattoos. The eight-foot-square waiting room was furnished with two split vinyl love seats that looked as if they'd been rescued from someone's garbage pile. On the walls were sketches of hundreds of tattoos to choose from.

Stan scanned the pictures carefully, looking for the spider.

"Be right with you." The voice was deep and phlegmy, and Stan turned to the curtained doorway separating the waiting room from whatever was behind it. A man who must have weighed four hundred pounds stood holding the curtains out of his way with one pudgy hand, a cigarette hanging from his mouth. "Know what you want?"

"I'm looking for something in particular," Stan said. "A spider."

The man pushed the curtain back and came through, giving Stan a once-over. "Spider, huh?" He pointed to one that Stan hadn't noticed yet. "Like that there?"

"Yes." Stan stepped closer to examine the lines of the drawing. "You do many of those?"

"What are you, some kind of cop?"

Stan studied the man, wondering why his simple question would have led him to that assumption. He pulled his shield from his pocket. "Stan Shepherd, Newpointe P.D. Do you do many tattoos on necks?"

"Newpointe? Ain't you a little out of your territory?"

"I'm investigating two homicides we had there last night."

"Blacks?" the big man asked.

Stan frowned. Why would he ask that? "No, actually. Both white women. Why?"

The man shrugged. "You lookin' at spiders and talkin' about necks and murder investigations. They usually only kill blacks. They can't get the spider 'til they do."

Stan didn't want to appear ignorant, but he needed information. "*They* being some kind of white supremacists?"

"You might call 'em that," the fat man said.

"How many of these have you done?"

"That's privileged information."

Stan smirked. "There's no law protecting tattooer confidentiality."

"No written law, maybe. But there's a law, all right, and if you violate it, you get dead. Besides, I don't keep lists. They come in and pay me, I do my job, and I never see 'em again."

"Do they talk when they're here?"

"Some do, some don't."

Stan pulled out a copy of Hank Keyes's mug shot and showed it to the man. "Remember doing one for this guy?"

"All the faces just blend together after a while."

Stan smirked, reached into his back pocket, pulled out his wallet, and held out a twenty-dollar bill. "Does this help your memory?"

The man took the bill. "It's coming back to me. Still a little blurry, though."

Stan handed him another twenty, then closed the wallet and slid it back into his pocket.

"What do you want to know?"

"What kind of gang it is he belongs to. The name of it, the code they have, anything you can give me."

"That's easy. Why didn't you just ask?" The man began to laugh, a wet, phlegmy laugh that ended in a coughing fit. Stan considered calling an ambulance before the coughing finally subsided. "They're called the Slashers, and they're mostly former military dudes. Hate blacks, and they have to kill one to earn their spider."

"What about women? Do they have anything against white women?"

"They like 'em." Amused, the man laughed again, which once more threw him into a round of coughing.

After that Stan got nowhere. Fearing reprisals, the tattooer wasn't about to give Stan any specific information about the Slashers—where they met, the names of any other members, anything that would be useful to Stan in his investigation. As he drove back to Newpointe, he struggled to make sense of things. Why would a skinhead—who'd killed at least one black person to earn his spider—want to kill two white women? Was there anything in what he'd just learned that supported the theory that these murders were just a drug deal gone bad? Had the Nazi-like group decided to start killing off Caucasian women, or were these murders unrelated to the Slashers? If the murders were gang-related, then he'd have to charge Keyes—and maybe his roommate, too—with conspiracy, as well as murder one.

He was bone-tired. He hadn't slept all night. Maybe he should get some sleep and let someone else interrogate Hank's roommate, now that they had the killer off the streets.

No, he thought. Not yet. He wanted to make sure no one dropped the ball. This was too important, and he didn't want Keyes to slip through their fingers just because something wasn't done right.

Chapter Sixteen

● ● ●

The funeral services were scheduled for two days later, back to back in Calvary Bible Church, the little nondenominational church in the heart of Newpointe. Brother Nick Foster sat at the big table in the firehouse kitchen and stared with tears in his eyes at the telephone in front of him, on which he had just spoken to Cale Larkins. Cale wasn't one of his church members, nor had Jamie been, but since the Larkins had no church home, Cale had asked his friend Nick to officiate at Jamie's funeral. Earlier, George Broussard had made the same request for Martha's funeral, but George's request had been natural, expected. From the Sunday they'd joined Calvary, Martha and George had been active members of the small church, and Nick would have much to say about the woman who had so often demonstrated tireless service and devotion to God.

But Jamie was another story. Nick hadn't known her well, which meant that he would have to find people who had and ask them for things to share at her funeral, good things about the woman that would make them smile or nod, that would give them hope or encouragement. On the phone, he had asked Cale a question that had been plaguing his mind since her death. "Cale, where was Jamie spiritually?"

"Oh, she was a real spiritual person, Preacher," Cale said. "Really. She was real interested in angels and swore she had her own personal guardian angel. She talked to her sometimes, right out loud. And she wore that cross around her neck most of the time, with a little crystal right next to it, because she said it had healing powers, in case she ever got sick."

Nick had groaned inwardly. "Cale, did Jamie ever pray, that you knew of? Did she study Scripture?"

"Everybody prays sometimes, don't they, Preacher?" Cale asked. "She wasn't much of a reader, though." His voice had cracked then, and there was a long moment of silence. "I know what you're gettin' at, Nick. I've been to church enough in my life to see what you're leadin' up to. You're tryin' to decide whether she went to hell or not."

Nick was speechless, something that didn't happen often. Quickly, his mind searched for some type of verbal Band-Aid. "Not at all, Cale. That's not up to me to decide. I just didn't know her very well, and I'm trying to find out as much as I can about her."

"Still . . ." The silence hung like a cloud over the phone line. "Don't you think the way she died would have been hell enough? I mean, wouldn't a lovin' God—the kind you preach—have mercy on somebody who was . . ." His pitch rose and his voice cracked. ". . . murdered like that?"

Since he'd become a preacher, Nick had often wished that he didn't have to be bivocational, that he could devote all of his time to shepherding his flock. But right now, he wished the opposite—that he were just a fireman, and not a preacher at all. He was supposed to give honest truths to people who asked him spiritual questions, but this was a tough one. The man was in the depths of grief and needed comfort desperately. And Nick wasn't sure he could give him any.

"Cale, where are you? I'm on duty right now, but as soon as I get off, I'd like to come talk with you, face-to-face."

"That's it, then, huh? You do think she's in hell, but you don't want to say it over the phone."

"Cale, I can't pretend to know where Jamie's soul is."

"You know where Martha's is, don't you, Preacher?"

"I knew her better than I knew Jamie." It was a lame, weak response to a complicated question, and he wished he'd studied more, gotten deeper into Scripture this week, prayed harder this morning . . .

"It all boils down to the sentence, don't it, Preacher?"

"Sentence?" Nick asked. "What sentence?"

"The prayer sentence. The one where you say you accept Jesus as your Savior. I grew up in church, Preacher. I know all the rules. And you expect me to believe that if my Jamie didn't say that one sentence some time in her life, that she's burnin' in hell right this minute?"

Nick rubbed the tears from his eyes and realized that his hands were trembling. He closed his eyes and asked the Lord for an extra helping of wisdom. "Cale, the gospel has little to do with a bunch of words strung together. It's a heart's commitment, an emptying out of self, and being filled, instead, with the Holy Spirit. It's not about repeating a sentence. I don't know what condition Jamie's heart was in, and I would never pronounce her to be in hell. Besides, Cale, neither of us knows what might have happened in her heart and soul in her last moments."

"That's right," Cale said. "We don't know." He grew quiet again, then asked, "Preacher, do you think if I got my heart right, that I could pray and ask God to put her in heaven, just in case she ain't there, after all?"

"We're each responsible for our own souls, Cale," he said sadly. "The only person you can pray out of hell is yourself."

"Yeah, that's what I figured." Cale drew in a deep, shaky breath, then sniffed hard, and said, "She was a good person, Preacher. She loved me. She had a lot of friends, and loved to laugh. She was a good person."

"I know she was, Cale. I know she'll be missed."

"You don't know the half of it." Cale was sobbing now, and Nick wished they were face-to-face so that he could offer the man more than hollow words. Handling needs such as this over the telephone made Nick feel so awkward, so helpless.

"Cale, I'm so sorry this all happened." Nick's own voice cracked, and he rubbed his face. "If there's anything more I can do for you—if you need to get away, I can borrow my uncle's boat, and we can go sit out in the middle of the lake for a few hours, and think and talk . . ."

"Yeah, I'll keep that in mind," Cale said. "I'll get back in touch."

Now, sitting in the kitchen of the firehouse, Nick wondered what Jesus would have done. He closed his eyes and tried to think. Jesus wouldn't have pulled any punches with the truth, he thought. He would have told Cale exactly like it was. Then maybe he would have taken Jamie's hand, brought her back to life, and forgiven her sins.

But Nick wasn't Jesus. He was just a man, and he'd never healed anyone, much less raised anyone from the dead. Today, he couldn't even provide the simplest comfort. Maybe he was just fooling himself into believing he was called to be the shepherd of this little church in this little town. Maybe he should resign, and just fight fires.

As he always did when his soul cried out, he opened his Bible and began to search for God's answers to the painful questions that plagued him.

• • •

It was getting close to lunchtime when Aggie Gaston got out of her big lavender Cadillac. As she opened the back door to retrieve the groceries she'd bought on her way there, she saw the front door of the firehouse open. Mark Branning hurried out.

"Aunt Aggie, I'll get that."

They pampered her here, as if she were an old lady, but she didn't mind. To most people, eighty *was* old. But most eighty-year-olds didn't walk five miles a day, or have the entire fire department as their adopted sons. Those things kept her young. She reached for a hug as Mark got to the car, and gave him an extra pat because of the bad news.

"Where y'at, Mark?" she asked in her thick Cajun accent.

"Awright, Aunt Aggie."

"You okay?" Still holding him and examining his face, she said, "You lookin' mighty tired, *mon ami*."

"I'm fine," he said. "We're all a little shaken up."

"With good reason." As he bent in to get the groceries, she said, "Careful with dat, now. I'm makin' a gumbo for tonight—a little lagniappe to cheer everybody up."

"You're a princess."

Aggie beamed and followed him in. As she cut through the firehouse, each of the firemen greeted her with a hug and asked what was for lunch, and she told them just enough to whet their appetites before she started cooking.

Like Aunt Bea in Mayberry, who cooked all the meals for the residents of the town's jail, Aunt Aggie had a reputation for mothering the firefighters, but that was where the similarity ended. Though she seldom mentioned it herself, it was well known around town that she had been Miss Louisiana back in 1938, and she had held onto her figure and good looks. She still watched her weight and carried herself as if she had an Amy Vanderbilt book of etiquette balanced on her head. When she was sixty, she'd had a face-lift that made her look forty, and now that she was eighty, and looked sixty, she wanted to have another one. But she couldn't find a doctor who would perform it on a woman of her age—a fact that she considered quite an insult. Despite her efforts to cling to her youth, she had long ago allowed her hair to turn white, but only because it was a pure white that looked glamorous—and because she secretly hated the humiliation of sitting for an hour in the chair at the beautician's with her hair all pasted on top of her head while peroxide burned her eyes and color trickled down her temples.

Besides, the men she served each day seemed to like her hair the way it was. They told her daily how good she was looking, and she never ceased to believe it. They also complimented her taste in clothing and her exquisite talent for creating fine cuisine. It was the only payment she required. Every day, including weekends, she pampered the firefighters with crawfish bisque, lobster tails, and a million other Cajun concoctions that had brought a little culture into the otherwise boring little firehouse. It had started over forty years ago, when she'd tired of hearing her husband complain about the meals other men cooked in the firehouse, so she had begun then to bring meals so often that they stopped cooking entirely and came to depend on her. They never worried about how much money she spent on the food—she was independently wealthy, having first inherited her father's money and then made a substantial ground-floor investment in a little company called Microsoft. Besides, she considered this the closest thing she had to a "calling." Had she believed in God, she would have sworn this was the job he had foreordained for her.

But she didn't believe in God. She considered herself a fine example of someone with strong moral fiber and a good life, none of which she attributed to church, an institution she considered a waste of time. She proudly boasted that she hadn't darkened the doors of any church in four years, not since Celia, her great niece—the only one in town who had a blood right to call her Aunt Aggie—had married Stan Shepherd. Still, she fed Nick Foster, Celia's preacher, when he was on duty at the firehouse, and treated him as kindly as she did any of the others, even though she thought he was probably no better than a car salesman peddling his congregation a weekly bill of goods. Still, she liked Nick, and she was glad he'd kept his day job so he'd have something to fall back on when his proselytizing got old.

As if her very thoughts had conjured him, she found him sitting at the table in the kitchen when she went in, looking as if he'd seen better days. The books all spread out on the table in front of him, Bibles and notebooks and whatnot, didn't seem to be offering him much help. She stepped over the phone cord and gave him a hug. "You awright, *mon petit?*"

"I'm okay, Aunt Aggie. How are you?"

"Dandy. I'm gonna cook you some good eats, make you feel better."

Nick gave a faint smile. "I'm looking forward to it."

Mark left the groceries on the counter, pulled out a chair, and sat down with the preacher. "Was that Cale you were talking to?"

"Yeah," Nick said, rubbing his eyes. "It wasn't an easy conversation." He looked up at Mark. "He wanted to know if I thought Jamie was in hell."

"Oh, heaven's sake," Aggie spouted. "I hope you didn't say yes!"

"Of course not," Nick said.

"Then you told him she was in heaven or wherever it is he wants to believe people go?"

Both men looked up at her, and she realized she'd stepped on some toes.

"No, I couldn't tell him that, either, Aunt Aggie," Nick said. "I would never just tell someone what they want to hear to make them feel better."

She pursed her lips and decided to bite her tongue, though she didn't know how long she would manage it. "Whatever happened to preachers havin' compassion, what I want to know," she muttered under her breath.

She heard a chair scraping back, and Mark appeared beside her, that charm-your-socks-off grin on his face. "Aunt Aggie, Nick has compassion. And he believes the things he preaches."

"How would you know?" she asked, looking up at him. "Accordin' to Celia, you ain't been to church in months."

Mark's smile crashed. "It hasn't been that long." He glanced self-consciously back at Nick. "Nick, tell her it hasn't been that long."

The preacher's gaze locked on the small Cajun woman. "What are you getting at, Aunt Aggie?"

"Just that all these *grande* convictions do get shaky when times get rough."

"Aunt Aggie—you're saying I'm a hypocrite," Mark said, with the same hurt-little-boy look on his face he'd have had if she'd spat on him.

She considered him for a moment. He was a handsome man, always had been, even when he was fourteen on the junior-high football team, scoring touchdowns and driving the girls crazy. He had been one of her husband's favorite local athletes, and now he was one of her favorite young men. "*Mon petit*, I'd never call you somethin' that mean. I just don't understand all the rules, and all the mumbo jumbo. No better'n voodoo, y'ask me. Seems to me at a time like this, when a friend needs a little comfort, you'd just give the comfort any way you could."

"Just because I fail, Aunt Aggie, doesn't mean what Nick preaches isn't true."

She patted his back with affection, and began unloading the groceries. "Awright, darlin'. It's just . . . Cale is one of *mes enfants*, too, and I hate to see him hurtin'."

"What about George?" Nick asked, catching her attention again. She turned back to him. "Aren't you concerned about him and the baby?"

"Of course I am," she said. "I just know Cale's all by hisself. Not like George."

"Why do you say that?" Nick asked, and she knew he was trying to make a point.

"Okay," she said, giving him his little victory. "Because of his church, that's why. He has all them folks rallyin' 'round him, bringin' him food, keepin' him company, offerin' him hope and comfort. He won't be shunned like Cale will."

"Shunned?" Mark asked. "Why would Cale be shunned?"

"Because he ain't one of you."

Nick looked down at his Bible for a long moment, then began to nod. "Thank you, Aunt Aggie," he said. "You've just given us a challenge. We need to make Cale one of us, even if he wasn't before. We need to bring him into the fold and love him and minister to him, just like we would to George. That's what Jesus would do."

Aunt Aggie smiled and turned back to her food. She hoped they would do just that, even if she didn't believe in Jesus or heaven or any of those other things. There were some good things about church. It had done a lot to heal Celia, her niece, after some great tragedies in her life, and she'd seen more than once how it embraced members of the community in times of crisis, and helped them through it. She knew they could help Cale. False hope, she supposed, was better than no hope to people at some points in their life. She didn't begrudge anyone the chance to lessen their grief.

Mark kept standing beside her, staring down at the counter with pensive brown eyes that almost broke her heart. She looked up at him and asked, "What is it, Mark?"

He seemed to shake out of his reverie. "Nothing," he said. "I just hate that I'm coming across as a hypocrite. I admit things haven't been quite right since my marriage broke up, but my beliefs haven't changed." He turned back to Nick. "You realize that, don't you, Nick?"

Nick looked as if the day was getting too heavy for him. "There are a lot of dynamics going on in your life right now, Mark. I understand that."

Whatever that means, Aggie thought with disdain as she turned back to her cooking. That was why she didn't trust preachers. They could never be counted on to say the right thing.

Patting Mark's hand, she put on her biggest smile. "Quit worryin', Mark, darlin'. You're as fine a Christian as anybody walkin' the streets of Newpointe."

But she could tell that her words didn't do anything to improve his mood as he pushed off from the counter and left the kitchen.

• • •

Outside, Mark found a tree stump and sat on it, looking out over the bayou that snaked through the back lots of the city property. It was a well-maintained bayou, not like the serpentine swamps covered in algae that characterized so much of south Louisiana. In the summer, a stretch of it further down was used for water skiing, but in this part, fishermen often drifted down the narrow channel in their boats, seeking both a catch and a little solace.

Mark glumly scanned the trees draped with long Spanish moss and tangled with catalpa webs, and watched a squirrel run from one of them up toward the city jail on the other side of the police station. Several hundred yards down, from the windows at the top of the basement cells of the city jail, he could hear inmates yelling and cussing. The jail was overcrowded because they'd brought in so many lawbreakers from the roadblocks the night before, and now they didn't know how they were going to process them all. Eventually, he suspected, they would have to let most of them go.

Funny that he felt as imprisoned as them, even though his separation from Allie was supposed to have given him freedom. He'd never felt so constrained, so much in bondage. He'd never had such anxiety, such dread, such hopelessness.

And now Aunt Aggie's comment had dragged him even deeper into his abyss of self-pity and self-deprecation. She hadn't called him a hypocrite, had even gone out of her way to deny that she'd meant that. But the comment about his church attendance from someone who watched from a distance—it had shaken him, made him realize that maybe he had fallen farther than he'd imagined. Were there others out there—other nonbelievers—who were watching his example, seeing him in the bars, following his marriage woes, recording his transgressions? Were they using him as an example of their conviction that Christian zeal was a temporary thing, that it always faded eventually, that it was an emotional exercise that waxed and waned as seasons changed?

Was he being punished for all of that?

The thought, itself, seemed so arrogant, so selfish, that he hated himself all the more. All of this intended as punishment for him? As if God would take two women so that Mark's resulting fears and anxieties would bring him back into step. There were bigger things going on here, and he doubted God even had time to notice his insignificant little lapses.

He heard the back door squeak open and looked over his shoulder to see Ray Ford coming toward him. "Aunt Aggie sent me to get you. Said it's time for lunch."

"I'm not hungry," Mark said. He looked up at his friend, whose dark skin was impressed with lines that hadn't been there days before. "Ray, the truth, no holds barred. What do you and Susan think about me these days?"

Ray looked genuinely surprised by the question. After a moment, he dropped down on the dirt in front of a pine tree across from Mark and looked him in the eye. "Where'd that come from?" he asked.

"Just wondering," Mark said. "Allie's opinion might be contagious."

"If we caught an 'opinion,' Mark, it was from you, not her."

Mark felt himself tensing, growing angry, even before Ray had answered the question. "And what would that opinion be?"

"That maybe, just maybe, you've forsaken your first love."

It wasn't an indictment, wasn't even said in bitterness, but still Mark reacted defensively. "The separation wasn't my idea, Ray. She threw me out over something I didn't even do. She's not interested in counseling; she doesn't want to talk about reconciliation—I don't know *what* she wants, Ray. Maybe blood. But don't condemn me because of things I can't control."

Ray only stared at him for a long moment. "How long since you been in the Word?"

Mark rolled his eyes. "What's that got to do with it? I've been busy, okay? Things haven't exactly been smooth sailing lately."

Ray nodded and got back up, dusted off the back side of his uniform. "Maybe that's why," he said, and started back up to the firehouse.

"What does that mean?" Mark called after him. "Really— what does that mean?"

Ray spread his arms innocently, then motioned for him to come on in. "It means I love you, bro, and I think you know better. Aunt Aggie's waiting."

But Mark didn't go in. He had no appetite.

Chapter Seventeen

● ● ●

The morning of the funerals, Blooms 'n' Blossoms buzzed with activities as patrons stopped in or telephoned by the dozens to send flowers to the church for both families. Allie had called in everyone who had ever worked part-time for her during Valentine's or Mother's Day—all three of them—and had them running deliveries for her or taking orders, while she worked feverishly in the back to finish in time for Mark to pick her up.

She heard the front door open and the bell jingle, then Jill Clark appeared in the doorway of the back room. "I had a feeling you'd be up to your elbows in funeral sprays."

"You were right." She put the finishing touches on the spray she was working on, attached the card, then moved it to the side of the room where five other sprays waited to be loaded onto the van. "I figured you'd be up to your elbows processing all those reprobates they threw in jail the other night."

"You were right, too," Jill said, leaning against the doorway. Allie looked up and realized that Jill looked more exhausted than she'd ever seen her. It seemed that everyone in town had aged a decade over the past few days. "I was interviewing clients all night at the jail, and I've been in court all morning, but fortunately the judge wants to go to the funerals, so he recessed for the rest of the day. I just wondered if you wanted to ride with me."

Allie stopped what she was doing and stared down at the flowers in her hand. "Can't. I'm going with Mark."

"With Mark?"

Allie looked up again and saw the surprise in her eyes. "Yeah, he asked me to go with him. I'm not sure why, but it seemed like the right thing to do."

"Well, that's interesting." Jill came further into the fragrant room and leaned on the table, which was covered with cut stems. "You think he's coming around?"

"I don't know," she said. "He's in this protective mode, all of a sudden. Acting real concerned about me, worrying ..." She let the words trail off, and released a long sigh. "It's kind of confusing."

Jill considered that for a moment. "Well, maybe it took the murders to make him realize what he was giving up."

"Don't get your hopes up," Allie said. "I'm not."

"Yes, you are."

Allie met her friend's eyes and saw that she was smiling. But Allie couldn't muster a smile of her own. "Jill, if we got back together out of fear over a couple of murders, how long do you think that would last?"

Jill got quiet. "I don't know, Allie, but you didn't get married out of fear. There was something else there."

Allie's face softened, and she looked back down at the flowers. "We got married because we couldn't stand to be apart. No matter where I was or who I was with, I would rather have been with him."

Jill leaned back against the door casing and smiled. "I remember when he announced your engagement, back when he was leading our singles Sunday school class. He said, 'In one of the greatest acts of kindness known among humans, that beautiful lady in the back has agreed to marry me.'"

Allie almost smiled, but refused to let herself get nostalgic. "Yeah, Mark's always had a way with words. I'm sure Issie appreciates it. I ran into her the other day, you know. She was all smiles. No remorse at all. Superior, like she knew she'd won."

Jill frowned. "Allie, he's not just a bowling trophy or something. She can't win if he doesn't let her."

"But he has. That's just it."

Jill shook her head. "I'm not buying that, Allie. Not yet. I'm just not convinced that Mark can so easily set aside his Christian—"

"People justify their sins all the time, Jill. And that serpent is just waiting, saying, 'Surely you will not die.' Mark's lost his focus. As Nick would say, he believes the lie."

Jill looked disturbed. "Still—if he liked her better, how come he's taking you to the funerals?"

Allie went back to working on her spray. "You act like he's taking me on a date."

"He didn't *have* to ask you, Allie. He could have gone alone."

"He's trying to nip the gossip in the bud."

"Too late for that. Everyone in town already knows you're separated."

Allie breathed a sardonic laugh. "Thanks, Jill. You always know what to say."

"You can't keep secrets in Newpointe. I say he's taking you because he wants to be with you. You said yourself that he's been worrying about you. All symptoms of love, Allie. Not the signs of a man whose heart is somewhere else."

Allie closed her eyes, trying to sift through the signs and signals—and the contradictions.

Just then, Jesse Pruitt, a retired teacher who had come in to help her this morning, breezed into the room, slightly out of breath and sweating. "You ready for me to take these?" She started gathering up the funeral sprays Allie had finished.

"Yes," Allie said. "Two are for Martha, the rest for Jamie."

As Jesse began moving them out to the van, Jill asked, "Is there anything I can do to help?"

Allie looked down at herself. "I had hoped to change clothes before Mark picked me up, but it doesn't look like I'll get to."

"You look fine," Jill said, then smiling slightly, added, "and you smell like the Garden of Eden." Jill touched her friend's cheek, a look of concern on her face. "I would say 'cheer up,' but under the circumstances, I won't. I'll see you at the funeral. Call me if you want to talk afterwards."

Allie waved good-bye, then went into the rest room and looked at herself in the mirror. Would Mark see the fatigue, the depression, the despair on her face, or would he see whatever it was that he used to like about her? Did it really matter? And should she even think about such things when they were on their way to bury the wives of two of Mark's friends?

She got her purse, dug into it for her lipstick, applied some, then powdered and tried to lighten the dark circles under her eyes. But even as she did, she felt the futility of it.

She wasn't sure there was any hope for the two of them.

Chapter Eighteen

• • •

When Mark pulled into the parking lot, Allie was just putting the "Closed" sign in the window. He thought of waiting in the car for her, but then decided against it. When they were dating, she had refused to come out unless he came in to get her. To not do so today would seem like an insult, and he didn't want to annoy her now, not when their emotions were already so frayed. Besides, he liked going into the shop. It was fresh and bright, and it smelled like Allie, and he never went through the doors without remembering the way they had dreamed of it and worked for it, and finally made it a reality. It had been as much his dream as hers—a great supplement to his insubstantial fireman's salary, and a place to work on his off-days.

But now it wasn't his anymore. Not really. He supposed that, if there was going to be a divorce, he would let her have the shop in the settlement. She could run it just fine without him—she had for the past two months—but he couldn't run it without her.

He went through the front door, making the little bell ring, and saw her across the floral arrangements. "You ready?" he asked.

"Just a minute," she said, looking preoccupied at the cash register. When she'd finished locking it, she got her purse. "Okay, I guess I am."

He stood there looking at her for a moment, wanting to tell her that she looked like a million bucks, that the blue in her dress brought out the stark blue of her eyes, but something stopped him. Was it pride? Fear of more rejection, like he'd suffered with her the night of the murders? He honestly didn't know.

His perusal seemed to make her feel self-conscious. "I didn't want to wear black," she said, her voice strained and hoarse. "Martha was a Christian, and we're not supposed to grieve as those who have no hope."

"No, we're not," Mark said.

"But then I thought of Jamie, and I wasn't sure if I'd be offending Cale if I didn't wear black."

"You're fine," he said. "I'm sure Cale won't be offended."

"But his parents . . ."

"If you'd feel more comfortable changing . . ."

"Do you think I should?"

"There's not much time, but if you want . . ."

She checked her watch and shook her head. "No, no. That's all right. I'll just wear this." Finally, she met his eyes. "I guess I'm just stalling."

He didn't blame her.

"Let's go," she said. She closed the shop's door behind them, set the dead bolt, and followed him to the car.

A steady stream of cars threaded into the already crowded lot at Calvary Bible Church. They saw Patricia Castor, the mayor, getting out of her car and shaking hands with others as they headed for the door.

Mark pulled into a space beside Ray Ford's car, then sat for a moment, straightening his tie.

"This is awful," Allie whispered. "We're supposed to say good-bye to old people and those who've been sick. Not healthy women in the prime of their lives."

Mark gave up on his tie and took a deep breath, then let it out slowly. "I guess we'd better get in there."

She nodded, and glanced at the car next to theirs. "The Fords are already here."

He took her hand as she got out of the car, and like nervous children who borrowed from each other's strength, they walked into the church where they had been married four years before. Ray Ford met them at the door, acting as usher, and Allie reached up to hug him. "Where's Susan?" she asked.

"She'll be here shortly," Ray said. "I came early to usher."

"We'll save you a place," she said. "Just point her to us when she gets here."

But several minutes later there was still no Susan, and the organist began playing. As the church filled up, Allie had to surrender her saved seats to those pressing in. By the time the service began, she assumed that Susan had found a seat of her own further back in the crowd. Forgetting Susan for the moment, Allie concentrated instead on this quiet moment of closeness in the midst of grief—Mark was sitting beside her, and he was holding her hand.

•   •   •

Across town at the Ford house, Susan's phone rang, waking her up. She had sat down for just a moment to rest before getting ready for the funeral, but sleep, which had seemed so scarce lately, had overtaken her. She looked at the clock on the wall, and gasped when she realized the funeral had started long ago.

Just then she heard the side door open.

"Ray?" she called. "Ray, I fell asleep. I'm so sorry."

There was no answer.

She started for the kitchen, then felt a chill come over her, and fear traveled through her veins like a drug. Someone was in the house, and it wasn't Ray.

Turning, she bolted toward the back of the house. She took one quick look back over her shoulder—and a muffled gunshot *whoofed* through the air. Her back exploded with scorching, ripping pain. The impact threw her forward, and she hit the floor. *I've been shot*, she realized in terror. *But I'm not dead. Not yet.*

She lay motionless in her own blood, face down, afraid to make a sound for fear that he would finish the job.

And then she heard him crying. At first it was a soft whimper, then it grew louder, more sloppy, more anguished, until the killer was sobbing. She heard him moving around her as he did; she smelled the gasoline . . .

Still she lay motionless, not breathing . . .

"I'm so sorry," the man sobbed in a high-pitched voice. "I'm so sorry, Mary. So sorry."

She heard the match striking, heard the quiet whoosh of the fire igniting in a circle around her. She felt her energy seeping out in the puddle of blood beneath her, felt her life slipping away. She began to pray, even as darkness overtook her.

• • •

Martha's funeral, though sad, was a celebration of a saint going home. The church choir, of which Martha had been a part, sang "It Is Well with My Soul," and Nick Foster told stories of Martha's devotion to Christ, her sacrificial acts of mercy around the town since arriving in Newpointe, her selfless acts of service to her church in the short time she'd been a member. He told of the miracle of the baby she and George had prayed for, and reminded the congregation that, reckoned in eternal time, she would only be separated from that baby and her husband for "a few minutes" before they would be reunited in heaven. He promised that some good would come of this death, whether the killer intended it or Satan wanted it, because God promised that all things would "work together for good to those who loved the Lord and were called according to his purpose."

After the service, they assembled at the grave site in the small cemetery adjacent to the church. There, George held Tommy in his arms and wept as they lowered the casket into the ground. He and his parents and Martha's parents stood accepting condolences from those who chose to give them. As friends and neighbors and church brothers and sisters hugged George or shook his hand or cried with him, they offered words intended to comfort and support—but those words often fell far short.

"Consider it joy," Sue Ellen Hanover, one of the clerks at the local post office, told him, and George swallowed and nodded mutely. Standing nearby and watching, Allie knew that regarding his wife's murder with joy was one of those God-sized tasks George hadn't yet grasped.

"Think how many were led to the Lord through this funeral today," Joyce Drake, who owned the cleaners, told George.

He bounced little Tommy and said, "Martha led lots of folks to Christ when she was alive."

"But maybe more will come through this," the woman insisted.

It was a nice thought, and most likely true, but Allie doubted that George's heart was ready for that kind of speculation.

When she and Mark worked their way close enough to George, Allie reached up to hug him tight, choosing not to say anything. "She's in heaven, man," Mark said with tears in his eyes. "And as hard as it is for you to be separated from her, it's not that long before you will see her again."

George glanced self-consciously at those in line behind them, then lowering his voice, said, "Wonder if she's really there, or just asleep 'til . . ."

Mark stepped closer and touched George's shoulder. "He said, 'Today you will be with me in paradise.' Not hundreds of years from now, but today."

Allie shot him a look, surprised that he still had any spiritual impulses.

George let his words soak in. "He did say it, didn't he?"

"She's there, buddy."

George tightened his lips and looked down at the baby, who was just nodding off in his arms. "We gon' be okay, you know. Tommy's a miracle baby, and God ain't gon' forsake us now."

Allie struggled to hold back her tears, but she failed. Wiping her eyes, she asked, "Is there anything we can do for you, George? Anything at all?"

George's face changed, and his eyebrows lifted. "Yeah, matter of fact. There is."

"What?" Mark asked. "Anything, man."

"Put yo' marriage back together. Some of us don't got a choice. Don't just th'ow it away."

Allie looked down at the floor, avoiding Mark's eyes. "We're doing the best we can, George," Mark said.

"You ain't doin' enough," the grieving man said. He patted Mark's shoulder, then forced a smile. "I can say these things 'cause I know you won't deck me today."

Mark breathed out a strained laugh, then his smile quickly faded as he looked at Allie. Squeezing his friend's arm, he took Allie's hand and led her back to the church.

They were silent for a long moment, then finally, Mark said, "Leave it to George to nail us like that today of all days."

"He just doesn't know all the facts," she said in a flat voice.

"No, he doesn't."

So they did agree on something, Allie mused miserably.

She looked up at the parking lot, and saw a whole new string of traffic pulling in for Jamie's funeral. While most of the town had come for both funerals, some had known Jamie better than Martha and had only come for the second one. "How long before the next funeral?" she asked.

Mark checked his watch. "About half an hour."

"I'm gonna go try to repair my makeup," she told him. "I'll meet you inside the church."

Chapter Nineteen

● ● ●

Susan struggled in and out of consciousness as the flames grew hotter around her and the smoke grew more smothering. As her consciousness returned, she forced herself to move. She was still bleeding, and her hand slipped through the wet puddle beneath her. Summoning all her strength, she turned her head—and saw the flames creeping across the carpet toward her. She had to move. She had to get out of the house while she still could.

She pushed with her feet, triggering unimaginable pain, until she managed to rise up on her knees. Blackness overtook her again, and she fell. But her consciousness hung on, and she pulled herself into a weak little ball and forced herself to roll with all the momentum she could gather—right through the flames that surrounded her.

She felt them singeing her hair and scorching her back, but she managed to keep rolling until she was out of the circle of fire the killer had made for her.

The flames were catching hold of the curtains and climbing the couch. Susan pushed with her feet and clawed with her hands until she reached the table next to the couch. She groped for the telephone cord, found it, and jerked the phone down. The phone fell off the table with a crash and a ring, and she dragged the cord until she had her hands on the base.

Darkness was coming again, sucking her under, but she managed to punch out 911. She couldn't reach the receiver, didn't know where it was. Smoke was filling the room, choking her, burning her lungs, and she felt the heat of flames licking close to her again.

"911, may I help you?"

She knew that the dispatcher could help her, but she couldn't get the words out.

"Hello? May I help you?"

"Help ..." The word was too faint, and she knew the dispatcher didn't hear. She groped for the coiled cord to the handset and pulled the receiver closer. "Help ..."

The darkness was too thick and the smoke too smothering, and she couldn't get a breath. Finally, the darkness closed in on her, leaving her no escape.

Chapter Twenty

• • •

Ray Ford grew concerned when the crowd had thinned out and Susan was still nowhere in sight. He wondered if she had fallen asleep at home and missed the funeral. She hadn't been sleeping well since the murders, and he wouldn't be surprised if she'd lain down for a few minutes and failed to open her eyes again in time.

He went to the church office to call home, but someone was using the phone. No problem. He had time to run home and get her up before Jamie's funeral began.

He trotted out to his car, pulled out of the packed parking lot, and headed down the street between the rows of cars parked on the sides of the streets. When he reached his house, he saw that Susan's car was still there.

A dull buzzing noise sang from inside the house, and as he realized it might be the smoke alarm, he broke into a run. He reached the back door and flung it open. Smoke billowed out.

He yelled for his wife as he stumbled into the kitchen. His heart jolted when he saw the flames dancing in the living room. He grabbed the tablecloth from the kitchen table and the fire extinguisher they kept under the sink, ran into the living room, and began smothering the flames, yelling, "Susan! Susan!"

Then he saw her, lying facedown in a pool of blood in the only part of the room that wasn't yet engulfed.

"No!" His scream shook the house. He dropped the extinguisher, gathered her up, and crashed out the front door. As he collapsed with her on the grass, he saw that her face was blood-splattered and her chest was soaked with blood. He heard a siren as he searched her neck for a pulse. "Susan, hang on, darlin'. Don't leave me, baby."

Finding a pulse, he bent his head and began praying as the sirens grew closer. A fire truck stopped in front of his house, then an ambulance, and the paramedics rushed to take her from him. "She's not dead," he told them. "She's not dead." His voice cracked as he tried to speak. "You've got to save her. Please."

But as they tried to stabilize her for rapid transport, he wondered if it was too late.

Chapter Twenty-One

● ● ●

Because no one knew for sure whether Jamie Larkins was a believer—and from her behavior, most assumed she was not—hers was a funeral of despair. Though Nick tried to offer hope, it was a floundering attempt at best. Nick had confided to Mark before the service that, as hard as he'd tried to come up with kind, hopeful words to say about her, most of what he'd heard from her friends and family had been wild stories about how "carefree" she was, how she loved life, how she would rather spend a night on the town with good friends than just about anything.

Empty sentiments for a life that would leave little legacy, Mark thought as he watched the pastor struggle with the eulogy. The difference between Cale's face now and George's at the previous funeral was profound. Though both were in agony, and neither could boast of much peace, George seemed to hold together better than Cale did.

Mark wished now that he had felt more concern about the Larkins's relationship to God, but all those nights he'd gone to Joe's Place and shared drinks with them, it had never crossed his mind that their need to find God might be urgent. He wasn't sure where his mind *had* been, but he knew it hadn't been on spiritual life—his own or anyone else's. Not for a long time. He felt as guilty as if he'd had something to do with Jamie's death himself. He'd moved a long way since his last Promise Keepers rally, he thought. An awful long way. In the wrong direction.

Allie was crying. Instinctively, he put his arm around her. She didn't recoil, as he'd half expected, and he wished he could take her home and hold her through the night, comfort her and let her comfort him . . .

But these moments—sitting here so close to her, holding her, touching her—were no longer reality. And when reality set back in, he and Allie would once again go their separate ways, despite George's admonitions.

After the service, they headed to their car for the procession to the grave site on the other side of Newpointe, which was not in the churchyard since the Larkins weren't members there. Mark opened the door and helped Allie into his car, then got in and pulled into the procession forming in the parking lot. At the front of the line, just behind the hearse, was Johnny Ducote, another fireman, driving the big limousine—his "moonlighting" job when he wasn't on duty. He had offered his services free for both families today, but Mark doubted that it gave them much comfort.

Before the hearse began to move, Mark saw Slater Finch pull out of the procession and make a quick U-turn. Several cars back, another car pulled out.

"Must be something going on somewhere to pull them away from this," Mark said, reaching to turn on the scanner he kept under his dash. He kept it on most of the time, as many of the firemen and police officers did, to the chagrin of their wives and families, but he had turned it off before he'd picked up Allie.

"You'd think they could let the on-duty guys handle it," Allie said. "It's not like this is a football game. It's the funeral of their colleague's wife, for heaven's sake."

"Shhh. Listen." He turned it up and tried to tune to an active frequency.

He found a police frequency first, heard an excited cop practically yelling into the radio. "The fire department is working on the fire, and we've got the ambulance taking Susan to meet the Medicoptor so they can get her to the hospital in Slidell. But I don't know, the gunshot wound was pretty bad. If Ray hadn't come home when he did and found her . . ."

"Susan and Ray?" Allie shouted, turning the radio up. "Not the Fords. Not Susan!"

"Oh, no." Mark closed his eyes and covered his face. "Not again. They caught the guy! He's still in jail."

Someone behind him in the procession tapped his horn. Mark jumped and opened his eyes. The cars ahead were moving, and he was holding the line up. Jerking his steering wheel hard to the right, he pulled out of the line.

"Where should we go?" Allie's voice was high-pitched, panicked.

"I don't know. House or hospital?"

"The hospital," she cried. "Oh, Mark. Hurry!"

Chapter Twenty-Two

• • •

Television vans were rapidly filling the parking lot at Slidell Memorial Hospital. Technicians scurried around setting up for live broadcasts as camera crews and reporters hurried toward the emergency room, providing a morbid sense of melodrama as Mark and Allie tried to find a parking space. The case was no longer just another murder, so common in south Louisiana. Now it was a serial killing, and the whole nation would follow the story.

Mark finally parked on the street, took Allie's hand, and headed into the emergency room. It wasn't easy—photographers and reporters were already crowded in elbow to elbow, some taping already, others calling in stories on the two pay phones or their own hand-held cell phones. The handful of people who'd come for treatment—a man with a cut arm, an asthmatic baby wheezing in his mother's arms, and a woman who appeared to be close to passing out—seemed incidental to the news the reporters sought.

Mark and Allie pushed through the crowd to the information desk where a frazzled nurse sat. He started to ask her if Susan had made it to the hospital, then overheard a reporter taping for the six o'clock news: "... here in Slidell Memorial Hospital, where this bizarre serial killing, targeting only wives of firemen in the Northshore town of Newpointe, is taking a new twist. We're told that Susan Ford, the newest victim, has a serious chest wound. She came very close to being burned as well, and if her husband had not found her when he did, she may have lost her life. She remains unconscious ..."

The haggard nurse pulled a pencil from her beehive hair. "Sir, if you're a reporter, I'm going to have to ask you to move over there."

Mark swung his attention from the news anchor. "No, I'm a friend of Susan and Ray Ford. Do you know where Ray is?"

"Yes, sir, he's here," the woman said in a nasal twang. "But everyone here wants to see him. We're not allowing anybody back."

"Oh, please," Allie said, bracing her hands on the reception desk. "He shouldn't be alone through this. We're close friends, and he needs someone with him."

The nurse sneered at them. "You reporters are reprehensible. I don't know how you sleep at night."

"We're not reporters!" Mark insisted. "I'm a fireman in Newpointe and I work with Ray."

Her face changed, and she crossed her big arms and chewed on her pencil for a moment. "A fireman, huh?"

He pulled out his wallet and showed her his I.D. "Yes. Mark Branning. And this is my wife, Allie."

It was as though he had changed channels on the woman's personality. Instantly, she softened. "Oh, you poor thing. You must be scared to death that you'll be next."

Mark looked at Allie, and she looked back. He put his arm around her shoulders. Three firemen's wives shot. He'd worried before that there was a killer on the loose in Newpointe. For the first time, he realized the killer was actually targeting—

"Excuse me!" The loud voice turned them around, and a reporter stuck a microphone in Mark's face. Blinding lights were suddenly on them. "I'm Clive Southerlyn from WDSU-TV in New Orleans," the man said in his familiar broadcast voice. "Did I hear you say you're on the fire department with Ray Ford?"

"That's right," Mark said.

"Sir, why do you think this killer is targeting your wives?"

He started to answer, but other reporters began to gravitate toward him, sticking more mikes in his face. "Uh . . . well, I didn't realize until Susan was shot that he was . . . that is . . ."

"Do you know who could be doing this?" someone shouted.

"No . . . uh . . ."

A reporter jabbed a mike in front of Allie's face, almost hitting her in the mouth. "What's your name, ma'am?"

"Allie Branning," she said, trying to back away.

"How do you feel about being a target for this killer, Mrs. Branning?"

"I'm not sure that's what I am."

"Are you going to stay at home tonight?"

"Were you friends with the other three women?"

"Do you know if Susan Ford was involved in drugs, as well?"

As Allie burst into tears, Mark struggled with the anger moving red-hot through his veins. He pushed away the cluster of mikes. "Please! We just want to know how our friend is doing."

He pulled Allie along with him toward the double swinging doors leading to the examining rooms. No one stopped them as they burst through, but when the reporters tried to follow, two security guards appeared and held them back.

They stopped in the corridor. Allie was shaking, and she wiped her eyes with a trembling hand. "Are you all right?" he asked.

"I'm scared, Mark," she whispered.

"Me, too."

"What does this mean? What's going to happen? Is he really targeting *us*?"

Mark shook his head. "I wish I knew. We have to find Ray," he said. He looked past her down the long antiseptic hallway, and saw Ray slumped over in a folding chair. "Ray!" He let Allie go, and they both ran to their friend's side. Still wearing his dress blues from the funeral, though they were soaked with blood, Ray stood up and accepted their fierce hugs.

"How is she?" Allie asked.

"Alive," Ray said. "I went in and saw the smoke, and she was layin' there ... fire all 'round her ..."

"Thank God you found her."

"I have thanked him, believe me." He wiped his rough face and shook his head as he sank back down. "But she ain't conscious yet. They got her in surgery, and they're tryin' to see how much damage the bullet did to her lungs." He looked up at them, his lips thin as he bit the words out. "Shot her through the back, you know. Poured gas in a circle around her. But the fire spread away from her instead of toward her." He looked up at Mark, his eyes tormented and anguished, and he asked, "Why, Mark? Who *did* this?"

"I don't know."

"It ain't the guy they got locked up, that's for sure. And it don't have nothin' to do with drugs. It's us, Mark. Somebody's comin' after our wives!"

The double doors opened again and the nurse came back escorting a distraught Vanessa, the Ford's fifteen-year-old daughter. Behind her was Sid, Ray's brother, still in his cop's uniform, who looked as if he, too, had wept all the way from Newpointe.

"Daddy?" Vanessa cried when she saw her father. "Is she dead, Daddy?"

Ray got up and she ran into his arms. "No, honey," he said. "No, she ain't dead. But she's in bad shape. We're waitin' to hear how her surgery comes out."

Vanessa wailed against her father's shoulder.

Sid patted his brother's back. "I called Ben. He's on his way from Baton Rouge."

Ray nodded, still clinging to his daughter. Finally, he looked back at the rest of them over Vanessa's head. With pleading eyes, he said, "Don't waste your time here, Mark. Take Allie and go back to Newpointe. Call a meetin' of all of the firefighters and their wives, and brainstorm 'til you figure this thing out. Somebody knows somethin'. Somebody will have some idea who might be doin' this. Mark, we can't let him get any of the other wives."

"You're right," Mark said. "But I'd rather stay here until I know how Susan is."

"I'll call the station and let y'all know," Ray said. "But time's wastin', Mark. We have to *do* somethin'."

Reluctantly, they left Ray with hugs and empty words of comfort. Then, hand in hand, they pushed back through the reporters. Other firemen and their wives had come in by now and were surrounded by cameras and microphones. As Mark pushed through the doors leading out, one of them called, "Mark, what did you find out? How's Susan?"

"Still in surgery," he said. "Ray wants us back in Newpointe. He wants us to call a meeting with all the firefighters and their wives, and figure out some kind of strategy."

"How are you going to protect your wives, Mr. Branning?" one of the reporters asked.

Without answering, Mark pushed out through the double doors, pulling Allie beside him.

Uneasy now that they were out into the open, he found himself with his arm around Allie, holding her close as they walked. Yes, all three wives had been at home alone when the killer had gotten to them, but now he must know that they were onto him, and that it wouldn't be so easy anymore. What if he got desperate or overconfident or anxious and started coming after them wherever he could find them? His eyes scanned the cars in the parking lot as he headed to his own.

Allie picked up on it immediately. "He wouldn't come after us in broad daylight out in a parking lot, Mark. He's doing this in secret."

"You're assuming he's consistent," he said, "This guy's too unstable to be predictable. Anyone who would murder a woman and then set her on fire has a loose wire somewhere. There's no telling what he might do."

He opened the driver's door of his car, guided Allie in first, and then slid in next to her. He checked the rearview mirror for anything out of the ordinary, then turned his key in the ignition.

"I wonder if he'd count me," she said in a flat, pensive voice as he pulled out of the parking space.

"What do you mean?"

"As a wife," she said. "Maybe I'm safe because we're not married anymore."

That almost sent him over the edge. "We *are* married, Allie."

"On paper," she said miserably as tears filled her eyes again. "Maybe he knows that. Maybe that exempts me from all this madness."

"Maybe," he conceded. "We can hope."

She covered her face with a hand, and her shoulders shook as she wept quietly.

He could feel her trembling next to him as her tears came harder. "I never thought there would be a blessing in our separation," she whispered.

He swallowed the emotion in his throat, but couldn't find a response to that. So he said nothing.

He concentrated on breaking into the traffic on Highway 90. They traveled for several miles in silence before he finally turned on the radio.

They listened to the news of Susan's shooting and the fires and the two other wives. Mark gritted his teeth. To the reporters, these women were just statistics—not real people with husbands, children, friends. When he realized that they were just repeating the same information over and over, he turned the radio off.

"As soon as we hit town, we'll go by the fire station and ask the chief to schedule a meeting. Then we'll go home and pack our bags."

"Bags?" she asked. "What for?"

"We can't be where he expects us to be tonight. I'm supposed to go on duty at five, but I'll get somebody to cover for—"

"Mark, every fireman in town is going to want to take off tonight. They're not going to let you."

"Then they'll have to fire me," he said. "I'm not leaving you alone tonight."

He wasn't sure what to make of her silence. "Mark, this isn't necessary," she said finally. "Believe me, I'm scared to death. I'm not going to stay at home alone. I'll stay with Jill or something."

"Two women alone could be just as bad as one. No way."

"Then I'll stay with Celia and Stan. What better place to be than with the detective who's investigating the murders?"

"He won't be home. Celia will be looking for a place to stay, too. She'll probably stay at Aunt Aggie's, and that's no help."

"Maybe we could *all* stay together. All the wives of the men who are on duty tonight. We could rent a hotel suite somewhere and hide until they catch him."

"No. Too easy. He could get you all in one swoop."

She shivered. "Don't be so morbid, Mark. I'm trying to find a solution."

"The solution is that I'm going to stay with you. We'll go get a room on the Southshore, where he won't be looking for us. I'm not going to leave your side until this is over."

Instead of relieving her, his insistence seemed to make her angry. "That's very touching, Mark, but I don't think it's a good idea. I don't want you suddenly caring about me because someone's trying to kill me. If you can't care about me every day, then it doesn't mean anything. There are other people who can protect—"

He slammed his hand against the steering wheel. "I *do* care about you, Allie," he shouted. "Every day. You're just too blind to see it."

As soon as the words were out of his mouth, he regretted them. They wouldn't help his cause. But he couldn't pull them back.

"And I suppose falling in love with another woman was one of the caring acts I was too blind to see?" she cried.

"I did *not* fall in love with another woman!" he shouted. "How many times do I have to tell you?"

"Don't tell me, *show* me," she yelled. "That's all I've been asking all along. And what I've seen is just the opposite. I'm not blind, Mark, you just wish I were."

"So you want me just to throw you to the wolves and pretend like you're not my wife?"

"You've been pretending it just fine for the past two months, Mark. I have friends, lots of them. I can stay with some of them, and I'll be fine."

"But *I won't*," he rasped. "*I won't!* Every time we get a 911 call I'll worry that it's you. Every minute I'll wonder if he's seeking you out, if he's found you. I'm not working tonight, Allie, and I'm not letting someone else do the job that I'm supposed to do. I promised to honor and protect you, and I intend to do that."

"You fell way short of the honor part," she cried. "Why is the protection part so important? Does it make you feel more like a man?"

He opened his mouth to shout a reply, then stopped. He breathed deeply a couple of times, then lowered his voice to a barely controlled monotone. "You won't insult me out of this, Allie. When you decided our marriage was over, I left. When you told me you wanted to quit going to counseling, we stopped. Until now, you've called most of the shots, but now *I'm* telling *you!* You're going home and packing a bag, and you're coming with me to New Orleans tonight, if I have to physically carry you."

"So you're going to protect me if it kills me?"

"That's right," he said.

To his relief she said nothing else. It wasn't until they passed the "Welcome to Newpointe" sign that he realized that he'd meant every word he'd said. Nothing on this planet could keep him from staying with her tonight. He just wasn't sure what her stubbornness was going to cost him.

Chapter Twenty-Three

● ● ●

A s soon as Aggie Gaston had heard about the meeting for the firefighters and their wives that evening, she'd started working to prepare enough food for all of them—and she'd been at it all day. She'd had no way of getting it all into the courtroom at city hall, where the mayor had suggested they hold the meeting, since none of the rooms at either the fire station or police precinct were big enough. One of the firemen had suggested that she borrow a gurney from one of the ambulances to cart the food on—an idea that had seemed distasteful at first, but after she'd wiped it down with Lysol and gotten all the food loaded on, she had found it quite a handy thing to have. She even toyed with the idea of buying one herself, in case the need ever arose again. She unloaded the pots and bowls onto the defense table, then set all of her china on the prosecutor's table, complete with silverware and cloth napkins folded in the shapes of swans. She had to admit that it had exhausted her to do all this, and she would no doubt sleep like a baby tonight, but it was worth it, because she knew it would be appreciated. They must all be starving to death, what with the murders and the fires, and that poor little Susan lying up in the hospital fighting for her life. And she should know, of all people, since she knew their appetites better than anyone else.

The courtroom smelled like a Creole restaurant by the time the firemen and their wives began arriving. In another room in the courthouse, Lynette Devreaux, a rookie cop, baby-sat their children. The courtroom filled up as they filed in, all eighteen married firemen and their wives, as well as the seven bachelors. Craig Barnes, the fire chief, was among them, as well as Jim Shoemaker, the police chief, and Patricia Castor, their esteemed mayor who liked to be at the center of everything important in the town, if for no other reason than to campaign for the next election. Stan and Celia were there, too—Stan, to answer questions and help with the brainstorming process as the detective working on the case, and Celia, because she was Aunt Aggie's great niece and a friend to everyone there—and because she had insisted on helping to clean up.

To Aunt Aggie's chagrin, few of those who came seemed to have appetites, and over half of them took their places without even looking at the food. She briefly considered taking the leftovers down to the jail, but changed her mind when she realized that that's just what Aunt Bea would have done.

When Patricia Castor finished her plate of crawfish etouffee and took her place in the judge's seat, as if she were in charge here instead of the police chief or the fire chief, Aunt Aggie took a seat in the defense attorney's chair, turned it so that she could see everyone in the room, and waited for Jim Shoemaker to tell them who was killing the firemen's wives.

•   •   •

Mark and Allie sat side by side in the courtroom—with several inches between them, since both were still angry over their fight in the car. In the end, she had capitulated—they had gone by the house and she had packed a bag. But, to Mark's annoyance, before they had settled into their seats in the courtroom, she had looked for someone else to stay with. It wasn't to be, however, since none of the wives intended to stay in their homes that night. All of them had plans to go into hiding until the culprit was caught. Allie was stuck with him, Mark thought angrily.

As if she were the judge reading out a verdict, Patricia Castor, in a pullover cable-knit sweater and a pair of khaki pants, banged the gavel on the judge's desk and insisted it was time to get down to business. "Now, I know ya'll are upset by these killings," she drawled, raising her voice since she didn't have the microphone she usually had when she spoke in public. "We all are. But we cannot panic. I've been hearing some of you men saying that ya'll refuse to go on duty until the killer is caught, but that is simply out of the question. We have to have firefighters on duty. We can't leave Newpointe without its protective services. That would present a crisis for our town. So the shifts will proceed as scheduled."

Jim Shoemaker, the plump, bald-headed police chief who leaned on the railing in front of the jury box, rolled his eyes. "We've taken care of it, Patty. The unmarried firemen on the force have agreed to work until the killer is caught, so that the married firemen can tend to their wives. Newpointe won't go up in a blaze of smoke, and you won't come out with egg on your face. Don't worry—if you lose the next election, it won't have anything to do with this."

The mayor's face reddened, and she leaned forward condescendingly. "Jim, I'd suggest that you start looking for the killer instead of worrying about our firefighters' schedules or my next election." She glanced at Craig Barnes, the fire chief. "Craig, do you always let the police chief do your job?"

Craig Barnes, whose eyes and nose were red, as if he'd had a weeping bout of his own over the killings, bristled at the accusation. "No, Patty, I do not. And I, personally, don't like the idea of keeping the same crew on duty until this person is caught. It could take weeks, and my men would be exhausted. I've tried to think of alternatives, and to me, the best solution is to let the wives whose husbands are working stay together with a twenty-four-hour guard. You can handle that, can't you, Jim?"

"No way," Mark called out, looking around at the others. "I don't want Allie anywhere near the other wives. No offense, but she's not gonna be a sitting duck."

"The wives could leave town," Patricia said. "Just take a vacation until it all blows over. Visit relatives or something. Why should the bachelors work consecutive shifts without a break?"

"They can sleep when they're not out on a call, Mayor," Mark said, "and they'll eat better than ever while they're at the station anyway."

Aunt Aggie beamed.

"I don't care," the mayor said. "There has to be another alternative. We will not jeopardize the protective services in this town."

"And *I* will not jeopardize my wife's life!" Mark yelled, jumping to his feet.

Everyone got quiet, and the mayor, who hadn't given Mark the time of day since her last campaign, pinned him with a look. But Mark would not back down.

"Two women are dead and another is fighting for her life. I don't give a rip about schedules and shifts. I am not going on duty tonight when some maniac wants to see my wife dead!"

Stunned, Allie looked up at him.

The mayor banged her gavel again. "It appears to me that your wife is the least endangered, since you don't even live together!"

Mark breathed an exasperated laugh and shook his head dolefully. "And here I thought that the mayor had too much to do to worry about all the town's gossip."

Pastor Nick Foster, always the peacemaker, stood up. "Mayor, as one of the unmarried men in the department, I can say that I'm more than willing to work as long as necessary, provided I can get off for a couple hours on Sunday morning to preach. There's not a lot I can do, but at least I can do that."

"That's nice of you, Preacher," Patricia said, "but you're not the only bachelor we're talking about."

Dan Nichols cleared his throat, getting the mayor's attention. "Uh, Mayor, I'm one of those single men, too, as you know, and I'd very much like to work in my friends' places while they take care of their wives. It's no problem. We get plenty of sleep on most normal nights. These women are my friends, too, and it would do me good to know that I was helping in some way."

"Me, too," Jacob Baxter, a young widower, added. "I'd feel a lot better about it. Don't seem right these women should be in danger just because their husbands are city employees."

The other two bachelors chimed in, and finally, Shoemaker tried again. "It makes the most sense, Mayor. And Craig, no offense intended, but if you force these men to leave their wives and work tonight, you might be asking for mass mutiny. If you make these husbands work, and then something happens to one of the wives, well . . ."

Craig looked at Jim as if he'd like to step outside and settle the matter with his fists. His jaw popped as he turned back to his men. "You're firefighters. *My* firefighters. And firefighters are public servants—which means they do their jobs when their jobs need to be done. Without good firemen, people die. Now, this is a critical time in Newpointe. If people hear that our firefighters are turning tail and running—"

Mark stood up, his heart pounding in anger and frustration. He concentrated on regaining his cool. "Look, Chiefs, Mayor—I know all three of you have a ton on your shoulders because of these murders. You're at the top of the protection chain in this town, and you have to think of the whole town, not just us." If anger wouldn't work, he would try flattery and charm. He didn't want to see Allie—or any of the other wives—jeopardized just because of a clash of egos among those at the top. "I understand that you don't want to start a panic, and that it's important for everything to look normal. I understand about job commitment and scheduling and public confidence. I love my job. I've wanted to be a firefighter since I was a kid. And I've given this job and this town everything I've had since the day I was hired, without complaining about the low pay and the toll it can take on my personal life." He glanced at Allie. She was watching him skeptically, and he knew that she wondered if this speech was sincere or just a means of manipulating her. He suddenly felt defeated—she always jumped to the wrong conclusion.

He forced himself to continue. "But I'm asking for a favor now. Let me protect my wife. Let all of us. You can't possibly believe we should make our work schedule a priority over the lives of our wives. Not in a family-friendly town like this. Mayor?"

Pat Castor's expression had softened during his speech, and now she looked torn. "Family-friendly" was one of the most-used phrases in her last campaign, so she couldn't dismiss Mark's point. "Well, I always do say that this is a family town. And of course I don't expect you to prioritize like that. That wasn't our intent. We do care what happens to your wives."

He turned to Craig, his arms spread, palms up. "Chief?"

The fire chief, who had never been married, stared back for a long moment, then looked around at the grieving, frightened couples in the room. "All right," he said, almost grudgingly. "You can have some time off. Jim, you'd better find this guy quick, because I can't work with one crew indefinitely."

"I'll do my best."

"Why don't you tell us how you plan to do that?" Pat Castor asked.

Jim nodded to Stan Shepherd. "Stan, you're the detective working on these cases. Tell us what you know."

Stan stood up from his front-row seat and turned to face the crowd, his back to the mayor. "Well, I hate to say it, but it does look like we got the wrong guy when we arrested Hank Keyes. We transferred him back to Bogaloosa this afternoon, where he's being held on drug charges. But he's no longer a suspect in the murders."

"No!" Marty Bledsoe bellowed, and a murmur went up over the room. "Why would you go and do a thing like that?"

"Because he couldn't have gone after Susan Ford while he was in jail."

"But the paper said he was in a gang," Mark argued. "Maybe his roommate did it, or another gang member."

"These murders don't fit that gang's profile," Jim Shoemaker said. "They're known for race crimes."

"So Susan Ford is black!"

"But Martha and Jamie aren't," Stan said. "Or—weren't," he corrected himself awkwardly. "We're beginning to think that Jamie Larkins's purchase of that cocaine from Hank Keyes had nothing to do with the murders. We searched his car and didn't find the murder weapon, and while we did find some guns in his apartment, they were registered and none of them was what we were looking for."

"If it isn't him, who is it?" Mark demanded.

"That's where we need your help," Stan said. "Everything is speculation at this point."

"You don't have any leads at all?" Craig Barnes asked.

"Few," Stan said, and a murmur rose from the crowd. "Our killer has been pretty good at burning all the evidence. We don't know if he's setting the fires to do just that, or whether it's some kind of statement or signature. And at this point, we have to consider everyone a suspect. If any of you has reason to think anyone could be connected with this, we need to know."

The room got uncomfortably quiet as each of them tried to identify plausible suspects among their neighbors and friends.

"We're not expecting anyone to point a finger right here, right now, but if you have any hunches we hope you'll come to us in private and let us know as soon as possible. You don't have to be right. But just bringing up the name could help. We'll rule him out if he's the wrong guy."

"Sounds like a witch hunt to me," Dan Nichols said.

"It's not a witch hunt," Jim Shoemaker piped up. "We just have to start somewhere."

"Meanwhile, we need to talk logistics," Stan added. "Do's and don'ts. Listen carefully, people, because these things just might save your lives."

Chapter Twenty-Four

● ● ●

Mark and Allie were on their way out when Stan and Celia Shepherd stopped them. "Can I talk to you two for a minute?" Stan asked.

"Sure," Mark said.

Celia, a pretty woman with hair so fair and blonde that it looked like baby hair, touched her husband's arm. "I'll just stay here and help Aunt Aggie clean up."

Stan regarded the gurney on which Aunt Aggie had loaded the food. "I think she's got it under control, and some of the guys are helping her. Why don't you come with us?"

"But isn't this police business?"

He looked uneasy at the question, then said, "Look, I'm feeling as uneasy right now as the firemen are about leaving my wife alone. Just come with me, okay?"

Celia looked from Stan, to Mark, then to Allie, and finally said, "Okay."

"You're worried he's going to cross over to the police wives next?" Mark asked softly as they walked out of the courthouse and crossed the street to the police station.

"I don't know what his motive is, or why he's targeting the fire wives. The truth is, we can't be sure that we *know* what his pattern is yet—he could be targeting city employees' wives, or wives of emergency personnel. Who knows? I'm not willing to take the chance."

Celia took in a deep breath and put her arm through Allie's. Arm in arm, the two friends followed their husbands into the interrogation room.

When they had sat down, Allie beside Mark and Celia beside Stan, Mark asked, "So what's this about, Stan?"

Stan rubbed his face and looked at his friends for a moment. He was tired, Mark could see, and he realized that Stan had probably gotten even less sleep than the rest of them in the past few days. He, after all, was the one on whose shoulders this whole investigation fell.

"I have a favor to ask."

"What?"

"I want to use your house tonight. See if we can trap the killer."

Mark sat stiffer in his chair, and gaped across the table at the detective. "You've got to be kidding."

"I can't see any other way, Mark," Stan said. "We haven't caught him, and we don't have any serious leads. But we might be able to trap him. Now that we can see that he has an agenda—"

"To kill our wives," Mark added.

"Looks that way. And now that we can see his agenda, I'm thinking that maybe we can start trying to think like him. Anticipate his next move."

Allie's face was pale as she stared at Stan through fear-stricken eyes. "And you think *I'm* going to be his next move?"

"Not necessarily," Stan said. "But so far, all of the shootings have been very close to each other. Houses just blocks from city hall, right in the heart of Newpointe. All of the other families live a little farther out. You're the only one left who lives in the center of town. Whether that means something to him or not, I can't say. But if it does, and he hits your house, we'll be there."

"No way," Mark said, standing suddenly and pulling Allie to her feet beside him. "No way are you going to use my wife for a decoy. This guy isn't playing. He sets fire to houses and puts bullets into defenseless women. He doesn't wait to make sure there aren't cops hiding in the other room."

"You're getting me all wrong," Stan said. "Sit down, okay? Sit down and let me explain what I'm suggesting."

Allie wiped her eyes with a trembling hand. After a moment, Mark took his seat again beside her. This time he reached for her hand and held it, as if through their hands he could communicate that no one on this earth was going to endanger her. Not while he was still breathing.

Stan tried again. "What are your plans for tonight? Were you going to stay in town?"

"Nope," Mark said, brooking no debate. "We're leaving town, so you'd better find someone else's house to use."

"Fine. Go. That's what I want you to do. Just give me the key to your house, so we can make it look like Allie is still home. Turn on some lights, leave the car in the driveway, turn the sprinkler on in the yard. All signs that someone is home. We'll be waiting for him."

"What if he burns down my house?" Allie asked. "What if he kills one of you?"

Celia turned her worried eyes to her husband, but said nothing.

"I'm a cop, Allie," Stan said. "I know what I'm doing. As for your house, his MO seems to be that he shoots first and then sets fire. If we catch him before there's a victim, there will never be a fire. Guys, it's the only way I can think of right now to catch him quickly. We have to draw him out."

Mark looked at Allie again. "What do you say, Allie? It's really your house now."

She looked down at the table. "The thought of him coming anywhere near my house ..." Her voice cracked, and she swallowed hard. "But he's got to be caught, or I can never go back there myself." She rubbed her eyes, long ago tear-washed free of any vestiges of makeup. "Oh, what he did to Susan. And Martha, and Jamie." Her voice got higher in pitch with each word. "I want him caught, Mark. If this is the way ..."

"It's the fastest way, if it works," Stan said. "And it may not. He may not come. Or, like the mayor said, he may not count you, Allie, since you two are separated. It's a sick mind we're dealing with, so we can't know for sure. But it's a start."

Allie wiped her eyes again, then dried her hands on her skirt. "The thought that I might be next . . ." Her voice broke off. "Let's do it."

Stan fixed his eyes on Mark. "Are you okay with this?"

Mark didn't like it. None of it. But if it worked . . . "I guess so."

"This means that you can't tell anyone you're leaving town. No one. Understood?"

"Stan, I just announced in that meeting that I'm not leaving Allie's side. So no one will expect her to be home alone."

"Then let's make him think you had another falling out. Allie can storm out of here with you right behind her, Mark, where everyone can see. You can say something like, 'Okay, then protect yourself! I've had it!'"

"Man, they'll think I'm such scum."

"We'll clear it up later, Mark. For now, I need your help. We can leave lights on at your apartment, and the television, too. If he checks, he'll think you're home. He'll buy it. Everybody in town knows you're separated."

Mark bit his lip. The idea that the trouble in his and Allie's marriage was apparently so widely discussed infuriated him, but he supposed he deserved it. He hadn't made a secret of his maintaining a separate residence, or of his nightly visits to Joe's Place.

"What do I need to do?" Allie asked.

"Nothing. Just give me the key, then fake a fight as you both run out of here, and I'll take care of the rest," Stan said. "You two slam into the car and screech away. They'll think you're taking her home, Mark, but go ahead and leave town instead. Allie, we'll get your van home, since it's still at your shop."

"What about the press people out on the sidewalk?"

"I'll pick the moment you leave to give them a statement," he said. "It'll distract them."

Allie reached into her purse for her key chain and handed it across the table. Stan dropped the keys into his pocket, then crossed his arms on the table. "Look, a lot of people in town are praying for you," he said. "Both of you, and all of the other families. Do me a favor, though, would you? Pray for me, too. I really want to find this guy." He took Celia's hand, squeezed it, and said, "He's got to be stopped."

"We will," Allie said. She got up and hugged Stan tightly, then Celia. "Be careful, okay? Both of you."

Celia clung to her, her body shaking with a renewed onslaught of tears. "I love you guys. And I know this'll all be over soon."

Chapter Twenty-Five

● ● ●

Are you okay?" Mark looked at Allie as he drove. Her head leaned against the window, and she nodded mildly. Their orchestrated argument at city hall had gotten the attention of several of the firefighters and their wives, but it seemed to have taken a lot out of her.

"Yeah. I was just thinking."

"Thinking what?"

She hesitated, and a few minutes passed. "About what George said to us at the funeral."

"About getting back together?" he asked.

"Yeah. And I know it isn't going to happen. But it would be nice if we didn't have to air our dirty laundry in public the way we just did."

"I'm not crazy about it, either, especially since I came out looking like a major-league jerk. But like Stan said, we'll clear it all up after this is over."

"Will we?" she asked. "As we go our separate ways, we'll let the town know that we weren't really at each other's throats? We were just helping Stan? You think that'll really change their opinion of you, Mark?"

He bristled. "*You* threw *me* out, Allie. I was in it for the long haul."

"Till death do us part?" she asked cynically.

He started to retaliate, then stopped, watching her out of the corner of his eye as the lights of passing cars and street-lamps cast her face in light and shadow. For a long time, the silence held. Finally, Mark spoke again. "I don't want death to part us, Allie."

Her face had turned back to her window, and he knew she was crying. He hated it when he made her cry. "Look, we're tense," he said quietly. "Our nerves are frayed. Let's just try to get along, okay?"

"You don't have to stay with me tonight, Mark."

"Yes, I do. You're my wife."

A tense silence caught them again. Finally, Allie asked, "Where are we going?"

He shrugged. "New Orleans," he said. "We can get lost there."

•   •   •

The long drive on I–10 over Lake Pontchartrain was quiet, and Allie leaned her head against the window and watched the shadows and lights dancing off of the water. Something told her that her life had taken a drastic turn, that things were never going to be the same again. She'd never go into her house without locking the door again, and she'd never feel comfortable alone. She would never take for granted any of her friends. And she'd never take her own life for granted again.

She looked at Mark and saw that he, too, was lost in his thoughts. What was he thinking? Was he wondering what he was going to do with her? It was clear that he worried about her safety, something that surprised and gratified her. But there was still Issie Mattreaux. Where was she, and was Mark worried about her, too?

The thought filled her with that familiar mixture of pain and outrage, and she looked out the window again.

"Do you have any place in particular that you'd like to stay when we get there?" Mark asked.

The only place she had ever stayed on the Southshore was the Marriott, where they'd shared their honeymoon four years ago. They'd gone back occasionally to see a Broadway traveling show or celebrate a birthday or anniversary. In fact, on previous trips, there'd never been any question of where they would stay; it was always the same.

But this time, *they* weren't the same.

"I'm thinking the Marriott," Mark said when she didn't answer. He gave her a moment, then glanced at her. "It's secure and safe. At least, it feels that way. And we're familiar with it."

"It's expensive," she said.

"I think there's a little room on our credit card. No, wait— if we check in with a credit card, we can be traced. I'll swing by an ATM machine and get a cash advance on the card."

"Fine," Allie said quietly. "But Mark, get something with two double beds, instead of one king-sized."

He stared out the windshield. "We're married, Allie."

"Not really," she said.

He didn't protest, and her gaze drifted out the window again. Her eyes misted over. How sad—they would be sleeping in the same room, but yards apart. She had missed sleeping next to him, feeling his warmth when she was cold, touching him for reassurance when she woke in the middle of the night. She would miss it even more tonight, so near and yet so far. It would be better—if she'd been brave enough—to insist that they get separate rooms. But she wasn't that brave. There was, after all, a killer on the loose. Despite her protests, she wanted Mark to be there, in the same room, watching over and protecting her.

But they couldn't touch—not if she was going to hold on to her sanity. They couldn't pretend to be man and wife, love each other, cling together, then go back to their separate lives and their separate homes. She couldn't let her heart find hope in him—not when he was sure to let her down, as he had before.

They got cash from an ATM and checked into the hotel under fake names—just in case the killer was looking for them—then rode the elevator up quietly and found their room.

"We should call home and see if Stan is there, and if he needs to know where anything is," she said as she set her purse on one of the beds.

Mark dropped the bags. "I'll call him. I'd like to know if anything's happened yet, anyway. Want me to order room service first?"

She shook her head. "No, I'm not hungry. I think I'll just get ready for bed."

He nodded, then picked up the phone.

• • •

Hours later, in Newpointe, Stan Shepherd sat at the table in Allie's house looking glumly at Sid Ford—Ray's brother, who therefore had a personal stake in the investigation—and Lynette Devreaux, a rookie cop who had Allie's coloring and hairstyle, making her a good decoy. While they waited for something to happen, they were going over everything they knew about the murderer. There were too many missing pieces, too many problems with every lead they'd followed. Although they had lifted quite a few fingerprints from all three houses, they still knew little. The same firemen and police officers had been in and out of all three homes, and even though they'd been careful not to disturb evidence, some of them had touched things inadvertently. The same caliber bullet had been used for each of the women, and in all three homes, according to the fire inspector, the fires had been started with diesel fuel. Diesel fumes didn't rise the way gasoline fumes would have, which had allowed the killer time to get out of the house unscathed after he'd set fire to it. There had been several shoe prints found—all belonging either to the residents of the homes or to the fire and police personnel who had come in afterward. The crime lab had examined all of the fibers vacuumed from the carpet of the Broussard house—since it hadn't been set on fire, there was more evidence to collect—but again, the only supposed clues wound up being related to the Broussards or to the firefighters and police officers who had responded to the call.

"What we don't know," Stan said, rubbing his tired eyes and staring down at the lists on Allie's kitchen table, "is whether he rang the bell and was invited in—in which case, he's someone they knew—or whether he picked the lock."

Sid stared quietly down at the papers spread out on the table. "My gut tells me there was an element of surprise. Susan was shot in the back, as if she was running away. Jamie was in bed. I can't see her getting up to let someone in, then getting back in bed."

"And that diaper bag in the middle of the floor at Martha's. Like she dropped it," Lynette added.

"Okay, then. Where does that leave us?" Stan asked wearily. "He may or may not know the victims. May or may not have been invited in. May or may not have worn gloves or shoe covers to keep from leaving prints."

"We know he's not afraid of being seen," Lynette pointed out. "Twice he entered homes in broad daylight."

"But both times there was some major event going on in town, so neighbors weren't as likely to be home. The parade and the funeral."

"We need the guest books at both funerals," Sid said. "We could at least use them for elimination. Whoever's on those lists isn't guilty."

"I'll get George's," Stan said. "You're right. But we need more than a process of elimination—we need a list of active suspects. And other than Hank Keyes, we don't have a single name."

"Hank Keyes may still be guilty."

"I don't think so," Stan said. "It doesn't fit. He's just a punk who thinks he's a big shot. Sure, he needs to be locked up for something, but I don't think it's this."

The radio they had turned down low on the table gave out a burst of static, and Stan reached to turn it up. "Yeah, this is Stan," he said into the mike.

"We might have some activity," came the low voice of Anthony Martin, who was sitting in the car parked in the garage across the street, keeping an eye on the outside of Allie's home. "Somebody's walking up the driveway. He left his car four houses down at the vacant house."

Stan and the others sprang up and reached for their weapons. "Can you get a picture?" he asked.

"No, the streetlight's out and I can barely see him. He's almost to the door."

Lynette was shaking as she went into the kitchen and pretended to wash the dishes she had put there earlier. Though the curtains were closed, they wanted the noises inside to be authentic, to make the killer feel sure that she was home, and alone. Stan and Sid got on either side of the door and held their breath, waiting.

The doorbell rang, and a tentative knock followed. Lynette froze. "What do I do?" she mouthed.

Stan shook his head, warning her to do nothing. Then he watched as, breathing hard, she pulled her gun with a trembling hand and held it at the ready, aimed toward the ceiling, as the bell rang again. He felt a bead of sweat trickle from his temple, down the side of his face.

They heard the knob rattle slightly. Although the volume on his radio was turned down so that its static wouldn't be heard, he whispered into it, "Back us up, Anthony."

The knob jiggled. They heard a key being inserted. Stan's heartbeat flew into triple-time. A bead of sweat trickled down his temple.

Then the knob turned. The door began to push open. Stan and Sid both stood back, guns drawn and ready.

The second the intruder's foot stepped over the threshold, Stan heard Anthony Martin's voice outside. "Freeze! Put your hands over your head and get down on the floor!"

The suspect jerked, startled, at the sound of Anthony's voice, then did as he was told. Anthony followed him in.

The intruder was face-down wearing a fireman's hat and bunker coat. Sid frisked him roughly while the others kept their guns trained on him.

"It's me, you idiots." The voice was muffled against the carpet. "It's just me!"

Stan grabbed the man's hair and pulled his head up to get a look as Sid kept up his search for weapons.

Craig Barnes's face was crimson, and he was gasping for breath. Stan turned him all the way over and gaped down at him. "What are you doing here?"

"I was checking on Allie, you fool!" Craig cried. "I just came from a call and was feeling nervous about her after their fight at the courthouse today."

Sid pulled a .38 automatic out of Craig's coat pocket. The fire chief sat up, cursing. "Yeah, I'm carrying a gun. Everybody and his dog is carrying a gun tonight."

"I asked what you're doing here," Stan bit out.

"And I told you! I'm on duty tonight. I was coming from a call and I thought I'd drive by and check on Allie. This is as much on my mind as it is on yours, Stan, maybe more, because it's *my* men who are losing their wives." They let him up, and he slipped out of the hot bunker coat and tried to catch his breath. "When I came by here I saw Allie's car and the lights on. I got concerned and drove around to Mark's apartment, and it looked like he was home, too. I figured he had meant it today when he said she could fend for herself. I wanted to check to make sure she was all right, and see if I could help her find an alternative to staying here alone." He looked around at them, one by one. "What are *you* guys doing here? Staking the place out?"

"Yes." Stan was getting confused, so he tried to shake his head free of the conflicting signals. "Craig, how did you unlock the door?"

"With a key!" he said, opening the door and showing them the key that was still in the lock. "When she didn't answer the door, what was I supposed to think? She could have been lying dead in here. I decided to look for the key and come on in, but I have to tell you I was nervous. I know this guy is just killing women, but I didn't want to wind up dead myself if I happened to catch him in the act. So I came in as quietly as I could—and then you guys scared the livin' daylights out of me."

"Why'd you park so far down the street?" Anthony asked, obviously not convinced. "Why wouldn't you want anyone to see your car here?"

Craig gaped at them, as though in disbelief. "You guys think *I'm* the killer? Chief of the fire department? I just lost seventy-five percent of my force because of this. You think I'd orchestrate all that and put myself in this kind of bind? You've got to be kidding."

"Answer the question about your car," Stan said.

Craig rubbed his hand through his hair. "The sprinkler was running—getting the whole driveway wet, and the street in front, too. I didn't want to get wet, so I parked in that driveway. I figured if I parked in front of any of the other houses, somebody would see me and call the police." He sat down and slumped wearily. "Look, we're all tired. We're all a little on edge. I need to get over to Eastside, because they've only got two of the usual three on a shift over there."

Stan looked from one of the cops to another, and saw that they had relaxed and were buying the story. Even Anthony Martin. Stan still wasn't sure, but after a moment, he nodded. "All right, Craig. But don't go breaking into anybody else's home, or I'll haul you in."

"Believe me, I'll never pull that again."

"You could have gotten your head blown off."

"Tell me about it." He got up, dusted off his uniform, then started for the door. "I hope you catch the real guy tonight. I'm ready for this to be over."

They watched him go out and closed the door behind him.

For a moment, all four cops stood looking at each other. "What do you think?" Stan asked.

"I believe him," Lynette said. "It made sense. Everybody's so strung out about all this, I guess nobody's really acting all that rationally."

"He's got to be concerned about his men and their families. I buy it," Sid said.

Stan looked at Anthony, who had gotten a distant look in his eyes. "Anthony?"

Anthony shook his head. "I don't know. He sure did look suspicious walking up to the house. But he's right about the sprinkler."

Stan had his doubts—but he needed more than doubts to justify an arrest. "All right, Anthony. Go back across the street, and let's try it again. Let's just hope that little fiasco didn't scare off the real guy, or we'll have wasted this whole night."

Chapter Twenty-Six

● ● ●

Because Mark was unwilling to take a room any higher than a ladder truck could reach in the event of a fire, their room at the Marriott was on the third floor, making all of the ground noise of Canal Street audible during the night. Allie lay awake in her bed on her side of the room as flashing blue lights occasionally colored the walls and sirens screeched by. Now and then, she could hear a jazz band somewhere in the Quarter, its music fading in and out like a dream.

Across the room, Mark lay in his own bed, tangled in the covers. He wore a T-shirt and white boxer shorts, and his hair was in disarray. He appeared to be sleeping soundly, though he didn't make the soft, snoring noise he usually made when he slept. It had taken her three weeks after he'd moved out to get used to sleeping without that sound. Now she longed for it. She turned on her side and watched him in the moonlight spilling in through the window. It was the first time she'd known him to sleep in a T-shirt, but she supposed their estrangement had created an unnatural modesty between them. She had always slept in his T-shirts, but tonight she wore a big LSU jersey and white leggings. Now she wished she'd worn something a little more attractive. As angry and hurt as she was at him, it hurt her to think that all of the attraction and chemistry were gone.

She got up quietly, went to the big picture window, and peered out into the night. She could see the lights of cars passing by on Canal Street, and establishments lit up in neon. Some were raunchy, decadent places that sold unspeakable things, and as she often had before, she asked herself how one city could have so much beauty and so much ugliness at the same time.

She heard a siren not far away and wondered if someone had been murdered. How often did those police cars have to rush to the scene of a homicide? Was life less valuable here than it was anywhere else? Was it growing less valuable in Newpointe?

She tried to picture what Martha, Jamie, and Susan must have gone through. Had they seen his face? Had they spoken to him, pled for their life? Had the two deaths been instant, or had they suffered that lingering awareness that it was all about to end and there was nothing they could do?

She covered her face with both hands and tried to muffle her sobs. Then she heard the creaking of the mattress behind her. She didn't turn around.

Warm, familiar, comforting arms turned her around, and she let herself relax into them. Mark held her for a long time, letting her weep against his chest, letting her cry out all the fear and rage and confusion that plagued her. After a while, the fear and rage were gone, and she cried, instead, out of grief, not for her friends, but for her husband. Even as he held her, she missed him.

When he kissed her, she had no power to resist, and all the old feelings came rushing back on a tidal wave of memory. The campfire where they'd first kissed, being carried in his arms to their car after the wedding, her long veil dragging the ground, the overwhelming love she'd felt for him as they'd moved into their first home and set up housekeeping, the conversations and plans and anticipation of children ... all of those things were still there, in that desperate kiss, and her heart raced with hope. But there was sadness, too. And that sadness was grounded in reality, whereas the hope seemed as empty as a child's balloon.

When the kiss broke, she looked up at him, her face wet and her eyes swollen, and she felt more vulnerable than a toddler standing in rush-hour traffic. She knew she should say something, but nothing came to her.

"It's been a long time," Mark whispered, his fingertips cupping her chin. "I've missed you." There was deep emotion in his face as he spoke, and she wanted to trust him. But Mark had always been a charmer. He had charmed her when she'd met him at a youth camp her senior year of high school. He had told her he loved her then, and had held her just this way when she'd had to go back home to Georgia. He had whispered that he would miss her, just as he whispered it now.

She had been swept away then, certain that he was her life partner, the one God had chosen for her. But God wouldn't choose a man who could forsake his vows so easily. He wouldn't have set aside a man who professed to be a Christian but drank too much and avoided the church they had both loved. She had made a mistake in marrying him. Somehow, without realizing it, she must have deposed God and followed her own agenda. And now she was paying with the deepest pain she'd ever felt.

She backed away, grabbed a tissue, and blew her nose, deliberately breaking the mood. He stood in his boxer shorts and T-shirt, watching her, waiting for the response she wasn't able to give. She pressed the wadded tissue to the inside corners of her eyes, trying to stop the tears. But she couldn't speak, and she couldn't look at him.

Finally, he moved into the bathroom. She heard water running, and in a moment he was back at her side, holding out a glass for her. "Here," he said softly. "Drink this."

She took it gratefully, drank it until it was empty, then set the glass down on the table next to her bed. She sat down, looking at the floor. Mark stooped in front of her and looked up into her eyes. He, too, seemed to be at a loss for words. Gently, he swept her hair behind her ear.

"Do you think you can sleep now?" he asked finally.

She drew in a deep breath and decided to lie. "Yes."

"If you can't, tomorrow we'll see about getting something to help. Maybe a mild tranquilizer just at night."

She nodded and slipped back into the bed. It seemed so big, so cold, without him beside her. She realized as he covered her that she would like nothing more than to have him slip in beside her and hold her until she fell asleep. But she couldn't let that happen. Not when their marriage was nonexistent. Not when there was another woman in the picture.

She closed her eyes and listened as he got back into his own bed. She couldn't wait for morning.

•   •   •

Across the room, Mark lay in his bed with his back to her, fighting the longing to climb into her bed and hold her so tight that the memories of the last two months would flee. That kiss had been a mistake, he thought. It had almost done him in. As if it had opened the floodgates, it had brought back a rush of feelings that he wasn't sure he could control.

He had felt her reaction, too, but then he'd felt the hesitation, the despair, then the separation.

Confusion dominated his mind as his heart mourned for the woman who was within his grasp, yet so far away that he feared he would never reach her again. Had their marriage been ruined beyond repair? In the words of the ceremony that had bound them, had they been torn asunder? Or were they still one, as his heart seemed to claim?

He honestly didn't know.

He thought of turning over, looking to see if she was still awake, hoping that maybe she was still distraught and needed him again. Only then could he go to her. Unless he knew that she needed and wanted him too, his fear of rejection was too great.

But he didn't hear her crying, didn't hear her wrestling with the bed covers . . .

She didn't need him, he thought miserably. Without that, he couldn't go to her. They were destined to spend this time together . . . all alone.

And as the night ticked by, he realized that he already knew the answer to his question about whether they were still one. He felt as though his soul had been ripped in two. Yes, they had been torn asunder. And it was probably too late to put them back together again.

Chapter Twenty-Seven

● ● ●

At two-thirty A.M., Officer R.J. Albright, who was patrolling Newpointe, drove down Purchase Street, which housed the Midtown fire station, police department, city hall, and courthouse, then turned onto Jacquard Street, where the Blooms 'n' Blossoms shop was. Allie's flower van was there, and a dim light shone from the back room. He turned into the parking lot. Had the rumors been true, about Mark abandoning her tonight? As his headlights lit up the small gravel parking lot, he saw someone coming from behind the building.

He radioed his location to the dispatcher, then pulled his car further in to get a better look. He got out, his hand on his gun, his heart pumping hard, and saw the man stop in the shadows, waiting for him.

"Hello, R.J." It was Dan Nichols's voice, and as the tall man walked out of the shadows, he saw that he was dressed in his fireman's uniform and carrying a crowbar. "I was just about to call you guys."

"Yeah?" R.J. asked. "What for?"

"Somebody tried to break in here," Dan said. He sounded excited, out of breath. "I was down the street at the station, and I came out for some fresh air. I could have sworn I saw someone moving around the door, but when I ran down here, I guess I scared him off."

R.J. examined the door. The lock was scratched, as if it had been tampered with. The dead bolt inside kept the door from opening, but someone had tried to pry it open. He turned back to Dan and regarded the crowbar.

"I found this in the back," Dan explained. "I was looking around, and I saw it lying a few yards from the shop. He probably dropped it as he ran away."

R.J. was mildly suspicious, despite his years of friendship with Dan. "So you're sayin' you *saw* someone? What did they look like?"

Dan hedged. "It's not that I saw anybody, just movement. I *thought* I saw something."

"Why didn't you call us right then?"

"I don't know," he said. "Didn't want to take the time to run back in, I guess. I saw Allie's light on and thought maybe she was inside, so I wanted to get over here quick."

"And when you got here, you didn't see nothin'?"

"No. Like I said, I think I scared him off."

R.J. stared at him for several seconds.

"Well, are you just going to stand there, or are you going to call in some other patrol units to search the woods back there?" Dan asked, irritated.

"Why ain't you sweatin'?" R.J. knew the question seemed to come from left field, but he had to ask it.

Dan frowned. "What?"

"I asked, why ain't you sweatin'? You said you ran down here. If you did, why ain't you sweatin'?"

"It's less than a block, R.J., and it's cold out here. Are you suggesting I'm lying?"

"Just askin'."

"Terrific. Remind me not to get involved the next time I see someone's business getting broken into." He flung down the crowbar and headed back up the street toward the station. "Glad you boys have so much time on your hands that you'd suspect fellow public servants instead of looking for the real killer."

But R.J. wasn't listening. Deep in thought, he went to his car and grabbed the radio mike.

Chapter Twenty-Eight

● ● ●

Jill Clark had just sat down with her first cup of coffee of the morning when the telephone rang. "Hello?"

"Jill, this is Dan Nichols. I'm sorry to call so early, but I thought you'd want to know."

A sick feeling washed over her, and setting her coffee cup down, she braced herself. "Not another murder."

"No, not that," Dan said quickly. "But last night there was almost a break-in at Allie's shop. I thought I saw someone over there and I apparently scared them away. But to me it indicates that Allie's definitely in danger. She might even be next on this guy's list."

Jill's skin turned cold, and she got to her feet and began to pace. "Are you sure, Dan? I mean, did they go in?"

"No, but they used a crowbar to try to pry open the door, since it was dead-bolted."

"But maybe it was just a simple robbery. I mean, it was apparent that she wasn't there, wasn't it?"

"Not really. Her van was parked there, and there was a light on in the back. He may have thought she was inside."

Jill closed her eyes and sat back down. "Have you heard anything? Are they any closer to finding this guy?"

"Haven't heard, and they're not really telling me anything. I think R.J. even suspects me, since I was at the shop when he got there last night. But we had a real quiet night at the station. Only a couple of calls, and those were for minor things. So I was out in the garage lifting weights, and I walked out into the fresh air. That's when I saw."

"Quiet night? At least there were no more murders."

"All the wives are out of town. Makes you wonder how bad he wants them dead, and if he's going to start going after them where they are."

She shivered.

"Look, do you know where I can reach her and Mark to let them know?" Dan asked.

"No, I don't. They didn't tell me where they were going."

"Well, if you hear from them, tell them what I said. They need to really be on guard. And hey, if they need a place to stay, tell them they can use my house. It's out in the country, and no one will look for them there."

"All right, Dan. I'll tell them."

After she hung up, Jill sat praying that Allie could somehow escape this madness. Someone insane enough to try to kill three women—two in broad daylight—might not stop until he had finished the job, regardless of what obstacles they threw in his way. Did he even care about getting caught? Was he rational enough to lie low?

Quickly, she started to get dressed. She would go to the police station and find out what they knew. Maybe something would give her—and Allie—a little hope.

•   •   •

While Mark was in the shower, Allie called her best friend in Newpointe.

"Hello?"

"Jill, it's me. Did I wake you up?"

"No. Allie, I'm so glad you called. I wanted to get in touch with you, but I didn't know how."

Allie stood up. "What's wrong? Is it Susan? Did something happen?"

"I don't know," Jill said. "I haven't heard a word about Susan. But I just talked to Dan Nichols, and he told me that someone tried to break into your shop last night."

"*What?*"

"Dan scared him off, so he didn't get all the way in, whoever it was—but Allie, he probably thought *you* were in there. The light in the back was on."

Allie's heart began racing. "I've gotta go, Jill. I've gotta call Stan Shepherd and see what he can tell me."

"Allie, don't come back here. Wherever you are, stay there. I'm scared to death for you. This guy's getting bold, and he isn't going to give up."

"I know," she said. "Look, I'm thinking about going to Georgia, to stay with my parents until this blows over."

"Do it. Get as far from here as you can."

"You be careful, too, Jill. Don't stay alone."

Jill hesitated. "I'll do what I can. But I'm not married to a fireman."

"If he can't get to us, he might start on others," she said. "Don't take the chance, Jill."

She hung up as Mark came out of the bathroom, his hair wet and a towel flung around his neck. He was wearing a pair of jeans and a clean T-shirt and smelled like soap. She felt rumpled and frumpy and wished she had gotten up earlier to put herself together. She'd be willing to bet that Issie Mattreaux never looked like this in the morning.

"Who was that?" he asked.

"Jill. Mark, the shop was broken into last night."

He stared at her in amazement, then grabbed the phone from her hand. "I'm calling Stan."

As he dialed, she said, "Mark, I want to go to Georgia. I think it would be a good time for me to visit my parents."

"Maybe you're right." He was quiet for a moment. "Stan Shepherd, please. This is Mark Branning." Turning toward Allie, he said, "Pick up the phone in the bathroom so you can hear."

Allie had often chuckled at the oddness of bathroom phones in hotels. Now she was grateful for it as she sat on the toilet lid and waited for Stan to pick up.

"I heard about the break-in," Mark said when Stan was on the line.

"Which one?"

Mark was stunned into silence.

"What do you mean, which one?" Allie asked.

"Well, there was the attempt at the shop. If Dan Nichols had called the police instead of trying to be a hero, we might have caught the guy. And then there was the one at your house when we were there, but it turned out to be Craig Barnes, checking on Allie. If your friends would stay out of our way, we could do our job."

Mark was getting impatient. "Stan, was the shop broken into or not?"

"It was an attempted break-in, and yes, there's plenty of evidence. A broken door, for starters, scratches on the knob, a crowbar that just happens to have Dan Nichols's fingerprints all over it, since he found it and didn't take precautions to protect it—"

"What about the house?" Allie cut in. "You said it was broken into?"

"Like I said, Craig Barnes was just checking on you. He heard the fight you two faked and worried that you were alone. When you didn't answer the door, he decided to come in and see if you were all right."

"But whoever broke into the shop was probably the killer," Mark said. "Does this mean Allie is supposed to be his next victim?"

"Might have been if she'd been here last night. Then again, it could have been just a routine burglary."

"No, too coincidental."

"Not really. Any fool kid looking for drug money would assume that the fire wives are all out of town."

"Were any other homes or businesses broken into that you know of?"

"No. We did a check of all of their homes this morning, and didn't find anything."

Allie heard Mark swallow. "Look, Stan, Allie and I have decided to get her out of the state. The farther the better."

"Good idea," Stan said.

"I'll call you later and see if you've come up with anything."

He hung up, and Allie came out of the bathroom and stood looking at him, fear and frustration illuminating her eyes. "I'm coming with you," he said.

"To Georgia? No, Mark, that wouldn't work."

"Why not?"

"Because . . ." She hesitated to tell him the real reason, then had to admit to herself that lying would be futile. "My parents are so angry at you right now."

His face changed instantly. "Why? What exactly have you told them?"

"I told them the truth, Mark."

"And just what is your version of the truth? That I was sleeping around?"

"No . . ."

"Then what? I haven't done anything wrong, Allie. There is nothing you could have told them about me to turn them against me—not anything true. What *did* you tell them?"

"I told them about my walking in on you and Issie at the fire station. I told them you moved out, that you were interested in someone else, that you'd started drinking and quit going to church, and didn't care about our vows anymore. I told them the truth, Mark!"

She turned away and started packing her suitcase. She could feel him standing there behind her, watching her, angry and so hurt—but denying nothing. Finally, he said, "You're wrong about what you saw at the fire station, Allie. But we've been through all that. I'm here right now. I'm sticking by you. Doesn't that count for something?"

"Don't do me any favors," she said. "Other people are watching over me, too. Dan Nichols, apparently, and Craig Barnes, and who knows who else. I can do without you, Mark."

She knew that stung him, and she was glad. But the satisfaction only lasted a moment. She knew Mark well enough to know that he might just leave her out of pride now, and then she would have to face all of this alone. She turned back to her bag and zipped it up.

Behind her, she heard him packing, too, and then he picked up the phone and dialed again.

"Econojet Airlines," he said. He wrote the number down, dialed it, then waited again. "Yes, I'd like to make reservations for two on the next flight from New Orleans to Atlanta this afternoon."

She swung toward him. "Mark, I *told* you! We only need one ticket."

He put his hand over the phone, and through his teeth said, "And I told *you*. I'm not leaving you."

"You already left me! You're only with me now because you're afraid I'm going to be killed. I don't want you staying with me out of duty!"

"Reservations for two," he repeated into the phone again. "Mr. and Mrs. Mark Branning."

She threw up her hands and went back into the bathroom and began brushing her teeth with a vengeance. In the other room, she heard him say, "No, it has to be today. Don't you have *any* seats? Yes, they have to be together."

She closed her eyes in frustration.

"All right, tomorrow then. Yes, that'll be fine. What time?"

When he hung up, she came out of the bathroom. "They were booked up today?"

"Yes," he said, staring down at his shoes.

"What about Delta or American or—"

"We can't afford them, Allie. Our credit cards are almost maxed out. We can only afford Econojet."

"My parents will pay for me."

"But not me."

"What about your dad? Maybe he could give you a loan."

Mark's laughter was bitterly sarcastic. "You've got to be kidding. My father hasn't got two dimes to rub together. Allie, we're just going to wait until tomorrow and take Econojet and pay for it ourselves. Meanwhile, we'll check out of here and go to Slidell, and see about Susan. We'll stay someplace else tonight. It isn't wise to stay in the same place two nights, anyway."

She sighed. She knew he was right, and the truth was, she didn't want to travel alone. "All right," she said finally. "I guess we have no choice."

Chapter Twenty-Nine

● ● ●

Jill got little information from the police department regarding the attempted break-in at the florist, so she walked over to the fire department to see Dan Nichols. Aunt Aggie stood in front of the stove making Monte Cristo sandwiches for the firemen. Jill watched her drop the batter-covered turkey sandwiches into the hot oil to fry them, then scoop them out and smother them with powdered sugar. A side dish of marmalade went on every plate for dipping. She wondered how any of them managed to keep from looking like Pillsbury Dough Boys. Actually, most did show a little pudginess from the rich food Aunt Aggie made them each day, but Dan remained thin. Why had no one in town snatched him up yet?

"Can I talk to you privately?" she asked him quietly, and he looked at the other firemen sitting around the kitchen.

"Sure," he said. "Let's walk out back."

She followed him outside, walked to a bench halfway across the lawn, and sat down. "I talked to Allie this morning," she said.

"Did you tell her what I saw?"

"Yeah. She was pretty upset."

"Where is she?"

"Headed to Georgia to stay with her parents until this blows over."

"Georgia? I didn't know she was from there. What part?"

"Atlanta."

"When's she leaving?"

"Today sometime, I think."

"Is Mark going with her?"

"She didn't say." She looked up at him, her eyes wide and pensive. "I called the hospital in Slidell this morning, and they're saying that Susan's still comatose. They don't know if she's going to come out of it or not."

"Yeah, I heard."

"Dan, last night when you saw the guy at the florist—why didn't you chase him down? Why didn't you call the police right away?"

"I was trying to get a look at the guy when R.J. pulled up. In his patrol car, he probably still could have caught the guy on the other side of the woods, but he was so busy trying to make me out to be the culprit that he let him get away."

Jill frowned. "They suspected you?"

"Yeah, you believe that? They stopped because they saw *me*. I might need a lawyer before this thing's over."

"Well, you know how to reach me. But I don't think you have anything to worry about. I'm just glad you ran the guy off."

"I would rather have caught him."

"Yeah, well. Don't beat yourself up."

"You know, with all these media people around, some people in this town might not want the killer caught. Apparently murder is good for business."

"Yeah, every motel in town is full, and the restaurants are bursting at the seams. Give me our sleepy little town any day of the week," Jill said. "This kind of attention we don't need."

Aunt Aggie came to the door and called out, "Eats is ready, *mon ami*. Jill, stay. There's plenty."

She stood up. "Are you sure?"

Aunt Aggie laughed with delight. "Where else can you enjoy the company of six bachelors at one time?"

"Six?"

"Sure. The chief is one, too."

Jill grinned and glanced at Dan. "How can any self-respecting woman pass up an invitation like that?"

• • •

Before they left New Orleans, Mark and Allie went to Pat O'Brien's for lunch. Though it was quiet now, this was one of the hot spots at night, when tourists and local party animals packed in to guzzle Hurricanes and dance to the band whose equipment was set up in a corner of the open brick courtyard. Now, only a guitarist, a bass player, and a saxophone player droned out a New Orleans flavored jazz medley that made them almost forget their troubles for a while.

When the waitress came to take their order, Allie saw Mark hesitate over the wine list. He looked up, apparently sensed her disapproval, and closed it again. "I'll just have a Sprite," he said, then told the waitress his lunch order.

When the waitress had gone, he met Allie's eyes again. "I don't drink that much, Allie. I just thought a glass of wine might relax me a little."

She let her eyes drift to the ensemble in the corner. But she could feel him watching her, could sense his frustration and his desire to launch into a conversation that she knew would prove both unproductive and unpleasant.

"Allie, I don't like you thinking I'm a drunk."

"I never said you were a drunk," she said, keeping her eyes on the musicians.

"You might as well say it. You act like I'm an alcoholic or something, and that's not true."

She looked at him again. He was asking for it. "Mark, remember when we started seeing each other, and I lived in Georgia and you lived here, and you had been to visit my parents, but you never wanted me to come home and meet your father?"

He lowered his eyes to the wrought iron table and traced the pattern with his finger. "Yeah, so?"

"I was hurt, because I thought you didn't want him to meet me. And then I found out that the real reason you wouldn't bring me home was that you didn't want *me* to meet *him*. When you finally told me the real reason, do you remember what you said?"

"No, Allie, I don't," he said on a note of sarcasm. "Why don't you tell me?"

"You said that your father drank too much, and you were embarrassed by him. You said that he was an alcoholic, and that your poor mother had to live with the stigma of being a drunk's wife until the day she died. You said that he wouldn't admit he had a problem, that he claimed he didn't drink that much and could stop anytime he wanted to."

"All right, Allie. You've made your point."

"No, I haven't," she said. "You also told me that you would never drink as long as you lived, because you saw how easy it was for alcohol to get its claws into you—because it had ruined your father's life, and your mother's life, but it wasn't going to ruin yours."

He compressed his lips and stared across the tables to the musicians on the stage. "Alcohol isn't ruining my life, Allie. It's a result of our problems, not the cause of them."

"So when you started going to Joe's Place with your buddies after your shift, when you started having those long heart-to-hearts with Issie, you were doing it because we were having problems?"

He hesitated, started to speak, then stopped and shook his head as if the argument was too futile to continue.

"Because I distinctly remember that our problems started *after* you made Joe's Place and Issie your daily habit."

"I wasn't drinking then, Allie. I just went to be with my friends. If coming home had been more pleasant, I wouldn't have found other places to go."

The blow was low, and she almost flinched with the force of it. She stared at him for several seconds, fighting the rage that seemed so familiar these days. "And why was coming home so unpleasant?" she bit out.

"Because you kept harping on the fact that you wanted to have a baby but we didn't make enough money for you to sell the shop and stay home, that you wanted me to get a better job, that you were having to work so hard to make up for the money that I didn't make, that the shop was barely breaking even—on and on and on. It was always the same. But you knew when you married me that I wanted to be a fireman, had always wanted to be a fireman. You don't go into that job for the money."

"So you were justified in going to bars every night with your friends?"

When he didn't answer, she added, "I wonder if that's how it started with your dad."

She knew that would hit him where it hurt, for his father had been a fireman, too, as his father before him had been. The realities of the job, particularly the low pay, had to have caused problems in their marriages, too.

"It's not the same, Allie. I'm not a drunk. I told you, when I first started going to Joe's Place, I didn't even drink. I just wanted some pleasant conversation, some companionship."

"And you chose to have that with another woman?"

He rolled his eyes. "And here I thought we were talking about drinking."

Tears welled in her eyes, but she wouldn't let them spill. She focused on a schefflera plant hanging from the ceiling. A soul-deep sadness filled her heart, weighing her down, and she wondered where things had gone wrong. Had she really turned into a nagging wife that made life so unpleasant that her husband had to seek out comfort in other women? Was it really her fault?

These were all issues that they hadn't been able to deal with in marriage counseling, primarily because either of them had the option to leave when things got too hot. Now they seemed stuck together by grim circumstances, trapped, unable to leave.

Their food came, and they both picked at it as the jazz music played on. Neither of them had anything to say.

"I should call my parents," she said finally. "Tell them we're coming."

"Warn them *I'm* coming."

She slid her chair back and dug into her purse for her calling card. "I'll be right back."

"No, I'm coming with you."

"But we haven't paid the bill."

"Then wait," he said. "We're not that far from Newpointe, Allie. I don't want you to be alone."

She bit back her objection and waited for their bill, amazed at his unwavering determination to protect her, even when being around her seemed painful to him. She regretted bringing up his dad's drinking; she wished she had tried to be more pleasant, more fun to be with, but there was nothing pleasant or fun about their circumstances. It was bad enough that their marriage had come to a halt. But the added stress of the killings made things a dozen times more confusing.

She looked up at him and met his eyes—and wished she didn't see contempt, guardedness, and anger there. Last night, when he had held her and kissed her, when she had melted in his arms, it hadn't been there then. But that moment had had little to do with reality.

The waitress brought their bill and Mark paid it, then they both walked to the nearest pay phone.

He stood close to her as she dialed, and in her peripheral vision she noted the fatigued slump to his shoulders and the tired lines around his eyes. This was hard on him—and he didn't have to do it. He could be in Newpointe working his shift, near Issie, but he had chosen to stay here with her. Warmth flooded through her, but she tried to shove it away.

Her mother answered on the first ring. "Mom? It's me."

"Allie, where have you been? We've been hearing all the reports about the murders, and we've tried to call, but we couldn't get you—"

"I'm fine, Mom. I'm in New Orleans right now, just trying to keep low until they catch the killer, but I'm catching a plane tomorrow to come there. I think I need to be out of the state for a while."

"Yes," her mother agreed. "Yes, this is exactly where I want you to be. But honey, be careful. If this man wants you dead—"

"Mark's with me," she said, not certain if that would put their fears to rest or not.

"Mark? Why?"

"He's worried." She met his eyes awkwardly, then looked away. "He hasn't left my side since this whole thing started. He's coming with me to Georgia, Mom."

"Are you two back together?"

"No. Nothing like that. It's just a safety thing."

"What about the woman?"

Her mother was blunt, as always, but Allie hoped Mark hadn't heard. "We'll talk about it later, Mom."

"So do I need to make up one bed or two?"

He'd heard that, and now he watched her, waiting for an answer. "Two, Mom, if you don't mind."

"I'll tell you what, I'm going to give him a piece of my mind when I see him. You should have divorced him already, and then maybe you wouldn't be on that maniac's list."

"Mom, we're not coming to fight. Please, we've been through enough lately."

"Then I have to bite my tongue?"

"I'd appreciate it."

"Oh, really, Allie, you can't be serious."

"Mom, there are more pressing issues to deal with right now. Be glad that I'm not coming alone."

"All right," her mother conceded at last. "I'm glad. But I still might tell him what I think of him if I get the chance."

When she hung up, Allie turned back to Mark. She could tell from the look on his face that he'd heard what her mother had said.

"So, is she going to let me in?"

"Not without telling you off first. Mark, if you want to back out, I'll be fine. Really."

"No way. I'm going with you and that's final. I can deal with your parents."

"All right," she said, "but I warned you."

He seemed thoughtful, and she knew that he dreaded the confrontation tomorrow. They both needed something to distract them. "Let's go to Slidell and check on Susan," she said. "At least we'll feel like we're accomplishing something."

Chapter Thirty

● ● ●

Television vans filled the parking lot of Slidell Memorial Hospital, and a crowd of reporters waited outside the front door for a story. CNN was among those lined up at the edge of the lot. "CNN? This is making national news?" Allie asked.

"Take a look over there," Mark said. "NBC, CBS—I guess it's big-time. 'Serial killer hitting all the wives of the firemen in a sleepy little southern town.'"

"I think I'm gonna be sick."

He stopped the car, let it idle for a moment. "We don't have to go in there."

"Yes, we do. I have to see Ray. I have to know about Susan."

"Look at all the reporters still here—that must mean she's alive."

Allie's face went from dejected to hopeful. "Do you think so?"

"Of course. They wouldn't hang around here if there wasn't a story. They'd be back in Newpointe."

She studied the crowd. "I don't know if I have the strength to walk through them again."

"Don't talk to them. Just stick close to me and keep your eyes on the door. It looks like the security guards are keeping them out of the hospital now, so once we're inside we should be all right."

She pulled down the visor and took a look at herself in the mirror. She had dark circles under her eyes and wore little make-up. "I look terrible. I don't want to wind up on national news."

Mark reached across the seat and touched her cheek. "You look pretty good to me."

Her eyes met his, and they locked there for a moment. Finally, he looked away. "Come on. Let's get this over with."

They got out of the car, and he took her hand and led her toward the door at the far end of the building, away from the crowd of reporters. Some correspondents doing stand-ups in front of their cameras noticed them, and Mark and Allie hurried faster to avoid them.

Once inside the doors, they navigated the halls until they were at the front desk where two elderly volunteers sat. "May I help you?" one of them asked.

"Yes. We were wondering about Susan Ford. Could you tell us where she is now?"

The gray-haired woman eyed them suspiciously. "Reporters?"

"No, ma'am," Mark said. "I'm a fireman with Ray Ford in Newpointe, and this is my wife."

"I have to ask for I.D. before I give you any information," one of the ladies said. "Our hospital administrator wants the media kept out."

"Sure." He reached into his wallet and pulled out his driver's license, as well as his firefighter I.D.

"All right," the woman said. "ICU is on the fourth floor, and Captain Ford is waiting in there."

They thanked her and took the elevator up. In the ICU waiting room, dozens of people waited in various stages of weariness. They saw Ray in a little cluster of people at the back of the room and hurried through.

Craig Barnes was there, along with George Broussard. Mark slowed as he reached them, and Ray looked up at them. His eyes looked as if he'd wept an ocean of tears in the last few hours, but he managed a smile. "You two back?"

"Yeah," Mark said. "How is she, Ray?"

His bloodshot eyes misted over again. "She ain't out of the woods. She's still unconscious."

Allic turned to George and hugged him. "It's nice of you to come here, George, when you've got griefs of your own."

He swallowed. "I thought nothin' would take my mind off my troubles like bein' here to help a brother with his. My folks got Tommy."

"It's gotta be hard for you," Allie said.

"Yeah." George sank down onto a vinyl chair. "At least Martha didn't suffer."

Allie sat down next to him. She took his big hand and held it tightly as she looked back up at Ray. "Has she come to at all?"

"No," Ray said. "Not at all. But I ain't leavin' here, and they promised me that if she does wake up, they'll call me. Other than that, I have to wait until six o'clock tonight to see her again." He blinked back the fresh tears in his eyes. "Anybody talked to the preacher?"

"He was at the meeting," Craig said. "He can't come, Ray, because all of our unmarried men are working to give the rest the chance to protect their wives."

"Good idea," Ray said. "Yeah, that's a better use of his time than bein' here with me."

"I know he's praying, Ray," Allie said. "Lots of people are."

Ray nodded. "I've tried, but it just seems like a chant or somethin'. I can't seem to concentrate."

"I've had the same problem," George said softly. "I know who can give me comfort. I know who can give me peace. But I can't seem to let go of all the anger and confusion long enough to talk to him about it."

"We could pray with you both," Allie offered.

Something about that suggestion made Mark uncomfortable. It had been a long time since he'd prayed with others . . . in fact, he hadn't done a lot of praying alone lately, either. Still, he did what he knew he should do, and nodded. "Sure, we could."

Ray sat slowly down, and Craig Barnes looked for a moment as if he might find an excuse to leave. But Mark sat down next to Ray, and after a moment, Craig followed.

For a moment, they sat there quietly, reverently, while the noise of the waiting room continued around them. Telephones rang, the intercom blared, people talked . . .

Mark looked at Allie; she was looking at him, waiting for him to lead them. He swallowed the lump in his throat and suddenly felt dirty, unrighteous, though he wasn't sure why. Knowing that it was cowardly, he passed the baton to his wife. "Allie, will you lead us?"

He could see her disappointment in him, but he also saw that she wasn't surprised. She bowed her head, closed her eyes, and began to pray.

None of their eyes were dry as she entreated God to intervene on Susan's behalf, prayed for peace for Ray and George, and asked the Almighty to stop the killer from killing again, and to aid the police in finding him.

When the amens came, all of them were weeping. Craig Barnes was so overcome that he had to excuse himself and head for the men's room. Allie dug into her purse and handed each of them a tissue.

"Thank you, Allie," Ray whispered.

"Yeah, *merci*, darlin'," George added. "I needed that."

In a moment, Craig came back, his face dry, but his eyes still glassy and red. "I guess I'd better get back to the station," he said. "I'm short on captains, so I need to be available."

Ray shook his hand and patted his shoulder. "Thanks for coming by, man."

"I'll be back tomorrow," he said. Craig turned to Allie. "You take care, okay?"

"I will," she whispered. "We're flying to Georgia tomorrow morning. Seems right to get out of town."

"I think you're right," Craig said. "But why are you waiting?"

"Econojet," Mark said. "They were booked till then. Anyway, we wanted to come here."

Craig shook Mark's hand. "See you later. Let me know if you need me."

Mark appreciated the sentiment—but he also remembered Craig's objection to the husbands taking off work, so he took those words with a grain of salt.

• • •

Moments later, Allie moved to sit in the empty chair next to Ray. "Where are the kids?" she asked him.

"Ben's takin' a shower," he said. "We been here all night. And Vanessa . . ." He nodded toward a window across the room, and Allie saw the girl sitting on the sill, staring out. "She's takin' it real hard," he said. "Think you could talk to her, Allie? I ain't been able to do much good."

"Sure, I will."

She zigzagged between chairs and clusters of people until she came to the pretty teenager whose only concern just days ago had been getting permission to drive. She touched Vanessa's shoulder, and the girl looked back.

"You okay, Vanessa?" she asked.

She moved her gaze back to the window. "She gon' die."

"We can hope not. They're taking good care of her here—"

"It's my fault."

"*What?* How?"

"Because I'm bein' punished. God's fed up with me so he's teachin' me a lesson."

"What lesson?"

"That if I don't value my mama he gon' take her away." She broke into a sob and turned back to Allie. "Yesterday I called her Ms. Hitler. I said I had the worst mama I knew of. I didn't know those'd be the last words I'd ever say to her, Allie! I didn't know she'd die thinkin' I hated her guts! They was just words."

"Vanessa, there hasn't been a single moment in your life when your mother thought you hated her." Allie's mind drifted back to all the hateful words she and Mark had exchanged—

words of contempt and bitterness. "Words can be pretty powerful, though, can't they?" she asked weakly.

"I just want another chance," the girl whispered. "Just one more chance, to tell Mama I love her. I don't care if she never lets me drive."

Allie pulled the girl into a hug and held her tightly, and they both wept.

"I can't pray for her," Vanessa cried. "God won't hear me, 'cause he gon' teach me a lesson."

"He does hear you, Vanessa. And what happened to your mom was not to punish you, honey. There's a sick man out there, and he's not doing God's business for him. You can pray for your mom, and I know God will listen."

The girl wiped her eyes and flipped her long black weaves back over her shoulder. "You really think so?"

"I know so."

Again they embraced, long and hard.

• • •

From across the room, Mark watched. The gentle way Allie spoke to the girl made him remember how he had wanted to have children with her, how strongly he had believed that Allie would be a wonderful mother. He had almost forgotten.

Now it came back to him how those discussions had led to Allie's desire to stay home with their children, which inevitably led to their conclusion that it was impossible because of his low income, which caused her to work extra hours at the florist to pay the bills, which caused him to feel inadequate and frustrated . . .

It was an endless cycle of discontent, all of it diverting them from their original course: loving and being committed to each other. It was what had made Joe's Place—and ultimately Issie—so attractive to him.

Ben, Ray's son, came back from his shower, and Mark smiled weakly and shook his hand. The boy's eyes were red, and he looked more like a scared little boy than a college track star.

"Any word?" Ben asked his father.

"No, son. No word."

Nor was there any change all that afternoon.

Chapter Thirty-One

● ● ●

Since money was getting low, Mark and Allie stayed in a less expensive, more obscure hotel near the French Quarter that night and ate hamburgers that they'd picked up on the way back. The room came with only one bed, which infuriated her.

"I'll sleep on the floor," she told him when they unlocked the musty room and spotted the one bed.

"That's a little silly, don't you think, considering that we shared a bed for four years? It's not like I'm going to attack you in your sleep."

"I don't want to sleep in the same bed with you," she bit out.

They were both irritable, and he hadn't shaven. Thick stubble shadowed his face, and he looked as if he hadn't slept in days. "Allie, the minute my head hits that pillow, I'm gonna be out. It'll be just like you're alone, if that makes you feel better."

"But I don't think it's right, Mark. Sharing a bed is a privilege between a husband and wife, and we are not husband and wife. We haven't been in eight weeks."

"For heaven's sake, Allie. I'll sleep on the floor then!"

He grabbed the pillow off the bed and threw it onto the stained carpet. She jumped when she saw a roach migrating across the room. Mark stepped on it, then threw it away.

"Long way from the Marriott, huh?" he asked.

He went to the closet for a blanket and threw it down on the floor next to the pillow. The thought of roaches crawling on him while he slept sickened her. "Mark, you can't sleep down there."

"Watch me. I could sleep anywhere right now. There's no choice, anyway."

"All right, sleep on the bed," she said finally.

He sighed, then leveled his red eyes on her. "I'll sleep on top of the bedspread so we don't accidentally touch. How would that be?"

She recognized the sarcasm, and it made her angrier. "Sounds good to me."

"Fine."

She went into the bathroom to take a bath and brush her teeth, and when she came out, Mark was already asleep on top of the covers, facing the window. She got in on the other side and lay still for a long moment.

When he began to snore, she tried to feel irritated, but some secret part of her found comfort in that. Turning her back to him, she closed her eyes and tried to sleep.

• • •

A thud against their door woke her. She sat bolt upright in bed and listened. The glowing clock beside her told her several hours had passed since she'd fallen asleep.

She heard footsteps in the hall.

"Mark," she whispered. "*Mark!*"

He didn't hear, so she reached for the lamp on the bed table to turn on the light, but she knocked over a glass.

Mark woke up. "What is it?" he muttered.

"I heard something outside."

He got up and padded across the room to the door. She followed him, listening.

They heard the sound again, footsteps, then a thud, and a scraping sound.

Mark went to the door and looked out through the peephole.

Allie came up behind him and touched his back, as if that could protect her. He turned around. "Come look," he whispered, then pulled her toward the peephole.

She stood on her toes and peered out. A man was standing at the door across the hall from them. He was obviously drunk and barely able to stand, repeatedly trying and failing to get his key into his door.

As she watched, someone opened the door, and he almost fell into the room.

"Where have you been?" a woman shouted.

He muttered something about a bar downstairs, and she slammed the door behind him.

Allie turned around. Mark was leaning on one arm against the door, close, too close, and she looked up at him in the darkness. "Guess it was a false alarm. I'm sorry I woke you."

"It's okay," he whispered. "No problem. I'm sorry he woke *you*."

The kindness in his voice almost did her in. She realized that her coldness gave him reason to treat her with contempt—which, ironically, she was better able to handle.

"Well, no point in standing here. Let's go back to bed."

He took her hand, as if he sensed that she was still frightened, and led her to the bed. She slid in, and he covered her up, then went around to his side.

She lay there on her side, shivering.

"Are you cold?" he asked, his voice a gravelly baritone against her ear.

"No. Just still shaking from the scare. But you must be cold."

"A little," he said.

She knew he waited for her to invite him under the covers, but something inside her, some hurt, self-protective part of her, refused. Finally, he did it without asking. Before she could object, he had slid up behind her, set his knees at the back of hers, and slid his arms around her.

"Mark . . ."

"Shhh," he said. "I'm just trying to warm you up and make you stop shaking. Just relax and quit trying to be mad at me. Close your eyes."

Trying to be mad at him? The thought almost made her smile. It sometimes did take an effort, when things were going well and he was so much like he used to be. But then she remembered walking in on him holding Issie, remembered him lying his way out of it, remembered the sick despair that had crushed her as she'd tried to decide what to do.

She stiffened. "I can't sleep with you touching me," she said.

He let her go and backed away. "You used to sleep like a baby when I was holding you."

"I've gotten used to sleeping alone."

A moment passed, and then she felt him turn over, slide out from under the covers, and drop back on top of the spread. Not another word was spoken until morning.

Chapter Thirty-Two

● ● ●

Mark stood inside the airport looking out onto the tarmac at the aircraft they were about to board, a small commuter jet that looked tiny compared to the massive airliners around it.

It was starting to rain, and he wished they had thought to bring an umbrella. He looked at Allie and saw the distant, worried look on her face.

"What's wrong?"

"Nothing," she said. "I just had this sick feeling. I don't know if I'm more afraid of getting on that little plane in a storm or of taking my chances with the killer."

"The plane is fine, Allie. It's all we could afford."

"If it weren't raining, I wouldn't be worried."

"We could wait. But the tickets are nonrefundable."

Chilled, she rubbed her arms, and he fought the urge to put his arm around her to warm her. After last night's rebuff, he had decided she would have to make the next move. "I'll be all right," she said.

"Are you sure? You didn't eat much breakfast. Maybe you need something in your stomach."

"No, there's no time."

"I don't want you to get—"

"I *said* I'll be all right!"

He sighed, disgusted, and turned back to the window. What was he doing here with a woman who didn't want him near her? His very presence seemed to keep her so tense that she couldn't eat or sleep. So far, he hadn't really protected her from anything. Was all of this wasted effort?

Their flight number was called, and Mark picked up their bags. Allie started for the gate, and he followed.

A handful of others trotted down the steps onto the tarmac ahead of them. The rain was picking up; thunder boomed above the sound of the jet engines; the scent of fuel and exhaust washed over them as they hurried toward the plane. Allie walked rapidly in front of him, carrying her purse in one hand and a small bag in the other.

Mark heard a crack from his left, and the bag flew out of Allie's hand. She screamed and spun around. *A bullet!* he thought. *Someone shot at Allie!* He dropped the suitcases and hurled himself forward.

Allie fell beneath him, still screaming.

He covered Allie entirely with his body. "It's okay, baby, it's okay," he chanted, trying to reassure her. But it wasn't okay. Another shot cracked the air. The bullet hit him, whiplashing his head sideways.

Lord, protect her, was the last conscious thought that cried through his mind before blackness overtook him.

•　•　•

Allie's screams shrilled into a higher, more desperate pitch as she felt the impact of the bullet move Mark's body. Then he went limp, and she saw the blood dripping onto the concrete. Screaming in a voice that seemed distant, apart from her, she rolled him over. Forgetting the threat of being struck by another bullet, she knelt beside him and tried to wake him.

Chaos surrounded them as people screamed and ran for cover. "Help me!" she screamed. Mark lay limp, lifeless, blood gushing from the side of his head and pooling on the asphalt.

"Somebody please help me!" She clutched his head with trembling hands, trying to stop his bleeding.

Time seemed frozen, and no help came. Finally, security guards appeared, then a rescue unit and police officers. Someone pried her hands from his wound and tried to pull her away, but she fought them. Even so, she soon found herself sitting on the ground a few feet from him. "I have to stay with him. He needs me!"

"You can, ma'am. But we need to check you first. Were you hit?"

She watched them working desperately on Mark. "Please, you've got to save him! Please."

"Ma'am, are you hurt?" they asked, examining the scrapes and bruises she'd received from being thrown to the ground.

"No!" she shouted, pushing their hands away. "Help *him!*"

But there *were* people helping him. It just wasn't enough. He was going to die. She knew it.

An officer with a badge that said Jefferson Parish Sheriff's Office bent down to her. "Ma'am, did you see the shooter?"

"No."

"Then you can't say how far away he was?"

"No. I . . . I think it came from over there." She pointed in the direction from which the bullet had come. "My bag . . . got hit first."

Several other officers clustered around the bag, and she turned back to Mark. "Is he alive?" she asked.

"Yes, ma'am."

That was all she could get out of them as she watched them lifting him onto a gurney.

She got to her feet and found that her legs were weak. She followed as they loaded him into a rescue unit. "It was meant for me," she told them, as if they would realize the mistake and clear the whole mess up. "*I'm* the fire wife."

"Fire wife?" A cop was in her way at once, but she pushed him aside and climbed in next to Mark. "Guys, she's a fire wife!" he shouted.

The paramedic closed the doors. Allie sat out of the way as they worked on him, putting tubes down his throat, an IV in his arm, applying pressure to his wound. One paramedic barked out vitals on the radio to the online physician at the hospital where they were headed.

He was still alive; she clung to that reality, and from somewhere she found the strength to pray. She reached between the paramedics to touch Mark's hand. Hers was still covered with his blood. His was warm, though limp. Sobbing, she closed her eyes and sent up her pleas to God, offering him bargains and promises and sacrifices, all peppered with terror and rage and confusion and desperation.

They were at the hospital in moments, and she followed them out of the ambulance as if in a fog, only dimly aware of the handful of reporters who shouted questions that she ignored.

They whisked him away from her before she had time to tell them how urgent it was that they save him, how she needed another chance with him, how good a man he was . . .

And they whisked her into an emergency room stall where they began to check her scrapes and bruises, her blood pressure, her temperature, asking her questions that she couldn't understand, couldn't answer, couldn't think about . . .

All she could think of was her husband, and the fact that she might never have the chance to make things right with him.

Chapter Thirty-Three

● ● ●

The television set in the living area of the Midtown Station in Newpointe blared the news report as WVUE-TV broadcast live from the New Orleans airport. Nick Foster, the room's only occupant, looked up from the notes he was making for Sunday's sermon, his attention caught by the urgent tone of the news correspondent. "John, the airport is teeming with police and airport security personnel as they comb the area from which the bullet seems to have been fired. Just over my left shoulder is the area where the shooter probably stood, although there doesn't seem to be any witnesses. The Jefferson Parish Sheriff's Office responded to the call, just after the shooting, but we're told that the Kenner Police Department is investigating the case. Police have determined that the shooter did not come through security; otherwise his gun would have been found. Instead, they believe he came through the gates leading to the tarmac and found a place on which to perch that would give him a clear shot of his victim. He is believed to be the Newpointe serial killer, since the victim was a Newpointe fireman."

Nick threw his notes aside; they fluttered across the floor. "Slater! Dan! Hey, anybody!" he yelled.

"Witnesses say that the first bullet hit Allison Branning's bag, at which point her husband, Fireman Mark Branning, flung himself over her to protect her."

"No, not Mark," Nick whispered, slowly rising to his feet.

"The second bullet fired, and he was hit in the head. It's clear that both bullets were intended for Mrs. Branning. Fortunately, she was not injured, but we have no word on Branning's condition. We'll have more for you later, John, as this bizarre case continues to unfold."

Nick almost tripped on his chair as he rushed to the door. "Mark's been shot!" he shouted to anyone who could hear. "He got Mark!"

He found Slater Finch lying on a bed napping, and Slater sat up and squinted at him. "What?"

"Mark Branning's been shot!"

He ran to the bathroom where there was a light under the door, and banged for whomever was in there. "Mark Branning was shot at the airport!"

Frantic, he searched for others. *Where was everybody?*

Slater was on his feet now, following Nick. "How do you know? Where did you hear this?"

"On the news." Nick's hands were shaking, and he rushed around a corner and ran into Junior Reynolds. "Mark Branning—"

"I heard you," Junior said, breathless. "Is he dead?"

"I don't know," Nick said, rushing to the phone. "I'll call."

He started dialing information as Bob Sigrest and Issie Mattreaux came in from the garage. "What's going on?" Bob asked.

"Mark's been shot."

Issie uttered a loud curse, then dropped slowly into a chair.

By the time Nick had been connected with East Jefferson Hospital's intensive care unit waiting room, all of the firemen and paramedics on duty, except for Dan Nichols, were in the room. He asked for Allie, but no one came to the phone. Nick hung up, frustrated and desperate. Some of them were now gathered around the television waiting for updates, while others ran next door to tell Stan, in case he hadn't heard. Issie just sat motionless, staring into space.

"I've got to get up there," Nick said, picking up the phone and dialing Craig Barnes's beeper. "I've got to go sit this out with Allie."

"You can't, man. You've got to stay on duty," Slater said. "That was the deal."

"But I'm their pastor! This is the kind of thing I'm supposed to be there for!"

"Craig is never gonna let you off. Not unless you get a replacement. Pat Castor will have a fit if she thinks we're operating with less than a full crew."

"Then I've got to call someone else in."

"They're all gone with their wives. You think they're gonna leave their wives alone after they hear about this? It means he knows, man. He knows where they are. What they're doing. He can find them."

Nick was feeling nauseous. "I'll call George Broussard."

"George? After what he's been through?"

Nick put the phone back down. "You're right." He stood motionless for a moment, lost in thought, then grabbed the phone again and tried the ICU waiting room. "But Allie can't be there alone. This guy will stop at nothing."

But despite how much he wanted to go, he knew he wasn't going to get to. He had a job to do, and he was stuck with it.

•   •   •

A little over an hour later, Dan came jogging back in, drenched from head to foot in sweat. He saw the others clustered around the television set, and stopped cold. "What's going on?"

Nick looked up at him. "Where have you been?"

"Out jogging," Dan said. "What happened?"

Issie wiped the tears on her face. "Mark's been shot."

"Mark *Branning?*"

"Yes, Mark Branning," Nick said. "He was shot at the airport as he and Allie were about to get on a plane."

Dan dropped his towel and gaped at his pastor. "Is he dead?"

"I don't know."

Dan's face reddened, and his mouth fell open as if in a silent groan. "I don't believe this," he muttered finally. "It can't be happening. What hospital is he in?"

"East Jefferson. I tried to call but couldn't find out anything."

Dan's eyes were misting over, and his cheeks were mottled now in blotchy patches of red. Sweat ran from his wet blonde hair down his face. "You couldn't find out if he was dead or alive?" he yelled. "Don't they know?"

The door opened and Craig Barnes ran in, his face twisted with emotion. "Did you guys hear about Mark?"

All eyes turned to him. "Yes," Slater Finch said. "We were just listening to the news. Do you know anything?"

"Is he dead?" Dan demanded.

"The news reports didn't say. But he got shot in the head. Doesn't sound good."

"In the *head?*" Dan shouted. "He got shot in the head? Man, I've gotta go there! Chief, you've got to let me go!"

"No," Nick said firmly, taking off his glasses and wiping his own eyes. "I've got to go be with Allie, Craig. I'm her pastor. She needs me. Dan, you know she does."

"He's my best friend!" Dan yelled.

"You can't both go," Craig shouted over them. "Only one of you. Now calm down."

Nick turned to Dan, entreating him. "Dan, I need to pray with Allie. I need to calm her down. She's bound to be a wreck, and you know it. You can't help right now. You're as upset as she is."

Dan knocked a chair over with a clash and kicked it. "I want to be there!"

Craig picked up the chair, and Nick could see that he, too, struggled with the emotion on his face. Compassion wasn't an emotion they commonly saw in their chief's face, but today none of them seemed able to fight it. "Dan, Nick's right," Craig said. "Let him go."

Dan banged his fist on the wall then leaned back hard against it. "No offense, Nick, but I'm in better shape to guard Allie. That bullet wasn't meant for Mark. This guy's getting desperate. He's not going to give up now."

Nick bristled. "Just because I don't spend most of my waking hours working on my body like you do, doesn't mean I can't defend Allie Branning."

Dan took a menacing step toward him. "I stay in shape, which is more than I can say about you. There's a killer out there, Nick! Do you really think you're ready to take him on?"

Junior Reynolds popped up from his seat in front of the television and stepped between them. "That's enough. Why don't you both just shut up?"

Craig intervened then. "Allie doesn't need either one of you protecting her. She's safe in the hospital, and if she did need protection, it wouldn't be from a fireman. Dan, you go get back in uniform before I dock your pay, and Nick, you get out of here before I change my mind."

Dan wilted and picked his towel up off the floor. "Tell Allie I wanted to come," he said.

Nick suddenly hated himself for being drawn into such a childish exchange. Pride wasn't supposed to be one of his weak points. He was supposed to be immune. He set his hands on his hips and looked apologetically at his friend. "I will, Dan. I'm sorry for what I said, okay?"

Dan drew in a deep breath, then let it out quickly. "Yeah, me, too," he muttered.

"I'll let you know the minute I know Mark's condition."

Dan couldn't speak, and Nick glanced with shame at Craig and saw the red rims of his eyes and the tears he was fighting to hold back.

Nick could have kicked himself as he headed out the door, praying that God would overlook his little display of spiritual bungling and still give them a miracle. He wasn't up to conducting his third funeral in a week.

•   •   •

On her way to meet Stan at the police station, Celia Shepherd rushed into Jill Clark's office to tell her what had happened. Jill's secretary tried to stop her, but Celia ignored her and burst in.

"Jill, have you heard about Mark and Allie?"

"No, what?"

"Mark's been shot! He's in surgery at East Jefferson Hospital in Metairie, and Jill, they're saying it was a head wound. I'm headed to the Southshore right now to be with Allie. Do you want to go?"

"Yes." She closed the file on her desk and came around it. Tears were already filling her eyes.

"Stan had the key to her house, so he went by to get some of her things. He's meeting us at the station. He's coming with us."

Jill grabbed her purse and headed out the door, shouting back to her secretary, "Cancel everything. Don't know when I'll be back."

Chapter Thirty-Four

• • •

Mrs. Branning?"

Allie gasped, startled. She looked up into the compassionate eyes of the nurse who, sometime before, had brought her coffee and a blanket. Lost in thought, Allie hadn't heard her approaching.

"Mrs. Branning, there are some police officers out front who need to speak to you about what happened. Do you feel up to seeing them now?"

"Yes," Allie said, trying to hold the now-lukewarm coffee without spilling it. "Yes, please. They have to catch him. They have to catch him before he kills all of us."

The nurse disappeared, and in moments, two Kenner detectives—Peter Blanc and Lou James—came in and introduced themselves as homicide detectives.

"Homicide?" she asked, still shivering. "He's not dead. It wasn't a homicide."

"We know, ma'am, but we got to assume it was an attempted homicide. This person's killed before."

She listened, then focused inward as thoughts whirled in her mind. "You think he's going to die, don't you?" she asked, her mouth twisting as she tried to control her tears. "What have they told you? I have a right to know."

"Nothing, ma'am. Really."

She spilt her coffee and one of the men took it from her, set it down. She covered her face with both hands and let her sobs rise up into her throat, reddening her face and threatening to

explode out of the top of her head. "He was shot in the *head!*"
she cried. "People don't survive things like that! Of course he's
gonna die!"

She forgot about the two men as she wept, thinking only
of Mark and of their lost chances, but sometime later she
glanced up and saw the two men looking awkwardly at one
another. Remembering how important it was to catch the person who did this, she tried to pull herself together. Still sobbing, she wiped her face. "We were headed to Georgia, to stay
with my parents until they caught the killer. I can't think who
we told . . . who knew that we were going . . . what plane we'd
be getting on." She shook her head, trying to clear her
thoughts. "I told my parents, and then I told my best friend
Jill that we were going, but I didn't say when or which flight.
And Mark told Stan, our detective in Newpointe. Maybe Jill
or Stan told someone, and they figured out which flight." She
drew a deep, painful breath. "It was meant for me. That bullet
should have hit me instead. But he threw himself over me."
She fixed her pleading eyes on them. "Did they find him? Did
they find anything?"

"No, ma'am. He never went in the airport. Came through a
gate to the runways and climbed to where he shot from. But we
can't figure out how he got past security. We're wonderin' if
maybe he had some kind of airport employee identification, or
a uniform that looked like the ground crews—somethin' that
woulda kept someone from asking for his I.D. We're checkin'
with the security agents on duty now."

"It all happened so fast," she said. "I didn't see anyone. All I
saw was Mark, lying—" She shook her head sharply, then said,
"You should call Stan Shepherd in Newpointe and compare
notes with him. He's been around for the last three shootings.
And now Mark . . ."

One of the detectives scooted to the edge of his chair, his
long legs making him seem uncomfortable. "We're doing the

best we can, Mrs. Branning, and I'm sure the Newpointe P.D. are, too. Just take care of yourself until we can find him."

Feeling hopeless, she shook her head. "There's no stopping him. He goes where he wants to, shoots whoever—"

But the detective held up a hand to stop her. "Mrs. Branning, you'll be safe here. There's security at the entrances. No one with a weapon can get in here."

She looked wearily back at them. They just didn't understand. Security at the entrances—it wouldn't make any difference. There'd been security at the airport, too.

The two men got up to leave, and Allie got to her feet, too, still clutching her blanket around her. She started out behind them, but the nurse stopped her. "Mrs. Branning, what can I get you?"

"My husband," she said. "I want to see my husband."

"He's in surgery, and I've made sure that the surgeon knows to call you as soon as he has any information. If you'll just wait in there, there's a phone, and it'll ring right to you. Plus, you can call out if you need to."

Gently, she led Allie back into the room. "My parents," she said. "I need to call my parents. And my pastor. People have to pray. There's no time to waste." She broke down weeping again, and the nurse pulled the blanket more securely around her. "Call your parents first," the woman suggested gently. "Here, I'll dial the number for you if you want."

Allie nodded weakly and told her the number.

Chapter Thirty-Five

● ● ●

Self-recriminations, white-hot and scalding, lashed through Allie's mind as she sat in the small waiting room. She was being punished, she thought, for rebuffing Mark's efforts, for resisting his advances. She was being taught a horrible lesson, though she wasn't sure what it was.

She pulled her feet up onto the vinyl sofa and hugged her knees as she cried out to God, pleading with him to let the judgment be hers alone, begging him to spare Mark. As her mind turned her own judgment inward, she felt smaller and smaller, less significant, rabidly infected by her own thoughts.

A sound startled her, and she looked up as Jill, Celia, and Stan rushed into the room. She fell into their arms, weeping with them, as she tried to tell them what had happened in broken sentences that she knew made no sense. Moments later, Nick Foster came in, his presence providing a fragile peace.

After only a few minutes, Stan left to go to the police department to see what they knew. Nick organized them all into a circle near the telephone—in case the surgeon called—and started them praying earnestly for Mark's recovery. Allie couldn't pray—not while her thoughts and emotions and fears were tangled in such a terrible knot—but she listened gratefully as the others prayed for her. When each of them had prayed, Nick led them in Psalm 23, offered as a prayer. "Yea, though I walk through the valley of the shadow of death, I will fear no evil. Thy rod and thy staff, they comfort me ..." Allie quoted it with them, trying to let that peace which transcends all understanding fall over her, trying to cling to the words that she knew gave life itself.

When they were finished praying, Nick stooped in front of her and made her look him in the eye. "Who's in control, Allie?"

"Feels like Satan," she admitted.

"Feels like it," Nick acknowledged. "But who do *we* know has already won the victory?"

"God."

"And if God is in control, what's going to happen?"

She wilted. "I don't know."

"He's going to watch over those he loves. He's going to make all things work together for good to those who love him and are called according to his purpose."

"That's just it!" she cried. "We weren't acting like people who loved him. We weren't doing much of *anything* according to his purpose. He's punishing us. He's judging me!"

"Allie," he said, not allowing her to look away from him. "God loves you, and he loves Mark. Do you believe that he *sent* some maniac to punish *you?*"

She couldn't answer, just hiccuped her sobs as she stared at him. After a few moments, she whispered, "You're right. Why would he have even bothered? I'm not that important."

Nick gripped her tighter. "You're his *child*, Allie. That's how important you are. And so is Mark. Jesus grieves over your pain. Allie, what does the Bible tell us about Christ interceding for us?"

She couldn't answer, just shook her head.

"That he prays for us ..." He paused to let her finish, but she didn't. "With what, Allie? Romans 8:26. You know the verse. He prays for us with what, Allie?"

"Groans that words cannot express," she whispered.

"If he were the kind of God who sent an assassin to gun you or Mark down, would he be the kind of God who prays for you with groans that words cannot express?"

"No," she whispered. She tried to let that sink in, but her heart rejected the comfort.

What if Mark's death now was part of God's plan?

•   •   •

After a while, Nick offered to go to the cafeteria to get her some tea. Jill and Celia stayed behind, holding her hands.

Allie checked her watch. She had been there for almost three hours, and still there was no word.

Celia got up, took Nick's seat across from Allie, and looked her in the eye. "Allie, I've been sitting here asking the Lord if I should tell you something I've never told anyone else in Newpointe, except for Stan and Aunt Aggie. I've decided that it would help you to know."

Jill got up. "I'll let you two talk alone."

Celia took her hand to stop her. "No, Jill. I know I can trust you both."

Jill sat back down.

Breathing deeply, Celia leaned forward, her elbows on her knees. Her baby-fine blonde hair fell into her eyes, and she swept it behind an ear. Celia's eyes were smeared with mascara from her tears, but Allie didn't suppose she looked any better herself.

"See, I've been in your place before, Allie. I was married before Stan. And my husband was murdered."

Allie's mouth fell open, and Jill leaned closer to her friend. "Celia, I never knew . . ."

Tears came to Celia's eyes. "He was poisoned," she said. "They never caught the killer." Her mouth trembled as she smeared the fresh tears away. "I remember sitting in the hospital up in Jackson, waiting, praying, wondering who would do such a horrible thing. I know how you feel, Allie. I kept trying to bargain with God. I kept wanting to throw myself on the altar as a sacrifice, to convince him to let Nathan live. It was one of the worst nights of my life."

Something about that shared experience gave Allie comfort. Celia had come through the pain. She had found light again after wandering through the same darkness Allie wandered through now. Allie put her hand over Celia's. "Celia, I'm so sorry. I remember when you came to town. You seemed so broken, so sad. But no one knew anything about you, and Aunt Aggie wasn't talking."

"She was so good to me," Celia said. "I found healing here, and I know God led me here so I could meet Stan. But I didn't tell anyone for a lot of reasons, one of them being that I didn't want to talk about it."

"I know that feeling," Allie whispered.

"I'm just telling you this, Allie, so you'll know that you can talk to me. I've been here, where you are. I've felt that kind of pain. I've prayed those prayers."

"But yours weren't answered," Allie said weakly.

"Yes, they were," she said. "Nick was right. God is still in control. He didn't answer them the way I wanted him to, but he did make things work together for good. I miss Nathan, but he was a Christian. I know I'll see him again. And God provided."

Allie leaned back in her seat and put her head against the wall. "I don't want God to provide anything but Mark. I don't want to have to get used to him being dead." She started to cry again. "All this time, he's been staying with me, and I've been so cold to him. I made him sleep in a separate bed most of the time, and every time he's tried to touch me I've pulled away. I wouldn't have blamed him if he'd left me to fend for myself. But he didn't. Why didn't he?"

"Because he loves you," Jill whispered.

Allie nodded. "I kept wondering how much. Now I know. Enough to take a bullet for me. He saw it coming, and he took it on purpose. He chose to take it."

"If that's a picture of his love for you, Allie, then it's some picture," Celia said.

Allie covered her face as she wept.

•   •   •

Not long after, the doctor came in. The very sight of him in his scrubs, with his blue mask pulled loosely down under his chin, alarmed Allie. "They said you were gonna call. Please, he's not—"

"He's good," the doctor said gently, cutting into her anticipation. "He's a lucky guy."

She caught her breath and looked up at him, not believing. "Really? He's alive?"

"Yes. The bullet didn't penetrate his brain; it was a glancing shot. It looked bad and he lost a lot of blood, but the damage may be minor in the long term. We've had a plastic surgeon patching up the damage to his face—his right temple and half of his forehead—so he has quite a few stitches. The bullet did cause a concussion, which is why he's unconscious. We're going to keep him in ICU until he's awake, and we'll watch closely to make sure no infection sets in. We're also concerned about his brain swelling from the impact. In head trauma such as this one, sometimes the brain can be shaken so hard that some damage occurs. That's why he's not entirely out of the woods yet. But I'm optimistic."

She burst into tears again, but this time they were tears of gratitude. Throwing her arms around the doctor, she said, "Thank you. Thank you so much."

The doctor looked awkward at the embrace, and patted her back. She let go of him, then turned to her friends.

They all clung together as if the very force of their embrace could keep Mark alive.

Chapter Thirty-Six

● ● ●

Mark's father, Eddie Branning, made it to the hospital before they allowed Allie to go see Mark. He sat with her in the waiting room, his hands shaking. She knew he longed for a drink, but she was thankful that he had abstained today, of all days. His leathery face was wrinkled beyond his years, and he was skinny to the point of emaciation. Since his wife's death and his retirement from the fire department, he hadn't taken very good care of himself. Most days, he sat in his recliner drinking the day away, watching talk shows and game shows and forgetting to eat.

His relationship with Mark had not been good, and although they lived in the same town, Allie knew that Mark hadn't spoken to him in nearly a year. Had he even heard that she and Mark had been separated? He must have—he often ventured out at night to a little hole-in-the-wall bar called the Pop-A-Top Lounge, where he drank with his buddies; someone would have told him. Even so, as he sat with her now, he didn't mention it.

For the first time since she'd met him during her engagement to Mark, she felt compassion, rather than disgust, for the man who had raised her husband. It hadn't been easy for him to come here, but Mark was, after all, his only son. She pictured him hearing about the shooting during an episode of Jenny Jones, thought of him stumbling around the filth and clutter of his decaying house to find something clean to wear to the hospital, forcing himself not to take the drink that would have made things easier to bear ...

When the doctors finally allowed her to go in to see Mark, she leaned over to her father-in-law and touched his shaking hand. "Eddie, would you like to come in with me?"

He shook his head. "No, that's okay. He's your husband."

"He's your son."

Tears filled those red eyes that looked so much like Mark's, and he wiped them quickly. "He won't want me there."

"Please, Eddie," she said. "*I* want you there."

He looked up at her, stricken with emotion, and she wondered how long it had been since anyone had shown him compassion. She had failed as a daughter-in-law. She should have been drawing him into their family, instead of avoiding him as if his presence would contaminate their marriage. Funny how they'd managed to contaminate it without him.

Eddie cleared his throat, then stood up and nodded toward the door. "Okay," he said. "You lead the way."

Filled with trepidation, she headed out of the waiting room, wondering what condition she would find her husband in. A nurse met them at the double steel doors of ICU and escorted them back to the three-walled room where Mark lay, still unconscious, under a tangle of wires and monitor cords.

For a moment, she thought they had led them to the wrong room. The man on the table had little resemblance to Mark. His eyes were bruised, and she could see the bare, bristly skin of his shaved scalp above the bandage that covered one side of his face. His color was deathly pale against the black of the bruises. Looking down at him, she went numb.

"He's very lucky," the nurse said as she made some notations on his chart. "If that bullet had changed its direction by even a centimeter ..."

"But ... he looks so different. It doesn't look like him."

"It will."

Allie stood paralyzed, staring, unable to grasp the idea that this helpless, wounded, unconscious stranger was her husband, who had been so protective of her just this morning. She heard a garbled sound behind her and turned to see that her father-in-law was doubled over, his hand covering his mouth as he muffled his own sobs.

Quickly, she went to embrace him. "I . . . can't," he said. "I'll . . . I'll be in . . . the waitin' room."

"Okay," she whispered. "I understand."

She let him go, and he fled from the unit.

She turned back to Mark and touched his face, then bent down to kiss his cheek. His skin felt warm, and the stubble was thicker than it had been earlier. It felt rough, familiar, beneath her lips. She closed her eyes and kept her lips there, wishing she'd had the grace to make such a move when he was awake, wishing the kiss could stir him to life. But Mark didn't move.

"If he's doing so well, why isn't he conscious?" she asked the nurse. "Is he in a coma?"

"No," the nurse said. "He's been awake for a minute or so a couple of times since the surgery. The concussion is the main reason he's out."

Allie looked hopefully up at her. "Did you talk to him? Ask him questions?"

"He wasn't talking yet," she said. "He was very groggy. But if he wakes while you're here, ask him questions like who he is, where he lives, what your birthday is, things like that. We'll be able to tell a lot about his condition when he wakes up."

The nurse began to describe the purpose of all of the machinery in the room, and a heaviness came over Allie's heart. So many instruments waiting for something to go wrong. So many things that *could* go wrong.

"I have to go talk to some other families now," the nurse said, "but if he wakes up while I'm gone, let me know, okay?"

"Should I try to wake him up?"

"Yes. It's important that I evaluate his progress."

Allie held her gaze. "He could still die, couldn't he?"

The nurse hesitated to answer. "Everyone in here is in pretty critical condition, Mrs. Branning. But we have a high success rate."

She left them alone, and Allie stood beside his bed, gently stroking her fingers along the side of his face. "Mark?" she asked, close to his ear. "Mark, wake up. Wake up and let me see that you're all right."

He didn't stir, so she tried shaking his arm.

"Mark? Wake up, Mark."

The silence and limpness of his body made her despair even more, and as a sob rose to her throat, she dropped her forehead to his chest. The terrible, irrational fear that he would die without knowing that she loved him overwhelmed her. "Why did you do it?" she whispered against his face. "Why didn't you take cover?"

He didn't have to answer. She knew why. It was because he loved her. From the beginning of this ordeal, he had been there, worrying and protecting and watching over her. If he'd loved Issie, he would have been watching over her, but he'd given no indication that he'd even thought about Issie in days. And Allie hadn't made it easy for him.

It was so simple, despite all the pain, and the betrayal, and the fact that she had biblical grounds for divorce. The Bible never mandated divorce in the case of adultery. It only allowed for it. The simple fact was that Mark loved her, despite how he had strayed. He had spent the past two days proving it.

A tear rolled down her cheek and dropped onto his. "I love you, too, Mark," she whispered. "I do. And I'm so sorry for all the things I've said and done. How I've acted toward you. I do love you."

There was no change in the expression on his face or in the position of his body.

In a broken voice, she whispered, "Oh, Lord, please let him wake up."

It occurred to her that she had almost no right to ask for that, when she had been willing to throw her wedding vows away without a fight. She had behaved as if her vows were contingent on his. But her vows hadn't included "as long as you keep your vows to me." In their wedding ceremony, she had said, "Till death do us part." And now that there was a real chance of that very thing happening, she realized that she didn't want it to end. Could God hear her prayers now, when she'd been so out of touch with him that she'd almost broken the most important earthly commitment she'd ever made?

She pressed her face into the sheets, muffling the words that she knew God heard clearly. "Forgive me, oh, God. Please forgive me for letting my marriage fall apart. Lord, if you'll just give me one more chance, I'll make my marriage work, I promise. I'm committed now, Lord, whether he is or not, whether he does what he should or not, whether he admits to me that he had feelings for Issie or not. Even if he doesn't change anything, I'll change, Lord. Please, just let me have one more chance."

She was wiping her eyes, trying to pull herself together, when she noticed the other families beginning to leave. Her time was up, and it wasn't enough.

The nurse came in, and Allie asked in a heartbroken voice, "Can't I stay? He never woke up."

"No." The nurse touched her shoulder and met her eyes with compassion. "But I'll tell you what. If he wakes up before I get off tonight, I'll let you come in for an extra visit."

"Will you?" she asked, wiping her tears. "You promise?"

"Yes. And if that doesn't happen before you come in for the eleven o'clock visit, let one of the new nurses know that you haven't seen him awake yet, and she'll do the same thing."

She took in a deep cleansing breath. "All right. I'll be right out there. I won't leave."

"You need to eat," the nurse said. "It won't do him any good if you get sick."

"I can't cat," she said, and went back into the waiting room.

She saw with some relief that her parents had arrived and were talking with Celia, Jill, and Nick. They were waiting for her to return, but she dreaded telling them how bad things were. Eddie sat off to himself, still obviously distraught, but unable to speak to anyone. Her heart welled with love and compassion for the man she had never gotten to know very well. She wished she had some good news for him.

When they spotted her, Allie's parents rushed to intercept her from the crowd coming back from ICU. They pulled her into a family hug, and she clung to them with all her might.

"We got here as soon as we could," her mother said as they broke the hug. "How is he?"

"I don't know," she said. By now, Celia, Nick, and Jill had joined their cluster, waiting eagerly for some positive word. She racked her brain for something to tell them. "His vital signs are good." There. That was it. The only positive thing she could think of.

"Is he awake?"

"No."

"Has he been?"

"Only for a second. They're gonna call me if he wakes up again."

Allie's mother, Mattie Miller, had given birth to Allie when she was eighteen years old. She was only forty-three now, and people often marveled at how young she looked. Her father, still handsome at forty-five, didn't have a gray hair on his head, and he worked out to avoid the paunch that many men his age carried.

Though they looked more like yuppies than potential grandparents, when it came to their daughter, they both behaved like typical parents.

"Honey, your mother and I talked about this all the way down here," her father, Robert, said. "We're worried. Someone is trying to kill you. Coming to Georgia was a good idea, and we still want you to do it."

She looked up at them, surprised. "Now?"

"Yes," her mother said emphatically. "There's a killer out there, and he's after you, Allie. There's nothing you can do for Mark here."

She stiffened. "No way. I'm not leaving him."

"He's the one who left *you*. Two months ago."

"*Today* he took a bullet for me!"

Her mother shot her father a look, and he sat down next to Allie, set his hand on her shoulder, and stared intently into her face. She could see that he struggled with his words. "Allie, what Mark did was admirable. I'm grateful to him for it. You'll never know how grateful. But right now, for his action to have any meaning, you have to think of your own safety."

"You don't have to feel any guilt, honey," Mattie piped in. "You're not even really married anymore. You have no obligation to stay here with him."

Allie closed her eyes and told herself to stay calm. They meant well. She knew they did. "We *are* married until we have divorce papers, and neither of us has filed," she bit out. "I'm not leaving."

Eddie looked up from his stooped position a few seats down, and Allie saw the pain on his face.

"Allie." Jill's voice stopped her mother's reply, and Allie saw that Jill was staring, stricken, toward the door. "What is it?" Allie asked.

Jill looked as though she didn't quite know what to say. "Uh—looks like you have a visitor."

Allie looked through the doorway. Issie Mattreaux stood at the desk. Allie's heart crashed like a lead ball. She didn't have the energy to deal with this now.

"Who is it?" her mother asked cautiously.

Allie hesitated. If she told her mother who was waiting outside, Mattie would launch out of her chair to "give that woman
a piece of her mind."

Celia and Nick, both of whom knew of Issie's role in the
Brannings' marital problems, stood up as if to divert whatever
confrontation was imminent. Nick started toward her. "Allie,
you just sit and rest. I'll do it."

It was tempting to let her pastor handle it, but something
reminded Allie that she had made a commitment to God, despite
what Mark had done or what had happened with Issie. Now that
she was committed to her marriage again, she felt a sense of
compassion for Issie, instead of the rage and resentment she
might have felt earlier. Had God empowered her already? "No,
Nick, that's okay," she said, getting up. "I'll go talk to her."

Allie was dimly aware of everyone's surprise as she walked
toward the front. The receptionist, who was still talking to
Issie, pointed back toward her. Issie turned and saw Allie coming toward her. Looking unsure of herself, she met her halfway.

For a moment, the two women stared at each other. Allie
saw the trepidation in Issie's eyes. She didn't know whether
Issie's coming here showed an incredible amount of gall or an
incredible amount of courage. Breathing a silent prayer for
strength and wisdom—and an extra measure of gentleness—
Allie reached her.

"I had to come," Issie said. "I just wanted to see how he is.
And how you are."

Issie's eyes were red, and Allie knew she had been crying.
People cried when their friends were in trouble. It didn't really
reveal anything about her relationship with Mark.

"Mark's still unconscious," she said. "But the bullet didn't
penetrate his brain. He's got a bad concussion, but they're
expecting him to recover—or at least that's what they say. We'd
appreciate your prayers. Until he wakes up, we can't be sure
how he is."

Issie looked at her hands, where she clutched a shredded tissue. "I don't know how effective my prayers will be, but I'll give it a shot."

Allie swallowed and followed her eyes to the floor between them.

"I'm glad you weren't hurt," Issie said. "It must be awesome knowing your husband loves you so much he'd give his life for you."

Allie looked up, soaking in the words, the meaning, the intent. Did Issie even know that she was the main reason for their breakup? Or was she in denial, too? Was she, like Mark, pretending that nothing had ever happened between them?

Her heart began to stray down that dangerous path, and she jerked it back, reminding herself of her commitment just moments earlier. Regardless of Mark's feelings, regardless of his behavior, regardless of his admitting or denying his relationship with Issie, Allie was committed to her marriage.

The silence stretched, and eventually Issie said, "I probably shouldn't have come."

"No, no, it's nice that you did." Allie locked eyes with Issie again. "I'm sure it'll mean a lot to him."

Issie was quiet, probably sifting Allie's words for some sign of sarcasm, but Allie had intended nothing malicious. Issie's coming *would* mean a lot to Mark.

"Not as much as you might think," Issie whispered.

Allie held Issie's gaze, looking deeply, and seeing the sincerity there, and reassurance, and even promise. Issie was not out to steal her husband away, Allie realized suddenly. At least, not anymore.

The thought made Allie uncomfortable, for it had been easy to think of her as the malicious other woman, the one who had finagled her way into Mark's affections, the woman who had rejoiced when she'd heard that Mark had moved out. Now Allie saw a different picture—one that confused her.

"Why don't you come sit down and wait with us?" Allie asked. "They're going to call me when he wakes up."

Issie looked over Allie's shoulder to the people in the back corner. Allie glanced back and saw that her parents were watching, arms crossed like judges. They had figured out who Issie was, and she didn't blame them for their feelings. She had vented to them so much about the woman that it wouldn't surprise her now if they stormed over and ordered Issie out. Guiltily, Allie realized that she had created their hostility, giving them a bitter play-by-play of what she'd seen and heard and thought. No wonder they felt no allegiance to Mark.

Issie forced a smile and blinked back the tears in her over-bright eyes. "No, I really need to go. I just wanted to come by for a few minutes."

Allie didn't mention that Issie had driven almost an hour just for those few minutes. She knew Issie wouldn't be comfortable staying.

"I'll have someone call you and give you a report when he wakes up, okay?" Allie didn't know what had made her say that, but now she would have to do it.

Issie gave her a surprised look. "I would appreciate that."

The two women stood with eyes locked for a moment longer. Finally, unable to keep her tears at bay any longer, Issie leaned forward and hugged Allie. Reflexively, Allie hugged her back—a tight, warm hug that somehow felt like an apology. When Issie let her go, she looked embarrassed, then took a step back. "I'll talk to you later, Allie. Hang in there, okay?"

"You too."

Issie headed back down the hallway and disappeared.

• • •

Nick Foster watched from his seat across the room, moved at how gracious Allie had been to the woman who had almost destroyed her marriage. He had expected such a different reaction. Perhaps one like he'd experienced earlier when Dan had insulted him.

And Issie seemed to have no ill will toward Allie, either. Though he wouldn't have advised her to come had she asked him, he saw that it might have been for good. He saw Issie struggling with tears, saw her hug Allie . . .

And then he watched her walk out.

He didn't know why, but he felt the need to go after her, to comfort her in some small way. He didn't know her that well. What he did know about her was that she was unchurched and uninterested, that she spent a lot of time at Joe's Place, that she did have an unhealthy interest in a married man.

But if she was lost, then why should he expect her to act any differently?

He excused himself and followed her out into the hall. She had already stepped onto the elevator and the doors were just closing behind her. He pressed the button, and the elevator next to it opened.

He rode it down, and as the doors opened, he saw her walking out across the lobby.

"Issie," he called. She turned around.

Tears mixed with mascara stained her face, and she wiped them away self-consciously, then dried her hands on the pants of her uniform. She looked at him suspiciously, as though she expected him to lecture her about having the gall to show up here. "I know, I know," she said. "You don't have to preach me a sermon, Nick. I know I shouldn't have come."

"No, no," he said softly. "That's not why I came after you."

"Then why?" she asked.

She looked up at him, and he searched his mind for a reason. "I just . . . wondered how I could pray for you."

"*Pray* for me?" She looked at him as if he'd just offered to read her palms. "Why would you pray for *me?*"

"Because ... I know that you and Mark ... well, I mean ... I just know that you cared for him, and—"

"And you want me to think that doesn't disgust you?" she returned.

He realized he was digging himself into a deep hole. "Well, no, actually, it does. I care a lot for Mark and Allie, and I want to see them work things out. I don't think you've helped much with that."

She nodded while he was speaking, as if she might have expected that exact speech from him.

"But I also don't think you set out to break up their marriage. I don't see you as a malicious person, Issie. I see you in emergencies all the time. You do care about people."

She was growing more agitated, and her eyes filled with tears again. "What do you want, Nick?"

He racked his brain. What *did* he want? "I don't know. I guess ... I just wanted to tell you that I appreciate what you did up there. It took a lot of courage."

She swallowed. "Yeah, well. Nothing ever happened between us, you know. I mean, nothing physical. And before you go putting me on some list for sainthood, I should tell you that it wasn't because I didn't want it. But Mark loves Allie. Enough to take a bullet for her." She wiped the tears spilling over her lashes. "Nobody ever loved me like that."

"Oh, yes, they did. Somebody loved you just like that."

She looked at him like he was nuts. "Who?"

"Jesus."

She breathed a laugh, shook her head, then looked back up at him. "I should have seen that coming."

He grinned. "Yeah, I guess so. But it's true." He cocked his head and gazed down at her. "You know, that smile looks pretty good on you. Even when it's mocking."

She couldn't seem to shake it from her face as she looked up at him. Finally, she reached up and took his wire-rimmed glasses off of his face. The surprisingly personal act made his heart jolt, and he asked, "What are you doing?"

"Cleaning your glasses," she said as she wiped them on her shirt. "You're not seeing clearly."

He laughed then, and realized he was, once again, behaving like a teenager instead of a minister. He wondered if she could see the heat climbing his face.

"You know what Dan said earlier? About you being out of shape?" Issie asked.

His smile crashed and he made a mental vow to start a diet immediately.

"You look just fine to me. For a preacher, that is."

She reached up and shoved his glasses back on, and he stood stock-still, too pleasantly moved to know how to react. She gave him a wink, then turned and headed out the door.

Nick stood frozen until she was out of sight. He told himself that he'd better stay as far away from her as he could in the future. It was a bad sign when a preacher reacted to a woman with wet palms and a runaway heartbeat. A real bad sign.

•   •   •

In the ICU waiting room, Allie saw that her parents were staring at her with shock. Feeling more peace than she'd felt all day, she started back toward them.

"What was *that* about?" her mother asked. "What did she want?"

"Just to see how Mark was doing." She sat down and looked at Jill and Celia. Both women offered her sweet smiles that told her they admired what they had just witnessed.

Her mother was livid. "Honey, are you sure you're okay? You're not thinking clearly." She looked at the others. "Has she eaten today?"

"No, not since she's been here," Jill said.

"That explains it. Her blood sugar is so low that it's paralyzing her brain cells."

Allie almost smiled. "I've always had a problem with sluggish brain cells, Mom. It has nothing to do with food."

Jill tried to hide her grin. "Allie, do you want to go down to the cafeteria and get a bite?"

"No," she said, serious again. "I'm going to fast until I know for sure Mark's okay."

"I'll join you," Jill said, and Celia agreed to do so, as well.

Her father looked at them all as if their neurons had collectively misfired. "Are you crazy? Allie, you *have* to eat."

"No, I don't."

"Why not?"

"Because praying and fasting is all I can do for Mark right now, and I'm going to do it. God will honor that."

"God doesn't need you to fast. That's an Old Testament thing. People don't do that anymore."

"Well, maybe they should."

"He could stay unconscious for a week!"

"Then I'll go a week without eating."

Her mother shifted in her seat and huffed out a sigh. "I'm going to ask the doctor for a sedative for you."

"And risk paralyzing more brain cells?" Allie asked with a half-smile. "Mom, I'm glad you're here, but I really need you to support me, not challenge me at every turn."

Her parents shot each other eloquent looks. Finally, her father patted her hand. "How about if we shut up?"

Allie smiled.

They all sat quietly, awkwardly, for a while, flipping through magazines, until the receptionist called Allie's name over the intercom. They sprang to their feet and together headed for the front desk.

"Yes?" Allie asked.

"The nurse just called to tell me your husband is awake." The receptionist smiled warmly as Allie caught her breath. "You can go on back."

Without another word, Allie shot for the door.

She pressed the button that opened the double metal doors leading into ICU, and saw a nurse waiting for her. "He's awake?" she asked.

"Yes, and asking for you."

Allie laughed softly and hurried to his bedside.

His eyes were closed, but a nurse stood over him, talking gently. "Mark, your wife is here."

His eyes opened as Allie went to his side and took his hand. He squeezed it, and she wilted into tears.

"Hey, what's wrong?" he whispered with the slightest hint of a grin.

"Oh, nothing," she said, laughing quietly as she wiped her tears. "So what do you mean going and getting shot?"

He closed his eyes. "Is that what happened?"

"Yes."

He was silent for a moment, and it looked as if he'd drifted back off to sleep. Allie looked up at the nurse. "How is he?"

"Doing very well," she said, keeping her voice low. "He had appropriate answers to everything we asked. Knew his birthday, your birthday—but he doesn't remember what happened to him."

"Yes, I do," he whispered, surprising them both.

Allie touched his face. "You do?"

"Most of it," he said. "I saw the bullet knock the bag out of your hand." His voice was weak, losing energy with each word.

"You saved me," she told him. "You threw me down and covered me, and the next bullet hit you."

"Gave me a raging headache," he said, barely audible, and Allie smiled. He closed his eyes again, but this time, the calm look on his face vanished, and his mouth twisted. She saw the tear rolling from his eye.

"What is it, Mark?" she asked.

He squeezed her hand harder. "I'm so glad . . . you're all right."

"He thought you were dead," the nurse whispered. "It was his first question."

Overcome, Allie rested her face on Mark's chest. "I'm glad you're all right, too," she cried. "I'm so glad."

She looked up at him. One slick, wet line went from the corner of his eye into his hair, and she smeared it away.

"I'm sorry, Allie," he whispered.

"For what?"

"For not being able to protect you now."

"I don't need protection. I'm safe here. They have security at the doors."

"No," he whispered. "You need to go somewhere else. Somewhere that he won't look for you. You need to—"

"No, Mark," she cut in emphatically. "I'm not leaving you. Nick's here, and your father, and my parents, Jill and Celia, and Stan's in town and will be back soon."

"I want to see him," he said. "I want to see Stan."

"All right," she told him. "If he's back at the next visiting hour, I'll let him come in with me."

"No, now," he said. "I need to see him now."

"What for?"

"Just call him."

"Okay," she said, trying to placate him. "I will."

"When's the doctor coming?" he asked the nurse. "I need to see the doctor."

"He'll be in shortly," the nurse said. "Why do you need to see him?"

"Because I need to go home. I have to get out of here. I have to protect my wife."

"You can't get out tonight, Mark," Allie said. "You're in ICU. You have to be still. Just relax . . ."

"Have to . . ."

He was getting weaker but more agitated. Allie stroked his forehead. "Mark, shhhh. You need to rest. Calm down."

Her gentle touch and soft words seemed to have the effect she wanted, and his eyes closed again.

"Shhhh. Get some more sleep, honey. Rest so you can get better."

His lips moved again as he tried to speak, but no sound came out. Finally, his breathing settled, and she knew that he was asleep.

"We'll be rousing him every hour," the nurse whispered. "He won't like it, but we have to do it. But we'd prefer you waited until visiting times to come back. We'll try to get him good and awake before the next one."

"Okay." Allie knew that was her dismissal, but she wasn't ready to leave. "Could I have just a minute alone with him before I go?"

"Sure," the nurse said. "Just don't be too long."

She watched the nurse leave, then laid Mark's limp hand on his stomach and set her hand on top of it. Closing her eyes, she thanked God for letting him wake up, for the possibility that she might get that second chance. And she prayed that he would continue to heal Mark—and take divine vengeance on the killer who had done this.

Feeling as if a million pounds had been lifted off her shoulders, she headed back into the ICU waiting room to tell the others that things were looking up.

Chapter Thirty-Seven

● ● ●

The Homicide Unit at the Kenner Police Department was as depressing as Stan had expected. The huge dry erase board on the wall had columns headed by the names of each of the homicide detectives. Beneath each name, listed in red ink, were all of the active homicide cases he had been assigned, the date of the crime, the name of the victim, the means of death. As the crimes were solved, the ink color was changed to blue—incentive for each detective to solve his crimes as quickly as possible, for those red cases were a source of shame and aggravation.

For the first hour Stan had been here today, Peter Blanc, the Cajun detective assigned to the airport shooting, had bemoaned the fact that he'd been given a case that wasn't really a homicide, since Mark Branning wasn't dead. He didn't appreciate having another red name on his list. He was quite familiar with the Newpointe killings, and immediately wanted to send someone to interview Hank Keyes in the Bogaloosa jail. Despite Stan's insistence that Keyes was no longer a suspect, Blanc was intent on proving he could be. He wanted to solve this crime, and soon. He had other cases—cases involving dead bodies, cases that really were in his jurisdiction, cases in red that he needed to change to blue.

Realizing that he wasn't going to get far with Peter Blanc, Stan haunted the crime lab for the rest of the afternoon. He learned the bullet that had hit Allie's bag had been retrieved from the concrete a few yards from where Mark was hit, and from that they had determined that the gun had been a .38—the same caliber used in the other three shootings. The ballistics report, evaluating the angles at which the bullets had struck Allie's purse and Mark's head, identified the possible areas from which the gun could have been fired. Kenner P.D. had also collected tape from the security cameras just inside the airport in that area, in the hope that the killer could be seen through the window. Stan viewed all of the tapes during that time, only to find that none of the cameras covered the exact area in question.

However, Stan noticed in the file that there was a witness—a guy who'd been loading luggage onto the small plane Allie and Mark would have gotten on, who claimed he had seen a man in uniform running down a ladder that led up to an air conditioner unit, and that the man had cut across the tarmac and around the airport terminal. The witness had taken cover behind the plane and peered out from under it to see if he could spot the source of the gunfire. While everyone else was scurrying out of harm's way, the man in uniform had been running the wrong way.

Thirty minutes after reading the report, Stan was at the airport interviewing the witness himself. "What kind of uniform was it? Did it belong to a ground crew worker?"

"Nope," the man said, spitting on the ground. "Wasn't a jumpsuit like mine. No, I think it was blue or gray. Might have been a pilot without his coat."

"A pilot?"

"No, come to think of it, the pants weren't black like a pilot's. The pants were, like, gray or something. Like a cop or a mailman."

A cop or a mailman? Ordinarily, he would have found the comparison amusing. But nothing about this was funny to him.

He climbed up the ladder to the air conditioner unit that the witness had pointed out. It was a perfect perch from which to fire at someone. Easily accessible, yet inconspicuous. Was the uniform an air conditioner repairman's uniform? Is that how he had gotten in without being stopped? Or was he, indeed, a cop, which would have kept anyone from asking questions? Or could he actually have been a mailman?

He went back to the homicide unit, hoping once more to put his head together with one of their detectives, even the cynical, hardened Blanc. To his frustration, none of them took him seriously enough to give him the time. He was, after all, the only detective on a small-town force—a small town which, until last week, averaged zero to one homicides a year. Stan had once taken pride in that, as though it somehow reflected well on him. Now, seeing the contempt and disinterest of the Kenner cops, who each had up to a dozen cases at a time in red, all murders within the last month, he couldn't help feeling inferior.

Stan pulled out his case file again, and sat down with a pen and paper to list all of the clues they had. Fibers from the Broussard and Larkin houses, though they had no one to match them to. A generic shoe print that could have matched a million size-ten feet. No fingerprints. No weapon. No motive . . .

"Stan Shepherd?" a detective called from across the room. He turned around and scanned the desks and faces of the dozens of people milling around the room.

"Yeah?"

"Telephone," the man yelled out, as if he hated being bothered.

Stan closed the file and carried it to the man's desk. "Hurry up, I've got work to do," the man bit out.

Stan ignored him. "Stan Shepherd," he said into the phone.

"Stan, it's me. Allie."

Stan stiffened, bracing himself for news of Mark's death. A sense of defeat and dread fell over him. "Allie."

"Mark woke up, and he's asking for you."

His heart jolted. "He's awake? All right!" He looked around for someone to tell, but no one was interested. "He wants me?"

"Yeah," she said. "He made me promise to tell you that he wants to see you. The next visiting hour is at eleven tonight, and they promised they'd rouse him for it. If you want to go in with me, you can."

"I'll be there. Allie, how is he?"

"He's great," she said, her voice cracking. "He looks like he's been in a train wreck, but he's talking and making sense, worrying."

"Thank God."

"You said it. God was watching over him, Stan. He's still in ICU. Anything could go wrong, but they're keeping a close watch on him."

"Is Celia okay?"

"Yeah, she's right here. Wanna talk to her?"

"Yeah." He told his wife he loved her and to stay right there, not to leave the waiting room under any circumstances, and not to allow Allie to. When he hung up, he felt a chill. His wife was so close to a marked target, someone the killer wanted dead. He hoped the security in that hospital had been reminded of the danger. Selfishly, he thought how glad he'd be to take Celia home after he saw Mark tonight.

Chapter Thirty-Eight

● ● ●

Because Mark insisted on it, the nurses called Allie for a visit at eight-thirty instead of making her wait until eleven. Since Stan had just arrived, she let him and Nick come in with her.

The nurse met them at the door. "He's doing much better than I would have predicted," she said with a smile. "But remember—let him rest."

The two men, shocked by Mark's appearance, hesitated at the door, but Allie went right to his side and hugged him. He hugged her back weakly, the gesture giving her a world of hope.

"Did you bring Stan?" he asked.

She had wondered if, with the concussion and head trauma, he would forget. Apparently he hadn't. "He's right here. Nick, too."

They came on each side of the bed, and Mark took both of their hands and squeezed them. "Thanks for coming, guys," he said in a gravelly voice that reminded her of the way he sounded when he woke up in the mornings. She had missed that voice.

"You don't look so good," Stan said with a grin.

"What can I say?" Mark asked weakly. "I've always wanted a cleft in my chin, but I didn't expect one across the side of my head."

The men laughed with relief—he still had his sense of humor, and Allie felt an overwhelming joy. He was still Mark, the Mark she'd fallen in love with once, the Mark she had married, the Mark who had, once upon a time, been able to make her laugh—until the fears and anxieties and disappointments of the last few months had interfered.

"So," Stan probed, growing more serious. "Did you remember something about the killer?"

Mark shook his head. "I wish. No, I'm worried about Allie, man."

Allie blinked back the mist in her eyes. "Why, Mark? What do you mean?"

"I've been watching over you since the murders started. Now I can't, and I don't like it. So Stan, I wanted to ask you a favor."

"What?" Stan asked. "You know I'm doing whatever it takes to find the killer."

"I know. But I want you to find Allie a bodyguard. I'll pay him whatever it costs. I'll sell my car if I have to. I can ride my ten-speed to work, or walk. But I want someone watching over my wife while I'm in here."

Allie took his hand, and he closed his fingers around hers and pulled it to his lips.

"I can do that, buddy," Stan said. "No problem. I'll call T.J. Porter. He's always looking to make some extra dough, and he's got a bunch of debts to pay off. Besides that, he's a giant, and looks menacing enough to scare off the meanest scumbag."

"Yeah, he'll do fine."

Allie wasn't sure she liked the idea of someone being with her twenty-four hours a day. "Mark, don't you think I'll be okay as long as I'm here?"

"No, I don't," he said. "You aren't safe anywhere." He looked up at Stan. "Hire him, and get him here tonight, okay? I know it'll be late, but you're a big, important cop, and you can coax security into letting him in, right?"

"I'll do my best. I'm more worried about getting him to come on such short notice. He may even be on duty."

"I'll be forever beholden, Stan. Think if it was your wife."

Stan had thought of that. "You got it. Somebody'll be here, even if it's me. But Mark, they won't allow a gun in here."

"Not even for a cop?"

"For an on-duty cop, maybe, but not for a Newpointe off-duty bodyguard."

Mark looked distressed. "Well, a gun wouldn't have done me any good today. But I managed to keep him from hitting Allie. I want someone who'll do that."

"T.J.'ll do it, if I can get him. I'll do my best."

Mark seemed to rest at that idea. "Okay. I'm counting on you." He turned to Nick. "So, Nick, are you gonna pray with me, or what?"

Nick grinned. "You bet I am."

Holding hands, they all prayed together for God's victory in all of this.

Chapter Thirty-Nine

● ● ●

They were on their way back into the waiting room when Stan's beeper began to vibrate. He checked the number. It was the Kenner Police Department where he'd spent the afternoon, and the extension was for Peter Blanc. He quickly went to the phone and called the detective back.

"Blanc," the man barked.

"Blanc, Stan Shepherd. Did you page me?"

"Yeah. We gotta witness, called in just a while ago. Said she remembers lettin' in a man in uniform right before the shootin'. Said he was a fireman and was answerin' a call, so she let 'im right in."

"A fireman? Did you check with the fire department to see if they really had any calls?"

"I know how to do my job, Shepherd. Yeah, I checked, and there was no calls from the airport today, 'cept in regard to the shootin'."

"A fireman," Stan repeated, incredulous.

"Said he was wearin' a bunker coat hangin' open and fireman's hat with that clear mask down."

"She didn't think that was odd?" Stan asked.

"Said she was busy and took 'im at his word."

"What was his description?"

"Average height, she says, somewhere 'tween five-eleven and six-two. Didn't notice eye or hair color under the hat and mask. Says she prob'ly couldn't ID him."

"Did she see him again after the shooting?"

"Nope. Says she was distracted and takin' cover. One thing," Blanc said. "She said his shirt under the bunker coat was gray. Our firefighters wear blue. What they wear in Newpointe?"

Stan closed his eyes, letting the horror sink in. "They wear gray." He felt nauseous. "How come the other witness didn't mention the bunker coat?"

"I was gettin' to that," Blanc said. "We searched that air conditioner unit he was on again, and found a bunker coat and hat wedged down between the unit and the building. He prob'ly ditched it before he started shootin'. Guess what fire department was identified on the hat?"

Stan didn't want to know, but he forced himself to ask. "What?"

"Newpointe," Blanc said. "Our man may be one o' your firefighters."

Stan couldn't speak. "Look, do me a favor, will you, Blanc? Don't leak this. We don't have that big a fire department in Newpointe. If the media gets hold of it, they'll blow it for us. I have to be careful, or we'll spook him and lose him. Can I have your word that you'll keep this just between us?"

"You think you can narrow it down?"

"Yes. Do I have your word or not?"

"All right, you got it. I got better things to do than start a frenzy."

Stan hung up and tried to think. His head was beginning to throb, and he was shaking. Someone touched his shoulder, and he jumped. He turned around and saw his wife. "Celia."

"Honey, are you all right?"

"Yeah, fine. I have to call T.J. Mark wants a bodyguard for Allie. But I have to get back to the Northshore. I've got a lead on the killer."

Nick was standing nearby. "A lead? Really?"

"Yes." Stan tried to remember if he'd eaten. He felt light-headed. Vaguely, he remembered eating something ... lunch? Breakfast? He wasn't sure. "Look, Nick, can you stay until T.J. gets here, assuming I can get him?"

"I think so."

He dialed information to get T.J.'s number.

Moments later, Stan headed back across the waiting room to Allie. "T.J. is coming, Allie. I called down to security, and they said the doors will stay open until ten. He should be here before that, although he might be cutting it close because he's on duty and has to wait for a replacement."

"Okay," she said.

"I'll stay with you until he gets here," Nick said. "Then I'll head back to the station."

Stan fought the urge to tell Nick what he knew, so that he'd be careful whom he trusted. But he couldn't. Everyone was suspect.

As he and Celia left, Stan had the feeling that his real work was just beginning.

• • •

A few minutes later, while Allie was saying good-bye to Eddie, who was shaking so badly he would undoubtedly head straight to the nearest bar, the waiting room phone rang and someone called out, "Branning family."

Jill was closest to it and took the phone. "Hello? This is Jill Clark."

"Jill, hi. Dan Nichols. I just wanted an update."

She smiled. "Hi, Dan. Well, let's see. Mark is conscious, and there doesn't seem to be any apparent brain damage. He's talking a lot, making demands, worrying about Allie."

"You're kidding. He's doing that well?"

"Yes. God was really with him."

He let out a heavy breath. "Man, I thought it would be—I don't know. A whole lot worse." His voice cracked.

"We all did."

"Cale and George just came in to relieve some of us. I'm about to get off for the night."

"Really?" she asked. "Are they ready to come back this soon?"

"Said they needed to get back to work to get their minds off their problems. George said Tommy's already asleep and his parents are baby-sitting, and he says he hasn't been sleeping so well. Anyway, they insisted, so I thought I'd come down there and hang out for a while."

Her heart leapt slightly, but she told herself that was silly. He was just a man. "Well, okay. You'll have to hurry, because I think they lock the doors at ten. And I'm not sure you can get out if you're in past that time."

"So I'll stay all night. I can sleep anywhere. Besides, I've worried about Allie all day. She shouldn't be alone, not with this guy out there still running loose. If he'd shoot in broad daylight at a crowded airport, he could be capable of anything."

"Already taken care of. Mark got Stan to hire T.J. Porter to be her bodyguard. He'll come as soon as he can find a replacement. He's on duty right now."

"Well, why don't I call and tell him he doesn't have to come? I could stay with her all night, and he could come in the morning. I wouldn't have a weapon or anything—"

"They wouldn't let you, anyway."

"Well, right. But my presence might be a deterrent if the creep tried to pull anything tonight. I'm no Hulk Hogan, but I don't think your average Joe would want to take me on."

Jill grinned. Maybe the rumors about his vanity were true.

"I know Allie would appreciate it, Dan. And Mark would feel good knowing you were the one here. Frankly, I'd appreciate it, too. I was planning to stay all night with Allie, but I've been a little concerned, too. I'm not much protection. Nick's here now, but he plans to go back to work tonight."

"Tell him help is on the way. I'll be there in half an hour."

"It takes at least forty, Dan."

"Not the way I drive," he said.

It was the first time Jill had laughed in days.

Chapter Forty

● ● ●

Dan looked like a breath of fresh air when he blew into the ICU waiting room wearing his gray firefighter's uniform. Just having him here made Allie feel closer to Mark, for Dan was his closest friend.

She noted the unusual grin on Jill's face when Dan came in, and she wondered if there was some interest developing there that her friend hadn't confided.

"Thanks for coming, Dan," Allie said, kissing his cheek. "When Mark asked for a bodyguard, I really dreaded it. I like T.J. and everything, but I don't know him that well. I'm glad you came instead."

"No problem," Dan said. "I should have changed clothes, though. This uniform caught a lot of attention from the press downstairs. Guess all us Newpointe firefighters are celebrities now, whether we want to be or not." He sat down and crossed an ankle over his knee. "CNN called the station a while ago. Wanted to interview some of us. I couldn't go on national television until I'd had a haircut though, so I passed."

Allie was surprised. "Your big chance to be discovered, Dan, and you passed?"

He winked. "I figured I'd let the others have a chance. Maybe after the haircut. Anyway, thank goodness for Cale and George or I couldn't have come."

"How are they?" Jill asked.

"Down. But they're okay. Cale really needed to get back to work, be around his friends, get his mind off of things. And

George just wanted to help in some way." He gazed down at Allie. "So how are you doing?"

"I'm okay."

"Have you eaten?"

She shook her head. "I'm not hungry."

"Allie, you have to eat."

"She's fasting," Jill said. "It's okay. She knows what she's doing."

Jill didn't mention that she was fasting, too, but Allie understood why. Somehow, the privacy of the decision lent more reverence to it—something that was just between God and them.

•   •   •

At eleven P.M., the families were called in for their last visit of the night. Dan walked Allie to the door of ICU, then he and Jill went to the window looking down onto the small courtyard behind the hospital.

"It's gonna be a long night," Jill whispered, looking out on the lights flickering off the surface of the pond. It all seemed surreal—her being here, knowing that today her best friend's husband had been shot in the head.

"You'll make it shorter," Dan said. "I'm sure Allie appreciates your friendship right now. How long have you two been friends?"

"About five years," Jill said. "Since she and Mark got engaged." She smiled at the memory. "You know how it is. Most of my friends from high school moved away. I got to know Allie at church, and we just hit it off. She and Mark were constantly trying to fix me up with some friend or other."

"Really?" he asked. "Wonder why they never fixed you up with me?"

She laughed. "Maybe because I put a stop to it after the third or fourth time. I convinced them I could wait for Mr. Right to find me."

His grin was so disarming she had to look away. "And has he?"

"Nope," she said. "Still waiting."

"So how'd you feel when they split up?"

"Depressed," she said. "I always thought if there was ever a couple whose marriage was made in heaven, they were it. I haven't given up yet, though."

"I've wondered if you were planning to represent Allie if they had a divorce."

"I would, of course, but I really hate for it to come to that."

"Yeah, me too," he said. "Maybe this shook them up enough to change things."

"I don't know. I gotta tell you, I've been amazed at the way he's tried to protect her through all this. Maybe we all need a glimpse of life without someone we love once in a while, just to teach us not to take them for granted."

"So you think they'll get back together when this is over?"

"Who knows?" she said. "A woman doesn't fast and sit in a waiting room all night keeping vigil for her husband if she doesn't love him. She doesn't fall apart the way I saw Allie do today if she's lost her feelings for him. And a man doesn't take a bullet for just anybody."

"Well, no one ever thought they didn't love each other. But they had some pretty fierce differences. He got to where he didn't like to go home anymore. Said she was always nagging him about things."

Jill bristled. "He called it nagging. But she had a right to confront him about his time in bars with his friends from work, about the fact that he wasn't pulling his weight in the shop on his days off from the fire department, about his relationship with other women—"

"Boy. She didn't leave anything out, did she?"

Jill was a little embarrassed that she'd said so much. "We're close. We talk a lot."

"Yeah, well." Dan crossed his arms and looked at his reflection in the window. "That's one of the reasons I'll never get married. The minute you tie the knot, you've got that other person telling the world every little thing you do in private. Your life is thrown out there for everyone to criticize."

"Oh, come on. Don't tell me Mark didn't talk to you about Allie."

He abandoned his reflection and turned back to her. "Of course he did. That's what I mean. They did it to each other. One of them did something wrong, and the next thing you know, they're telling their friends what a jerk the other one is. And a guy like me, who's never been married, stands back and watches, and thinks they'd all be better off if they were single."

"Single isn't all it's cracked up to be," Jill said. "Before their breakup, there weren't many days when I wouldn't have traded places with Allie in a minute. Not to be married to Mark, but just to belong to someone, to have that hope of having a family."

"A family would be nice," Dan said with a soft chuckle, "if it weren't for that pesky marriage thing."

Jill looked seriously at him, wondering if she'd misjudged him all those times she'd seen him in church.

"No, don't get me wrong," he said. "I'm thinking of Paul, and his encouragement to stay single. He felt marriage distracted people from God's work. That's why it was preferable not to be married."

"But that wasn't God's instruction to his children," she said. "It was Paul's opinion, that was all. The whole point of that passage was to tell us how focused and devoted we should be to Christ—not to tell us that marriage is wrong. God loves marriage and family. Even in Eden, his first commandment was to be fruitful and multiply."

"True. But the earth is populated now. We don't have to fill the earth with our offspring anymore."

"So marriage is obsolete?" she asked with a smirk.

He shrugged. "No. I just think it's a lot less complicated to be single. Look at all these guys in the fire department. Most of them are going nuts protecting their wives, scared to death of losing them—and they might. It may be a good thing that there's nobody I can lose that would make me grieve like that."

"And you're determined to keep it that way?"

"Well, yeah, sort of. I like being unattached. Hey, if I want to take off for a trip on my days off, I can. I don't have to make arrangements, leave instructions, call home every night ..."

"Don't you ever wish you had someone to call home to—or better yet, take with you?"

He laughed, and she noted the laugh lines crinkling out from his eyes. "Sometimes. But then I remind myself that there are strings attached in every relationship. Conditions. Expectations."

"And you stop wishing?"

"Something like that."

She didn't know why that disappointed her so. "I'm glad it's so easy for you," she said.

Dan got quiet for a moment. "So if you wanted to get married, Jill, why didn't you?"

She shrugged. "I could have. I was serious about someone in college. But I had dreams of going to law school, and we broke up, and he married someone else. Since then, I've been in a few relationships, but they're either self-centered, or they're sports-centered, or they're big around the center ..."

Dan laughed.

"None of them were Christ-centered. Really, I don't know. Guess I never found the right person."

"Like me."

"No, not like you," she said. "I'm looking. You're not."

"I thought most professional, independent women denied that they were looking."

"Well, I could lie. But there's nothing I'd like better than to fall head over heels in love and get married and have children and live happily ever after. I know it isn't politically correct, but I don't make apologies for it. All my life I've wanted that, and someday I'm going to have it."

He turned back to her and met her eyes. She saw the gentleness there, the sweetness, and her heart reacted despite her better judgment. "Well, I hope you do," he said.

She leaned her face back against the glass and looked out on the courtyard again. A man and woman, both in scrubs, sat on a concrete bench. The woman leaned her head on his shoulder, and he held her and stroked her hair. Jill yearned for that kind of human warmth. It was too bad Dan felt the way he did. He had seemed so gallant, so masculine, so caring. And he wasn't too hard on the eyes, either.

Which was exactly why he wasn't her type. He went for anorexic blondes with beauty titles, she mused. Not plain-Janes with law degrees.

The doors to ICU opened, startling her, and she looked up and saw the others milling out, some with tears in their eyes, others laughing in relief and joy. Allie trailed at the end, her eyes tired but hopeful.

"He's awake," she said. "Dan, he wants to talk to you."

"Me?" Dan asked. "Why?"

"I told him that you came instead of a bodyguard, so I guess he wants to give you instructions or something." She grinned and lifted her eyebrows. "I'm trying to humor him. You just have a few minutes."

"All right," Dan said, and started through the doors.

"I have to go with you," she said. "That's one of his rules. Come on, Jill. You come, too."

Jill felt awkward as they went through the doors and around to the cubicle where Mark lay. She caught her breath at the sight of him, then told herself that a man who'd been shot in the head probably had a right to look pretty rough. His eyes were closed.

She hung back and let Dan go to his bedside, as Allie took the other side. "Mark, here's Dan," she said. "And Jill."

Mark opened his eyes and saw Jill at the foot of the bed. "How's it going, Jill?" he asked weakly.

She smiled. "Great. You feeling okay?"

"Been better." He looked up at Dan and reached for his hand. "Hey, buddy."

Dan leaned over and lowered his voice. "Man, I thought you were ugly before, but I think you could win the championship tonight."

Mark laughed. "You try a one-on-one with a bullet, see how you look."

"No thanks, man."

Mark's face sobered, and his eyes grew more serious. "Well, you hang around us long, brother, and you might wind up doing it. No kidding."

"I'm okay with that," Dan said.

"I appreciate it. And I'll pay you, man."

"No way."

"Yes way. I'm paying you, or I'll call T.J. myself. I know *he'll* take my money."

Dan laughed. "What are you gonna do? Get up and go to a pay phone?"

"Don't test me," Mark said. "I can do it. Now do we have an understanding?"

"Whatever you say."

"And you gotta promise me that you won't leave her side, not for a minute. I know you've got to sleep, but if you sleep out there in the waiting room, keep one eye open, will you? No kidding. He's after her. I don't even think he's afraid of getting caught. You've got to watch over her, man, because I can't."

"Don't worry. I've got this under control. I'm not going to sleep tonight at all. I brought a book to read, and I'll sit right next to her and keep my eyes on the door."

"And the windows. Are there windows? What floor are we on, anyway?"

"We're on the third floor. I won't let anything happen to her, buddy."

"Promise me."

"I can do that. I promise."

Mark seemed to relax. "What about the killer. Have they got any leads yet?"

"I don't know. I haven't talked to Stan today."

"Man, they've got to. Pray, okay? Pray hard. With your eyes open."

Dan chuckled. "I will. Now get some sleep. We expect to see you looking a lot better in the morning."

Allie kissed him good night, and they all headed back into the ICU waiting room, where they were given blankets. The lights were turned down, and Jill took a seat and tried to get comfortable in her recliner.

Dan sat between her and Jill, reading a novel.

As she drifted into a light sleep, Jill told herself that no harm could come to Allie here. Dan was watching over them both.

Chapter Forty-One

• • •

Our man may be one of your firefighters.

The words played over and over in Stan's mind as he took Celia to stay with her Aunt Aggie. Once he was sure they were both safe and settled in, he drove back to the police station and sat at his desk. *Not one of our firemen,* he thought. *It couldn't be.*

The bunker coat could have been stolen. It didn't mean that the killer was one of theirs.

Besides, why would the killer wear something so identifiable? What was the logic? He rubbed his eyes, trying to focus his thoughts. Maybe the uniform gave the killer anonymous access to places he couldn't normally go. It *had* gotten him onto the airport tarmac without a security check. After he'd fired on Mark and Allie, he had escaped during the confusion. Anyone who'd seen him probably thought he was responding to the emergency and ignored him.

But that didn't mean he was a firefighter. It only meant that he owned a uniform. These days, any yahoo off the street could walk into a specialty shop and buy any uniform he wanted, without authorization.

Stan needed advice. He needed to know what kind of person he was dealing with. Maybe his old friend Jake Logan, a psychology professor at Tulane who specialized in criminal behavior, could help. Jake had helped New Orleans police with profiles of murderers before. He could help Stan put together some kind of psychological profile on this killer. Stan dialed information and got the man's number.

He checked his watch. It was nearing midnight, but he couldn't wait. The phone rang once, twice—

"Hello?"

"Jake, this is Stan Shepherd. Hope I didn't wake you."

"No, Stan. In fact, I've been wanting to talk to you. I was going to call tomorrow to see if I could offer any help on this serial killer case."

"You sure can, man. I don't know what I've got on my hands here. That's why I'm calling."

"I've been following the case," Jake said. "I'm particularly interested in the pattern of the murders—he kills them first, then sets them on fire. My guess is he's trying to tell us something with that pattern. It means he's a thinking man, and in my experience, I'd say that he feels some sort of high purpose for what he's doing."

"High purpose? Like what? How can anybody justify what he's doing?"

"I didn't say he was thinking rationally. Just that he's thinking, planning. It's very important to him to follow the murder up with a fire."

"I figured he just wanted to destroy the evidence."

"Then why didn't he burn the Broussard house down? No, I think it's more than that. It could be that he's involved in the occult in some way, and that he considers these to be sacrificial murders. When you find him, you're likely to find evidence of obsession of some kind. A collection, maybe, of clips and articles about the fire department, or pictures of the women he's targeted, or some sort of evidence of occultism, or books on a certain subject. I studied a case once where a guy killed six 7–11 workers in three states, because he believed in his heart that 7–11 stores were part of a conspiracy for Iran to take over our country. He believed he was killing for his country. At his home, they found stacks and stacks of articles from the Internet about conspiracies and attempts to overthrow the government. He felt he had a mission to fulfill, and he set out to do it."

"Would people know about this obsession?" Stan asked. "I mean, would the people he's around every day think he's strange? Would there be clues?"

"Maybe not. Serial killers often live very normal lives, and later their friends and acquaintances are stunned to learn that they've done such brutal things. But in this guy's case, I'd say he's going to start making mistakes soon. One would almost think that he *wants* to be found out, judging by the way he went after that couple in broad daylight at the airport. If I were you, I'd be worried: his carelessness means that he intends to keep his agenda, whatever the cost to him."

Stan rubbed his forehead, trying to process all of this. "There's one new development, just between you and me," he said. "It seems that the guy at the airport was wearing a New-pointe firefighter's uniform. I'm trying to figure out if he's one of our guys, or if he's just using the uniform. I know all of our firemen, Jake, and I can't think of one that would do something this bizarre."

Jake was quiet for a moment. "I don't know, Stan. It doesn't make sense that he'd steal or buy a uniform, unless that was one more piece in the puzzle. Part of the statement he's making, if you will. Is there any other evidence that it really could be a firefighter?"

"Well, he uses diesel fuel to start the fires, which is safer for the arsonist, because the fumes don't rise as fast as gasoline. Not everybody knows that, but firemen do. He knows when the husbands won't be home. And today he knew where to find Mark and Allie. Seems like it's someone who knows them well. And why are the firemen's wives the target? Why no one else?"

"Do you have any bitter widowers who've lost their wives, so they want to deprive everyone else of theirs?"

"Well, yeah. We have a couple of widowers."

Jake was getting excited. "Were either of their wives shot or burned to death?"

Stan frowned. "No, I'm sure they weren't."

"Oh." Stan could almost hear the wheels turning in Jake's brain. "That blows that theory. I thought maybe these were murders of revenge—a firefighter who had a vendetta, and wanted his coworkers to pay for something. Maybe not." He thought for a moment. "Did the fire department lose anyone in the last couple of years? Fire victims, I mean. Anyone they didn't save?"

Stan thought for a moment. "Yeah. Three people. A few months ago two kids died of smoke asphyxiation before the fire department got to the scene. And before that, probably a year ago, a woman burned to death in a fire."

"The father of the children!" Jake said. "Where is he?"

Stan saw where Jake was going with this and shook his head. "The mother was single—as in, father unknown."

"Okay, what about the husband of the woman who died?"

"Dead. Was killed a few months ago, too, in a car accident. I think we're barking up the wrong tree."

Stan wondered if he was any closer than he'd been when he made the call. "Look, I appreciate your help, Jake. Can I call you back if I get anything new? Maybe you can help me brainstorm some more."

"I hope you will," Jake said. "This is fascinating. Simply fascinating."

"Yeah, well. Look, keep that bit about the fire uniform between us, okay? I don't want that leaked."

"You mean, don't make this a case for my classes to solve?" He could hear the smile in Jake's voice.

"I'd appreciate it if you'd hold off."

"Will do. I won't say a word until you've locked the guy up."

When Stan hung up, he walked out the back door of the police station, where a full moon painted the bayou behind them in grays and blacks. He looked into the yard behind the fire station. Two of the guys were out there now, one of them smoking a cigarette. He watched the red, glowing ember blaze more brightly, hang in the darkness as the man puffed, then drop to the grass where it was ground out with the toe of a foot.

Not a fireman, he thought. *It couldn't be a fireman.*

He went back to his desk. Closing his eyes, he tried to reconstruct the events on the day of Martha's and Jamie's murders. There was the parade first ... He got a pen and began to jot down the names of all the firemen he remembered seeing in the parade. That was difficult since they'd been made up like clowns, so he moved his thoughts to Martha Broussard's house, and the people who had been on the scene while they were sifting through the rubble. He had seen Mark Branning and Cale Larkins and Ray Ford, all men whose lives would be irrevocably affected by the events that began on that day. He remembered seeing Craig Barnes, and Nick Foster had been there— without makeup, since he'd been on the skeleton crew at the fire station that day—and Dan Nichols and Junior Reynolds had been with him. He closed his eyes tighter and tried to remember the others—which ones had gotten there sooner, which ones later, who they were standing with, whether they were in uniform, civilian clothes, or dressed like clowns.

Could one of them have been the one who'd shot Martha Broussard, dragged her out to a storage house, and set fire to her? Could one of them have been the one who came into Jamie Larkins's house at night and killed her, then buried her in flames? Had one of those men shot Susan? Then Mark?

The thought made him shudder, so he tried to think clearly, despite the fatigue that made his entire body ache. Since most of the firemen were accounted for on Fat Tuesday, he discarded the process of elimination. He tried a different tack: Did the evidence point to anyone in particular?

And then he remembered the other night, when Dan Nichols had been caught with a crowbar in his hand at Allie's shop, and the building had almost been broken into. Had Dan lied? Had *he* been the one breaking in?

And then there was Craig Barnes, who had gone into Allie's home the night of the stakeout. Had he lied about what he was doing? Did his suspicious behavior make him a suspect?

He rested his face in his hands and tried to think. First, he needed the personnel records of all of the firemen on the force. Maybe just examining their histories, their job performance, their beefs, their reprimands, could help him finally eliminate some of the firemen and target others as possible suspects. The first two files he would look at would be Dan's and Craig's— with the hope that he could rule them out.

But how would he get those files quietly? If the press heard that the detective on the case was asking for firefighters' personnel files, they'd have a field day. It would destroy the whole investigation and jeopardize their search for the killer. Even if he did it in private, he'd have to get those files through Craig Barnes.

He looked around the room. Ah—LaTonya Mason, the skinny little rookie cop who was always looking for something important to do. He slid his chair back, went to her desk, pulled up a chair, and sat close enough to her to speak in a low voice without being overheard. "I need your help," he said.

She looked up at him, her black eyes suspicious. "Oh, yeah? Whatchu want?"

"I need for you to get some files for me first thing in the morning. I want the personnel files of all the firefighters in town. But I don't want anyone to know who requested them. I want it to seem routine. Tell the chief we're ready for another round of drug testing, and we need the files so we can decide who to test. Got that?"

"Sure." She wrote down what she was to say, then looked up at him, folding her fist and propping her chin on it. "So what's the real reason? Somethin' to do with these murders?"

"I can't say just yet," he said. "But this is all confidential. You're not to talk about this with anybody, even another cop. That clear?"

"Sure."

"And whatever you do, don't let Barnes know that I requested it. If he asks you, just say that you don't know who will be doing the testing. That'll be evasive enough."

"Do we always request all the files before we do drug testin'?"

"I haven't got the foggiest idea," Stan said. "But if we don't, we should. Tell him we've decided to start."

"Will do."

"Thanks, LaTonya. Put them in a closed box on my desk, and I'll see them when I come in tomorrow."

"Yeah, if you go home in the first place. Everybody worked like you, we wouldn't need shifts."

Stan headed back to his desk. What LaTonya had said was true. But it was hard to go home and sleep comfortably when two friends were fighting for their lives in the hospital, and at least a few more were on some killer's hit list.

Still, he was exhausted. Since he couldn't get those files until morning, maybe he should go home and sleep. Besides, he was worried about Celia. Even though she wasn't a fire wife, he was uneasy. Presumably, the killer knew Stan was on the case. What if he decided to hit Celia, too, just to slow Stan's investigation? The thought, as unlikely as it seemed, plagued him.

He went home, punched in the phone code that would forward calls to his cellular phone, and went to Aunt Aggie's to be with Celia.

Celia was already in bed in the guest room. Stan got undressed, set the phone on the bed table, and climbed in beside her. She snuggled up to him, her warmth giving him more comfort than he'd had in days. Slowly, he drifted off to sleep.

• • •

The phone chirped, startling Stan out of sleep. Forgetting where he was, he glanced groggily to where the clock should be. How long had he slept? It rang again, and Celia stirred. "I'll get it."

"No, I've got it." It was still dark, not morning yet. Fumbling, he reached for the cell phone.

"Shepherd." He reached for the light, turned it on. His watch read three A.M.

"Sorry to wake you, Stan, but I thought you'd wanna know." The voice belonged to LaTonya Mason at the precinct. "There's been another murder."

His heart plummeted, and a wave of dizziness passed over him as he got slowly to his feet. "Who?"

"Marty Bledsoe's wife, Francis."

Another fire wife. He sat down on the side of the bed, and Celia slid her arms around him from behind. He took her hand. "They were in hiding," he said. "They weren't even in town."

"They was in Slidell stayin' at her mama's. He broke in and shot her in the head, while Marty was lyin' in bed right next to her. Must have had a silencer, because Marty didn't even wake up till a few minutes later, when he found the room on fire."

Stan reached for his clothes hanging over a chair. "When did you hear?"

"Just now. It all happened within the last hour."

"All right, give me the address. I'm headed to Slidell."

Chapter Forty-Two

● ● ●

By the time Stan arrived at the crime scene in Slidell, the media had descended. Armed with cameras and microphones, they stood just outside the area marked off by police tape. The moment he drove up, they surrounded him, as if he were a celebrity arriving on Oscar night.

Vultures, he thought, shoving them back with his car door as he got out of the car.

"Detective Shepherd, has tonight's murder produced any new leads on the Fire Wife Killer?"

"Excuse me," he said, trying to find an opening in the crowd around him.

"How many wives are left, Detective?"

"Are any measures being taken to protect the others?"

"Wouldn't it seem that the killer knows the victims, since he was able to find this one's hiding place?"

He shoved himself between two of them and ducked under the crime scene tape. He quickly flashed his badge at the officer standing there trying to keep order. "Stan Shepherd, Newpointe P.D. Who's in charge here?"

"Detective Madison is the supervising officer, sir. He's inside."

Stan ignored the questions being shouted at him and headed for the door.

He was stopped by the logging officer before he entered the house. He showed his identification and asked for Detective Madison. Madison, who had worked with him on an occasional case that crossed from one town to the next, seemed glad to see him. "I figured you'd be showing up soon, Stan."

Stan stepped into the house and looked around at the handful of officers collecting evidence. "Where's Marty?"

"Out back. He's pretty strung out. We had to take his mother-in-law to the hospital. Her blood pressure was stroke level. She took the twins with her, and Marty's parents are supposed to go get them."

"Did Marty see anything?"

Detective Madison shook his head. "He woke up, saw the fire, and tried to get her up. That was when he realized she'd been shot."

"Right there beside him? He didn't feel her body jerk or anything?"

"Claims he sleeps like the dead. Didn't know firemen could sleep like that."

Stan rubbed the back of his neck, wondering how they got Marty up at the station when they had a call in the night. "Well, truth is, none of us from Newpointe have slept all that sound lately. He was probably so tired he just zonked out. I was almost that way myself tonight."

He went into the bedroom, where one of the evidence technicians was photographing the scene. The body was still lying on the sheets, apparently untouched. Stan had last seen Francis at the meeting at the courthouse, looking as worried and scared as the rest of them. She looked oddly peaceful now, pretty even, as though someone had arranged her hair on her shoulders and folded her hands across her chest. He swallowed and fought the urge to look away. He needed to look. Maybe there was something there, something that would help him get to the bottom of this.

He made himself step closer and examine the bullet hole in her forehead. ".38?" he asked Joe Madison, who had come in behind him.

"Yep. Fired at pretty close range."

Stan leaned back against the wall that hadn't yet burned and looked up at the ceiling. A char pattern from the flames had shot up the other wall and climbed across. "They were hiding. How could he have known where? Marty didn't even tell *me* where they were."

"Stan, I think you need to start looking at someone who knows all of these victims. Someone who knows them real well. And the first place to start is by asking Marty who he told. It's probably a short list."

"You're right," Stan said. He thought of telling Joe about his suspicions that it was another Newpointe firefighter. But someone might overhear. If that word got out, the resulting panic would render the fire department useless in Newpointe—people would rather let their houses burn than call 911. "Look, don't say that to the vultures out there, okay? I don't want them to start speculating."

"I'm not talking to them," Madison said. "I know better."

Stan turned away from Francis's body and headed back through the house to the patio where Marty sat with his head hanging down between his knees. He touched his friend's neck, and Marty looked up at him.

"How's it goin', buddy?"

Marty rubbed his eyes. "How could this happen?" he asked. "How, Stan? We was hidin'. How did he find out where? He come in and shot her right next to me. How could I have slept through it?"

"That's what we have to figure out," Stan said. He found a chair and pulled it up to face Marty. Sitting close, he asked, "Who did you tell where you were?"

"Nobody!" Marty said. "I didn't tell nobody. We just came."

"All right, did anyone know where Francis's mother lived?"

He closed his eyes. "Well, yeah. I mean, lotsa folks knew she lived in Slidell. I guess if they knew her maiden name it wouldn't be that hard to find out the address. And then my car was in the driveway."

"All right, let's think, Marty. Can you think of anyone, say, in the fire department, who knows Francis's maiden name and that her mother lives here?"

He thought for a moment. "Well, it wasn't no secret. Few months ago when her daddy died, I took off work a week or so while he was in the hospital. I reckon everybody in the department knew where we were, and why."

"How about flowers?" Stan asked. "Did any of them send you flowers when he died?"

He tried to think again. "I don't know. I can't remember. There were so many flowers. They might have. Why?"

"If they did, then we know they knew your wife's maiden name. It wouldn't be a stretch to think they could have found out the address."

Marty began to stiffen, and looked at him as if he'd just suggested something ludicrous. "You're thinkin' this guy is somebody in the department?"

"I didn't say that. Don't you tell anyone I said that."

"Then what? Why would one of us be doin' somethin' like this? Instead of lookin' at us, you need to be out there findin' the real killer."

Stan looked from side to side, to make sure they hadn't been overheard. "Marty, do you have any idea where Francis's mother might have kept the guest book for the funeral, or the list of people who sent flowers?"

He rubbed his eyes again, trying to think. "Uh ... maybe. Yeah, in there in the dinin' room. She keeps lots of stuff like that in the drawers of the hutch. Pictures she hasn't put in albums, that sort of thing. She mighta stuck it in there."

"Okay. I'll go look."

"Stan?" Marty grabbed the lapel of Stan's sport coat as he started to stand up. "When are they gon' do somethin' with her? They can't just leave her lyin' there. It's wrong. All those pictures they're takin', and all those cops gawkin' at her. Please, can't you tell 'em to leave her alone?"

Stan sighed. "They're taking the pictures for evidence, Marty. It might keep anyone else from getting killed the same way. And when we catch this creep, the pictures'll help us nail him."

Marty dropped his head back into his hands. "Oh, why didn't he shoot me, too? Havin' t' see all this—it's cruel, man."

Stan couldn't answer. It did seem cruel. Almost intentionally so. Was the whole thing for that purpose? To somehow make the firemen suffer when they found their wives dead? If so, why? Why *hadn't* the killer shot Marty, too, or his mother-in-law? Why had he not hurt Tommy Broussard?

He went into the dining room and found the hutch. He pulled on the latex gloves he'd brought and began to go through each of the drawers until he found the guest book from Marty's father-in-law's funeral. There was a stack of cards stuffed inside it in a ziplock bag. He pulled them out and began to thumb through them. Some of them were small florist's cards. He went through the cards one by one, noting who from Newpointe had sent them. There was one from Nick Foster. One from all the guys at the Midtown Station, signed by each of them individually. He checked the address on the front, then compared the handwriting to the signatures. It looked as if Dan Nichols had been the one to address the card. Where had he gotten the address? He flipped a few more cards, found one from Mark and Allie Branning, one from Craig Barnes, one from the Fords.

Joe came into the room. "Got something?"

"Maybe, maybe not. I'm gonna take this bag of cards for evidence. It might help me figure out who in Newpointe knew where Francis's mother lived."

"All right, Stan. Just log it in, so we'll know where it is."

A uniformed cop came in and said, "Detective Shepherd?"

"Yes," Stan said.

"Someone from your office is looking for you. They said to tell you that Susan Ford just came out of her coma. She wants to talk to you."

Stan's heart leapt. "All right, now we're getting somewhere."

"That the woman who survived the shooting?"

"That's right," Stan said, dropping the ziplock bag into a paper sack and pulling off his latex gloves. "And she just might be able to tell us who's doing all this."

Chapter Forty-Three

• • •

Back on the Southshore in the ICU waiting room, Jill woke up and felt the pangs of hunger, the chill of the room, and a slight disorientation. She looked around. Allie was lying two chairs down from her, her vinyl recliner back as far as it would go. She thanked God that Allie was sleeping. She needed rest, and the energy that would come from it.

She stretched and tried to move into a more comfortable position, but there weren't many choices. Dan, who had been between them when they'd fallen asleep, wasn't there. She looked around, trying to adjust her eyes to the dim light, to see where he'd gone. Surely he hadn't gone far—not when he'd promised Mark he wouldn't leave Allie's side. Her eyes strayed to the doors marked "Men" and "Women." He must have gone there.

Closing her eyes, she let her consciousness drift as sleep came back over her.

A while later, she stirred awake again, this time to see Dan ambling slowly back in with a canned drink in his hand. He smiled when he saw that she was awake, and sat back down between Allie and her. Leaning close, he whispered, "Hi."

"Hi," she said. "Where'd you get that?"

"In that little kitchenette area over there. I know every nook and cranny of it. There are some stale muffins in there if you want some."

"No," she whispered. She didn't tell him she was fasting. "Is that where you were? I woke up a while ago and you were gone."

"I was over at that window overlooking that courtyard. I was bored and didn't want to read because the light might disturb someone. So I took my book out there and read for a while. If anybody had tried to get into the waiting room, they'd have walked right past me, so you and Allie were safe. If I'd stayed in here, I would have just fallen asleep. I promised Mark I'd be alert."

She lay the side of her head on the back of her recliner, but it wasn't comfortable, so she shifted again. "Come here," he whispered. He put his arm around her and guided her head to his shoulder. He was warm, and his uniform had the faint scent of aftershave and a lingering hint of smoke. He'd probably put out a fire today—he must be exhausted. Yet he was willing to give up his sleep to come here and guard Allie. The thought warmed Jill.

It wasn't long before sleep overtook her again, but this time, instead of cold, she felt the deep, soul-stirring sense of warmth that Dan had given her.

Chapter Forty-Four

● ● ●

Even though it was four-thirty A.M., the security guard at the Slidell Hospital let Stan in as soon as he showed him his identification. Stan rode the elevator to the second floor, where Susan Ford's room was. The moment he stepped off the elevator he saw Sid, Ray's brother, sitting in the corridor beside the door, still wearing his Newpointe P.D. uniform.

"How's it going, Sid?" Stan asked in a low voice, taking Sid's hand in a casual shake. "I hear she woke up."

"Yep," Sid said. "And she got some stuff to say. You ain't gon' believe this."

Stan looked past him into the room and saw Ray sitting on the side of Susan's bed, holding her hand and kissing it and talking softly to her. Vanessa and Ben stood on the other side, leaning over the rail, their expressions poignant. At the foot of the bed, two nurses spoke softly and recorded pertinent information for her chart.

Stan stepped inside the door and rapped lightly, and Ray looked up.

"Hey, Stan. Thanks for comin', man. How'd you get here so fast?"

Stan hated to tell him that he'd already been in Slidell because of Francis Bledsoe's murder. "I was already here working on the case when I got the call," he said. "I hear she woke up."

"She sho' did," Ray said with a chuckle, then turned back to his wife.

Stan went to the bed rail and looked down into Susan Ford's face. She had an oxygen mask on and looked frail, but her eyes focused on him as soon as he came into her view.

"Stan." Her voice was weak, so weak he almost couldn't hear, so he braced his elbows on the rails and leaned over her. She groped for her mask and pulled it off her face. "Need to ... talk to you."

"She been askin' for you ever since she woke up," Ray said softly. "Stan, she remembers gettin' shot."

Reluctant hope surged through Stan, and he told himself to stay calm. "What do you remember, Susan?"

"He ... he came in ... I couldn't see his face ... he was aimin' for my head, but I swung around and ran—"

"You couldn't see his face?" Stan asked.

"No ... a mask."

Stan leaned closer, trying to hang on every word. "Mask? Like a Mardi Gras mask?"

"No," she whispered. "No, not that. Like Ray's mask. The oxygen mask."

Stan looked up at Ray, questioning. "What does she mean?"

"The face piece they ... wear in fires," she said before Ray could answer. "Had on that face piece, that mask, and a bunker hood that covered his head."

Stan looked up at Ray again. "Does she mean ... like a fireman's hood? The mask you wear in fires?"

"Sounds like it," Ray said.

Stan's heart was hammering. "Susan, you didn't see his eyes? Any identifying marks on his body? What he was wearing?"

"Bunker coat," she said. "I just ran ..."

Tears rolled out of her eyes, and Ben wiped them away. "It's okay, Mama."

Vanessa turned away and began to sob, and Ray got up to embrace his daughter. "Honey, you want to go out and talk to Uncle Sid?"

Vanessa shook her head. "No, I'm stayin' with Mama. I wanna hear."

Susan took her hand and squeezed it. "My baby. Thank goodness . . . you weren't home."

"Put the mask back on, Mama," Vanessa coaxed. "Please put it back on."

Susan put the oxygen mask back on and closed her eyes for a moment, resting. Stan stepped back from the bed, his mind racing. So it *was* a fireman, without a doubt. But which one?

"He cried," Susan said after a moment, her eyes opening again.

Stan wasn't sure he'd heard right. "He what?"

She pulled the mask down again. "He cried. After he shot me . . . and I was layin' there . . . he thought I was dead . . . I wanted him to think so . . . and he cried, and started prayin'."

"Praying?" Stan asked. "He was *praying?*"

"Some kind of Catholic prayer, I think," she said. "He was prayin' to Mary. Sayin', 'I'm sorry, Mary. I'm so sorry.' I thought . . . he might have me . . . mixed up with somebody named Mary . . . but now I think he was prayin'."

"Why would he cry?" Vanessa asked, her eyes full of tears. "Why would some maniac shoot my mama and then cry about it?"

"I don't know," Stan said.

Ray's face was confused. "Stan, do you think this killer is one of our firefighters? Somebody I sleep and eat and go to church with?"

"I don't know, but I'm gonna find out," he said.

"Hurry up, will you?"

"I'll do my best. Look, you can all do me a big favor by keeping quiet about this. If it is a fireman, and I'm not saying it is, we don't want to start a panic. And we sure don't want to clue the guy in that we've got his number and risk having him disappear."

"I won't say nothin', man," Ray said. "Look, how's Mark? I been wantin' to call, but I been so busy here—"

"He's gonna be fine. The Lord must've had an army of angels around him when he got shot."

"Him and Susan both."

Stan squeezed Susan's hand. "I appreciate your calling me. I needed to know this."

"You be careful, Stan, you hear?" she whispered.

"I will," he said. "Now you get some rest."

He left them all there, then stepped out into the hall. Sid got to his feet. "So what'd you think o' that?"

"I think it confirms some leads I've already gotten," Stan said quietly. "I didn't want to believe it was a fireman, but I can't ignore the evidence. Sid, I didn't want to tell Ray, but something else has happened."

Sid looked as if he wasn't sure he wanted to hear this. "What?"

"Marty's wife was shot this morning."

Sid backed against the wall. "Not Francis. Where was she?"

"Here in Slidell. Whoever it was came in and shot her in bed without ever waking Marty. He's in pretty rough shape. The killer knew where they were, Sid. And Marty didn't tell anyone."

"Wait a minute." Sid narrowed his eyes and stared at Stan. "Somebody shot her and Marty didn't wake up? That don't seem possible."

"It happened," Stan said.

Sid obviously wasn't buying. "But the bed woulda jerked, and the body woulda flailed at least a little." He frowned. "Was there a fire this time?"

"Sure was. That's what woke him."

"A bullet didn't wake him, but a *fire* did? Huh-uh, Stan. I don't think so."

"He must have used a silencer," Stan said. "Come on, Sid. You aren't suggesting that Marty's our man. What did he do? Set up the whole serial killer thing so nobody'd suspect him when he killed his own wife?"

Sid lifted his eyebrows, as though that was a possibility.

"No way," Stan said. "You don't know Marty. He's not a killer."

"Name somebody in the fire department who is," Sid challenged. "Can you, Stan?"

"No," Stan said. "I can't."

"Gotta be somebody, man. And I don't buy this business about your wife gets shot while you're sleepin' in the same bed and you don't even wake up."

Stan hadn't considered Marty to be a suspect—not the man he'd just seen grieving over his wife, who worried about her body and all the pictures being taken. But then he also couldn't explain why a killer would weep and pray, as Susan had said.

"I don't think it's Marty," he said finally. "I think he's covered during at least some of the other murders. But listen: I found cards that some of the firemen had sent when Francis's father died, so some of them had known earlier where her mother lived. It wasn't a big stretch to figure out they'd be hiding there. And there's something else, too. Yesterday, after Mark was shot, they found a Newpointe bunker coat at the scene."

Sid dropped his head back against the wall again and closed his eyes. "We gotta find him . . . stop him before he comes back for Susan. He might think she can identify him." He opened his eyes and fixed them on Stan. "Okay, look, if it ain't Marty, look at Dan Nichols. He's the one got caught at the flower shop the other night, walkin' around with a crowbar in his hand."

"I'm considering him," Stan said. "And Craig too. He's the one who got lured in with our bait the other night. But he's also the one tap-dancing to keep both stations running."

"Question all of 'em, Stan. Just take ever' one of 'em in and question 'em one at a time."

Stan knew that Sid's insistence came from fear and frustration, not from doubts about his ability to do his job. "Well, I'll get back to you. I need to get back to the office and put all this together. Let me know if Susan remembers anything else, will you?"

"Stan, you find him! 'Cause if I find him first, I ain't gon' be askin' no questions!"

"I'm working as fast as I can, Sid," Stan promised.

Chapter Forty-Five

● ● ●

Good news came that afternoon, when the doctor evaluated Mark and decided that he could be moved into a private room. There was a cot in there for Allie, so she could sleep beside him that night. Dan had gone home, and T.J. had come to replace him. The hulking cop had set up a chair outside the door in the hallway, where he could screen everyone who tried to come in.

As Allie tried to make Mark's room as comfortable as she could, she felt much the way she'd felt when they'd bought their first house together. Flowers had begun arriving early that morning, so she quickly reworked the arrangements to her satisfaction and placed them around the room where Mark could see them. Then she fluffed his pillow and filled his pitcher with ice water.

Because they all felt that Mark was out of the woods, Jill had broken her fast, and Allie intended to as soon as Jill brought something back for her to eat. As they waited for Mark to be brought from ICU, her parents sat on the couch, watching her do her best to domesticate the sterile little room. They had something to say, she realized, but their reluctance in saying it warned her that it was something she didn't want to hear. Finally, she sat down on the bed and regarded them both. "What is it, Mom? Dad?"

Her parents looked at each other and seemed to silently agree to tell her what was on their minds. "We just hate for you to have your heart broken."

"What do you mean?" she asked.

Her father seemed to consider his words carefully. "We understand why you would be so devoted to Mark after such a trauma," her father said. "Really, we do understand. But now that he's going to get better, we hate to see you acting like everything is fine between you. Like you're still married—"

"We *are* still married."

Her mother took the baton. "But honey, as soon as he gets out of here, he's going to go back to his apartment and that woman, and you're going to go back to yours."

She sighed heavily. "I really don't want to talk about that."

"We just want you to be safe, honey. We don't want your heart broken, or your life threatened by some killer. We were thinking . . ."

Her father touched her mother's hand, taking over again. It was uncanny how they finished each other's sentences, completed each other's thoughts. "We were thinking, honey, that you should fly back with us this afternoon. Mark will be fine. He has all sorts of friends who can take care of him, and that father of his—"

"I'm not going," she cut in. She couldn't find anything else in the room to do, so she reached for the remote and turned on the television. She hadn't seen the news since yesterday in the hotel room; the ICU waiting room had no television. "I'm staying here with my husband."

"And what if he just uses you until he's better?"

She couldn't believe their persistence. "Uses me? How?"

"To take care of him. He's not exactly in a position to tell you to hit the road."

"He's never told me to hit the road," Allie said with weariness. "I told *him* to, so he did."

"But that woman—"

"Mother," she said, using the name she called her only when she was getting angry. "I'm tired of hearing about this. I never should have told you all those things. It's my fault that you feel the way you do about him, but—"

"... *identified as Francis Bledsoe* ..."

The name blaring from the television grabbed Allie's attention, and she quickly stood, gaping up at the set in the corner of the room. "Oh, no," she whispered.

"... *victim number five in the bizarre case of the Fire Wife Killings. Victim number four, Mark Branning, himself a firefighter at Newpointe's Midtown Station, is still hospitalized after a bullet to his head, and victim number three, Susan Ford, is still in critical condition. Francis Bledsoe was found shot through the head in her mother's home, while her husband, firefighter Marty Bledsoe, slept beside her. The killer is purported to have started a fire, as he did in almost every other case. Sources tell us that Bledsoe woke after the fact and saw the fire. It was moments later that he realized his wife was dead in their bed.*"

"Oh, God, what is happening?" Allie cried, sinking to the floor. "Not another one! Not Francis! She had kids! She had those sweet little twins!"

Her parents were at her side in an instant, kneeling beside her and holding her while she wailed out her anguish and pain.

"What's happening? He's killing us all!"

"You're coming home with us today," her father said. "I won't take no for an answer. Mark will want it, too, if he really cares about you."

She shook away from them, got up, and tried to pull herself together. "I'm not going *anywhere*, do you hear me? He found her! He found her at her mother's. He found *us* at the airport. He'll find me wherever I go, so I might as well be here, with my husband!"

"Oh, for heaven's sake, Allie, listen to us!" her mother shouted. "Stop being a martyr. You won't do Mark any good if you're dead!"

"I have a bodyguard!" she argued, red-faced. "I'm doing what's necessary. But I made vows to my husband, and I intend to keep them. He took a bullet that was intended for me, Mom. Don't you understand that? I wouldn't be alive if it weren't for him. I'm going to stay with him and take care of him, and nothing—not you or Dad or some stupid wild killer—is going to make me leave him now. So either get that through your heads, or go on home. I have enough to deal with!"

Her parents backed away, and finally, her mother said, "Let's go for a walk."

Her father nodded. "We'll leave you alone for a while, honey. Eat something, okay? You'll feel a lot better."

She watched, sobbing, as they walked out of the room. Wilting on the bed, she began to pray—short, disjointed prayers that she feared made no sense, but she knew God heard. He knew she prayed for Marty Bledsoe and their little twins, for Mark to get well so they could renew their vows, for her parents to understand, for herself to cope, for Stan to find the killer, for the killer to have a conscience . . .

When she had finished, she washed her face, brushed her hair, and tried to hide the evidence of her tears before Mark was brought in. He didn't need to know about Francis Bledsoe. He needed to concentrate on getting better.

Not long after, they wheeled Mark in and moved him onto his bed. He saw Allie and smiled. "Hey . . ."

"It's not much," she said, her eyes glimmering, "but it's home."

"You mean they're actually gonna let us be together for more than fifteen minutes at a time?"

"That's what they tell me."

He grinned. His voice was gravelly, groggy, as he asked, "You think we can handle that? I'm better in small doses, they tell me."

She knew he was kidding, playing with her, but the challenge made her feel awkward. When he reached out for her hand, she took it and came close to the bed. The nurses worked around her, hanging his IV bag, taking his blood pressure.

He smiled up at her, but suddenly his smile faded. "Your eyes are red. Is that from fatigue, or have you been crying?"

"Fatigue," she said quickly.

"You slept in a chair last night, didn't you? Man, that's cruel. With all the beds in this place, you would think . . ." His voice faded out, and he began to shake his head. "No. That's not fatigue. Your nose doesn't turn red when you're tired. You *have* been crying."

She feared that the tears would come again. Desperately, she tried to blink them back. "I was just thinking about everything that's happened," she said, giving him a half-truth. "I guess now that I know you're out of the woods, I was able to let go and have a good cry." She reached over and stroked the hair that started behind his bandage. "Wonder what you're going to look like when the bandage comes off?"

"It won't be pretty."

The nurse left them, and his eyes grew serious as he looked up at her. "I really appreciate your staying here with me, Allie. I didn't know for sure if you would."

"Of course I would."

"So how's T.J. treating you? You two getting along?"

"Sure, we're fine. He mostly sits out there flipping through magazines, but he's careful not to let just anybody in. Dan was more fun."

"You just know him better. But T.J. will do a good job. Make sure you don't go anywhere without him."

"I'm not going anywhere at all. I don't want you left alone."

"Hey, the killer is after you, not me. I got in the way, remember?"

She swallowed the lump in her throat. "Still, I think I'll just stay here."

"Fine with me. Come here."

When he opened his arms, she bent down and went willingly into them, and clung to him for several moments, basking in the warmth of his strength. Tears filled her eyes again as she thought about how close she had come to losing him. "I'm glad you're going to be okay," she whispered.

He loosened the hug, letting her pull back enough to look at him. His eyes were soft, sweet, as he gazed up at her, and she wondered what he was thinking. Did he, too, want to renew his commitment to their marriage vows?

"I'm sorry you ever married me," he whispered.

Her expression crashed. "What?"

"I'm sorry," he repeated. "If you hadn't married me, you wouldn't be in this mess. Maybe you'd be off happily married to some rich guy with a big house, a minivan, and a couple of kids by now."

"What about you? Where would you be?" she asked soberly.

"Probably right where I am, since that maniac wants to kill my wife no matter who she is. On the other hand, there's probably nobody else in the world I'd ever take a bullet for but you."

"Sure there is," she said sadly. "That's the kind of guy you are. There are probably lots of people."

"Nope. Just you, kiddo." His eyes locked with hers for a long moment, and he reached up and stroked his finger through her hair, pushing it back from her face, sweeping it behind her ear.

The overwhelming urge to kiss him swept over her, drawing her toward him. Her heart pounded, and that old chemical ache that had drawn them together when they met began to pump through her again. She felt the slightest pressure of his hand on the back of her head, pulling her down to him . . .

Their lips met, and her heart soared like a bottle rocket in a fourth of July celebration, as all the love she'd felt for him and stifled, all the misery of their separation, all the joy of his survival, all the regrets of her part in their marriage, culminated in a moment of bliss even more poignant than their first kiss. The kiss lingered for several moments. Neither wanted to end it, and his fingers stroked the roots of her hair, as her knuckles moved across his stubbled jaw.

When at last the kiss ended, she pulled back a fraction of an inch and looked into eyes that were dark with longing for her. Joy burst through her heart that he could look at her that way again.

"How do you manage it?" he asked in a whisper.

"What?" she whispered against his lips.

"To give me a coronary workout when I'm flat on my back?"

She grinned, but his eyes remained serious.

"I meant it the other night," he said. "When I told you that I'd missed you. I know you didn't believe it then, but it's true, Allie. I've missed you."

He pulled her into another kiss, and a sense of supreme well-being, intense contentment, filled her.

"Knock, knock." It was her mother, back from her walk, and Allie sprang up as if she had been caught at something.

"Hey there, Mom, Dad," Mark said, surprised to see them. "Allie didn't tell me you were here."

Her mother assessed the situation, then shot her father another of those wordless, but eloquent, looks. "Uh . . . yes. We've been here since yesterday," her father said in a cool tone.

Her mother stepped closer to his bedside, but still hung back a noncommittal distance, as if she didn't want to be mistaken for someone who cared too much. "We're glad you're feeling better," she said, as if he'd had a head cold.

Allie hated the chill coming from her mother, the chill she didn't want Mark to feel, so she changed the subject. "Mark, can I get you anything? Water? A popsicle? I could call the nurse, and get her to bring one."

"No, I'm fine. Thanks." He looked back at her parents, who still stood there, so cold and uncommunicative. "Why don't you guys sit down? The remote control's probably around here some—"

"No!" Allie said, too quickly. "No television, Mom. Please."

Mark gave her a suspicious look. "Why not?"

"Because . . ." She felt like a thief caught in the act of stealing. But she didn't want Mark to know about Francis Bledsoe, not until he was better. "I just want some peace and quiet."

"But I'd like to watch the news," Mark said. "They might have some word on the hunt for the killer."

"They don't," she lied. "Mark, don't you want to rest?"

He stared at her for a moment, then looked at her parents and saw the volumes written on their faces. "What's going on? Has something happened? Was someone else shot?"

Allie glared at her parents to keep them quiet.

"Allie, tell me! What's going on?"

She wilted. "Mark, you really need to ignore the news. You need to concentrate on getting better. You can't do anything about the killer from in here, so there's no point in—"

"Who?" Mark asked, turning to her parents. "Who's the latest victim?"

Her father started to speak, but Allie stopped him. She took a deep breath. "It's Francis Bledsoe," she said, her mouth trembling with the words. "She was killed last night."

"Aw, no!" He closed his eyes and brought his hand to his eyes. "No, Allie, not another one. How many is that?"

"Including you and Susan, five. But there is good news, Mark. Susan woke up, and T.J. said that she's been able to give them some pertinent information about the identity of the killer. He won't say what that information is, but it must be a strong lead."

He let out a heavy breath, then slid his hand down his face. "Well, good for Susan. I'm glad she's gonna pull through. But how's Marty?"

"I don't know. I just heard about it all myself."

"His kids," he whispered in horror. "Those poor little kids."

Her mother got up and stepped close to the bed, her face suddenly softer. "Mark . . . we're worried about Allie."

"That makes three of us."

"We want her to come home with us. Today."

Allie's eyes filled with fire as she turned on her mother. "Mom, I've already told you," she said through her teeth. "I'm not going."

Mark took Allie's hand and made her look at him. "Maybe you should."

"Why? I have T.J. here, and you. The killer found Francis Bledsoe at her mother's in Slidell. What makes you think he wouldn't find me in Georgia?"

Mark closed his eyes and let that sink in for a moment.

"Mark, I'm not leaving, no matter what you say. I'm staying, and that's final."

He seemed to be undergoing some supreme struggle. She laid her hand on his chest. "Mark, I mean it. Don't even think about it."

Mark looked at her mother, then her father, who had approached the bed himself. Mark's eyes were deep with thought. For a moment, she thought he would agree with them and insist that she leave, and she wondered how in the world she would convince all three of them that her place was here.

But Mark surprised her. "She's right. She's really probably safer here, where there's a mob of press people downstairs and a bodyguard outside the door."

Her father's teeth came together, and through compressed lips, he said, "That's selfish, Mark! You want her here taking care of you, so you're letting your selfishness endanger her life. She's my daughter. I want her to be safe."

"She's my wife," Mark said. "And I want that, too. If I thought she'd be safer in Georgia—"

Her mother's tough facade shattered, and she turned away. "You don't even love her, Mark. You were going to divorce her just a few days ago. Why should we believe now that you'll do everything in your power to protect her?"

Allie's face was hot, and tears stung her eyes. "Mother, please—"

"You're right," Mark said, closing his hand possessively over Allie's. "My power is pretty limited right now. And there's no good reason you should believe me when I say that I'll make sure she's protected."

"Yes, there is, Mark!" Allie shouted. "There *is* a good reason." She swung around to her parents, her face raging red. "He almost died protecting me! He almost died! The least I can do—the very least—is to stay here with him now."

Mark tugged on her hand and turned her back around. She saw the pain on his face, and realized that he'd misinterpreted her words. "You don't owe me anything, Allie."

"No, Mark, that's not what I meant. But they can't pretend that you haven't protected me. That you haven't done everything in your power—"

"We appreciate what Mark did," her father said, more softly now, as if trying to appease her. "We do. But now it's our turn—"

"No, it's not! I've made my choice."

"You're our only daughter," her mother cried. "We don't want to leave you." Her voice broke, and she began to sob. In a high-pitched voice, she cried, "We may never see you again."

Suddenly, Allie understood the reason for her parents' domineering stance in this. They were terrified. Maybe even more terrified than she was. Melting, she whispered, "Oh, Mom," and went to her mother, hugged her, then pulled back and hugged her father. "Dad—I'm gonna be all right. Really. Please. Just go home. I'll call you every day."

"You promise?" her mother asked through her tears.

"Yes. You can pray for us, and trust that God is still watching over us."

Her mother, who had been the one to teach Allie to pray, nodded her head, unable to speak. Her father struggled with his own tears as he turned to Mark. "Don't let anything happen to our little girl, do you hear me?"

"Yes, sir."

He settled his gaze on his daughter.

"We'll go home," her father said. "We're just getting in the way here, and we're not going to see things eye to eye. But we love you, sweetheart."

"I love you, too." She hugged them again, and finally, he took her mother's hand and escorted her out.

She turned back to the bed and met Mark's eyes. Though they were still bruised, she saw clearly the longing in them.

"You know, you don't have to stay," he said quietly. "You don't have to take care of me. If you want to go with them—"

"I want to stay, Mark."

"Why?" The question seemed important, but she was too tired, too hungry, too depressed to answer it eloquently.

"For the same reason you want to take care of me."

The quiet seemed to bond them in some unspoken way as they gazed at each other with sad, questioning eyes. Questions needed to be asked, questions about where they stood in each other's hearts, what their next step would be, whether there would still be a marriage when all the dust settled. But those questions were never asked, because Jill came hurrying in with a Styrofoam plate in her hand.

"Allie, I'm so sorry it took so long to bring this back, but the line was long."

"It's okay," Allie whispered. But her eyes stayed locked with Mark's in sweet anticipation and fragile hope.

Chapter Forty-Six

● ● ●

Two days later, Aunt Aggie puttered in the kitchen at the fire station, making a thick gumbo that she didn't really have the heart for. These funerals were wearing her out. It was one thing saying good-bye, one by one, to people her own age who'd led long lives and were ready for the fat lady to sing, but it was another watching them bury a beautiful young woman with twin girls who would need their mama. The sight had broken her heart; it almost made her want to stay at home in mourning today. But her boys had to eat, and they, too, were in mourning. They needed some comfort, even if she could only offer it through their stomachs.

Nick had come in after the funeral and a visit to Susan Ford in Slidell, looking drained and sober. He looked worn and aged, too, she thought, even though he was only thirty. He needed a wife to take care of him and keep that soft heart of his pumping. He was a good man, even if Aunt Aggie didn't believe a word of the stuff he preached.

Dan Nichols hadn't gone to the funeral. He had stayed behind on the skeleton crew that kept the fire station open, as had Cale Larkins, who said he couldn't bear the thought either of attending another funeral or of staying in a lonely house. One by one, they had all returned to the station. It was quiet, deathly so—there hadn't been a call in hours, they'd said, not even a cat up a tree. She wished someone would turn on music or something, to break the quiet. She thought of humming as she prepared the meal, but she just had no hum in her.

She heard footsteps in the doorway and turned around to see George Broussard standing there in a pair of worn jeans and a gray sweatshirt, holding that little baby, Tommy, on his hip. The little boy looked freshly bathed, and his hair was slicked over like that of an older child. His face was so clean it shone.

"Oh, let me see *mon enfant*," Aunt Aggie said, rushing to his side. "Oh, George, how is he, bless his heart?"

George pressed a kiss on his cheek. "He's good, Aunt Aggie. He's gon' be awright."

"My heart break for him. And for you, too."

He swallowed and looked down at the baby, then asked, "Is Nick here, by any chance?"

"He in the back changin'."

"I need to talk to him," he said.

"I'll baby-sit for you," she said, "soon's I get the table set. Y'eat?"

"No, but I ain't hungry."

"Y'have to eat, George. You look like nothin' but skin and bones." She'd meant it to make him smile, since it was so obviously untrue. But it didn't work.

"I ain't been hungry."

"Neither has nobody." She hurriedly set the table, then reached for the baby. "Come here, darlin'."

Tommy puckered up like he was going to cry, and George shifted him to the other hip. "I b'lieve I'll just keep him with me."

"You sure?"

"Oh, yeah. No problem."

Aggie watched them disappear to the back. She heard a knock, and turned to see Celia standing in the doorway. "Aunt Aggie? What's wrong?"

She dabbed at her eyes with a corner of her apron. "Just George," she said. "And that poor little orphaned boy."

"He's not an orphan, Aunt Aggie. He has his daddy."

"But not his mama. We could set up a whole school full of young 'uns lost their mamas in the last week." She dabbed her eyes again. "How many is that monster gonna kill before Stan stops him?"

"He's doing the best he can, Aunt Aggie. You know he is."

She waved a frustrated hand. "Ah, it's takin' forever." She pulled a tissue from a box on the corner of the counter and blew her nose. "So what bring you here? You smell my gumbo all way across town?"

Celia smiled. "No. I was just talking to Allie Branning, and she said that Mark is doing so well that they might let him go home tomorrow."

"Really? After gettin' shot in the head?"

"The Lord was really looking out for him."

"Then why he got shot in the first place?"

"He was protecting Allie."

"No, no," Aggie said with frustration. "I mean, why did somebody go t' shootin' at him? If the Lord was lookin' out for him, why he got shot? And was the Lord not lookin' out for Martha and Jamie and Susan and Francis?"

She knew that her niece wasn't fooled. Everyone in town knew she didn't believe in the Lord, nor any other supposed higher being, and she sure didn't believe in divine intervention of any kind. Aggie was making a point, and she hoped she'd made it well.

"Aunt Aggie, I can't pretend to know what God is doing, or why he's doing it. I just believe that he is working somehow. Now, the reason I came is to ask you a favor."

"What favor, darlin'?" Aggie asked, suddenly contrite that she'd offended her niece. If she hadn't been so grouchy and irritable from the funeral, she wouldn't have.

"Well, I was just thinking. Allie was a little worried about where she and Mark would go when he gets out. They can't go home for obvious reasons. In fact, the farther from Newpointe they are, the better. And it's a little hard to recover in a hotel. They need a place with a kitchen so they don't have to go out. That got me to thinking about your apartment in the French Quarter."

Aggie's eyebrows arched. "You think they'd want to stay there?"

"I'm not sure, but we could offer. Oh, Aunt Aggie, it's such a romantic little place. It's just what they need. It was heaven for Stan and me on our honeymoon. I could stock the kitchen and get it all ready for them. That is, if there's not a tenant in it already."

Aggie had kept the apartment for her frequent visits to the Southshore. She rented it out through a real estate agent who specialized in tourism, but only for a week at a time. This time of year, between Mardi Gras and Easter, tourism was slow, so the apartment was vacant. "It's a good idea," she said. "I'll call the realtor and tell her we'll be usin' it ourselves 'til further notice. And I'll get the cleanin' lady I use down there t' go by and give it a once-over. Oh, and I'll have some fresh flowers sent over, to freshen it up a little, since Allie loves flowers. Me and you can go down there tomorrow mornin' and spruce the place up before they get there."

"Okay," Celia said with a smile. "What about feeding the guys?"

Aggie looked back at the food, still sitting on the table, cooling. "Nobody 'round here has much appetite, noway. Let 'em order pizza for a coupla meals; they'll appreciate my eats a little more when I get back."

Craig Barnes came in just then, his face as tired and preoc- cupied as all of the other firefighters today. He glanced at the table. "Where is everybody?"

"Nick's in back talkin' to George Broussard. Dan, Slater, and Cale's washin' the ladder truck. Jacob and Junior is out back shootin' hoops. Sit down if you hungry. Food's gettin' cold."

"No thanks," he muttered. "Not hungry." He disappeared into the back.

"Heaven's sake," she said. "Guess I'll be glad to get out of town tomorrow and do somethin' with my time that's worthwhile."

Celia set a time for them to meet, then rushed out to call Allie.

• • •

In the back room where the television set and a couple of recliners and rockers were, George rocked his baby. Nick sat across from him, elbows on his knees, his eyes locked into his friend's.

"I just wondered, Nick," George said, his voice cracking as he got the words out, "if you have any advice . . . on, you know . . . how to stop feelin' like I'm smotherin' in the dark."

Nick prayed silently for an answer. He'd counseled people before about dealing with death, but never after a murder. He felt helpless, inadequate. "Trust God," Nick said. "That's all I know. It's normal to grieve, George. Jesus grieved over Lazarus. But you have to trust God and know that things are working together for good, and that this grief will just be a memory some day when you're reunited with Martha."

Little Tommy's eyes were drifting shut as George rocked, the steady rhythm of the rocker the most soothing sound Nick had heard in days. "I do trust God," George said, stroking the baby's cheek with his rough knuckle. "I just wish he'd let me in on what he's up to."

"Don't we all?"

"I wish it didn't have to hurt so bad. I wish—" His voice broke, and he dropped his head and squeezed his eyes shut as a sob broke from his throat. "I wish Tommy would stop lookin' around me for his mama." He drew in a deep, wet breath, and wiped his face with a hard hand. "I wish I'd spent more time with him before it happened ... so's he'd be more used to me. But she was nursin', so I couldn't do the feedin's, and I was here every third night, and she changed most of the diapers and did most of what had to be done. I shoulda helped her more. I shoulda been there instead of actin' the clown in some stupid parade."

Guilt. It was a natural stage of grief, yet knowing that didn't give Nick a clue how to make it easier to deal with. Again, he prayed for strength. An idea came to him, and he sat back in his chair.

"Let's think about Martha for a minute, George," he said. "About where she is right now."

George brought his grieving eyes back up to Nick's. "She's in heaven. No question."

"What do you think she sees there? What's it like for her?"

George thought about that for a moment. "I couldn't say."

"All right," Nick said, taking it one step at a time, though he realized he was going way out on a limb. "Let's just think about it. If when we get there, we're reunited with loved ones, who do you think would have come to greet Martha?"

George was quiet for a long moment, and Nick began to think this line of thought might have been a mistake. Finally, the man said, "Her parents. She'll be glad to see 'em. Especially her mama. She just lost her last year, and it really hurt her. She wanted so much for her mama to see her as a mama herself."

"Wonderful. She's reunited with her parents. Who else?"

"Grandmaws and grandpaws, I reckon. And her sister who died when she was a teenager. I never knew her, but she was in a car wreck, and Martha always missed her."

"She's with her sister!" Nick exclaimed. "What a wonderful homecoming she must have had. Anyone else?"

George struggled with his thoughts for a moment longer. "Yeah." He looked up at Nick with a look of surprise as the thought came to him. "Martha had two miscarriages. Reckon those babies'll be there, too?"

Nick's eyes filled with tears. "I'm certain they are."

George managed to get out a smile, then a soft, poignant laugh as he wiped the tears from his face. "What do you know 'bout that? She'll get to be a mama, after all. And her mama *will* see it." He laughed again, and shook his head. "She'll have her work cut out for her, what with two babies and me not there to help her."

"But she's got her parents there, and her sister. And you've got your family here."

He nodded. "Yeah, I do. Maybe that's why the good Lord didn't let the killer take Tommy, too. He left one for me."

"And one day, you'll have them all together."

George looked down at the little baby, a sweet smile on his face. "Wonder if she has cellulite there?"

Nick didn't think he'd heard right. "Has what?"

"Cellulite," George said, chuckling and leaning his head back on the rocker. "She always said that she hoped when she got to heaven she wouldn't have no cellulite. Reckon she has any?"

Nick laughed softly. No matter how hard he tried, he couldn't think of a single scriptural reference to cellulite.

• • •

When no one had come to the table, Aggie had gone looking for them, one by one, insisting that the boys eat so that her gumbo wouldn't go bad. When she'd gone after George and Nick, she had heard the conversation going on in the TV room, and had hung back, listening quietly.

All that talk about heaven irritated her. It was a nice thought, but she didn't see the point in getting a man's hopes up about some fairy-tale future. Then she'd heard them laughing, and she'd peeked around the door and had seen the beginning of joy in George Broussard's eyes, and she decided that, fairy tale or not, it had chased the shadows from the grieving man's face. She didn't know how he was as a preacher, but Nick Foster would make a great shrink. Empty fairy tales or not, if hope made the man feel better, then she supposed she wasn't against it.

Miscarriages, two babies, the Lord leaving Tommy behind, the idea of reuniting a family of five when on earth it had only been a family of three . . .

Funny thing about Christians, she thought. They always managed to see good in the most awful circumstances. At least, some of them did. It beat everything she'd ever seen. Either they were master pretenders or master self-deceivers.

She went back into the kitchen, only to find the other men at the table with their heads bowed as Dan Nichols led them in a prayer of thanks for the food she had cooked. Shaking her head in frustration, she took off her apron, grabbed her sweater, and decided to go for a walk before she came back to do the dishes.

Chapter Forty-Seven

● ● ●

Allie was amazed at how quickly Mark had been able to bounce back from his run-in with the killer's bullet. He had gotten up and walked around the day after they'd moved him into a room, had eaten a full meal that afternoon, and had visited with his father who had come to visit. It was clear that Eddie had been drinking, but Mark was used to it, and didn't even let that bother him. Though he complained of a headache only when asked, he had insisted repeatedly that he felt well enough to go home.

The doctor told her that the minimal damage caused by the bullet did indicate a quick recovery, and that, under the circumstances, he thought Mark might actually recover more quickly if he and Allie were in a safer, less public location than a hospital. But he cautioned her not to let Mark get carried away—he had lost a lot of blood and was still in danger of infection. He needed rest, lots of it, and a stress-free environment.

But he didn't sleep well that night and seemed tired the next day as she loaded the car with their suitcases and flowers. Allie told herself his fatigue had more to do with his insomnia than with the trauma itself. His head was still bandaged, but the bruising around his eyes was clearing to yellow patches.

They said good-bye to T.J., who needed to get some rest before his next shift as a cop. They had agreed not to hire a replacement, since they had a good hiding place. Money was a problem—they just couldn't afford to keep a bodyguard. Still, Allie hoped they were doing the right thing.

Allie was jumpy as she drove across New Orleans, heading for the French Quarter apartment Aunt Aggie had loaned them. She watched her rearview mirror for some sign that they were being followed.

When they reached Canal Street, Mark told her to pull over.

"What?" she asked.

"Pull over. Right up there, next to that purple sign."

"But the apartment is still a few blocks over."

"I know. But I need to stop here. There's something I want to buy."

She did as he told her, even as she protested. "Celia stocked the apartment, Mark. We don't need to buy anything."

"Yes, we do."

As she pulled over next to the purple sign, she saw that they were parked in front of a pawn shop. She looked at him, confused. "Mark, what do you want here?"

"I'm buying a gun," he said, his tone brooking no debate.

She hated guns, always had, and the thought of having one in their possession frightened her. "Why a pawn shop? This isn't the best place to buy a gun."

"Because there's a seven-day waiting period in this state, Allie, and I don't have seven days to wait."

"So you're going to buy one illegally?"

"Yes. And if they want to lock me up for protecting my wife and myself—especially after I've been shot in the head—more power to them."

"Mark, are you sure? I don't like it."

"Yes. I'm going to protect you, Allie. And the only way to do it is to be armed, just like he's armed."

She let out a heavy breath. "But I don't know if I even believe in guns. It doesn't seem like Christians ought to be pistol packers. Jesus said, 'He who lives by the sword, dies by the sword.'"

"That's right. But look." He opened her purse, and pulled out the small Bible he knew she carried there. She waited as he flipped through to Nehemiah. "I was thinking about this yesterday, and praying about it, and I ran across this passage. Look here at chapter 4, verses 13 and 14. Nehemiah knew that the enemies of the Israelites were going to attack them to keep them from rebuilding the wall, and he says, 'Therefore I stationed some of the people behind the lowest points of the wall at the exposed places, posting them by families, with their swords, spears and bows. After I looked things over, I stood up and said to the nobles, the officials and the rest of the people, "Don't be afraid of them. Remember the Lord, who is great and awesome, and fight for your brothers, your sons and your daughters, your wives and your homes."'"

Tears came to her eyes as she watched him studying those verses again. Was her husband praying again? Was he searching the Word for his answers? As much as the thought moved her, she found it hard to believe that the Holy Spirit had led him to break a law.

He brought his soft eyes back up to her. "They can have my home, and my brothers can fend for themselves, and I don't have sons and daughters. But I plan to fight for my wife, Allie. I plan to fight with all I've got."

An unbridled warmth gushed through her. She reached across the van and touched his face.

"We need a gun, Allie. I'm not gonna go off the deep end and start waving it at everything that moves. But I need a defense."

"Okay," she whispered.

He swallowed and held her eyes for a moment longer. "It's not that I think we won't be safe there. We will be safe. He won't know where we are."

"I know."

"I'll just sleep better tonight."

She nodded. "I understand."

"Good." He opened the door and, weakly, got out. She hurried around the van to help him, but he waved her off.

"I'm okay."

She opened the door for him, and she tried to shove back her doubts as they both went in to buy the gun that they hoped would defend them from any more attempts on their lives.

Chapter Forty-Eight

● ● ●

If she had custom-ordered a perfect little romantic getaway, Allie could not have found an apartment more pleasing. Located on the outskirts of the French Quarter, away from the sleazy shops and loud bars, the apartment was on the second story. It had a sweet balcony that was covered in blooming jasmine, with antique wrought-iron chairs and a little round table.

Celia had left a fire in the fireplace—for effect, Allie imagined, since there was only a touch of chill in the air and no need for a fire. But it lit the romantically decorated living room in a yellow glow, and the little lanterns around the room accented that light. Hanging baskets of ferns and schefflera, and pots of vinca and impatiens in every shade of the rainbow colored the small rooms. The place was fragrant with floral scents, much like Allie's shop.

"This is perfect," Mark whispered, sinking down on the overstuffed couch that faced the fire. He pulled off his shoes and socks and let his bare feet slide across the lush carpet. "Absolutely perfect. We owe Aunt Aggie one."

Allie crossed the living room to the two doors on the opposite wall. She felt Mark's eyes watching her as she opened a door and peered in. "The bathroom," she told him. "It's lovely. An antique tub with claw feet, and a separate shower." She went to the next door and opened it.

It was the one and only bedroom, with a four-poster bed with a canopy, and lacy mosquito curtains hanging to the ground from the canopy and draped back with satin ribbons.

The bedspread, too, was made of satin and lace, as were the curtains.

She stepped into the room, taking in the sight of the scented candles around the room, the bright throw rugs on the floor, the Tiffany lamps.

"Beautiful." The voice came from behind her in a whisper, and she turned and saw that Mark had followed her in.

She swallowed. "It sure is."

He went to the bed, sat on the edge, then after a moment, pulled his feet up and lay down. His eyes slowly closed. "This sure beats a hospital bed."

She stepped up to the bed and ran her hand along the bedspread. "Yeah, and that couch sure beats that hospital cot. Maybe we'll both get some sleep tonight."

She started to walk away to check out the kitchen, but he reached out and caught her hand. His reflexes were quick for a wounded man, she thought, but she didn't tell him so. She found that she couldn't speak at all.

"You must be tired," he whispered. "Sleeping in a chair in the waiting room, and then on some vinyl cot."

"Yeah, a little."

"You're not sleeping on any couch tonight," he said. "That's silly."

She didn't know what to say. "I don't mind. That way you can stretch out. You need your rest, Mark."

He scooted over on the bed and pulled her on it beside him. She sat on her knees for a moment, looking down at him. "I can't rest unless you're beside me. That's the only way I can be sure you're safe."

That was true. She hadn't thought of the safety issue, but her heart's safety was what worried her now.

"Lie down," he coaxed in a voice that mesmerized her. "Come on. Just lie here with me for a minute."

She felt silly arguing with him about it, especially when she really was so tired, and the bed seemed so inviting. Slowly, she stretched out and lowered her head to the pillow.

He slid his arm under her neck, and pulled her onto her side until they were facing each other. Their eyes locked in longing, but neither of them could speak of it.

"I should fix you something to eat," she whispered. "You must be starving."

"No," he said, closing his eyes. "I'm not. Just stay here. Be still."

He scooted closer, until their knees were touching, and their faces were centimeters apart. He wrapped his arms around her.

She watched him as his eyes drifted shut, as his breathing slowed, as his body slowly relaxed next to her.

Such love burst through her that she thought she might weep at the very thought of it. As tears came to her eyes, she closed them, and felt the anxiety and stress and tension seep out of her, as well. For the first time in over two months, she felt as if she was truly home.

Safe in his arms, she let herself fall asleep.

Chapter Forty-Nine

● ● ●

The boys at Midtown Station were glad to see Aunt Aggie when she arrived that afternoon to make dinner. As if she'd been gone a week, they convened in the kitchen to find out where she'd been during the lunch hour that day, when they'd wound up having to order pizza.

"Was on the Southshore," she announced as she began to chop celery. "Girl needs culture ever now and then, you know."

Craig Barnes sat at the table with a clipboard, studying some paperwork he'd brought from his office. He looked tired, worn; they all did. Nick looked tiredest of all, and she pitied him. Dan Nichols had dark circles under his eyes, and she wondered if he was getting any sleep at all.

"Did you see Mark while you were there?" Dan asked her, sliding out a chair and sitting in it backwards.

She glanced at him over her shoulder. He had folded his arms over the back of the chair and propped his chin on it. She had long considered him the best-looking firefighter of the bunch, but he was looking a little worn around the edges, if you asked her. "Yep. Just before they let him out."

"He's out?" Craig Barnes asked, looking up. "This soon? How can that be?"

"You know them hospitals," she said. "They slap a Band-Aid on you and send you home."

"So is he back in Newpointe?" Craig asked.

"Not home, home. They stayin' in my apartment there. Me and Celia, we fixed it up, stocked the kitchen. They'll be fine there."

"You have an apartment in New Orleans?" Craig asked. "I didn't know that."

"There's a lot about me you fellas don't know. I got a life, you know. I like to go to the city ever now and then and take in a show or the opera. Don't just spend all my time cookin' for the likes of you, you know."

"Where in New Orleans?" Dan asked.

It wasn't until then that she realized she had said too much. Should she have told anyone that Mark and Allie were staying in her apartment? Could she really trust everyone here?

"Never mind. Mark and Allie are hiding, don't forget. I ain't gonna go around spoutin' out where they are to nobody who asks. Not with that killer runnin' loose shootin' people at airports and in their mothers' homes. Just makes your skin crawl to think about it."

"How are Allie and Mark getting along?" Craig asked, getting up and flipping with preoccupation through his papers.

"Nothin' like a bullet in the head to bond a couple. They might just work things out." Aggie nodded her head emphatically. "Yep, they just might."

Chapter Fifty

• • •

Mark woke at eight P.M. and found the apartment bathed in darkness. Both of them had apparently slept so deeply that they hadn't even awakened to eat. He opened his eyes and tried to let them adjust to the night. It took a moment for him to orient himself to the big four-poster bed with the white lace mosquito netting—and his wife lying beside him. She was on her side facing him, deep in sleep, and she looked angelic in repose. Though she was still fully dressed, as he was, all of the tense lines seemed to have melted from her face, and she was completely relaxed, her rhythmic breathing making her shoulder rise and fall. He smiled at the way one fingertip touched her lip in sleep. She probably didn't even know she did that. He had forgotten, but now it brought back such warmth, such personal truth, that his eyes filled with tears.

He didn't know how long he lay there watching her sleep, but eventually he realized that he was not going to be able to go back to sleep himself.

He reached for the gun he'd set on the table beside the bed, slid it into his pocket, and sat up on the edge of the mattress. His head ached, and he felt a little dizzy, but he got up and felt his way to the door. Closing it quietly behind him, he groped in the darkness for a lamp, found one, and clicked it on.

It bathed the room in a soft yellow hue and calmed the unease stirring in him. He padded across the lush carpet to the kitchen, looked in the refrigerator, and saw all the treasures Celia and Aunt Aggie had put there. He pulled out some cold cuts, lettuce and tomato, found the bread, and made a sandwich. It was the best thing he'd eaten since the killings had begun.

When he finished, he cleaned up, then went to the window and peered out between the blinds. The street was quiet, and a damp fog hung around the street lanterns, lending an eerie feel to the night. He saw their car parked on the street, and he suddenly wished they had rented a different one in case the killer was out looking for them, searching for their car in parking lots.

He shivered and abandoned the window.

He needed to go back to bed and bury himself in sleep, but suddenly he was too tense. He needed a drink. Just one drink would relax him, and then he could lie back down with Allie and sleep until morning.

He went to the refrigerator, sifted through the contents, and found a bottle of Chablis back in the corner. Good old Aunt Aggie. She'd known just what he needed. He pulled the bottle out and began searching the drawers for a corkscrew.

He moved quietly, so he wouldn't wake Allie; he didn't want her to catch him with the wine. It wouldn't help the already fragile situation. They had come so far in the past few days, and he never again wanted to see that look in her eyes he'd seen when they'd been at the diner before they'd gone to the airport the other day, when he'd perused the wine list, and she'd acted as if he was ordering up a syringe of heroin.

Unbidden, from somewhere in left field, thoughts of his childhood came to his mind. He remembered waking up in the night and going to the bathroom. He'd heard his father milling around in the kitchen. Rubbing his eyes, Mark had gone to see what he was doing. Entering the kitchen, Mark had startled his father so badly that he'd dropped the bottle of bourbon he was drinking from, which had shattered all over the floor, along with the bitter-smelling liquid. His father had cursed and sent him back to bed, and then he'd heard his mother getting up to see what had happened, and the fight had begun . . .

It had always been the same. His father was always the wounded party, misunderstood, not trusted. And his mother would apologize meekly to keep the peace, and pretend the next day that nothing had ever happened.

Had his father once been like him, drinking only occasionally, but getting up in the middle of the night and searching the kitchen for something alcoholic?

His heart sank, and he closed the drawer, abandoning the search for the corkscrew, and returned the wine bottle to the refrigerator. He didn't need it. He wasn't like his father.

He sank onto the couch and tried to think. They said that alcoholism was genetic, but he'd never believed it. Weakness could be genetic. Self-pity might even be inherited. And what about cowardice? Wasn't that what really led his father to drink? A fear of confronting the real issues of life that plagued him and everyone else on the planet?

He was different than that, he told himself. He knew better. He knew Christ. But maybe Christ had turned his back on him. Wasn't there a place in Revelation that talked about God spitting us out of his mouth?

Suddenly, he felt the overpowering urge to find that passage, study it, and determine whether God had already done that with him. Maybe that was why he'd been shot. Maybe he was being punished . . . or maybe God's protection had been lifted from him. Maybe the Lord was trying to teach him something.

He took Allie's little Bible from her purse. Going back to the lamp next to the couch, he flipped through the book until he came to Revelation. He scanned the letters to the churches and paused at chapter two, at the beginning of the red letters denoting Christ's words, and read the letter to the church in Ephesus. Praise, commendation, approval. But then he came to the rebuke, and he sat up straight and read the words out loud, realizing they were meant for him, that God had led him to this page tonight.

"Yet I hold this against you: You have forsaken your first love."

Sitting out behind the firehouse just a few nights ago with Ray—it seemed a lifetime ago—he had asked his friend what he thought of him now. And Ray had answered Mark with those very words.

"Maybe, just maybe, you've forsaken your first love."

And Mark had totally misunderstood. He grimaced, touching his forehead. That just showed how far from God he had truly strayed. He had thought Ray meant only that he had forsaken Allie. But Ray had been commenting on much more than that. It was his relationship with Christ that Mark had forsaken.

Mark turned the page and read on.

"Remember the height from which you have fallen! Repent and do the things you did at first."

What were those things? For one, Mark had abstained from alcohol, not wanting to repeat his father's mistakes. He had worshiped regularly. He had loved God and others. He had cherished his wife.

He read on, each of the letters to the churches, both the praise and the reprimands. He read God's warning that he would spit them out of his mouth, and he read that God rebukes and disciplines those he loves. Was the Fire Wife Killer God's way of rebuking Mark? Had God raised up a murderer—snuffing out lives, taking mothers from their babies, wives from their husbands, daughters from their parents—just to punish Mark for straying from his walk with Christ?

In his confusion, he cried out to God, and he felt the still, peaceful voice of his Savior whispering that the consequences Mark had created himself were discipline enough. Separation from God, the darkness of divorce, loneliness, regret, fear— those were disciplines that would teach him to follow Christ. But the evil wrought by a murderer's bullets were not part of some avalanche of judgment by an angry God. The father had not sent hit men to torment the Prodigal Son. He had allowed him the suffering he'd brought on himself, but all the while, he'd been watching, waiting, hoping for his return.

Wiping tears from his eyes to clear his vision, Mark read on, praying that God would show him his way back, that he would have the strength to get things right. There were things in his heart he had to pull out and hold under the light, things he had made into lies that had rubbed calluses on his heart.

Issie. Allie had accused him, and he'd hidden behind his righteous indignation, telling himself and Allie and even God that he'd been falsely condemned. He'd comforted himself with that thought when she'd asked him to leave. It had been his self-acquittal, his excuse for not keeping his commitment to love and honor her.

What had Allie ever really wanted from him? Fidelity. And he had sworn that he had been faithful to her.

But she had known better.

He wept harder as he closed his eyes and recalled the late-night talks with Issie, when they had bared their souls, even if their bodies had been clothed. He had shared intimacies with her in the form of conversation, had told her unflattering things about Allie, had told her just how unhappy he was in his marriage. He had enjoyed the attentions the pretty woman had shown him, had enjoyed the flutter of his heart when she had smiled at him or flirted with him, had appreciated that she wanted to spend time with him.

For so long, he had told himself they were just friends. But now he realized how deeply he had wounded Allie with that friendship. What would he have felt if he had walked in on Allie in another man's arms? Would he have listened if she'd told him it had been innocent? Would the fact that nothing more physical had happened really matter to him if she'd been unfaithful in her heart?

Lord, show me what to do, he prayed through his tears. *Help me get it right.*

And for the first time in his life, he read the Bible like a starving man, searching for words addressed to him, and answers that could restore him.

Chapter Fifty-One

● ● ●

Even though it was only eight-thirty, Aggie had shut off all the lights and was upstairs in bed reading when she was startled by the sound of a door closing quietly. For a moment, she thought she had dreamed it, but then she heard something else: the sound of a drawer closing, the floor creaking as someone moved across it . . .

She sat up in bed, listening, and didn't hear anything for several moments. Maybe it had been her imagination. But she'd never imagined anyone in her house before.

Quickly, she got up, grabbed the poker from the fireplace in her bedroom, and started down the stairs.

She heard a sound again, the sound of the drawer closing in her study. Someone was in there, she thought as she waited halfway down the staircase. The killer? The thought made her heart flip into triple-time, and she reached out for the banister to steady herself.

She heard another drawer close quietly; the sound of the rollers moving in and out on her file cabinet drawers was unmistakable. Summoning all of her courage and hoping her heart could stand it, she tiptoed toward the study, her poker raised, and saw that the door was closed.

She never closed that door.

She wanted to scream, wanted to run and call the police, wanted to burst into that room and catch whoever had had the gall to break into her home. But what if he had a gun aimed at the door, waiting for her? She would wind up the next victim, dead on the floor as he set fire to her house and burned it down around her.

She froze, unwilling and unable to move. She heard papers rustling. What was he looking for? Then she heard the sound of the window being raised, then shut again.

Silence followed, and she waited, still not moving. Had he gone out the window? Is that how he had come in?

Of course he had. Anyone who drove by could see that her front windows were usually open an inch or two this time of year, before it got too muggy and she had to depend on air conditioning. What if he came back?

Forcing herself, she slowly, carefully, pushed the study door open. The room was just as she had left it.

The windows were slightly open, as usual—except for one, which was closed. Was that the one he had gone out?

Quickly, she slammed all of the windows down, locked them, then rushed for the telephone. She dialed Stan and Celia's house.

"Hello?" It was Stan, wakened from sleep, but she made no apology.

"Stan, he was here. Somebody—maybe the killer. He come in my house, and he went out a window, and I didn't see him, but I heard him—"

"Whoa, wait a minute. Aunt Aggie, is that you?"

"Yes! Stan, come over here. Maybe there's fingerprints on the window or on my desk. I heard drawers openin'. Maybe the file cabinet. Maybe you could catch him now before he get too far."

"Aunt Aggie, I'll be right over. Meanwhile, don't let anyone in until I get there, okay? Don't touch anything. And lock those windows."

"Already did. What he wants with me? He killin' the wives of dead firemen, too?"

"If it was the killer and he wanted you dead, you'd be dead."

Aggie shivered at the realization of how close she had come.

Chapter Fifty-Two

● ● ●

By 9:30 Mark had managed to read all of First, Second, and Third John, as well as Jude, James, and First and Second Peter ... when the lamp began to flicker.

He checked the bulb to see if it was screwed in tightly, found that it was, then went back to his reading.

The lamp flickered again, and this time went out. He got up and fumbled for the cord, followed it in the darkness to the plug, and found that it was still plugged in.

Feeling his way to the bedroom door, he slid his hand across the wall until he found the light switch. He flicked it up, but there was still no light.

Had they somehow tripped a breaker? He stood in the dark for a moment, wondering where the breaker box was. Maybe the kitchen. He began working his way toward it. He stubbed his toe on a table he didn't remember being there, tripped on a cord, knocked over a plant. Finally, he made it to the kitchen and tried the switch there. Still no light. Was this entire apartment on a single breaker? He wished for a flashlight, but didn't have a clue where Aunt Aggie might keep one.

He was sliding his hand across the wall, feeling for the breaker box, when he heard a sound outside. Someone was at the door, scratching on the lock.

He pulled the pistol out of his pocket and groped for the telephone he'd seen hanging on the wall. Miraculously, his hand closed over it, and he jerked it up.

No dial tone.

His heart jolted, and he thought of running to the bedroom, waking Allie up, putting her out through the window onto the fire escape. But there was no time. The doorknob was turning, the door was pushing open—

He raised the gun, and in the darkness watched and waited for someone to come through. He smelled the faint scent of diesel as a shadowy form came into the room and bent over to set something down. A canister of some sort? A gas can?

His hand trembled, his head ached, and he felt dizzy as he stood frozen, holding that gun on the man who seemed unaware that he stood there, watching him. The man straightened and, like a shadow in the dark, started to steal through the room.

"Hold it right there, pal." The words sounded alien, distant, but Mark knew he had uttered them. A strange peace fell over him—whether from God's strength or from his own weakness he wasn't sure—but as the man twisted quickly toward him, a dim ray of light from a street lamp outside partially illuminated him. A fire mask covered the man's face. He was wearing bunker pants and boots, a bunker coat, and carrying oxygen on his back—all the things a firefighter would wear when fighting a fire.

The sight was staggering, and he almost lowered the gun—until he saw the man go for his own. Mark had no time to think, only to react, and his finger closed over the trigger, smoothly, quickly, without hesitation.

The gun went off, and the man fell backward.

He heard Allie scream behind the closed bedroom door, and he yelled, "Go out the fire escape, Allie, and call the police!"

If there was a response from Allie, Mark had no time to hear it. The man got to his feet and launched himself at Mark, knocking him to the floor. Mark's head jarred slightly with the impact, but he managed to stay conscious and keep fighting. The man's right arm was slick with blood, and he no longer held his gun. He lunged for Mark's gun, an ironclad grip on his wrist cutting off his circulation, challenging him to let it go.

Mark kicked him in the groin with his knee, making the bleeding man recoil. Still on the floor, Mark kicked him again in the right shoulder. The anguished groan that followed told Mark that his kick was aptly aimed, and the man loosened his grip on Mark's wrist, allowing Mark to roll away from him. Mark fired the gun again, but he knew even as he pulled the trigger that his shot would miss.

The man rolled away. Mark sat up and tried to shake the dizziness away. He heard a clattering. Something cold splashed against Mark's legs. He recognized the smell of diesel fuel. Mark could hear it gurgling out of the can, soaking into the carpet, into his jeans. He fired again in the darkness, but the bullet smashed into the wall. He heard a match striking, saw the flame ignite, saw it being thrown his way—

The carpet in front of him ignited, throwing him back. Flames erupted on his legs—

He fired the gun at a shadow on the far side of the flames, then hit the ground again and rolled, trying to put out the fire on his skin. He grabbed an afghan draped over the couch and smothered the flames on his body. Scalding agony charged through his body, but he tried to find the man through the flames again, to aim the gun and finish the job he had started.

He was gone.

"Allie!" Mark screamed, staggering back to his feet and running into the bedroom as the fire raged behind him. If Allie had gone out the fire escape, as he'd told her, the killer might have caught her by now. "*Allie!*"

The window was open, and she was gone.

Chapter Fifty-Three

• • •

The moment the gunshot woke her, Allie had heard Mark yelling for her to escape. Without hesitation, she had done what he'd said and gone to the window. After several tugs she managed to get it open, hurled herself out, and half-ran, half-tumbled down the steps of the fire escape to the ground. She tore around the building to the front doors and banged on the first one she saw with a light on. A couple of doors down, a man came out, and other neighbors emerged. She grabbed one of them and pleaded for their telephone.

Even as she spoke to the 911 operators, she saw the killer running down the steps of Aunt Aggie's apartment, dressed like a fireman answering the call. He headed up the sidewalk, blending into the shadows until she lost him. "He's running up Bienville in a fireman's hat and mask, and full bunkers like a fireman wears. Please—you've got to catch him. He's the Fire Wife Killer from Newpointe. Please hurry!"

"Ma'am, there's smoke coming from your apartment," the neighbor shouted. "I think there's a fire up there. We have to wake everyone in the building!"

Her heart raced as she told the operator to send a fire truck and ambulance, too, then took the fire extinguisher the neighbor thrust at her, and hurried up the stairs, praying that Mark was all right.

The apartment door was open when she got there; flames engulfed the carpet. From somewhere, she heard Mark's voice screaming for her. "Allie! *Allie!*"

"Mark, I'm here!" she called as she pulled the pin on the fire extinguisher and began to spray the flames. "Are you all right?"

"He got away!" Mark cried as he came out of the bedroom. "But I shot him. He's wounded. Maybe there's a blood trail."

He grabbed the extinguisher from her and quickly doused the flames. Dropping it, he stumbled back against the wall.

"Mark, are you okay?" She touched his face with both hands, trying to examine his bandage in the darkness and smoke.

He was weeping. "Thank God. Thank God he didn't get you."

He pulled her against him and held her, sobbing, until the police arrived. They came up the steps with flashlights, several of them shining their beams on the charred carpet as firefighters pushed into the apartment to make sure the fire was completely extinguished.

A paramedic stepped in front of them. "I need to look at those burns."

"Mark, you're hurt!" Allie cried, seeing the burns for the first time.

"I'm okay," he said. "I put it out real quick." Wiping the tears from his face, he raised his voice so the police could hear. "I shot him in the right arm or shoulder. There's got to be a blood trail—enough for a DNA test. This is the guy who's killing our wives."

The paramedics rolled in a gurney. "We need to take you to the hospital for these burns," they told him.

"No," Mark said. "I'm not going back to the hospital. I just got out. Treat the burns here with whatever you've got, and I'll be fine. I have to talk with Stan Shepherd. He'll want to hear what I've got to say."

Chapter Fifty-Four

• • •

Stan searched Aunt Aggie's house for evidence of the burglar's identity, but found none. There were no fingerprints, no footprints, and nothing taken—nothing except a few missing files from Aunt Aggie's file cabinet. She had determined that the files were nothing more than paid bills for everything from credit cards to her utilities.

He was looking for something, Stan thought, racking his brain for what that could be. A credit card number, or a bank account, or . . . an address.

His heart began pounding. Could it be that he knew Mark and Allie were staying in Aunt Aggie's apartment in New Orleans? If so, they were in serious trouble.

"Aunt Aggie, what's the number of your apartment in the Quarter?"

She rattled off the number, and he quickly dialed it.

"You think he was after that?" she asked. "You think he goin' after them?"

The phone began to ring, and he waited. "Was there anything in those files that would have that address?"

"I don't know. Well . . . yes. The records of them realtor fees. It would have the address. Oh, Stan!"

The phone kept ringing, unanswered. "Why aren't they answering?" he asked. "Is there a phone in the bedroom?"

"Yes. You don't think the line was cut—"

He finally hung up and dialed the number for Blanc's office at the Kenner Police Department. Blanc wasn't in. Quickly he dialed the number for the New Orleans police. "This is Detective Stan Shepherd, Newpointe P.D. I need for you to get a patrol car to this address." He gave them the address of the apartment, and explained his fears. They told him they'd check on Mark and Allie and get back to him.

He took Aunt Aggie to stay with Celia at his own house. Celia had a gun and had been instructed on how to use it. Then he headed back to the police station, a terrible sense of dread making him feel helpless and useless.

His cellular phone rang, and he jerked it up. "Stan Shepherd."

"Stan, this is Mark. You're not gonna believe what's happened."

"Mark, are you all right? I tried to call. I think the killer may know where you are—"

"You think right. I had a run-in with our man tonight, but he got away. Stan, he was wearing a complete bunker suit with a mask. I think you need to consider that this guy is a fireman."

"I already have," Stan said. "Mark, what happened?"

"I got him before he got me. Shot him through the arm or shoulder, and then he threw diesel fuel on the carpet and set fire to it. He got away, but the police are looking for blood evidence now. I'm at the station—Eighth District on Royal Street."

"Is Allie all right?"

"Yes, thank the Lord. She's fine."

"Were you burned?"

"Yeah, but not bad. Stan, did you say you'd already considered that this guy is one of us?"

"Yes. We have other witnesses who saw a guy dressed in Newpointe bunkers. Susan told me she saw the guy wearing a bunker coat and mask, and an airport employee saw a man in a gray fireman's uniform."

There was a stunned silence. Finally, Mark said, "Stan, don't you think that information might have been pertinent to those of us hiding for our lives?"

"Of course it was pertinent, Mark, but I couldn't start a scare. I didn't want the press stringing up some poor innocent guy and keeping us from nailing it down to the real one."

"I'm not the press, Stan. I needed to know this!"

"Mark, I'm doing the best I can. It was against my better judgment—"

"So do you know who the killer is?" Mark cut in, his voice teetering on the edge of rage. "Or are you going to keep that to yourself, too? You think you might let me in on it before I'm six feet under?"

Stan closed his eyes. "No, Mark, I don't know. Not yet, but I've managed to narrow it down a little."

"Stan, if you don't tell me *something*, so help me—"

"I will, but not on the phone, Mark. In fact, if you're feeling up to it, I need you and Allie here. I'll arrange a squad car to get you here."

"Fine," Mark said. "Whatever it takes to get this guy locked up. I don't care who he is."

"You might when you hear my hunches."

Mark got quiet again.

"Look, put one of the cops there on the phone so I can set up your trip home and compare notes with those guys."

"All right," Mark said. "You'll be there when we get there?"

"I'm not going anywhere," Stan said. "I've got a job to do."

Chapter Fifty-Five

● ● ●

The highway patrolman who drove Allie and Mark back to Newpointe was fascinated with the "Fire Wife Killer" case. He grilled them—and, since he had nothing to do with the case, Allie felt that his questions were based on mere morbid curiosity. He would get a lot of great gossip out of this.

"So you got brain damage from that bullet?" he asked around the tobacco stuck in his bottom lip.

"No," Mark said, trying to be patient. "I'm fine."

"You think fine now. But you still gon' be as sharp as you was before?"

"I don't know," Mark said. "I guess I wasn't all that sharp before. Probably won't be able to tell a difference."

Allie grinned.

"I mean, you cain't get shot in the noggin without havin' somethin' wrong with you afterwards."

"He's really fine," Allie said. "Please, he needs to rest."

Gratefully, Mark laid his head back on the seat and closed his eyes.

The patrolman peered at her in the rearview mirror. "I reckon you must be scared t' death, ma'am. Dude poppin' off them wives one by one, tryin' t' get t' you. You don't have no idea who it might be?"

"No idea," she said.

"Some psychopath from up north. They like to come south to do their killin'. Them Jeffrey Dahmer types."

"Dahmer didn't come south," Mark said.

"May have," the patrolman said. "Maybe they just ain't found the bodies. What kind of crazy would wanna leave a trail of dead firemen's wives? Downright bizarre. I heard he tortured 'em first, at least the ones he killed. Fed 'em dope and made 'em drink diesel—"

"That's not true," Allie said hotly.

"What I heard." The man spat into a Styrofoam cup on the seat next to him. "Don't know why my sources at N.O.P.D. would lie. They'd know, since they're investigatin' the case."

Mark's face was turning red, the most color Allie had seen on it in days. "The only part of this case *they've* investigated had to do with me, so why don't you just shut up and drive?"

Allie tried to suppress her grin as the patrolman muttered a benign apology, then did just what Mark suggested.

The car was quiet for a while, except for the roar of the engine, the crackle of the radio, and the occasional call that came through it.

"You okay?" Allie whispered to Mark.

"Yeah," he said.

"Tired?"

"Yeah. Thinking about what Stan said."

"About it being a fireman?" she whispered.

"Yeah," he said quietly. "That, and the possibility that I might be close to the killer."

She stiffened in surprise. "He said that?"

"Not in so many words."

"Then what?"

"He said I might not like hearing who he's narrowed it down to."

She got quiet a moment, her mind running over the men at the station, assessing them one by one. The thought that it could be a good friend gave her chills. "You're close to Ray, and it couldn't be him, since Susan was one of the victims. Nick isn't a killer. And you're best friends with Dan, but it obviously isn't him."

Mark was too quiet, too pensive, and she watched his face as he struggled through the possibilities. "Mark, you don't think it's one of them, do you?"

"Let's just see what Stan says," he told her.

• • •

It was 11:30 when Allie and Mark arrived in Newpointe. Stan was waiting for them in the interrogation room with a stack of files spread out on the table in front of him. He leapt to his feet when they came in, giving Mark a once-over from the smoke-stained, bloody bandage on his head to the charred remains of his jeans and the burns visible through the holes and rips. "Mark, you look awful."

"Thanks, man. You don't look so hot yourself."

"You should be in bed, if not the hospital."

"I want this guy caught first, Stan. Then I'll go to bed." He sank carefully into a chair, and Allie poured him a glass of water, then took the seat next to him.

"Stan, Mark said that you'd narrowed it down," she said. "Who are the suspects?"

Stan set both hands palm-down on the table. "I spoke to the detective at N.O.P.D. a few minutes ago, and they collected some blood samples from the carpet, the stairs, and the sidewalk. I'm about to send some of our uniforms out to bring three guys in for questioning. First thing we're looking for, of course, is the wound. That with hair fibers and a blood sample should satisfy any jury and get us a conviction."

"Just arrest him," Mark said weakly. "Get him off the street. Then worry about getting a conviction. My wife has been through enough."

Amazed, Allie looked at her husband—at the bandage on his head, at the pale cast to his skin and the burns on his legs. And he thought that *she* had been through enough?

"I need to ask you and Allie a few things," Stan said, rubbing his red, fatigued eyes. "First, who did you tell where you were staying?"

"No one. Absolutely no one. Only Aunt Aggie and Celia knew."

"I've already talked to them. Aunt Aggie said she did mention to some of the firemen that she had loaned you her apartment. But she didn't say where it was. Tonight, her house was broken into. Nothing was stolen except a couple of files from her file cabinet. My guess is they were looking for an address."

Mark leaned forward, his face intense. "Who was in the room when she told them?"

"Nick Foster, Dan Nichols, Slater Finch, Craig Barnes, Cale Larkins, Jacob Baxter, and Junior Reynolds."

"Seven people?" Mark asked, growing angry again. "Stan, if you'd *told* her it was a fireman, she wouldn't have spouted off like that. What were you thinking, keeping this information to yourself?"

Stan bristled and raised a cautionary hand. "I didn't know for sure. Now, do you want to hear the rest or not?"

Mark took a deep breath and nodded for him to go on.

"She said a couple of them asked her where the house was, but she wouldn't tell."

"A couple of them? Who?"

"Dan and Craig."

"Well, they were probably concerned. Both of them. Maybe they went out and mentioned it to someone else, who then broke into Aunt Aggie's house and came after us. It's not Dan—he's my best friend. He was with Allie all night when I was in intensive care, the night Francis Bledsoe was killed. And the chief of the fire department? Give me a break. These killings have caused him a ton of problems. Why would he do something like this?"

"There's another suspect," Stan said. "Marty Bledsoe."

Mark's mouth fell open, and Allie gasped. "Stan, you can't be serious," she said. "His own wife was a victim."

"But his account of her murder is suspicious," Stan said. "He didn't see or hear anything, didn't feel her body jolting when it was hit. Don't you find that odd?"

"Why would he kill the mother of his twins?" Mark asked. "Stan, *think*. It doesn't make sense. None of these guys could have done it!"

"I've checked everybody's whereabouts for each murder," Stan went on. "Around the time of Martha's murder, Dan was out jogging, and no one can confirm it. Marty and Craig both showed up at the parade late. When Jamie was killed, no one's sure where Craig was, and Dan claims he was home alone—no one can confirm that—and Marty was supposedly at home, but since Francis isn't here to confirm it, we can only take his word for it. We aren't sure who was at the funerals when, so we can't say if any of them could have left or come late after shooting Susan."

"What did you do? Ask them all for alibis?"

"No. I asked for an account of who was on duty during each emergency, and where they were if they were off duty. I told them the prosecutor might need to call some of them as witnesses. No one questioned it. Once I had their answers, I tried to confirm them."

Allie still looked disturbed. "Stan, what about the night Francis was killed? Dan was at the hospital with me that night."

"Allie, are you sure that Dan didn't leave at any time during the night that he stayed with you? Even for a couple of hours?"

"Positive. Both Jill and I were there. He didn't leave."

"Didn't you sleep at all?"

"Well, yeah. But not deeply. I would have known if he'd left for that amount of time." But even as she spoke, a memory seemed to come back to her.

Mark saw the change on her face.

"What?" he asked.

She looked at Mark, shaking her head. "He didn't do it," she said. "He's not a killer. But I was just thinking—one time when I woke up, he was coming back from somewhere, and he told Jill he'd been outside the door in the hallway, reading. Jill and I had both been sleeping. I didn't think anything of it, just went back to sleep."

"And you don't know how long he'd been gone?"

"Not long."

"How do you know, if you were asleep?"

She thought about it for a long moment. "Well, if it was him, why didn't he just kill me then? Why would he sit up with me all night? It doesn't make sense."

"No, it sure doesn't," Mark said. "I trusted him with my wife. He wouldn't have hurt Allie, or me for that matter. But neither would Craig or Marty."

"Mark, Allie, remember the night that we set up the stake-out in your house, hoping to lure the killer?"

"Yes," Allie said. "You said Craig Barnes showed up, that he was worried and was checking on me."

"Right. But he parked his car down the street, and he was wearing his bunkers, like he'd just come from a fire. Only I just did a check on emergency calls for that night, and there wasn't a fire within two hours of his showing up there."

Mark and Allie stared at him in disbelief.

"On the same night, Dan Nichols was caught sneaking around your shop with a crowbar in his hand, and there was evidence that someone had tried to break in there. Both men thought Allie was inside."

"Okay, but Dan was on duty when I got shot at the airport," Mark said. "He was on the clock. He couldn't have just left. And Craig was running both Midtown and Eastside. He couldn't have left town, either."

"Yet no one knows where Craig or Dan were at that time. Craig claimed he was at the other station, but no one at either station saw him during that time. At least, not that they can remember, and I have to leave some room for error since these have been hard days and people aren't thinking that clearly. But no one could find Dan, either. He came in some time later, all sweaty, and claimed he'd been out jogging."

"That's possible. He jogs every day," Mark said.

"But isn't it a coincidence that he did it right at the time when he'd need an alibi? And I can't find anyone who saw him."

"Well, what about tonight? Wasn't he working tonight?"

"He was, but he left early. And I sent someone to bring him in for questioning, but he wasn't home. At this hour of morning, where would he be?"

"What about Craig?"

"Not home, either, and not at either station. And Marty's not home, either. His parents live in Metairie, though, so I've sent some men to see if he's there."

"You're kidding."

"Wish I were."

Mark looked as if he was going to be sick, and Allie's eyes filled with tears. Finally, he rubbed his face. "All right, there's one easy way to tell. The killer has a gunshot wound in his arm or shoulder."

"It's none of them, Stan," Allie said. "You're wasting your time, and meanwhile, the killer may be going after someone else."

Chapter Fifty-Six

● ● ●

At first, the banging was part of his dream, a *whop, whop, whop* of a fireman's ax, chopping at wet, smoldering wood ...

Then the dream was gone, and Dan shifted in his bed. The *whop, whop, whop* was coming from the other room, and he raised himself up and looked at the clock. Midnight.

Only then did he realize that someone was banging on his door. Feeling as if he'd just slept off a three-day drunk, he slid out of bed, pulled on the jeans he'd dropped on the floor beside his bed when he'd fallen into it, grabbed a sweater and pulled it on, and stumbled to the door.

"Who is it?" he called through the door.

"Police. Open up!"

Frowning and squinting in the lamplight, he unlatched the door and pulled it open. The two cops standing there were old friends—he'd played football with both of them in high school. "Chad, Vern—what in Sam Hill—do you know what time it is?"

"Why didn't you open the door earlier?" Vern asked him.

"I was asleep. I've been on duty for days and haven't slept much. I haven't caught up yet. How long have you been here?"

"Long enough to think you weren't home."

"Have you been here all night?" Chad asked with a tone of suspicion.

"Well, yeah. Since about seven or so. I was working but I cut my hand—"

Chad and Vern exchanged eloquent looks.

"So they let me come home. What?" Dan asked. "What's going on?"

"We came by earlier and you weren't home."

"When?"

"About an hour and a half ago."

"No way. I was here. I was sleeping. Didn't you see my car? Anyway, what did you want?"

"We have to take you in for questioning," Vern said. "Stan needs to see you."

Dan stared at them for a moment, groggily assessing their faces. "Am I under arrest for something?"

"No. We just need to question you about some things."

"What things?"

Vern stepped into the house and looked around. "We also have a warrant to search your house and your car."

"Search—for *what?*" His eyes followed Vern as he walked from room to room. "Chad, what's going on? Has there been another murder or something?"

"Not a murder, but another attempt."

"Another—who was it?"

"Allie Branning."

"*What*—how is she?"

Chad looked at him suspiciously. "She's fine. They're both okay."

Dan paused for a breathless moment. "And they think *I* did it?"

"They're not jumping to conclusions of any kind, Dan. We just want to ask you some questions."

"Fine. Then ask. Why do you have to search my house and car?"

"Do you have an objection? Something to hide?"

"No!" he yelled. "Search all you want. I have nothing to hide. I just don't understand why you'd think it was me. I've been at the station for the past several days, practically nonstop, except for when I was at the hospital with Mark and Allie. How could I be out killing people?"

Vern looked down at the bloody bandage on Dan's hand. "What's wrong with your hand, Dan?"

"I told you, I hurt it at the station tonight. Cut it on some glass. That's why I called Cale in to replace me."

Chad looked at Vern, again exchanging silent observations. "Dan, would you mind taking off your sweater?"

"My sweater? What for?"

"Just take it off."

Agitated, Dan pulled the sweater off, wondering what in the world they were looking for.

"No wound," Chad said with a note of relief.

"Okay, but remember," Vern said, "people have been known to get overconfident about where and how they wounded someone. It was dark, and his adrenaline was pulsing, and he could have gotten it way wrong."

"Yeah, I know."

"Wounded?" Dan asked. "You think I did it, don't you? You think I've been killing those women. You can't be serious!"

"You're not the only one we're questioning, Dan. You can put your shirt back on now and calm down."

Dan pulled the sweater over his head, shaken and sweating now. "I want to call my lawyer."

•   •   •

The phone woke Jill on the first ring, for she hadn't been sleeping well. She had been too worried about Mark and Allie, and her dreams all night had been plagued with shadows chasing her, chasing Allie, chasing Mark, chasing Martha and Jamie and Susan and Frances.

She lifted up on one elbow and picked up the phone. "Hello?"

"Jill, it's Dan Nichols. I need a lawyer."

"Dan, what's wrong?"

"Vern Hargis and Chad Avery are here to take me into the police station for questioning, but they have a warrant to search my house and car. Jill, I think they're trying to pin these murders on me."

"That's ridiculous!"

"Tell me about it. Can you meet me at the station?"

"I'll be there," Jill said, already getting out of bed. "And Dan, don't say anything at all until I get there, okay?"

"Don't worry," he said. "I won't."

Chapter Fifty-Seven

● ● ●

Jill made it to the station moments after they had brought Dan in, just after one in the morning. She found a haggard Mark Branning slumped in a chair next to Allie. She caught her breath and rushed to them. "Allie, what happened?"

Allie looked wearier and more defeated than Jill had ever seen her. "The apartment where we were staying was broken into tonight. Mark fought the guy off and he got away—but not before he'd started a fire."

Jill's face drained of all its color. "Was either of you hurt?"

"Mark was," Allie said. "His legs . . ."

Jill saw the burns and winced.

"Jill, they've just brought Dan Nichols in for questioning."

"I know," she said. "He called me. That's why I'm here. Why are they interested in him?"

"Because the man who broke into the apartment had on a firefighter's bunker suit and a mask. The other day, at the airport, they found a Newpointe bunker coat. Stan's been trying to narrow it down."

"And he's narrowed it down to *Dan?* That's ludicrous. Didn't you tell him it couldn't have been him? He was with us all night the night Francis was killed."

"We told them," Allie said quietly. "But there's that time I woke up and he was coming back in from the hall. You were talking to him—you remember. They're saying that maybe he wasn't in the hall, maybe he had been to Slidell and back."

"Give me a break!"

"The guy who broke into our apartment tonight is wounded," Mark said weakly. "I shot him somewhere in the right shoulder or arm. It'll be easy to rule Dan out, if he's innocent."

"*If* he's innocent? Mark, you can't really think there's a possibility—he's your best friend!"

"Of course he is," Mark said wearily. "I didn't mean that."

She looked down at them for a moment, frustrated. Then she realized how painful those burns must be, and how tired and sapped for energy Mark was, just out of the hospital. His head was wrapped in a fresh bandage, but the yellow bruises around his eyes reminded her just how miserable he must feel. "Mark, you don't look so good. Shouldn't you be in bed?"

"What bed?" he asked. "We can't go home or we'll be killed in our sleep. We can't go back to where we were hiding. We can't get on a plane."

"Maybe they could find a place for you to lie down, at least."

"Forget it," Mark said. "I'm not closing my eyes until this man is caught."

A few minutes later, Jill found Dan in the interrogation room with Stan Shepherd, Chief Shoemaker, Vern Hargis, and Chad Avery. She walked in with an air of disgust, dropped her briefcase into a chair, and took the seat beside Dan. "All right, guys, let's get down to business so my client can go back home and get some rest."

"We just want to know where he was between seven and twelve tonight."

"I *told* them," Dan said. "I cut my hand around seven, then went home and went to bed. No witnesses. Can't prove a thing."

"Yes, you can," Jill said, looking directly at Stan. "Stan, surely you've checked him for that gunshot wound Mark says he inflicted on the killer. Does he have one?"

"He has a wound on his hand," Stan said. "Mark could have been mistaken about where the bullet hit."

She looked down at the small bandage wrapped around his hand. "Take the bandage off, Dan. Let us see it."

Dan unwrapped the gauze bandage and showed them the cuts on his hand. "Glass," he said. "Not a bullet—glass."

The cops weren't convinced. "Did anyone see you break the glass?"

"Absolutely. Nick did. He disinfected it and wrapped it for me."

Stan nodded for Vern to go and check, and he dismissed himself from the room.

While they waited, Dan looked at Stan. "Mark was in a gunfight with that guy? What happened? Was Mark hurt?"

"He was burned," Jill said. "But he seems okay. I just saw him outside." She glanced back at the detective and chief of police. "Surely you guys have other suspects. If you know it to be a fireman—"

"A fireman?" Dan cut in. "Is that what this is about? The killer is a fireman?"

"If you know him to be a fireman," Jill went on, "you must have a whole list of suspects."

"We have two others we're questioning tonight, Jill. We just haven't been able to locate them yet."

"Well, maybe one of them has a gunshot wound. Maybe you'll find him soon, and you'll see. Meanwhile, you must realize that Dan is not your man."

"I don't want to think he is," he said. "But Dan, there are pieces that don't fit. You can't prove where you were when Mark was shot at the airport."

"I was *jogging*, Stan. People saw me—"

"We can't find anyone who did."

"Stan, if I'd gone to New Orleans, shot Mark, then driven back to Newpointe, I'd have been gone two hours, at the very least. I wasn't jogging that long."

"Like I said, we can't confirm that. Besides, everybody knows you drive like Mario Andretti. And you weren't home when they came to get you earlier tonight, and the night Francis was killed, you were allegedly at the hospital with Allie and Jill, but you disappeared for an unspecified period of time . . ."

"*What?* I did *not*. I was there all night."

Stan focused in on Jill. "Jill, did you or did you not wake up to see Dan coming back from somewhere?"

Dan gaped at her. "Did you tell them that? That I left?"

Jill couldn't believe Stan had breached professionalism this way. "No, Allie did. Stan, he wasn't gone long. He was just in the hall. And I'd appreciate it if you wouldn't question me like a witness when I'm trying to defend my client!"

Stan wilted. It was pure exhaustion that had motivated him, she thought. They were all worn out.

"Can you prove that you were in the hall, Dan?" Stan asked.

"Prove that I didn't sneak out and kill Francis Bledsoe in another town? Yes, I can prove it! You bet I can prove it!"

"How?"

"Well . . . there were others in the waiting room that night. Some of them had to be awake. Somebody saw me, Stan. Somebody had to."

Stan looked doubtful. "Dan, Vern and Chad found a bunker suit in your trunk."

"Yeah, so?"

"So why did you have it with you?"

"Because I keep scanners in my car and my house. Sometimes I hear a call and I go to help. I keep the suit in case I need it when I'm off duty." He gaped at each of them. "Oh, come on, Stan. Most of the guys keep suits in their trunks, and you probably have a scanner at home, too."

"Even Mark has a bunker suit in his car," Jill cut in. "I saw one in his car just yesterday."

"Yeah," Dan said. "Even Mark."

"What about the night at the florist, when you had a crowbar—?"

"Aw, man." He sat back hard in his chair and rubbed his face roughly. "It happened exactly like I said. I saw somebody, Stan." He banged his hand on the table, then winced at the cut as it started to bleed again. Tipping his hand up to keep the blood from dripping, he said, "Here. You must have blood samples from the killer. Take some of mine, Stan. It'll rule me out. And give me a lie detector test, truth serum, whatever you want. I'm innocent."

Stan reached for the phone to call someone to do just that, when Vern came back in. "I just talked to Nick, Stan. He says he did see Dan cut his hand, and he bandaged it up himself. But I asked him if he was sure Dan hadn't left the station before that, and he said he didn't know, because he was sleeping. I asked him if Dan could have already had the wound and broken the glass after the fact—"

"*What?*" Dan shouted. "Why would I do that?"

"To cover for a gunshot wound," Vern said, raising his voice over Dan's outburst. "The killer wouldn't have to be a genius to go back to where he was supposed to have been all night, make a big deal out of breaking a glass and cutting his hand, and then he's got an alibi."

Dan just stared at him for a long moment. "You ought to be writing movies, Vern. Your talents are wasted here."

"Oscar caliber," Jill agreed. "Stan, if this is a bullet hole in his hand, how come it doesn't come out on the other side? It's on his palm, for heaven's sake, so it couldn't have been grazed. It's a *cut! Look* at it!"

"I have O positive blood, Stan," Dan threw in. "What kind did the killer have?"

"I don't know. I'll have to call New Orleans and see if they have any results yet."

"Do it," Dan said. "I don't like being in the hot seat."

• • •

Less than fifteen minutes later, the telephone in the interrogation room rang, and Stan picked it up. He listened and jotted down something on the pad on his lap, then brought his eyes back to Dan and Jill. Gravely, he hung up the phone.

"What is it?" Jill asked. "Is it the results of the blood test?"

Stan rubbed his eyes, thinking, then focused on them again. "They found two types of blood in Aggie's apartment," he said. "O positive was one of them."

Dan jumped up from his chair, knocking it over. "I don't believe this."

"The other one was Mark's blood type."

Dan picked the chair up and slammed it down on its legs, then plopped back into it and dropped his head into the circle of his arms.

Jill was silent for a moment. Then she spoke up. "Stan, O positive is the most common blood type. What about the DNA tests?"

"Not ready yet."

"So where does that leave us?"

Stan turned his bloodshot eyes to Dan. "I'm afraid we're going to have to book you, Dan."

Dan looked up, his face burning. "Stan, you must know you're making a mistake. You know me, man. We go to church together. I was in your wedding."

Stan nodded glumly as he looked down at his hands. "Go ahead and book him."

Vern got Dan to his feet again.

"Vern, we played football together. You know me, man!"

Vern didn't answer as he led him to the door.

"Dan, I'm going to get you out of here as soon as I can," Jill said. "I won't rest until I do."

Dan turned to her. "You believe me, don't you, Jill? I didn't do this!"

"Yes," she said without hesitation. "I believe you. And I'll make sure they do, too, before it's all over."

•   •   •

Dan was distraught as Vern led him out of the interrogation room. In the waiting area a few feet down, Mark sat in a chair with his bandaged head leaning back against the wall. Allie sat next to him. His pant legs were burned, and Dan could see blistering burns on his friend's calves. Dan's anger melted, and he took a step toward them.

"You don't think I did this, do you, Mark?" he asked.

"No!" Mark got to his feet. "Vern, what's going on?"

"We're booking him," Vern said reluctantly.

"Why? Dan, we both said that it couldn't have been you."

"So how come they weren't convinced?" He looked at them both with a misty heaviness in his eyes. "Allie, you told them I disappeared when I was guarding you in the ICU waiting room. How could you tell them that? How could you even think it?"

"Dan, that's *not* what I said. I told them you were with Jill and me all night. That you didn't leave. They just asked me if there was ever a time when I woke up and you weren't there, and I told them about when you had walked back in from the hall. I believe you, Dan. But I had to answer their questions. I want the killer caught."

"Well, I'm not him!"

"We know you're not," Mark said. "Vern, I shot the guy in his right arm. Dan isn't shot."

Vern lifted Dan's bloody hand. "It was dark, Mark. You could have just thought it was his arm."

Mark's fight drained out of him, and he stared, stricken, down at Dan's hand.

"Mark, I broke a glass. Nick was there; he'll tell you. It doesn't even *look* like a gunshot wound."

Dan jerked the bandage off and held out his hand. "You tell me, Mark. It's just a stupid cut—doesn't even need stitches. Does that look like a bullet did it?"

Mark couldn't answer. Dan weighed and analyzed the confusion on Mark's face, and realized that even his best friend had some doubts.

"Aw, man," he said. "I don't believe this."

He turned away from all of them and started up the hallway, where he would be booked as the serial killer that had terrorized the town.

Chapter Fifty-Eight

• • •

Marty Bledsoe's parents lived in a mobile home near Metairie, right outside of New Orleans. It took R.J. Albright and Anthony Martin an hour and a half to find the trailer park. When they finally did, they saw a Metairie police officer waiting to make the arrest with them, since they had no jurisdiction there. They pulled up beside his squad car and rolled the window down. "Thanks for comin'," R.J. said. "Sorry it took us so long to get here."

"No problem," the officer said. "You said it was about the Newpointe killin's. You think the serial killer's hidin' out here?"

"We ain't sure," R.J. said. "We just need to take him in for questionin'."

"Well, the trailer you want is up that-away to the right. I'll foller ya'll up."

R.J. pulled up ahead and turned into the driveway.

When he saw that Marty's pickup truck was parked out front, he knew they'd hit pay dirt.

A brisk wind swept up, chilling them, as they reached the door. R.J. knocked hard. It was after 1:30 A.M., so they waited, then rapped again.

R.J. was about to knock again when something metal touched the back of his neck. He jumped and reached for his gun.

"Don't neither of you move." It was Marty's voice, and R.J. realized he had a gun pointed at him. Next to him, Anthony stood frozen, as well. The Metairie officer cursed and spat.

"It's me, Marty—R.J. Put the gun down. Me and Anthony just want to talk to you."

"You didn't hunt me down at 1:30 in the mornin' just to talk to me," Marty said, his voice quivering. "What'd you come for? You gonna kill me and my kids now, too? You gonna kill my folks?"

"We ain't gonna kill nobody!" Anthony shouted. "Marty, we're here on police business. Put the stinkin' gun down!"

"Turn around."

The three cops turned slowly around and saw the fireman standing barefoot in nothing but his Fruit of the Looms. R.J. would have been amused if he hadn't had a deer rifle pointed at his head.

"Did we get you out of bed?" Anthony asked.

R.J. almost laughed at the polite question. Didn't Anthony realize Marty could blow them away?

"I come out the back way when you knocked," Marty said. "I ain't gon' sleep through another killin'. This time I'm ready."

R.J.'s amusement faded as he heard the pain and self-recrimination in Marty's voice.

"Marty, I don't blame you for bein' nervous. But Stan sent us. We have to take you in for questionin'." He kicked himself. How absurd, to tell Marty that when his finger was over the trigger.

"Me?" Marty asked. "Why would you wanna take *me* in? I'm one of the victims."

"We just want to ask you some questions. You aren't the only one."

The porch light came on, and Marty's father peered out. "I called the po-lice, son. They're on their way."

"These *are* police," Marty said. "They're sayin' they have to take me in. Do me a favor, Pop. Call the Newpointe P.D. and see if they sent 'em."

Marty's father disappeared, and they waited while Marty kept his gun on them.

"No wound," Anthony noted.

R.J. nodded. "I see that."

"What are ya'll talkin' about?"

"Mark Branning got into a scuffle with the killer tonight," Anthony said. "Mark wounded him, but he got away."

Marty's face twisted, and R.J. saw the tears reddening his eyes. "Did he get Allie?"

"No, she's okay."

His mouth quivered. "You think *I'm* the killer?"

"No," R.J. said honestly.

"Why would I *do* that?" He wiped at his eyes with the back of his hand. "Why would I want to do somethin' like that?"

Flashing blue lights lit up the trees around the trailer as another Metairie police car approached. About that time, Marty's father stepped out onto the porch. "They confirmed it, son. Stan Shepherd sent 'em. Put the gun down."

Slowly, Marty lowered the rifle as another Metairie cop got out of his car.

R.J. relaxed. "Why don't I go with you to put some clothes on, Marty, while Anthony fills him in. Then we'll take you in and get this cleared up."

Marty nodded, wiped his eyes again, and led R.J. into the house.

Chapter Fifty-Nine

●●●

With Dan Nichols locked up and Marty Bledsoe in interrogation—though they had ruled him out—Jim Shoemaker ordered Vern Hargis and Chad Avery to wake the judge to get a warrant to search Craig Barnes's home and patrol truck, while Stan tried to find Craig.

Stan tried to shake the misery as he stepped out onto the front steps of the police station at two A.M. Several cameras were setting up there, and a reporter dashed up the steps to meet him. "Detective Shepherd, we're told that you've made an arrest in the Fire Wife Killings."

"No comment," Stan said and trotted on down the stairs.

"Detective, can you confirm that it's a local firefighter?"

"No, I cannot." He reached his car and locked himself in, then tried to get his bearings as he cranked it and pulled away from the curb.

As he drove, his mind raced. As much as the evidence pointed to Dan, Stan didn't want to believe it. But he didn't want to believe Craig or Marty had done it, either, and the evidence suggested that it was one of the three.

He remembered Dan's face as Vern had taken him to be booked. Part of him hoped they'd done the right thing, or Stan would never be able to live with himself. The other part, the bigger one, prayed for some turn of events that would prove Dan's innocence. After all the prayer groups Stan had attended with him, all the Promise Keepers rallies . . .

He drove to Craig's house and found Vern and Chad already there. "He's not home," Vern said. "We're gonna have to bust in."

Stan thought that over. "No. Let me go back to the fire station one more time. I'll wake everybody up and see if anybody knows where he went. Meanwhile, you two go to the Eastside station and do the same thing."

They headed out in separate directions, and Stan prayed that they would find him. Maybe by now Craig was back at the station. Maybe he had sacked out there, and didn't have a clue that people were searching for him.

Stan cruised past the Midtown station; reporters still clustered around the door. He parked a block down the street, then cut through the yards until he reached the back door of the station.

The door was unlocked, so he went in and saw Nick and George Broussard sitting at the kitchen table. "Hey, guys."

They both sprang up when they saw him. "Stan, what's this about Dan getting arrested?" Nick asked. "I told you guys—he cut his hand on glass. I still have the broken glass in the wastebasket to prove it."

Stan didn't want to talk about it. "Look, can you tell me if you've seen Craig Barnes? Has he been here?"

"I haven't seen him," George said. "Stan, Dan would never have hurt Martha. You've got the wrong guy."

Stan went through the kitchen and into the back room, where three other guys slept. He turned on the light. "Wake up, guys. Come on, get up. I need to talk to you."

One by one, they woke up—Cale, Slater, Lex.

"What is it, Stan?" Cale asked, sitting on the edge of his bed and squinting into the light. "Has something else happened?"

"They've arrested Dan," George said. "Ain't that the most ridiculous thing you ever heard?"

"Dan?" Cale asked, standing up. "Is that for real?"

Stan wanted to evade as many of the questions as he could. He'd only come to find out one thing. "Look, I need your help. We're trying to locate Craig Barnes. Did he say anything to any of you about where he would be tonight?"

"Not me," Cale said.

He asked each of them individually, and all said no.

"How long since any of you has seen him?" Stan asked.

"I haven't seen him since supper," Nick said wearily. "Stan, why are you looking for him?"

"I just need to ask him some questions."

"About Dan?" Nick asked.

"No. Are you sure none of you has seen him since supper?"

"Absolutely," Cale said.

"Well, do you know of any place he might be? A favorite hangout, or maybe a woman—"

All of the men shook their heads. Did they really not know, or were they just covering for him?

"Look, guys, we're on the same side here. Are you being straight with me?"

"The same side?" George asked. "When you've already locked up one of us?"

"I'd give anything to prove Dan didn't do it," Stan said. "I don't like my job much right now, but I'm sworn to do it. All I'm trying to do is keep any more of our townspeople from getting murdered, and you can help me or you can stand in my way!"

"Stan, we don't know where Craig is," Cale said quietly. "But if we see him, we'll tell him you want to talk to him."

"Does Dan have a lawyer?" Nick asked as Stan headed to the back door.

"Yes, Nick. He has Jill." Unwilling to answer any more questions, he headed back out to his car.

Vern and Chad came up empty, too, and radioed Stan that they would meet him back at Craig Barnes's house. They were waiting there for him when he pulled up to the curb.

"He's still not answerin'," Chad said. "Time to break in?"

Stan thought for a moment. Barnes wasn't one to take it lightly if they did any damage to his house. If they broke the lock and splintered the door, they'd better be dead sure he was the killer. If he just had a key. . . .

A dim memory came to him of another key. The key Craig claimed he'd gotten under Mark and Allie's mat, the night he'd broken in.

"Just a minute, guys," Stan said, getting back into his car and grabbing his cell phone. He dialed the number of the police station and told them to get Mark to the phone.

Mark's voice was strained and hoarse as he answered. "Yeah, Stan. What is it?"

"I need to ask you something. Do you and Allie keep a house key hidden?"

"No, why?"

He wasn't surprised. "Not even under the doormat?"

"Especially not under the doormat. That's the first place anyone would look. Why?"

"I'll tell you later." Stan clicked off the phone and sat staring for a moment. Craig had lied. He'd already had the key. Did he have the Broussards', the Larkins', and the Fords' keys, too?

Despite the chill breeze, he was beginning to sweat as he got out of the car. "Let's do it," he said.

Vern got a crowbar from his patrol car and Stan broke the inner edge and splintered it until the door opened. Guns drawn, they went cautiously inside.

Stan turned all the lights on, and began to search the premises—for what, he wasn't sure. The house was clean, everything in its place, and it smelled of strawberries or apricots . . . A woman's picture—the only picture in the living room—sat on a table beside the recliner.

"Hey, that's Amanda Marigrove!" Chad exclaimed, bending over to get a closer look. "She died last year when her house burned down."

"Yeah, I remember," Vern said. "Pretty lady. Kind of quiet. Why would he have her picture?"

"Good question," Stan said.

"Wasn't she married?" Vern asked.

"Yes. Her husband worked offshore on an oil rig. He died a few months ago, though. He had moved to Gulfport. I heard he was in a bad car wreck."

Vern shot Stan a look. "Do you think she had a thing going with Craig?"

Stan shook his head. "No telling." He stood frozen for a moment, remembering the tragic circumstances of her death. Her house had caught fire in the middle of the night, and it was blazing out through the roof by the time a neighbor had reported it. The firefighters were told no one was home—the husband was out of town, and the neighbor thought Amanda was visiting her mother in Gulfport. Still, they had tried to search the house where it was possible, but by the time they had found Amanda, it had been too late.

The firemen at the scene had taken it hard, and Craig Barnes, who had not gotten there until after the body was found, had been outraged. But no one had suspected that his feelings were any more significant than those of the other firemen who grieved their failure. It was his department, after all, and everyone assumed he had taken the brunt of the guilt.

Could it be that, instead, he was grieving the death of his lover, and biding his time until he could take vengeance on the men who should have saved her?

Chad and Vern were checking out the other rooms now, and Stan went into the hall. There was a door there, and he nodded to the others to back him up as he opened it.

He swung the door open, and they saw a set of stairs leading up to the attic. The scent of strawberries seemed more pungent there.

Stan slid his hand on the wall until he found a light switch. When he flicked it on, a dim yellow bulb lit up the room above their heads, enough to see to climb the stairs.

Stan went first, his gun in one hand as he used his other hand to steady himself on the shaky banister. The smell of strawberries was getting stronger, and a strange sense of foreboding fell over him. He reached the top of the stairs and froze.

"I don't believe it."

Vern and Chad came up behind him, and they all froze, gaping at the scene: a shrine, built of tables and shelves, with a kneeling bench in front of it, and scented candles of all shapes and sizes surrounding the large portrait of Amanda Marigrove in the middle.

"Weird," Vern whispered.

Stan stared at the altar as a million fragments of the same puzzle whirled through his mind.

"*He was prayin' to Mary. Sayin', 'I'm sorry, Mary. I'm so sorry...'*"

Could it be that he wasn't praying to the Virgin Mary, but to someone else? Amanda Marigrove? Had he called her Mari?

A chill swept over him as he saw an ashtray full of keys, and a clipboard with a list on the altar. His heart hammered as he walked toward it. "It's a list," he said. "A list of women." He looked up at the other two men. "Fire wives."

"You're kidding."

With gloved hands, Stan picked up the clipboard, and he saw the list with women's names marked through. Martha and Jamie and Francis were all marked out. Susan was marked through with a question mark beside her name. And Allie was last on the list. "What do you bet these keys are to their houses? He probably had them copied while the firefighters slept at the station."

"It's him," Chad said without a doubt. "Craig Barnes is the killer."

Vern bolted down the stairs. "I'll call an APB on him. If we can get everybody on it, we'll find him before daylight."

Chapter Sixty

• • •

A hospital was a luxury Craig Barnes could not afford. But it didn't matter much anyway. Yes, the pain was great, and the blood loss had been significant. He was finding it hard to operate that right arm, and since he was right-handed, that presented a dilemma when he tried to drive.

He turned down rural roads and saw old man Radcliff's farmhouse sitting out in the middle of its acreage. The old man was half deaf, decrepit, and lived alone. As he drove past the house, Craig hoped he was a heavy sleeper as well. There was the big barn in the back, just as he remembered.

He left his car idling as he got out and opened the wide door on the side of the barn. The door was big enough to drive a tractor through—but the mayor had forced the old man to sell off his tractor after one too many accidents that had come close to killing him or others. Craig drove his car in, cut off the engine, and closed the door behind him.

Breathing more calmly in the safety of the barn, he unbuttoned his uniform shirt, peeled it off, and carefully removed the towels he had pressed over the wound, front and back, to stop the bleeding. The towels were soaked, and still he bled.

He was getting dizzy. Quickly, he reached into the glove compartment for the bottle of iodine he had borrowed from a rescue unit. He'd found the unit parked in the Delchamps parking lot a few hours ago and had simply driven up beside it and asked the attendants for some iodine. Because he was their boss, they had simply handed it over, no questions asked.

By now, Jim Shoemaker and his crew probably knew that Mark had shot someone. Too bad he'd left Mark alive to describe what he'd been wearing. It would lead them to him. He'd known that he would be caught eventually; he had long since adjusted to that idea. But now time was running out, and he wasn't finished. They would catch him and lock him up, and Susan Ford and Allie Branning would continue to live, and Mark and Ray would never know the pain that George or Cale or Marty had experienced—the pain that he, himself, had experienced over a year ago. They had to know. They had to understand the pain.

He poured the iodine over his wound, front and back, and screamed at the intensity of the pain.

It was a while before the pain from the antiseptic eased, leaving only the raw pulsating agony that had come with him from New Orleans. He wished he had some clean towels. He opened the car door and stumbled out. There was a bale of hay against one wall, and he staggered to it. He had to lie down. If he could just rest for a few minutes, he'd get a second wind. He could then go after Allie, and finish off Susan—and then they could catch him, because it wouldn't matter anymore.

Chapter Sixty-One

• • •

The safe house where Jim Shoemaker put Mark and Allie at 2:30 A.M. was guarded by four police officers. It was a small house that had once been owned by Patricia Castor, the mayor. She had long ago vacated it for a bigger place more in keeping with her image of authority and power. Though she'd tried to sell it, the furnished house had been vacant for some time, and Stan had gotten her to loan it to the department.

Mark was waning as Allie walked him in, and she realized that the things he'd been through tonight would have worn out a healthy person. In Mark's condition, it had to be agony. He complained of a headache, and walked with a limp. She was sure his burns were causing a lot of pain.

The house was dusty, but Allie told herself she'd take care of that later. Her first priority was to get Mark to bed.

That didn't take much persuading. As soon as he was horizontal, his eyes closed. In no time, he sank into a deep sleep.

Allie was tired, too. Climbing in beside him, she was soon asleep herself.

• • •

Less than an hour later, a killer headache woke Mark. He opened his eyes and found his wife beside him, her finger touching her lips again. The sight of her filled him with warmth, and he ached to reach over and pull her against him. But she needed her sleep.

He got up, feeling as sore as a man who'd been beaten. The blistered skin on his legs stung, the pain competing with his headache. He wished he had taken a pain pill. Then again, it was better that he hadn't. He needed a clear head in case anything happened. He padded into the kitchen and opened the back door. "Hey, R.J.," he said.

His old friend looked up at him, smiling. "Hey, Mark. You get enough sleep?"

"I think so," Mark said. "Listen, heard anything from Stan? Are they still holding Dan?"

R.J. looked as though he didn't want to disclose the information. "I think so. But they're lookin' for somebody else now."

"Who?" Mark asked. "Marty or Craig?"

The cop hesitated. "I think you'd better call Stan for information, Mark. I'm really not authorized to disclose it."

"Okay," he said. "But is the phone working in here?"

R.J. nodded. "The mayor never had it cut off."

Mark went back in and dialed Stan's number.

"Stan Shepherd." His voice was fatigued and gravelly, and Mark knew it had been a long time since he'd slept.

"Stan, what's the latest?"

"Who is this?" Stan asked.

"Me, Mark. I heard you were after someone besides Dan."

Stan was quiet for a moment. "Mark, we're still holding Dan. But we have strong reason to believe that Craig Barnes is the killer."

"No way."

"'Fraid so. And since we put the APB out on him, we've heard from two paramedics who said he came by their rescue unit and borrowed some iodine last night."

Mark let that sink in. "Was he bleeding?"

"They couldn't see. He didn't get out of the car at all, and it was night. He just pulled up to their window and asked them for it."

"Still . . . Craig Barnes? Why, Stan? It doesn't make sense."

"There was something interesting in his attic, Mark. A shrine set up to Amanda Marigrove—remember her?"

Mark thought for a moment. "Yeah. The woman who died in the fire last year. He didn't even know her, did he?"

"Must have. He had a shrine to her, complete with candles and a kneeling bench, and a list of some of the fire wives with lines crossed through the ones who've been killed."

"You're kidding."

"Wish I were. Mark, tell me something. Do you remember much about the fire Amanda Marigrove died in?"

Mark struggled to think back to that night, but it was so long ago that the memory was blurry. "I remember that the neighbor told us he had seen her leave, that she wasn't home. We still searched the rooms, but some of them were so engulfed that we couldn't get all the way in. If we'd had reason to think she was there, we might have tried harder to get to her. But I think she was dead before we ever got there."

"What was Craig like that night?"

He closed his eyes and tried to remember. Craig had shown up late after hearing of the fire on his scanner. He had been rabid when they'd told him about Amanda. "Oh, he was furious. Ranting and raving that we'd dropped the ball, that we'd let a woman die . . . real emotional. He disappeared and didn't come back to work for several days. We didn't know what was going on with him, except that he was so angry at us for letting it happen. Believe me, we felt plenty of guilt, but I don't think there was anything we could have done. The house was so far gone when we got there."

"Apparently, he was obsessed with her," Stan said. "Tell me something, Mark. Who was on the shift that went to the fire that night?"

Mark thought. "Well, I guess that's obvious, isn't it? Me, Ray, George, Cale, and Marty. And Barnes has targeted all of our wives."

"Guess we've got our motive. That's why the fire. He wants you to know what it's like to have the woman *you* love burned in a fire. Only it was hard to keep them there unless he shot them first. He's getting desperate to get Allie," Stan said. "The thing at the airport proves that. Just seeing her dead would have been enough, and even if he'd gotten caught it would have been worth it to him."

The realization washed like a black tide over Mark. Dizzy, he felt for the chair behind him and sat down. "Find him, Stan."

"That's not so easy. We have an APB out on him, and chances are, he's listening to his scanner to find out what we know. We're having to be real careful. But you're safe, Mark. He's not going to get past the guards we've posted there."

Mark realized he was drenched with sweat, and his hand trembled as he clutched the phone. "Stan, go out and find him. Don't let another minute go to waste. Come up with a plan. Draw him out somehow. I don't care how you do it, but keep him from finishing the job."

When Mark hung up the phone, his head was throbbing harder. He went back to the bedroom door, opened it quietly, and looked in on his wife. She still slept peacefully.

To his frustration and dismay, he began to weep as his exhaustion and the horror of Barnes's betrayal of them all washed over him. He closed the bedroom door and sank down on the plaid couch in the living room, covered his face with his hands to muffle the sound, and wept for several minutes. Finally, he leaned back and looked up at the ceiling, as if he could see God through it. "Don't let me lose her, Lord. Please don't let me lose her. I want my wife. Forgive me for treating my marriage lightly. Forgive me for ignoring my vows."

He wiped his wet face with both hands, then his body shook once again with the force of his remorse. He had forsaken Christ, he had forsaken Allie, and worse, he had blamed her for his indifference.

He'd had choices—and he'd made bad ones. He'd had chance after chance to set things right—and he'd ignored them. Even in counseling, when Allie had pleaded with him to tell the truth about his feelings for Issie so that they could put this chapter behind them, he had continued to deny it. He'd even told her that his marriage vows said nothing about choosing each other's friends.

And then he'd told Issie that Allie didn't want to work on their marriage, that she was materialistic and a workaholic, that their marital problems were Allie's fault. Maybe Allie was right—maybe his friendship with Issie *had* been building toward a sexual affair. It was the natural progression for a relationship like theirs, after all. And she'd made no secret of her willingness.

How far he had fallen, how despicable he had become. He hated himself—and for a moment, he wished that Craig Barnes had succeeded in killing him at the airport. Allie deserved so much better. Allie, who had not taken the easy way out and gone home with her parents. Allie, who had suffered so much grief and fear.

And now, the threat to her life only reminded him that his marriage was still too precious to lose. It was a viable, sacred union under God.

He fell to his knees, folded his hands in front of his face, and pleaded with God to forgive him. "I love her, Lord," he whispered. "I love her. Please give me one more chance. Keep her alive so I can convince her to stay with me, so we can have kids—and help us to teach them not to make the same mistakes we've—"

The door opened, and he looked up to see Allie, standing in the doorway.

"Mark? Are you all right?"

"No," he said, wiping his face. "No, I'm not all right."

She stooped beside him, her face panicked. "Do you need to go to the hospital? Do you need me to call an ambulance?"

"No," he said, almost laughing. "No, it's not my body. It's my soul."

"Your what?"

"Allie, can you ever forgive me?" he cried.

"For what?" she asked. He moved her up onto the couch, and knelt in front of her. His eyes were still full of tears as he looked up at her. "You were right, Allie. My relationship with Issie, though it was never physical—it was too close. It was out of line."

She touched his face. "Mark, you don't have to—"

"Shhh," he said. "I have to say this. It was wrong. And I should have distanced myself from her the minute you got uncomfortable with it. *I* should have gotten uncomfortable with it! I had no business having long intimate talks with another woman, and I had no business lying about it, and I had no business leaving you and our marriage and blaming you. That night at the station, when you walked in on us—we hadn't done more than hug, Allie, I swear it. But in our hearts, well—it was heading that way, Allie. You were right. In your eyes and the eyes of God, I was being unfaithful. But I'm so sorry. I love you, Allie, and I don't want our marriage to end."

He laid his head down on her knees, and she stroked the back of his head.

He looked up at her again. "Maybe it took the danger of losing you permanently for me to realize how much I love you, but I need your forgiveness, Allie. And I need another chance. I want to go home with you when this is over, and be your husband, and grow old with you. And you don't have to worry about the drinking, because it's over."

He reached for her, and she went willingly into his arms. For the first time, he had a full understanding of the concept of grace. "You have another chance," she whispered. "You've had it for some time. I promised God when you were in the hospital that I would make our marriage work, even if I had to do it by myself. I'm committed to this marriage, Mark. I'm committed to being your wife."

Gratitude seeped through him like warm honey, filling him with joy and peace. He kissed her then, a kiss that was like a gift, a wonderful gift that he neither expected nor deserved. When the kiss broke, he led her back into the bedroom.

There, they renewed their vows to one another and consummated the reunion that they both intended to last the rest of their lives.

However long—or short—that might be.

Chapter Sixty-Two

● ● ●

Craig Barnes tried to sleep in the hay in the big barn that smelled of manure. But sleep would not come. Even though he had bled out most of his energy, he could not sleep. The pain from his wound was too great, and he was alternately feverish and chilled. He needed a hospital, but that was out of the question. He'd be okay if he could just find enough energy to finish off Susan Ford and Allie Branning. He couldn't leave the job unfinished—he owed it to Mari. He had to let their husbands experience the horror of knowing their loved one died a painful, screaming death.

He had listened all night to the scanner crackling and police and firemen talking about the APB on him, and he'd heard someone calling in from the "safe house" where Allie and Mark were being kept. If he listened long enough, he might get some clue as to where that was. Then he would go there, kill Allie, and set her on fire. He would love to tie Mark to a tree out front, to make him watch the fire blaze and the building fall around his wife. Yes, that would be justice. That would be retribution.

The hospital would be trickier, but he would get to Susan somehow. He hadn't figured out a way yet, but he would.

Yes, they would catch him. That was inevitable. But it didn't matter to him as long as he got the job done. Then he could join Mari.

"I'm coming soon, Mari," he said to the empty barn. "I'll be there when I finish the job."

He looked forward to the end for himself. If they didn't catch him first, he would somehow get back to his house, up to his attic and the shrine to his beloved, and he would take his own life right there on the altar. He couldn't wait to see her again. The thought filled him with renewed vigor, and he got up, shivering from his fever.

In the shadows cast by the moonlight playing through the window of the barn, he saw a form taking shape, and Craig stared at it, trying to focus. It looked like the filmy shape of a woman, smiling and reaching out for him.

His eyebrows lifted, and he staggered toward her. "Mari? Is that you?"

It *was* her, he thought as he drew closer. He took her in his arms and held her. He heard music—their song, "Unforgettable," the old Nat King Cole version, sweet and mellow, and he began to dance with her. "I've missed you, Mari. But I've made them pay. Did you see how they paid?"

But he sensed that she wasn't happy, for he had not finished his job. Two of the wives were still alive.

"I was just going out to get them, Mari. They'll be dead tonight. And I'll be coming home to you."

She faded. Like an image sucked away in a vacuum, she retreated, slowly, quietly, fading out of view until he could no longer see her.

He wept at her disappearance, but he kept dancing to the song that played in his brain, swaying as if he held her, as if she'd never left.

He shivered again, and suddenly saw flames coming up through the hay, but he smelled no smoke, nothing burning. The building still smelled of cows and chickens. But he could see the flames, could see Mari right through them, standing in the center of them, screaming. "Save me, Craig! You're a fireman. You can save me! Please! Help, Craig! *Please!*"

"I would have, Mari!" he cried. "But I wasn't there. I didn't know until it was too late!"

She kept screaming, shrinking from the flames, and he stood helpless, watching her burn. If only he had been on duty and heard the call. If only he'd been with her when it happened. If only he had gotten there moments sooner.

But he hadn't, and she had died, and all those firemen who had been on the scene had as good as murdered her. They had pretended to be remorseful, had attended her funeral with sober faces and dry eyes, had recounted the events as if nothing more could have been done. But he had known better.

"I'll show them, Mari," he whispered. "I promise, I'll show them."

Staggering to the barn door, he opened it cautiously. He couldn't take his own car; they would be looking for it. He retrieved the scanner from his car and then made his way out the door, holding onto the building for support, and saw the dust-covered pickup truck old man Radcliff kept parked under the trees beside the house.

He crossed the pasture to the truck. He got in, leaned over, and with his left hand he pulled out the crucial wires and hot-wired the truck.

As he hoped, it cranked, and he backed out of the spot it had occupied next to the house for so long, leaving a rectangle of tall grass where it had been.

His right arm had grown virtually useless. He drove with his left hand. He knew all the back roads, and took them as he listened to the scanner, trying to figure out where Allie could be. *Someone* knew where she was—someone who could lead him to her.

Jill Clark? Did she know where the safe house was? If he followed her, would she eventually lead him to Allie?

Not likely. Surely they realized by now how important it was to keep the Brannings' location secret. No, it was more likely that only a handful of police officers knew where they were.

Which ones, though? He tried to think like the cops he had known for years, tried to imagine which ones Stan would entrust to guard Allie. It was difficult to guess. Stan, himself, was the only one Craig was certain about.

He would have to follow Stan Shepherd.

Chapter Sixty-Three

● ● ●

The moment the press learned who the suspect was, Craig Barnes's picture flashed all over the nation. It was just a matter of time before they caught him, Stan thought as he headed out of the station to his car at 4:30. The problem was, they didn't have time. Judging from the level of psychosis apparent in his shrine to Amanda Marigrove and the desperate urgency with which he had tried to commit the final two murders, time was running out.

But he had a plan.

In the car, he turned on his scanner as he switched on his engine. Routine calls came across the radio, and an occasional report from a cop who'd sought Craig Barnes at one location or another, to no avail.

There was still time to carry out his plan if Mark would go along with it. He had Sid Ford guarding them, along with R.J. Albright, two of the finest, most trustworthy officers on the force. Allie would be safe with them.

He checked his rearview mirror before he made the turn-off to the safe house, and wondered briefly if the pickup truck behind him had followed him all the way from the station. He turned onto the street where the safe house was and watched to see if the truck followed. It did not.

He breathed a sigh of relief.

He pulled into the driveway of the house where Mark and Allie were staying, looked out all of his windows to make sure no one had followed, then hurried in.

• • •

Craig Barnes turned the pickup truck around, and turned onto the street where Stan Shepherd had gone. He cut off his lights as he drove past the houses there, looking for Stan's car.

There it was, parked at the fourth house on the left. Mayor Castor's old house, before she'd decided that she needed something a little more opulent. He might have guessed.

He drove down the street and pulled his truck into the driveway of a house for sale, the Krafts' old house before Alex Kraft had been transferred to Houston. There he waited for the right time to make his move.

• • •

So what's this plan?" Mark asked Stan as they all sat around the kitchen table.

Stan hated to ask for his cooperation in anything, with his head all bandaged up, and those burns on his calves and hands. He looked tired and sick, but there was a strange peace about him as he sat next to his wife, his arm protectively around her. At least something good had come of this—it might have saved the Brannings' marriage.

"My plan is to use your flower shop to draw Barnes out. He's probably listening to the scanner. We can let something slip about you and Allie staying at the shop. Then you go there, Mark, and we send Lynette with you as a decoy for Allie. If he's listening, he'll go there, and we'll have the place staked out from every angle. We'll get him the minute he shows up."

Mark just stared at him for a moment, and Stan could see this might be a tough sale. "So what about Allie? Where will she be?"

"Here," Stan said. "With Sid and R.J. It's the safest place for her."

"But it isn't safe for Mark to be at the shop," Allie argued. "I don't want him there. Couldn't you set up a decoy for him, too?"

"No. If Craig's watching, he needs to see one of you, so it'll look authentic."

"But I don't want him there. He's still recovering, Stan, and I don't want him to risk getting shot again."

"He won't get shot. We'll never let Barnes get near him."

"Then let me go with him," Allie said. "Don't make me stay here. If it's so safe, let me be there instead of the decoy."

"No way," Mark said. "She's not coming. I don't want her anywhere near Craig Barnes."

"And I don't want *you* anywhere near him!"

"Allie, you're the one Craig wants," Stan said. "He'll stop at nothing to get to you. It's my job to protect you, and I want you here. Mark will be protected. The person who'll be in the most danger is Lynette, but she's willing. She's a good cop."

Mark sat stone still for a moment, thinking. He looked up at his wife, his eyes gentle as he touched her cheek. "If this might end this terror tonight, baby, I say we do it."

"But Mark, you need to be in bed—"

"I'm fine. I can rest a whole lot better after Barnes is caught."

Allie followed Mark to the door, and as Stan went out to his car, the two stood in the doorway and embraced for a short eternity. "I love you, Allie," he whispered.

Tears came to her eyes. "I know you do. I love you, too." She breathed in a sob. "Please be careful. Please don't do anything stupid or heroic. Don't stand in front of any windows. Just promise—"

"Shhh," he whispered, touching her lips. "Calm down. I'm gonna be fine. It's time to trust the Lord. He's taken care of us so far."

"But I don't know what his plan is," she whispered. "I don't know how he wants this to end. I don't know what he wants to teach us."

"Whatever it is, it's right. We have to trust in that."

He kissed her then, a long, gentle, familiar kiss. "I don't want you to go," she whispered.

"But I have to so that we can go back to our own home and start that family we both wanted when we got married, and get on with our lives. I have to, Allie, so you'll be safe again."

He hugged her tightly again, then with tears in his eyes, said, "I'll keep in touch on the phone, okay?"

She swallowed hard and breathed in another sob. "Okay." Then she hurried back inside to keep from seeing them drive away.

❧ ❧ ❧

From his driveway down the street, Craig Barnes watched the scene. At first, he thought that Allie was going out to the car with Mark and Stan, but at the last moment, she had stayed.

On his scanner, he heard Stan ask a car to patrol the Branning florist shop, and he laughed lightly, realizing that they were trying to draw him out by making him think that was where Mark and Allie were. It was a trap. But it wouldn't catch him.

It couldn't be more perfect. Even though Allie was guarded by at least two cops, he could get to her—even if he had to take both of them out. Then while all the commotion continued in Newpointe, he would drive to Slidell and finish off Susan Ford. He didn't care if he had to take half of the hospital along with her.

Then he would go back to his own house, to his altar in front of his picture of Mari, and he would sacrifice himself to her, once and for all. Then he would be redeemed.

Chapter Sixty-Four

● ● ●

An hour had passed and it was 5:30 A.M. Allie had spoken to Mark by phone twice, only to learn that nothing had happened. Craig Barnes hadn't shown up. Maybe he had the trap figured out. Maybe he wasn't going to bite.

Or maybe she just needed to be patient.

Sid and R.J. stuck so close to her that she felt claustrophobic, and she wished there were a television set to distract her. But Pat Castor hadn't left much in the house when she'd moved out. All they had was the police scanner, which Sid had brought in from his car to keep in touch with the outside world as they hid.

The smell of fumes drifted on the air, and she looked up at R.J. "Do you smell something?"

R.J. sniffed the air, and his face changed. "Diesel." He shot Sid a look. Sid looked around as he drew his own weapon.

Allie grabbed the telephone. "I'm calling Mark and Stan."

She brought it to her ear, but it was dead. She felt her skin grow cold, felt her heart race, felt herself growing dizzy. "He's out there," she whispered. "He found me."

Sid took the phone and listened, then slowly set it in its cradle. "She may be right," he told R.J. "Why didn't we have this house staked out, too? We knew he was smart."

"Calm down," R.J. said again. "We still don't know—"

The lights flickered, and all the power went out.

Allie screamed.

Chapter Sixty-Five

● ● ●

Mark was getting impatient. He'd been sitting at the shop with Lynette for over an hour, and nothing had happened. Sweating from anxiety, he paced the room back and forth, back and forth.

"You should sit down," Lynette said. "You need to rest."

"Where is he?" Mark asked. "Stan was so sure he would come."

"Maybe his wound has slowed him down. Maybe it was even fatal. We'll find him eventually, dead or alive, Mark."

"That's not good enough," he said. "I want Allie out of danger now."

"She is out of danger. She's safe."

"Wish I was as sure of that as you are." He picked up the phone and dialed the number again. Just hearing her voice would give him some peace. But this time, he got an obnoxious honking sound, more abrasive than a busy signal. The phone was out of order.

He suddenly felt nauseous. "The phone isn't working. Something's wrong over there." He slammed the phone down and frantically punched out Stan's number.

"Shepherd," Stan answered.

"Stan, the phone is dead at the safe house. I want to get over there right now."

Stan hesitated for only a second before he said, "All right, Mark. I'll be there to pick you up in less than a minute."

◦ ◦ ◦

Allie heard a faint pop, then the sound of a bullet smashing through the wooden front door. She hit the floor. Sid fell virtually on top of her, his gun drawn, guarding her with his body. R.J. was in front of them, aiming his gun with one hand while, with the other, he reached for his radio.

There was another shot and the door flew open, letting in a dim ray of light from the streetlight at the end of the driveway. Allie screamed, scooted out from under Sid, and crawled to the bedroom nearest them. She flattened herself under the bed and slid as far back against the wall as she could, knowing even as she did that it was one of the first places he'd look, since there weren't that many places to hide. She hoped the darkness would shelter her, that dawn wouldn't come soon and bring deadly light to expose her. Panicked, she closed her eyes and began praying.

She heard another gunshot, and someone's body thudded on the floor. She closed her hand over her mouth, muffling a sob. Another shot, another thud.

She heard footsteps coming into the room, saw a flashlight beam scanning the hardwood floor. From under the bed she could see the fire boots and bunker pants he wore, and the fumes grew stronger as he poured more diesel around the room.

Suddenly the bed slid, and she was exposed against the wall. She looked up into the light blinding her and closed her eyes, waiting for the gunshot that had been meant for her all along.

◦ ◦ ◦

A convoy of police cars headed with sirens blaring and lights flashing to the street where Pat Castor's old house was. Mark sat in the front seat of Stan's unmarked car, holding onto the dashboard to keep from being flung around the car as Stan tore through town.

They had heard R.J.'s frantic radio call that he'd been shot, and that he needed backup, and now Mark prayed desperately that Allie would be spared. But did Craig have her already? Had he already shot her and started the fire that would consume her?

They rounded the corner in a power slide, and came to a stop in front of the house. "Stay here!" Stan ordered Mark.

"No way!" Mark said. "I'm going in with you."

•   •   •

In the bedroom, Craig heard the sirens. He cocked the pistol. It wasn't too late to shoot Allie and start the fire. In fact, it would be perfect. Mark was probably standing out there now, and he'd have to watch while the house burned down around her. Craig couldn't have planned it better.

But what would he do about Susan?

He was sweating and shaking—not from fear but from weakness, for he'd lost too much blood. His whole side ached from the festering bullet wound, and he didn't have much energy left. He needed to get Allie and Susan both, and quickly, or his redemption would be forever lost.

But if he killed Allie here, the police would descend on him, and he'd never get to Susan. He froze for a moment, thinking.

"Don't do it, Craig," Allie pleaded. "Amanda wouldn't have wanted it. She was a good person. It won't bring her back."

The fact that she knew who he was, though the light blinded her, registered vaguely in his mind. She was crying, sobbing, and he wondered if Mari had cried when she'd realized her house was on fire. Maybe she'd never awakened at all. His energy revived when he thought of how casually the firefighters had fought the fire, as if there wasn't a human life involved, as if Amanda had meant nothing to anybody. He wondered if they'd treat this fire as casually.

Or the one at the hospital.

He heard more sirens, heard tires squealing to a halt outside, and through the windows saw the reflection of dozens of flashing blue lights. No, this wouldn't work. He should have gotten Susan first. But then they might have caught him at the hospital, and he wouldn't have gotten to Allie. He had to get them both. There had to be total redemption.

"Get up." His words were weak, breathless, and he hoped they didn't make him seem less in control. Allie had to fear him. "Get up!" he shouted, and she scrambled to her feet.

"Craig, please. I trusted you. I never would have thought—"

"Shut up!" He looked out the back window and saw cops scrambling into position. The house was surrounded. "You're coming with me," he said.

"Where?" she cried.

"To the hospital," he said. "I'm taking you with me. I can't let them stop me before I get there. If I have you as a hostage, they'll let me go."

Her face flashed on and off like a blue strobe light, flashing like the lights on the cars outside, and he felt as if he was about to pass out.

"Yes," she said. "The hospital. You need a hospital. I'll help you get there. Just give me the gun."

He managed to laugh and didn't lower the gun. "Not for me. I need to get there for Susan."

He put the gun in his right hand, which was growing weaker, and grabbed her with the other. "We're going outside," he told her. "We're going to get into one of the cars out there and head for the hospital. And I'm going to hold you close. They won't dare shoot me, or you'll die, too."

He pulled her against him and hoped she didn't sense how weak he was. "They're going to kill you," she said.

"Come on." He pulled her toward the front door. "If you make a move to get away, I'll blow your head off."

He could feel her trembling. That was good. She would be too frightened to try anything.

They reached the living room, and in the flashing blue lights still coming through the window, he could see the two cops he had shot, still lying there. He stepped over them, making her do the same, and headed for the door.

He pushed the door open with his foot and yelled, "I'm coming out!"

He could almost taste the tension in the air as he pushed her through the doorway ahead of him. Dozens of police officers stood with guns drawn, waiting. "I have a hostage!" he shouted. "Don't make a move or she's dead."

"Allie!" It was Mark's voice, and he heard the struggle behind one of the cars as someone wrestled Mark down.

"We're going to go out to get in one of your cars," Craig yelled. "And if anybody makes a move, she's dead."

He held her tightly beside him, as he headed out toward a squad car at the outer edge of the cluster of cars—the one that seemed easiest to get out. He moved slowly as cops with guns drawn and trained on the two of them slowly fell back and took new cover. When they finally reached the car, he opened the passenger door and pushed Allie in first. "You're driving," he said, closing the door behind him. "Crank it up."

She did as she was told, and he leaned close to her and pressed the gun against her ribs. "Head to the hospital," he said. "As fast as you can drive."

She put the car into drive and skidded forward. He looked back and saw Stan and the others jumping into their cars and pulling out. They would follow him all the way—but that was all right. As long as he had Allie, they wouldn't try to stop him.

• • •

In the safe house, Sid Ford heard the cars pulling away. The blue flashes faded. Had they forgotten him? Had they assumed he was dead?

The door flew open, and Issie Mattreaux and Bob Sigrest burst in, carrying flashlights. "Sid?" Issie asked. "Sid, where are you?"

"Here," he groaned.

Behind her, two more paramedics ran in.

"R.J.?"

No answer. He prayed that R.J. wasn't dead.

Issie fell to her knees beside him and began checking out his wound. "Were you shot more than once, Sid?"

"No," he managed to get out.

"R.J.'s alive," Bob yelled. "But he's losing a lot of blood."

Issie had a cuff around Sid's arm and was taking his blood pressure. He grabbed her shirt and pulled her down to him. "Susan. He's goin' after Susan."

"Calm down," she said. "We're gonna get you to the hospital. Your BP is real low."

"Susan," he said again. "Radio. He's headed for the hospital."

Issie hesitated. "Are you sure?"

"Yes. Radio. Have to warn Ray."

She pulled her radio out of its sheath on her hip. "Simone, this is Issie," she said to the dispatcher. "We have two police officers down at 232 West Lake Avenue. Sid Ford is conscious, and says that Barnes is headed for the Slidell Hospital to get to Susan Ford."

There was a moment of static, then, "Copy, Issie. I'll get the word out."

Before Sid could be sure that Ray had been warned, they were moving him onto the gurney and carrying him out to the waiting ambulance.

•   •   •

Traffic seemed to part for Allie as she drove down Highway 90, headed for Slidell. Craig kept that gun in her ribs, and she feared that it would go off at any moment, if only accidentally. Behind her was a convoy of police cars with flashing lights, and she worried that one of them would try to shoot Craig and hit her instead.

Next to her, Craig seemed to be getting weaker, and she prayed that she'd be given an opportunity to disarm him once they got to the hospital. Somehow, she would have to stop him from shooting Susan.

Perspiration trickled down her temples, and her hands trembled as she gripped the wheel. "Craig, you don't think they're going to let you waltz into that hospital and kill Susan. Every cop in Newpointe is behind us, and probably every one in Slidell will be waiting for us. They'll kill us both to stop you."

"No, they won't." He was panting hard. "They've lost too many already. They won't risk losing you."

She hoped he was right. She glanced at him, saw how pale he was, how he shivered with chills. His bullet wound must be causing him significant pain. Maybe if she just talked to him . . .

"I understand what you're doing, Craig," she said, tempering her voice. "I understand how angry you were that Amanda was killed. It wasn't fair."

"No, it wasn't. But I'm making it fair."

"What's fair about three women dead? Five if you kill Susan and me? How will that even things up, Craig?"

"That's how it has to be," he said. "It's the only way I can redeem myself to her."

"She's dead, Craig. You're not thinking clearly. She can't give you redemption."

"But I can get it for myself," he said.

"No, you can't. You'll only multiply your guilt. Craig, you're sick. You need help." She tried to calm her voice, tried to sound like a friend who cared. "No one knew how upset you were about her, how much you loved her. No one knew she was in that house. Killing those women hasn't helped, has it? It hasn't brought you peace."

"It wasn't peace I was looking for," he said in a dull monotone. "It was revenge. Retribution. An eye for an eye." He began to weep, a deep, guttural, wailing sound, and she found that she felt compassion for him even while she feared him.

"Craig, I'm sorry for your pain."

Her kind words seemed to calm him somewhat, and he wiped his tears away. "It's not personal, Allie," he moaned. "It's not about you. This is to hurt Mark. I'm not a cruel man. I'll make it be over quick for you. Not like it was with her."

Tears pushed to her eyes again, and she realized that there might not be a way out. He fully intended to kill her.

"What if you turned things around?" she asked, her voice quivering. "What if you found that peace you're looking for by giving Susan and me a way out—just what you would have wanted for her? What if you changed the ending, Craig—if you were the hero who saved lives instead of the killer who destroyed them?"

He was still weeping, but he kept the gun aimed at her. "If it was just you, I would. But then Mark would never learn. Ray would go on feeling no remorse."

"They've seen what it feels like, Craig. They've been afraid. You put them through it. You did. And you shot Mark and Susan. They've felt the pain. You accomplished what you set out to do. Isn't that what you really wanted?"

He was quiet, looking out the windshield, and she wondered what he saw. Was he weighing her words? Thinking about listening?

She saw the hospital up ahead. Her time was running out. "Craig? You don't have to go through with this. You can rest. You can go into that hospital and have them treat your wound. You can turn over your gun—"

"Pull up to the emergency room door," he said.

She didn't know if that meant that he was going to heed her words and get himself some help, or if that was just the only entrance he knew would be open.

The parking lot was noticeably clear of people, and she saw the scattering of police cars waiting for them. She put the car in park and closed her eyes, praying that God would watch over all of them, that no stray bullets would hit the innocent, that no one else would have to die . . .

"Craig, if you give me the gun right now, no one will have to know. We can go in, just like I'm your hostage, and once we're in, we can get you treatment. Don't you want help?"

He grabbed her arm. "Open your door."

She was trembling so badly that she could barely grasp the handle. "Craig—"

"Open it and get out."

She opened the car door and slid out, Craig's fingers still tight around her arm. Dozens of police officers crouched behind their cars, weapons drawn. Someone was going to shoot—some trigger-happy rookie would fire, and then Craig would fire, and there would be bloodshed all around.

Craig got out of the car, keeping his gun pressed into her ribs. As he put his arm around her neck, she tried reaching him again.

"Give me the gun, Craig. Give me the gun, and I'll walk you in. You don't have to kill anyone else, and you don't have to die. You know you're not ready."

He stood frozen beside her for a moment, holding her in an embrace of terror. For a split second, she felt how weak he was and thought he might drop the gun or give it over to her. Then she saw him shaking his head. "I have to keep my promise to Mari," he said. "I have to finish my list."

• • •

Mark crouched behind Stan's car, watching as Allie stepped out of the car. Then Craig came out beside her, staggering like a drunk man.

"He's weak," Mark said. "Somebody could get that gun away from him."

"He's expecting something like that. He'll be ready for it." Stan lifted a megaphone to his mouth. "Craig, this is Stan Shepherd. Don't go any further."

Craig didn't listen. He kept walking toward the entrance, with Allie tight against him.

Mark knew that if they disappeared inside that hospital, Craig would kill her. He looked around at the cops staked out in firing position, and realized that not one of them had the means to protect his wife once they were inside.

But he could.

Still crouched, he ran from one car to another, hiding to keep Craig from seeing him. As soon as he reached the building, he skirted the corner so that he was out of Craig's sight, and ran around to the admissions doors.

He burst through, and two police officers stopped him. "Don't go any further," they warned him.

"I'm Mark Branning," he said. "My wife is the hostage. What's the fastest way to the emergency room from here?"

"You can't go any further," one of them said.

"Watch me," he said, and headed down a hall.

He followed the maze of corridors from admissions, to the lab, to the radiology department, past a number of other doors and a dozen other halls. Finally, he saw a sign that said "ER," and an arrow pointing east.

There were several police officers already up ahead crouched in the corridor, watching the emergency room doors for Craig to come in with Allie. Mark tried to think. If Craig had come here to kill Susan, he would have to go to her floor. He wouldn't dare take the elevator—someone might cut power to it. No, he would take the staircase. He looked around for an exit sign, and saw it near the elevators.

Quickly, he ducked into the stairwell and waited.

•   •   •

Allie waited for something to happen. A gunshot, or another warning from Stan's megaphone . . .

Craig was leaning partly on her as he held her with one arm and kept the gun against her waist with the other. The emergency room doors opened automatically, then closed behind them, cutting her off from those outside who could have saved her. The security people normally stationed at the door were conspicuously absent. They had been warned to stay out of the way or risk getting shot, she realized. She hoped the police were hiding, waiting to disarm him.

"Where are we going?" she asked.

"Stairwell," he said. "Third floor."

She looked down at the gun pressing into her side. Craig kept that elbow against his side. He was clearly in a lot of pain, and Allie realized that he couldn't move his arm very well. If she hit him in that arm, it would send pain radiating through him, and maybe he would drop the gun . . .

But his finger was over the trigger. Just a slight nudge could make it to go off.

She headed for the stairwell, but stopped at the door.

"Open it," he said.

Dread rose up in her. They would climb those stairs to Susan's floor, and no one would stop them. Didn't they realize that they *had* to stop him? If he got to Susan, he would kill them both! Didn't they understand?

She opened the door and shuffled into the dark stairwell, wondering where the light switch was.

"Turn the light on!" he said in a panicked voice. "Find the switch!"

He moved with her as she felt around for the switch.

Suddenly she was hurled against the wall, and she spun as Craig was knocked away from her.

"Run, Allie!" It was Mark's voice, and she groped for the stair rail and began running up, as fast as she could, stumbling in the darkness as the staircase turned. Below her, she heard the sounds of a struggle, heard bodies thudding and curses and groans. She found the light switch at the top of the stairs and flicked it on, bathing the place in light—just as she heard the *whoosh* of Craig Barnes's silenced gun.

Allie screamed and threw herself back against the wall.

Chapter Sixty-Six

● ● ●

Allie slid to the floor, her hands covering her head, screaming hysterically. But over her screams she heard footsteps
coming up the stairs, and then there were hands on her shoulders, pulling her out of her fetal position, and a soft, soothing
voice saying, "It's okay, baby, he's dead. It's over, Allie. Come
here. It's over."

She surged upward and fell into Mark's arms. She wept as
he held her with all his might. Below them, she heard the many
voices of cops revved up with adrenaline, checking for a pulse,
shouting loud enough to wake the dead. One of them said,
"Forget it. He's dead."

Craig's plan for achieving his own redemption, doomed
from the start, would never be completed.

She heard paramedics rushing up the stairs, and the door
behind them opened as Ray Ford dashed in. He looked from
Allie to the body at the bottom of the stairs. He put a hand on
the wall to steady himself and sat slowly down on one of the
stairs.

"He's dead," Mark told him as he kept holding Allie. "It's
over."

She tried to control her sobs, but they came like hiccups as
Issie Mattreaux rushed up the stairwell. She touched Ray's
shoulder. "Ray, I just brought Sid in. He was shot, but I think
he's gonna be all right."

In shock, Ray looked up at her and nodded his head. "I
thought he was dead," he said. "They made it sound like—"

"He's asking for you," she said.

Ray got clumsily to his feet and went back out the door he'd come through. Issie came the rest of the way up. She stooped down next to them. "Let go of her, Mark. I need to check her, make sure she's not hurt."

"No," Mark told her. "Leave her alone. I've got her."

"But she could be injured. I need—"

"She was," he choked out, "but it's nothing you can fix, Issie. She's my wife, and I'll take care of her."

Issie stared at them, a dozen emotions passing over her face. "I understand," she said quietly. "I'm glad you're both all right."

Issie went back down the stairs. Allie realized that Mark seemed entirely uninterested. His only interest right now seemed to be in her, and in the words he muttered in her ear.

"Thank you, Lord, thank you . . . thank you so much . . ."

And she let that gratitude seep into her own heart as well. Gradually, the realization came that she was alive, and her marriage was renewed, and her life had a new start. It was a new day.

Chapter Sixty-Seven

● ● ●

Dan Nichols lay on the hard cot in the Newpointe jail cell, staring at the ceiling and wondering how on this green earth he had wound up in such a mess. The betrayal gnawed at him like a mole tunneling through his heart. Stan, Vern, Chad, Mark, Allie . . .

He heard his name and looked up to see Vern standing at the cell door. "Dan, you're free to go," he said, unlocking the door. "We found Craig Barnes. He's the killer, so we owe you an apology."

Dan hesitated. Were they going to make someone else the scapegoat now? "Just because Craig has a bunker suit doesn't mean he's a serial killer."

"He's dead, Dan."

Dan's face changed. "Craig Barnes is dead? How?"

"He shot Sid and R.J. and took Allie as a hostage. He was headed for the Slidell Hospital to finish Susan off, but Mark managed to get his gun away from him."

Dan slowly lowered back to the cot. "I can't believe it."

"Me, either," Vern said. He leaned in the doorway of the cell, then pushed off from the bars and stepped closer to Dan. "Look, man, no hard feelings, huh? We were strung out. We didn't know which end was up. We were desperate."

Dan shook out of his reverie and got to his feet. "You say I'm free to go?"

"You can walk right out." Vern held out a hand to shake, but Dan ignored it and pushed past it.

"Dan, come on. You have to understand—"

Dan spun around. "How could you think that I was a serial killer?" Dan stared him down. "No, I don't think I *can* understand that."

"But, Dan—"

Dan walked up the hallway, between the other cells, where drunk drivers slept it off and vandals waited for their parents.

Jill was waiting at the end of it. She'd been crying, he could see. Her eyes glimmered and her nose was red. "Dan, I'm so glad you're free. You're not going to believe what's happened. Allie almost got killed, and Craig—"

"I heard," he said coldly. "Where's my stuff?"

"Over here." She led him to the booth where he could pick up his watch, his wallet, the cross he wore around his neck. "Dan, are you all right?"

He looked down at her as he slipped his watchband on. "No, I'm not, Jill. I feel like the whole town betrayed me."

"I know, Dan. I'd feel the same way. But put yourself in their places."

"I don't care what their place was. If I'd been in the same position, I wouldn't have suspected Vern or Chad, or Stan, or Mark or Allie."

"You also wouldn't have suspected Craig. It was an unusual circumstance, Dan. The town doesn't know how to deal with so much tragedy. It went on for too long."

He headed out the door. Thankfully, all of the reporters had fled to the scene of the shooting, so he and Jill were alone on the steps, squinting in the morning sunlight. "Oh, great."

"What?" she asked.

"I don't have my car. They brought me in a squad car."

"I'll take you home, Dan," she said. Wearily, he walked her out to her car, took her keys, and unlocked her door. Then he got in on the other side.

He was quiet as she drove to the outskirts of town, where he lived. When she reached his driveway, she looked at him expectantly. "Guess I'll see you later."

"Yeah. Thanks for the ride." He got out and started up to his house, then stopped suddenly. Jill was the only person in town who had come to his defense, and he'd treated her like he was angry at her, too. Slowly, he turned back around.

She was still sitting there, waiting for him to go in. He went back, opened the passenger door again, and got in.

"Uh—I meant to tell you how much I appreciate you going to bat for me. It means a lot that you didn't seem to have any doubts about my innocence."

"Why would I doubt, Dan?"

"Mark and Allie did." She started to object, but he went on. "And you didn't. You went in there with both barrels loaded, like you knew beyond a shadow of a doubt that I wasn't the guy. I really appreciate that, Jill."

She was quiet for a moment as she regarded him. "It was easy," she said. "I'm a good judge of character."

He sat, thinking, as he gazed seriously at her. "Do you think, after this is all over, that you might like to have dinner with me some night? Maybe someplace nice on the Southshore?"

Her smile broke through the fatigue and tension on her face. "I'd love to."

"Okay then." He squeezed her hand, then got out of the car. "I'll call you."

"Get some sleep. And take care of that hand."

"Yeah, I will."

He went into his house and watched from the window as she drove away. He felt warm around her, close to her—a strange feeling for a man who dated widely but avoided feelings that might lead to something deeper than mere dating. He tried to shake it away, along with the fatigue and the distress, as he headed back to his bedroom.

Chapter Sixty-Eight

●●●

Nick Foster waited until Susan was out of the hospital— four weeks after Craig Barnes's death—before he held the memorial service the town so desperately needed to begin its healing after all of the deaths. Mark expected the whole town to turn out—except for Dan, who hadn't been to church or spoken to him at work since he'd been wrongly arrested.

He had left a dozen messages on Dan's machine, all of which had gone unacknowledged and unreturned, and had tried to convince Ray, who had taken Craig's place as fire chief, to assign them to the same shift, but Dan had managed to evade even that. He feared that Dan would never understand or forgive him.

"Who are you watching for?" Allie whispered, sitting on the pew next to him.

He started to deny he was watching for anyone, but then worried that she might think he was looking for Issie. "Dan," he said. "I sure wish he'd come."

"He'll come around," she said. "I know he will."

The service started, with Susan, Ray, Ben, and Vanessa sitting in the front row with Marty Bledsoe and his twins, George and Tommy Broussard, Cale Larkins, and Mark and Allie. Much of the town packed in behind them, until there was standing room only.

Mark held Allie's hand as Nick preached on healing, pressing on, looking forward instead of behind, and finally, forgiveness.

There wasn't a dry eye in the house when he was finished, and as each of them said a word to the crowd, the emotions grew even more intense. Mark wondered if he could even find his voice as he went to take his turn behind the microphone.

He cleared his throat—then simply stood quietly for a moment, looking out on the loving faces in the crowd, the people who were part of his family . . .

Allie's parents, who had forgiven him after he'd proven his remorse to them, were sitting on the second row. His father, dead sober though he trembled miserably, sat next to them.

There were firemen and cops, schoolmates and teachers . . .

And then he saw Dan, standing at the back in the crowd.

He cleared his throat again, and tried to find the words he'd been wanting to say. "As Nick said, bad things aren't all bad. I wish we could do some of it over. I wish I hadn't hurt one of my best friends because I was so panicked that anything seemed possible. I wish he could forgive me. Me and all the others— because we do know that he's incapable of such a horrible crime. We do know that, now that we can think clearly."

He saw Dan push through the crowd to the nearest door, and he was gone.

Disheartened, Mark tried hard to go on. "But some good came, too. I realized that I didn't want to live apart from Allie anymore. That I wanted to share a double rocking chair with her someday in that nursing home where our children would send us."

The crowd chuckled.

"I guess I owe that to Craig Barnes—or more likely, to the Lord. He can make something good out of something bad. And today, it's my pleasure to tell you, that Allie and I just found out we're expecting our first child. A Thanksgiving baby."

A round of applause went up over the congregation, and everyone cheered. Allie got up and came to his side, and Mark kissed the wife whom God had taught him to cherish. They had so much to look forward to. So many things to be thankful for. So much to rejoice in.

He only wished that Dan could rejoice with them.

• • •

Dan stood just outside the door to the small sanctuary, fighting his wildly conflicting feelings while Mark spoke. When the announcement about the pregnancy came, he smiled, surprisingly glad for Mark and Allie despite how he wanted to hang onto his anger.

Confused, he just stood, his mind shifting from his brief time in jail to the years he'd spent as Mark's friend. The amount of time he'd spent in jail wasn't the issue—it was the principle of the thing. He had the right to be angry.

Yes, he had the right. But he didn't *want* to be angry anymore.

The choir sang the final song, and then the memorial service broke up, and the crowd began to pour out of the small building.

He worked his way through the crowd back into the sanctuary. Mark and Allie stood at the front, hugging well-wishers with so much joy on their faces that he longed to share it with them.

He pushed toward the front, through the people, weaving back and forth against the flow of traffic.

Mark looked up, and their eyes met. Mark excused himself and started toward him.

They grasped hands first, then pulled each other into a tight hug, one that lasted much longer than either of them would normally have allowed. When Dan let Mark go, Stan was waiting, and Dan hugged him too. Then Vern and Chad grabbed him, then Nick, then some of the firemen—as if *he'd* been one of the injured ones.

And when he was done, Jill was standing nearby, looking so beautiful and so happy. He pulled her into a hug too, and laughed in her ear. Surprised, he found he didn't want to let her go. "So how about that dinner you promised me?" he asked, still holding her.

"Tonight?" she asked.

"Yes," he said. "Right now."

She laughed heartily against his shoulder, and made no attempt to get out of his embrace. "All right," she said. "Let's go."

•   •   •

Allie beamed as she watched two of her favorite people head out of the church together, and she breathed a silent prayer that something important would blossom between them. They both deserved so much happiness.

Celia touched her arm, and Allie turned and hugged her.

"I'm so excited for you," Celia said, her voice shaking. Allie pulled back to look into her friend's face.

"Celia, what's wrong?"

She tried to laugh off the tears. "I'm just so jealous," she said. "Stan and I have been trying to have a baby, too."

"You will," Allie said with excitement. "And they'll play together, and we can join some hokey mom's group and take our kids to the park. I'm selling the flower shop so I can stay home with the baby. We're going to have to cut way back, but it'll be worth it. And you and I can exchange recipes and baby-sit for each other . . ."

Celia threw her head back and laughed. "Oh, if it would only hurry and happen."

"It will," Allie said, as Mark walked up behind her and put his arms around her. "I know it will. And there's no rush. We have all the time in the world."

Or so it seemed—and that was good enough for them.

Afterword

●●●

As a Christian writer, I struggle with the balance between the message and the story. I don't want to preach to any of my readers, nor do I want to read stories that preach to me. But each time I finish a book, I experience the very real fear that someone will read my book and be spiritually moved, but not know where to go from there. Will they know they need something, and follow a false doctrine that might come along at just that time, a false doctrine that temporarily fills some void in their life, but keeps them from ever walking through the door that leads to salvation?

It's possible. So I include this page, to let you know that there is only one way to God, and that is through Jesus Christ, who is the way, the truth, and the light. There are many counterfeit religions, and they're dressed up in pretty packages. They promise great rewards. Some promise license to live as you want; others exalt *you* as God; others tickle your ears through psychics and New Age thinking; others lead you to angel worship and offer "spiritual guides" who seem safe but are, in reality, demonic. But perhaps the most counterfeit religions of all is the one in which you sit in church Sunday after Sunday and tell yourself you're a Christian, when you've never entered into a sacred covenant with Christ, never died to yourself, never lived for Christ, and never borne fruit. All of these counterfeits offer cheap hope, temporary pleasure, shallow fulfillment. They also offer a miserable eternity.

That wonderful salvation through Christ is not cheap, temporary, or shallow! Our doctrine deals with sin—my sin, your sin—and only through dealing with that can we come to understand why Christ had to die. Only then can we have the promise—not of feeling good and important and guilt-free and unaccountable while on this earth—but of having *abundant* life on earth, and *eternal* life in God's presence. The most wonderful worship experience I've ever had is just a sample of what my everyday life will be like in heaven!

But I'm like a prisoner on death row who's been pardoned. All I have to do is accept the pardon and walk out. I have a choice. Why would I deny a pardon that came at such a high price—in fact, at the cost of someone else's death—and insist on finishing out my sentence? I don't know. But day after day, millions and millions of people choose to do just that.

Don't be one of them.

Tell Christ you accept that pardon today, and walk out of your prison into freedom. And if you've already done that, tell someone else, so that they can be pardoned, too.

Coming April 2002

● ● ●

THE FIRST BOOK IN THE CAPE REFUGE SERIES
Cape Refuge

The air conditioner was broken at City Hall, and the smell of warm salt air drifted through the windows from the beach across the street. Morgan Cleary fanned herself and wished she hadn't dressed up. She might have known that no one else would. The mayor sat in shorts and a T-shirt that advertised his favorite brand of beer. One of the city councilmen wore a Panama hat and flip-flops. Sarah Williford, the newest member of the Cape Refuge City Council, looked as if she'd come in from a day of surfing and hadn't even bothered to stop by the shower. She wore a Spandex top that looked like a bathing suit and a pair of cut-off jeans. Her long hair could have used a brush.

The council members sat with relaxed arrogance, rocking back and forth in the executive chairs they'd spent too much money on. Their critics—which included almost everyone in town—thought they should have used that money to fix the potholes in the roads that threaded through the island. But Morgan was glad the council was comfortable. She didn't want them irritable when her parents spoke.

The mayor's nasal drone moved to the next item on the agenda. "I was going to suggest jellyfish warning signs at some of the more popular sites on the beach, but Doc Spencer tells me he ain't seen too many patients from stings in the last week or so—"

"Wait, Fred," Sarah interrupted without the microphone. "Just because they're not stinging this week doesn't mean they won't be stinging next week. My sign shop would give the city a good price on a design for a logo of some kind to put up on all the beaches, warning people of possible jellyfish attacks—"

"Jellyfish don't attack," the mayor said, his amplified voice giving everyone a start.

"Well, I can see you never got stung by one."

"How you gonna draw a picture of 'em when you can't hardly see 'em?"

Everyone laughed, and Sarah threw back some comment that couldn't be heard over the noise.

Morgan leaned over Jonathan, her husband, and nudged her sister. "Blair, what should we do?" she whispered. "We're coming up on the agenda. Where are Mom and Pop?"

Blair tore her amused eyes from the sight at the front of the room and checked her watch. "Somebody needs to go check on them," she whispered. "Do you believe these people? I'm so proud to have them serving as my elected officials."

"This is a waste of time," Jonathan said. He'd been angry and stewing all day, mostly at her parents, but also at her. His leather-tanned face was sunburned from the day's fishing, but he was clean and freshly shaven. He hadn't slept much last night, and the fatigue showed on the lines of his face.

"Just wait," she said, stroking his arm. "When Mom and Pop get here, it'll be worth it."

He set his hand over hers—a silent affirmation that he was putting the angry morning behind him—and got to his feet. "I'm going to find them."

"Good idea," Morgan said. "Tell them to hurry."

"They don't need to hurry," Blair whispered. "We've got lots of stuff to cover before they talk about shutting down our bed and breakfast. Shoot, there's that stop sign down at Pine and Mimosa. And Goodfellows Grocery has a light bulb out in their parking lot."

"Now, before we move on," Fred Hutchins, the mayor, said, studying his notes as if broaching a matter of extreme importance, "I'd like to mention that Chief Cade of the Cape Refuge Police

Department tells me he has several leads on the person or persons who dumped that pile of gravel in my parking spot."

A chuckle rippled over the room, and the mayor scowled. "The perpetrator will be prosecuted."

Blair spat out her suppressed laughter, and Morgan slapped her arm. "Shhh," Morgan whispered, trying not to grin, "you're going to make him mad."

"I'm just picturing a statewide search for the fugitive with the dump truck," Blair said, "on a gravel-dumping spree across the whole state of Georgia."

Morgan saw the mayor's eyes fasten on her, and she punched her sister again. Blair drew in a quick breath and tried to straightened up.

"The Owenses still ain't here?" he asked.

While Morgan glanced back at the door, Blair shot to her feet. "No, Fred, they're not here. Why don't you just move this off the agenda for this week and save it until next week? I'm sure something's come up."

"Maybe they don't intend to come," the mayor said.

"Don't you wish," Blair fired back. "You're threatening to shut down their business. They'll be here, all right."

"Well, I'm tired of waiting," the mayor said into the microphone, causing feedback to squeal across the room. Everybody covered their ears until Jason Manford got down on his knees and fiddled with the knob. "We've moved it down the agenda twice already tonight," the mayor went on. "If we ever want to get out of here, I think we need to start arguin' this right now."

Morgan got up. "Mayor, there must be something wrong. Jonathan went to see if he could find them. Please, if we could just have a few more minutes."

"We're not waitin' any longer. Now if anybody from your camp has somethin' to say ..."

"What are you gonna do, Mayor?" Blair asked, pushing up her sleeves and shuffling past the knees and feet on her row. "Shut us down without a hearing? That's not even legal. You could find yourself slapped with a lawsuit, and then you wouldn't even have time to worry about jellyfish and gravel. Where would that leave the town?"

She marched defiantly past the standing-room-only crowd against the wall to the microphone at the front of the room.

Morgan got a queasy feeling in her stomach. Blair wasn't the most diplomatic of the Owens family.

Blair set her hands on her hips. "I've been wanting to give you a piece of my mind for a long time now, Fred. I figured you could use the donation."

The people erupted into laughter, and the mayor banged his gavel to silence them. "As you know, young lady, the city council members and I have agreed that the publicity from the *20/20* show about Hanover House a few months ago brought a whole new element to this town. The show portrayed your folks as willin' to take in any ol' Joe with a past and even exposed some things about one of your current tenants that made the people of this town uncomfortable and afraid. We want to be a family-friendly tourist town, not a refuge for every ex-con with a parole officer. For that reason, we believe Hanover House is a danger to this town, and that it's in the city's best interest to close it down under our Zoning Ordinance number 503."

Blair waited patiently through the mayor's speech, her arms crossed. "Before we address the absurdity of your pathetic attempts to shut down Hanover House just because my parents refused to help campaign for you—"

Cheers rose again, and Blair forged on. "Maybe I should remind you that Cape Refuge got its name because of the work of the Hanovers who had that bed and breakfast before my parents did. It was a refuge for those who were hurting and had no place else to go. I think we have a whole lot more to fear from an ex-con released from jail with a pocketful of change and no prospects for a job or a home, than we do from the ones who have jobs and housing and the support of people who care about them."

Morgan couldn't believe she was hearing these words come out of her sister's mouth. Blair had never sympathized with her parents' calling to help the needy, and she had little to do with the bed and breakfast. To hear her talk now, one would think she was on the frontlines in her parents' war against hopelessness.

"Hanover House is one of the oldest homes on this island, and it's part of our heritage," Blair went on. "And I find it real interesting that you'd be all offended by what they do there out in the open, when Betty Jean's secret playhouse for men is still operating without a hitch."

Again the crowd roared. Horrified, Morgan stood up. Quickly trying to scoot out of her row, she whispered to those around her, "I'm sorry, I'm so sorry, I didn't know she was going to say that. She didn't mean it, she just says whatever comes to her mind—"

"Incidentally, Fred, I've noticed that you don't have any trouble finding a parking spot at her place!" Blair added.

The mayor came out of his seat, his mouth hanging open with stunned indignation. Morgan stepped on three feet, trying to get to her sister. She fully expected Fred to find Blair in contempt—if mayors did that sort of thing in city council meetings—and order the Hanover House bulldozed before nightfall.

"She didn't mean that!" Morgan shouted over the crowd, pushing toward the front. "I'm sure she's never seen your car at Betty Jean's, have you, Blair? Mayor, please, if I may say a few words ..." She finally got to the front, her eyes rebuking Blair.

Blair wouldn't surrender the microphone. "And I might add, Mayor, that your own parents were on this island because of Joe and Miranda Hanover and that bed and breakfast. If I remember, your daddy killed a man accidentally and came here to stay while he was awaiting trial."

The veins in Fred's neck protruded, and his face was so red that Morgan feared the top of his head would shoot right off. "My daddy was never convicted!" he shouted. "And if you're suggesting that he was the same type of criminal that flocks to Hanover House, you are sadly mistaken!"

Morgan reached for the microphone again, her mind already composing a damage-control speech, but her sister's grip was strong.

"After my parents inherited the bed and breakfast from the Hanovers," Blair said, "they continued their policy of never harboring anybody illegally. You know that my father works with these people while they're still in prison, and he only agrees to house the ones he trusts, who are trying to turn their lives around. Hanover House gives those people an opportunity to become good people who can contribute to society … unlike some of those serving on our city council."

Again, there was applause and laughter, and Morgan grabbed Blair's arm and covered the microphone. "You're turning this into a joke!" she whispered through her teeth. "Mom and Pop are going to be mortified! You are not helping our cause!"

"I can handle this," Blair said, jerking it back.

Morgan forced herself between Blair and the microphone. "Your honor … uh … Mr. Mayor … council members … I am so sorry for my sister's outbursts. Really, I had no idea she would say such things."

Blair stepped to her side, glaring at her as if she'd just betrayed her.

"But I think we've gotten a little off track here. The fact is that Hanover House doesn't just house those who've gotten out of jail. It also houses others who have no place to go."

Art Russell grabbed the mayor's microphone, sending feedback reverberating over the room. "I don't think Cape Refuge is very well served by a bunch of people who have no place else to go."

"Well, that's not up to you, is it, Art?" Blair asked, her voice carrying over the speakers.

"If I may," Morgan said, trying to make her soft voice sound steady, "the question here is whether there's something illegal going on at Hanover House. And unless there is, you have no grounds for closing us down."

The crowd applauded again, but Sarah, the swimsuit-clad councilwoman, dragged the microphone across the table. The cord wasn't quite long enough, so she leaned in. "If there aren't any dangerous people staying at the bed and breakfast, then how come *20/20* said Gus Hampton served time for armed robbery and didn't even complete his sentence? And how come your husband was at the dock fighting with your parents just this morning, complaining about Hampton? I heard it myself. Jonathan didn't want you working there around Hampton, and he said it loud and clear."

Blair's eyes pierced Morgan. "Why didn't you tell me this?" she whispered.

"It wasn't relevant," Morgan hissed back, "since I didn't think you'd be the one speaking for us."

The council members all came to attention, their rocking stopped, and they waited for an answer. "If there isn't any danger at Hanover House," Sarah continued, "then how come your own family's fighting over it?"

Blair tried to rally. "Well, Sarah, when Jonathan gets back here, you can ask him. But meanwhile, the question is simple. Do you have the right to shut down Hanover House, and if you do try to close it, are you financially able to handle the lawsuit that's going to be leveled at this town … and maybe even at each of you individually?"

"They can't file a lawsuit," Fred said, his face still red.

"Watch us," she bit out. "And the chances of your re-election would be slim at best, since the people of this town love my parents. Most everybody in this town has benefited from their kindness in one way or another."

The crowd applauded again, and cheers and whoops backed up her words. But Morgan realized that it wasn't the cries of the people that would decide the fate of Hanover House. It was those angry members of the city council, sitting there with their hackles up because Blair had insulted them.

"Some call that kindness, others call it naivete," the mayor said. "They'll believe anything anybody tells them. Just because some convict claims he wants to change, doesn't mean he will."

"Thank goodness they believed your daddy," Blair said, "or you might not be sitting on this island in some overpriced chair!"

As the crowd expressed their enjoyment again, Morgan pressed her fingertips against her temples and wondered where her parents were. If they would just rush in right now and take over the microphone, she knew they could turn this around.

While the mayor tried to get control of the crowd again, Morgan looked fully at Blair, pleading for her to surrender the mike and not do any more harm. But Blair's scathing look told Morgan that her sister was in this to the end. The burn scar on the right side of Blair's face was as red as the mayor's face. It always got that way when she was upset, reminding Morgan of her sister's one vulnerability. It was that imperfect half of her face that kept her unmarried and alone—and it had a lot to do with the hair-trigger temper she was displaying now.

"Order, now! Come on, people—order!" the mayor bellowed, banging his gavel as if he were hammering a nail.

The sound of sirens rose over the crowd's noise, cutting across the mayor's words and quieting the crowd. Those on the east side of the building, where Morgan and Blair stood, craned their necks to see out the open window, trying to figure out where the fire trucks and police cars were heading. As one after another went by, sirens wailing and lights flashing, Morgan realized that something big must have happened. The island was small, and the sound of sirens was not an everyday occurrence. But now the sound of several at once could not be ignored.

When the front doors of the room swung open, everyone turned expectantly. Police Chief Matthew Cade—whom friends called simply "Cade"—stood scanning the faces, his skin pale against his dark, windblown hair.

His eyes fell on the sisters at the front of the crowd. "Blair, Morgan, I need to see both of you right away."

Morgan's eyes locked with her sister's for a second, terrors storming through her mind.

"What is it, Cade?" Blair asked.

He cleared his throat and swallowed hard. "We need to hurry," he said, then pushed the door open wider and stood beside it, watching them, clearly expecting them to accompany him.

Whatever it was, Morgan realized, he couldn't or wouldn't say it in front of all these people. Something horrible had happened.

Melba Jefferson, their mother's closest friend, stood and touched Morgan's back. "Oh, honey."

Morgan took Blair's hand, and the now-silent crowd parted as they made their way out. Cade escorted them into the fading sunlight and his waiting squad car.

About the Author

• • •

Terri Blackstock is an award-winning novelist who has written for several major publishers including HarperCollins, Dell, Harlequin, and Silhouette. Published under two pseudonyms, her books have sold over 3.5 million copies worldwide.

With her success in secular publishing at its peak, Blackstock had what she calls "a spiritual awakening." A Christian since the age of fourteen, she realized she had not been using her gift as God intended. It was at that point that she recommitted her life to Christ, gave up her secular career, and made the decision to write only books that would point her readers to him.

"I wanted to be able to tell the truth in my stories," she said, "and not just be politically correct. It doesn't matter how many readers I have if I can't tell them what I know about the roots of their problems and the solutions that have literally saved my own life."

Her books are about flawed Christians in crisis and God's provisions for their mistakes and wrong choices. She claims to be extremely qualified to write such books, since she's had years of personal experience.

A native of nowhere, since she was raised in the Air Force, Blackstock makes Mississippi her home. She and her husband are the parents of three children—a blended family which she considers one more of God's provisions.

Seasons Under Heaven
Hardcover 0-310-22137-4

Showers in Seasons
Hardcover 0-310-22138-2

Times and Seasons
Hardcover 0-310-23319-4

ZondervanPublishingHouse
Grand Rapids, Michigan

A Division of HarperCollins*Publishers*

TERRI BLACKSTOCK

NEWPOINTE 911 SERIES

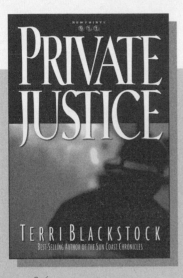

Softcover 0-310-21757-1

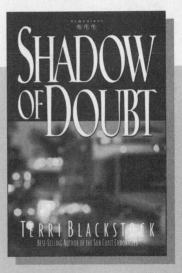

Softcover 0-310-21758-X

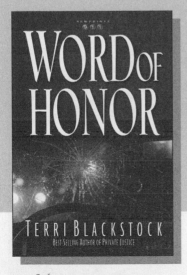

Softcover 0-310-21759-8

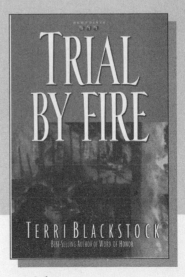

Softcover 0-310-21760-1

Check out these great books

from Terri Blackstock, too!

Softcover 0-310-20016-4

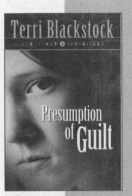

Softcover 0-310-20018-0

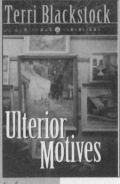

Softcover 0-310-20017-2

Softcover 0-310-20015-6

terri blackstock

seaside

A Novella

Seaside

Terri Blackstock

Seaside is a novella of the heart—poignant, gentle, true, offering an eloquent reminder that life is too precious a gift to be unwrapped in haste.

Sarah Rivers has it all: successful husband, healthy kids, beautiful home, meaningful church work.

Corinne, Sarah's sister, struggles to get by. From Web site development to jewelry sales, none of the pies she has her thumb stuck in contains a plum worth pulling.

No wonder Corinne envies Sarah. What she doesn't know is how jealous Sarah is of her. And what neither of them realizes is how their frantic drive for achievement is speeding them headlong past the things that matter most in life.

So when their mother, Maggie, purchases plane tickets for them to join her in a vacation on the Gulf of Mexico, they almost decline the offer. But circumstances force the issue, and the sisters soon find themselves first thrown together, then ultimately *drawn* together, in one memorable week in a cabin called "Seaside."

As Maggie, a professional photographer, sets out to capture on film the faces and moods of her daughters, more than film develops. A picture emerges of possibilities that come only by slowing down and savoring the simple treasures of the moment. It takes a mother's love and honesty to teach her two daughters a wiser, uncluttered way of life—one that can bring peace to their hearts and healing to their relationship. And though the lesson comes on wings of grief, the sadness is tempered with faith, restoration, and a joy that comes from the hand of God.

Hardcover: 0-310-23318-6

Mystery and suspense combine
in this first book of an exciting
new 4-book series by best-selling
author Terri Blackstock

Cape Refuge

Terri Blackstock

Thelma and Wayne Owens run a bed and breakfast in Cape Refuge, Georgia. They minister to the seamen on the nearby docks and prisoners just out of nearby jails, holding services in an old warehouse and taking many of the "down-and-outers" into their home. They have two daughters: the dutiful Morgan who is married to Jonathan, a fisherman, and helps them out at the B & B, and Blair, the still-single town librarian, who would be beautiful if it weren't for the serious scar on the side of her face.

After a heated, public argument with his in-laws, Jonathan discovers Thelma and Wayne murdered in the warehouse where they held their church services. Considered the prime suspect, Jonathan is arrested. Grief-stricken, Morgan and Blair launch their own investigation to help Matthew Cade, the town's young police chief, find the real killer. Shady characters and a raft of suspects keep the plot twisting and the suspense building as we learn not only who murdered Thelma and Wayne, but also the secrets about their family's past and the true reason for Blair's disfigurement.

Softcover: 0-310-23592-8

Pick up a copy at your favorite bookstore!

ZONDERVAN™

GRAND RAPIDS, MICHIGAN 49530 USA

WWW.ZONDERVAN.COM

We want to hear from you. Please send your comments about this book to us in care of the address below. Thank you.

ZondervanPublishingHouse
Grand Rapids, Michigan 49530
http://www.zondervan.com